BOOK 3 OF THE ALTERATIONS TRILOGY

PRIMAL WILL

BOOKS BY JANE SUEN

Children of the Future
Flowers in December

THE ALTERATIONS TRILOGY SERIES
Alterations
Game Changer
Primal Will

SHORT STORIES
Beginnings and Endings: A Selection of Short Stories

BOOK 3 OF THE ALTERATIONS TRILOGY

PRIMAL WILL

JANE SUEN

PRIMAL WILL: Book 3 of the Alterations Trilogy

Jane Suen books are available for order through Ingram Press Catalogues

www.janesuen.com

Printed in the United States of America

First Printing: August 2018

ISBN: 978-1-7323873-3-1

Ebook ISBN: 978-1-7323873-2-4

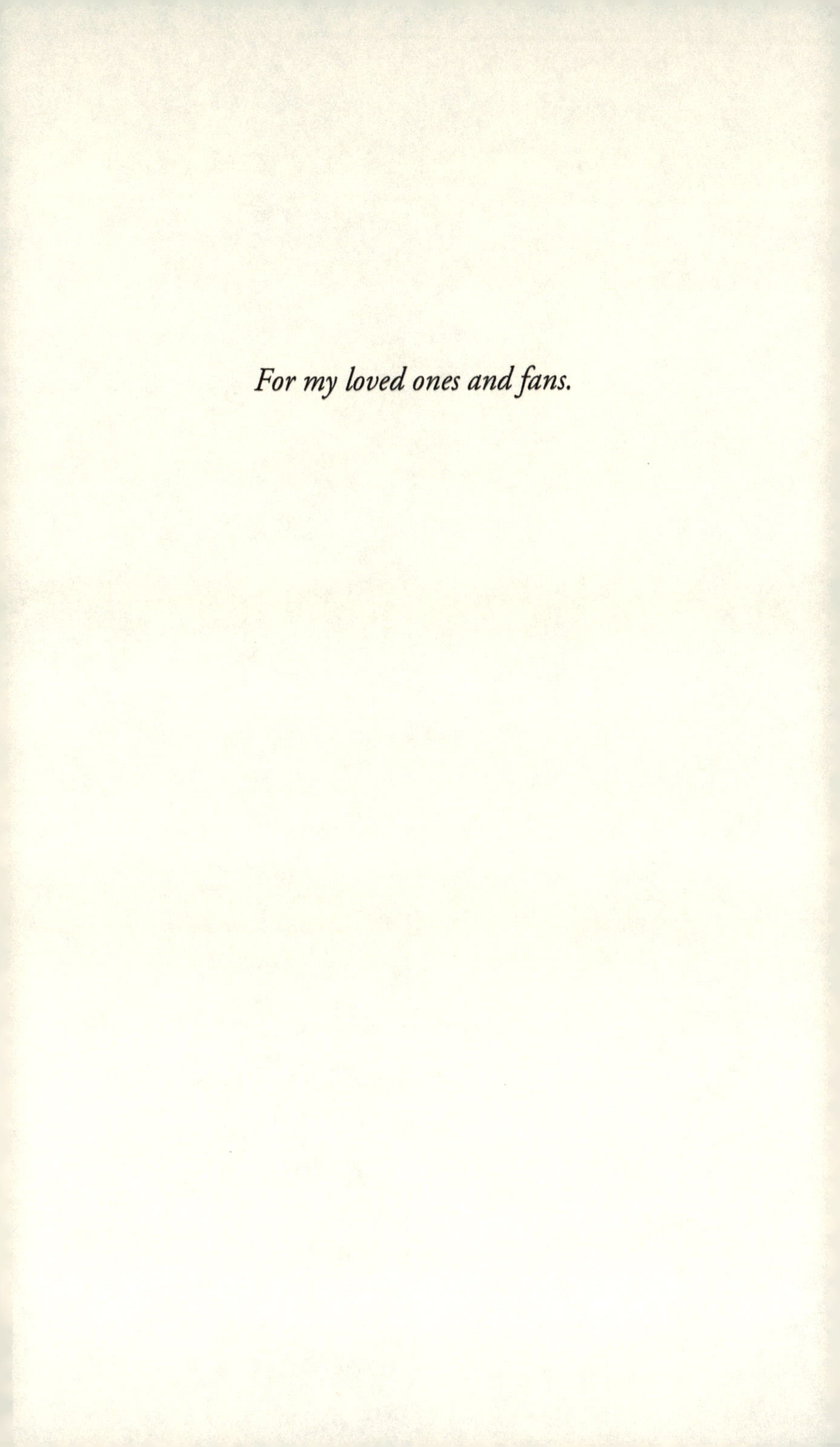

For my loved ones and fans.

Chapter 1
DR. KITE

"So, which one will it be?" Kite said, holding the two microchip injection pens, one in each hand. He offered them to her, a gift for his princess, as he had come to think of her.

Tiffany had heeded Lilly's warnings, expecting the worst in the man. She maintained her reserve and was on her guard. So far, Kite had been the perfect gentleman. The other day when she was dizzy and vulnerable, he took charge, making sure she got medical attention, remaining at her side. She had sensed—no, more than that—she *knew* he was interested in her, in more ways than just being friends.

She thought back to her last boyfriend. She had fallen crazy in love with him, his boyish charm, the way he tossed his hair to the side, his rebellious streak. He melted her reserves and took her on a roller coaster ride higher than she'd ever ridden. But, in the end, his immaturity broke her heart into bits and pieces, and she felt it would never be put back together again.

At this low point of her life, she found Lilly and enrolled in her program. Tiffany got through the pain, fought her way back, and started a new life. She graduated top in class. Kite had been her first assignment, a personal request from Lilly. She couldn't fail her.

Tiffany stared at Kite. He just stood there, not making a move to inject her, offering her a choice. She hesitated in the void of silence. *What will he do if she refused?* She exhaled, blowing a strand of hair away from her face.

Chapter 2
LILLY

She waited with a deepening sense of dread and worry for Tiffany's call. The decision to assign her to Kite had been calculated, dependent upon Tiffany's graduation from the program, one of two women in the first class. Tiffany was capable, smart, and quick-witted. She had more street smarts than book smarts, unlike Naomi. Tiffany was someone Lilly trusted. Someone she trained. Lilly had been patient, waiting for the right person, the right time.

She swiped a finger across her cell phone, checking one more time for missed calls.

Naomi was as different from Tiffany as night was from day. The two women had met in the program and trained together. They complemented each other, pulling on the other's strength where one was weak in a way that made them better together than separate. They survived the program, rising to outdistance the others until only the two of them remained in the advanced class. They had become close, as friends and supporters, in this endeavor.

It didn't come as a surprise when Naomi volunteered to find Tiffany after numerous calls went unanswered.

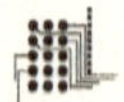

She picked up her cell phone and called.

"Naomi?"

"I'm in the car," said Naomi. Her voice was faint, surrounded by static and a hollow echo.

"Can you talk louder?" said Lilly, adjusting the volume, moving the phone closer to her ear.

"Yeah, I went to see Tiffany. I knocked on the door, but there was no answer." Naomi paused, steering the car down a narrow street. "She wasn't there. I looked in the windows and tried the door, but it was locked."

"Was her car there?"

"No."

"So where are you now?"

"Scouting the area. Looking for Tiffany."

"It's getting late."

"I'll stop soon to eat and find a place to stay tonight, then start back up in the morning."

"Did you check Kite's place?"

"The lights were all out."

"You be careful, okay?"

"Sure."

Chapter 3

ELLEN

To say she was nervous was an understatement. For months she had thought about Brad, throughout her pregnancy and after Angie was born. In moments of self-doubt over her impending role as a single mother, she had almost given in and reached out to Brad for help. But each time she had stopped before her fingers touched the phone.

She developed the rosy glow of pregnancy. Her baby became her first and most important priority. Gradually, the desire and connection to Brad diminished as the circumference of her belly increased.

She looked forward to the birth, as she'd made up her mind and resolved to be the best mom, to prove that she could do it. Ellen focused on this goal as the life inside her womb moved and kicked, exerting itself, extending a limb, exploring the boundaries of confinement.

Ellen tried to imagine what the baby would look like. Would she have the physique of her father, slim and muscular? Would the baby inherit the beauty of her mother?

Or would she carry Ellen's propensity for gaining weight and her fat cells? Would she have brains and beauty? Would she be healthy? She felt sure the baby would encompass the best of both parents. But she prayed, nevertheless, for this tiny life that she carried.

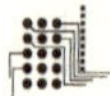

Ellen called her mother and father before she went to the hospital. When Angie was born, her mother was by her side, having gotten over the initial disappointment of Ellen having this baby without Brad.

Her mother had probed, tried to pry the details from Ellen. Ellen remained firm. Eventually, her mother stopped asking, knowing it was useless to push when Ellen had her mind made up. Mrs. Fulbright had raised Ellen to be an independent child. Finally, she'd let it go as her daughter came into motherhood on her own terms, and left Ellen to take this incredible journey without Brad.

As she gripped her mother's arm, beads of sweat gathered on Ellen's forehead. "Mom," she cried out, forcing the breath out in between the cramps that were coming closer and closer. Her doula was there, a young woman who had three children of her own.

"Push," the doula said.

Ellen nodded when it was time. Push she did, as hard as she could, again and again until the sound of crying erupted as the baby's tiny lungs released from her womb. She sank back on the pillow, exhausted, although she wanted to lean forward to catch the first glimpse of her baby, her Angie.

Someone fussed over her, fluffing her pillow, making her comfortable. In a brief moment, the nurse had measured and checked her baby, swaddling her in a blanket and placing a knit cap on her head, before laying her on Ellen's chest. She felt weak, the blood from her womb spotting the sheets as the nurse midwife sewed her back up.

The baby's heart pumped, pushing the blood through her arteries as Angie lay on top of her, right over Ellen's beating heart.

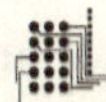

A knock at the door brought her back to the present. Ellen shifted Angie to her arm. When Angie was smaller, she had carried her in a sling. She chose it over the other baby carriers. It seemed like a perfect opportunity for mother-daughter bonding.

Now that Angie was a few months old, she held on, her legs clamping around Ellen's waist, tiny fists gripping Ellen's top.

"Angie, your dad's coming to see you," said Ellen.

She paused at the front door, turning to Angie. "You ready?" She planted a tender kiss on Angie's cheek before flinging the door open.

The clean-shaved, neatly dressed man at the door threw her a shy smile. He leaned in to greet her. "Ellen."

Ellen caught a whiff of his aftershave, his scent taking her back to the first time she met him, sitting next to her on the airplane. "Hi, Brad."

Last night Brad had tossed and turned in his bed, unable to sleep. The thought of meeting Angie for the first time, *his* daughter, the daughter he never knew he had, kept him awake for most the night. Between fits of sleep, he dreamed of her.

He crossed over the doorstep, looking at the baby in Ellen's arms, taking in her round chubby face, the long thick eyelashes framing her hazel eyes. "Angie," he said, as he beheld her dimpled arm and her tiny fingers. He held up a soft, stuffed puppy, the cutest one he could find with adorable eyes and big floppy ears.

Angie threw her head back and giggled at the sight of the toy, exposing the toothless gap in her little mouth.

His eyes lit up, relieved at her response. Brad let go of his fears and worries, and joined his daughter with boisterous laughter of his own.

Chapter 4
GIGI

Rex picked up the phone and called Steve Cosine. He had been surprised to hear from him. Last he'd heard, they had run into dead ends on the investigation of Gigi's accident. Now, the match on the fingerprints taken from the van used to transport Gigi to Hotel Seven sounded crucial and perhaps the missing link to discovering who was responsible.

"I've been expecting your call," said Steve, picking up on the first ring.

"We got your email. It sounded like you have an important breakthrough."

"I've been working with the detective assigned to her case. Although it's been simmering on the back burner."

"Heavy workload?"

"Our caseload exploded since the storm."

"I can imagine," said Rex, sympathetically.

"How's Gigi, by the way?"

"Gigi is good. The nightmares are gone, and they haven't come back. We're on vacation at the moment, our first together."

"Does that mean you're in a relationship now?"

"Happily as a couple," said Rex.

"Give her my best," said Steve. "Rex, when are you guys coming back to the city?"

"We'll be back on Monday."

"Could you do me a favor?"

"Anything, old buddy."

"When you get home, would you and Gigi meet with me?"

"To talk about her case?"

"Yes, I'd like to see you both, and I have some questions for her."

"I'm not sure she can shed more light on what happened that day," said Rex. "You know she was pretty shaken up after the car accident."

"I just need to sit down and talk to her. The match on the fingerprints is our big break, but there are still some missing pieces of information."

"I'll see what we can do, since it's that important."

"Hold on. I'm checking my schedule for the first of next week," said Steve. "I have some openings Monday afternoon at 3:00 p.m. and in the early evening."

"Can you come by our place? We'll be getting home just after lunch, and that'll give us some time to unpack."

"Sure, and, oh Rex?"

"What?"

"I'm happy for you, man."

Rex sported a grin as he ended the call, glad to be hearing from his old buddy and anticipating more good news when they meet.

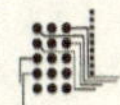

One thing about Steve was his excellent reputation with the police force, which carried through when he retired and became a consultant. Relentless. Persistent. His *modus operandi*.

In the aftermath of the storm that wreaked havoc in the city, Steve had been in demand. He didn't hesitate to jump in and help when they called him. In addition to his police work, his experience in insurance was a plus. His buddies on the force were all too glad to see him back. They were stretched thin, working around the clock. He was assigned to the vehicle recovery unit.

He worked his way down the vast list, compiled painstakingly from multiple sources of information. Each vehicle tracked down, and the owners notified. Sometimes they'd hit a stumbling block if the owner moved and the contact information on the registration was no longer current. Finding the owner took ingenuity and hard work, but it was the kind that Steve enjoyed. That, and sometimes strokes of pure luck. It was one of those days when he picked up the file on the white van, abandoned close to a warehouse that burned. Flipping through it, a name caught his eye. Raul.

Where had he seen that name? He rubbed his forehead, bent low over the paperwork. He was tired. So many cases, so few hours. Something about the name clicked. White van. He stared at the name, typed neatly on the paper, surrounded by white space. With a sigh, he closed the file and put it on top of his pile. He'd sleep on it and come back to it in the morning.

That night, Steve stopped by his favorite diner on the way home. He grabbed a quick bite since it was already past nine. Tomorrow Steve would be tired again if he didn't get more sleep and back on schedule.

Steve knew the route, it was the same one he'd taken for more than twenty years. The one that he knew by heart, every turn, dip, and corner. His mind wandered. The monotony of the road blending with the last rays of sunlight.

His headlights came on automatically. Unbidden, the thought came to him, the one that put two and two together. Bingo. He was staring at the face of Raul now, the man he'd visited after Gigi's car accident, the one whose white van had been stolen, the one with an expired registration.

In possession of the vehicle, he had taken fingerprints and sent it off to check for a match. Could this be the same van used to transport Gigi to Hotel Seven?

Steve was a patient man. He didn't like unsolved cases. Through his contacts on the force, the fingerprints from the white van got expedited processing. It got a match—to a dead man.

Chapter 5
DR. KITE

Tiffany waited for Kite's explanation. She wanted him to tell her. Lilly's warning had been loud and clear. Kite finally made his move and it was a big one. *Would he do something against her will? Would he hurt her?*

She searched his face for clues. Watched his body language, trying to get a read. She closed her eyes and counted silently to three. When she opened them, Kite was frowning at her.

"Tiffany, arc you all right?"

She held up her hand.

"Maybe you should sit down, if you're feeling dizzy."

She nodded, moving to the couch.

Kite opened his palm, displaying the pen. "This is a mini-syringe filled with a medication-tracking microchip. Injection is quick and painless, a tiny pinch like a mosquito bite. With a reminder programmed, the chip will send you an alert to take your meds."

"A reminder?"

"Yes, it'll be sent to your mobile device. I'll also get it."

"But, you know I didn't take my meds because I didn't have enough money. It wasn't because I forgot."

"It works the same in either case. The bottom line is to get you to take your meds when you've missed it."

She sighed, gesturing to Kite's other hand. "What about that one? What do you have here?"

Kite stiffened, sucking in a deep breath. "This is a prototype chip I'd been working on—you know my story, the storm, the fire destroying the warehouse."

She nodded.

"I thought I'd lost it all, but fortunately I had these two microchips with me, tucked in the inner pockets of my laptop bag." He paused. "This chip is pheromone-specific, a love potion, as some would say."

"Specific?"

"Yes, to the pheromones it detects at the time of injection."

"Why would I need that?"

"Um . . . it'll enhance pheromones."

"I don't see how that would help me," said Tiffany.

"Think about it. Then ask me any questions you have," said Kite vaguely.

"What if I change my mind, decide I don't want it?"

"That's simple; I'll remove it from your arm."

Tiffany knew that the moment had come. Lilly had warned her that Kite might try this. All the months of their planning came down to this. The decision rested with her.

Chapter 6

ELLEN

Monday morning, when she arrived at work, Ellen saw a folded note taped on her door. Snatching it off, she read, *Please see me. Andrew*

An involuntary shiver quaked through her body. Ellen entered her office, plopped down her briefcase, and sat. Just for a moment. She needed a few minutes to regroup, to think. Her mind ran wild. This special summons caught her by surprise. Andrew. So formal. Foreboding. What happened to his insistence that she call him Andy? Had she done something wrong?

Dreading the meeting, she snaked her way to the break room, hoping someone had made coffee. Thankfully, someone had left half a pot of the morning brew. She poured, filling her favorite green ceramic mug. Taking her cup of joe black today, she inhaled the aroma, eyes closed for the full experience, before swallowing a big gulp. Ellen dropped off the mug in her office on her way to see Andrew.

A knock on his door elicited an immediate, "Come in." Andrew was expecting her.

Putting on a cheerful face, Ellen entered. "Good morning." She left off her usual 'Andy' to be safe. Perhaps he preferred Andrew now?

Andy was sitting straight in his chair, arms crossed.

She held up his note. "I got your note."

He nodded, gesturing her to come closer.

"You wanted to see me?" She left out asking, *What's wrong?* The question was burning in her mind.

"Have a seat." He waited until she sat, prolonging the tension. "Is there something you'd like to tell me?"

"I . . . I don't understand," said Ellen, stuttering.

"You left suddenly during the social hosted by Ergon Towers."

Ellen raised her eyebrows, wondering what Andy was going to say next.

"I was worried all weekend. Is something wrong?"

Ellen breathed a silent sigh of relief. She thought she'd mucked up his big project, or worse. She shook her head. "I didn't mean to worry you. I'm sorry."

"Are you okay?"

She nodded. "Yes, I'm fine."

His clenched jaws relaxed a bit. "Are you mad at me?"

Ellen's mind took a sharp turn. So this was why! "Not at all. I'm sorry if I gave that wrong impression. You know I couldn't party all night like the rest of you."

He persisted. "You didn't say goodbye. You just left all of a sudden."

She gave a forced laugh. "I had to look in on Angie. She hasn't been feeling well." She added the fib about Angie, the words tumbling out before she could put a stop to it. Ellen didn't usually lie and hated doing so, but this came under extreme circumstances. Besides, she reasoned with herself; it *was* about Angie and her father. Her protective mother's instinct came out in full force. Ellen wasn't going to tell him about Brad. It was *none* of his business.

Chapter 7
LILLY

She chewed her lip, thinking about Tiffany. Sending Naomi may not have been the best move, but it was the quickest. Tiffany had been unreachable. If she needed help, Naomi would be reliable.

Lilly recalled the first day she met them. If she had to guess then, she would have been wrong. Tiffany was a mess, emotionally, coming fresh from a relationship break-up. The headiest drug wasn't some powder or pill; it was love, more powerful than anything you can buy or get. And Naomi, she was the opposite. Tight, buttoned up, a hard nut to crack. She didn't show her emotions. She came with baggage too. They all did.

The program attracted people who needed a fresh start. The first part took two weeks. It was grueling. A process to cleanse the body of toxins and waste products, and a sharpening of the conscious mind to the realm of the unconscious. It was taxing physically and mentally. Only those who were determined to finish made it to the end. The ones who dropped out; they just weren't ready. They were looking for hand-holding, sympathy, anything other than what the program required, and not prepared to do the hard work. But for those that did make it through, the end was satisfying.

Lilly had offered the second part of the program to the five women who finished. Three of the five weren't interested. These women had achieved what they came for, got what they needed, and they were ready to go back.

Picking up the calendar, Lilly stared at the date circled. In three days, it would be the end of the program. If she could leave now, she would. But she couldn't, not before it ended. The wait was going to be torture. Working quickly, she mapped out a new plan, one she'd see to herself. One she'd looked forward to with long-awaited anticipation and dreaded at the same time.

Chapter 8
DR. KITE

Kite didn't want to push her. He had never forced anyone, except for the ones who were incoherent, too drunk or high, or passed out—the ones the fake taxicab trawling the city at night picked up and brought to the warehouse. Kite wasn't proud of that, what he did. He rationalized away his guilt. He gave them a microchip, a night's sleep, and released them the next morning. In the name of science, he created novel technologies to cure illnesses, reverse aging, lose weight, and uplift moods.

As much as he wanted to inject Tiffany, he held back, giving her the time to decide. He just wanted to help her, right? Oh, right. He had his selfish motives. Tiffany was different, not like anyone he'd met. She was more than a guinea pig; he wrestled with his thoughts, his feelings. She was the one who brought him out of the utter depths he had sunk into after the warehouse burned to the ground. Even if he had any, Kite wouldn't have given her the mind-control chips, a problem since two out of three of the chips he'd implanted were defective.

"Hey, are you off in another world?" said Tiffany, touching his arm.

He shook his head, focusing on her.

"Talk to me, tell me more about the chips."

"You know what happened to the warehouse?" said Kite. She nodded.

"We had trawled the city at night, picking up people drunk or high, passed out on the sidewalk. They got injected with a microchip and spent the night there sleeping."

"Did you get consent before you injected them with the chip?"

Kite looked down, uncomfortable. "No, they were incoherent, too far gone, out of it." He paused. "I violated the ethics of human experimentation."

"You didn't give them a choice."

"They didn't even know."

The confession of his wrongdoing hung heavy in the air.

Tiffany broke the silence. "So, what happened next?"

"The next morning, we released them."

"And the fire?"

"Destroyed the warehouse—"

"What happened to the people?"

"Nobody died in the fire, because it happened later in the day after we'd released all of them."

Tiffany sighed with relief. She had dreaded asking the question and finding out the answer. She knew she had to earn his trust before he'd tell her the truth. *Could she have faced the man if he was a murderer, had blood on his hands?* This part of the assignment had been eating at her, one that made her sick to the stomach, one she wasn't sure she'd have the strength to deal with, had it come to that.

The other part of her assignment was to find out about the microchips.

"And your chips?"

"Burned in the fire."

"All of them?"

"All except the two that I have here. These are prototypes of two other types of chips. I had put them aside to work on the new mind-control chips instead."

"And you just found them?"

Kite nodded.

Tiffany looked into Kite's eyes. She saw truth, sincerity, and something else—a deliverance from the pain, guilt, and load he'd been carrying.

Chapter 9
GIGI

"Let's do something special today," said Gigi, turning to Rex. Sipping coffee at the kitchen counter, thinking they would be leaving tomorrow, brought a pang of sadness.

He nodded, knowing her well, and what she was thinking. How did nine days fly by so quickly? He tried not to dwell on the inevitable, to enjoy their remaining time together in this beautiful place.

"I remember picking up some pamphlets on a trip to town to get groceries, and I stuck them in the kitchen drawer." He got up to retrieve them, bringing them back to Gigi and spreading them on the counter. He scanned them now, stopping at one picture. A working ranch, one that advertised rides. Maybe Gigi would be interested. He pointed to it. "Have you ever ridden a horse?"

Gigi's eyes opened wide. "Me, ride a horse?" She was a city girl and had never been out to a ranch. The closest thing she got to horses was watching TV.

Rex smiled. He'd love to see this. "Why not try it? You're

the one who said you wanted to do something special today."

She picked up the pamphlet, turning it over to study the pictures and read the descriptions before making up her mind. "Okay, let's do it."

A quick call secured a reservation at the corral for the horseback riding lessons. Rex also got directions to the place.

"The owner said we could arrive earlier if we want to tour the ranch, feed the chickens, and see the animals. Do you want to do that?"

"Yes, that sounds fun."

Rex did a quick calculation in his head. "If we leave now, we'll have time to stop in town to pick up a picnic lunch, then head out to the ranch."

"Ooh," squealed Gigi, barely able to contain her excitement. "And a picnic lunch . . . yeah!" She reached over to hug Rex and planted a firm smooch on his lips.

He closed his eyes, enjoying Gigi's kiss, her sweet, soft, tender lips. He was conscious of her energy radiating through her body. Gigi's enthusiasm was infectious. He felt it. His body craved it. Man, he was happy. He kissed her back, wanting more of it. More of her.

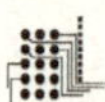

There were five horses in the corral. The trainer picked one for Gigi, the black one, Lucy. He saddled her, and the brown one for Rex, and one for himself.

As Gigi sauntered up to Lucy, the horse turned its head,

watching her. She could smell the horses now, the muck from the stables. Up close, Gigi came eye-to-eye with Lucy. Her large brown eyes and long lashes, the wind-blown mane between pointed ears.

Lucy shook her head and snorted. Her nostrils flared, the size of small pancakes, moist and soft.

Gigi jumped back, aware of how close they were, keeping her hands down as she didn't want to spook Lucy.

Rex stood beside her, giving her encouragement. "Let her check you out."

Gigi smiled nervously. "She's magnificent. So big and tall, I can't see over her."

"You'll be fine."

The trainer stepped forward. "First-timer?"

Gigi nodded eagerly.

"Let's get you up. Put your foot in the stirrup. I'll help you."

"Will she move?" asked Gigi, eyeing the saddle warily, in awe of Lucy's spectacular muscular back and long thin legs.

"Lucy is gentle and patient," said the trainer as he held the reins, giving Gigi the instructions. "I'll be riding beside you if you need me."

After a few tries Gigi was finally hoisted into the saddle, mounted and ready to go. Sitting on top of Lucy, she felt ten feet tall. As Lucy started to move, Gigi panicked for a moment. She gripped the reins tightly and turned to look at Rex.

Rex grinned as he nodded reassuringly. "Take it easy on the reins. Go slow. I'm right here."

Rex watched her, the stiffness of an inexperienced rider apparent, thinking she ought to lighten up. "Hey, I think she likes you."

"Really?" said Gigi, breaking into a smile as she looked down at Lucy. Gigi cooed, "Oh, Lucy." She called out Lucy's name several times, sure Lucy's her ears perked up with "I luva you."

"You're gonna talk baby-talk to a horse?" Rex pretended to be shocked.

Gigi laughed at his horrified expression.

Rex thought, *it's good to see her laugh, to have a break from her intense concentration.*

Soon Gigi was talking and singing to Lucy, almost nonstop because Lucy couldn't talk back.

It was hilarious, those two, thought Rex as he watched Gigi bounce in the saddle. He was pleased with how relaxed she had become once she got over her initial fear and nervousness.

"I miss riding horses. But you know, it's like riding a bicycle. Once you learn, you won't forget," said Rex.

"I love Lucy," said Gigi, laughing. She felt alive, invigorated. Rex knew her so well, knew what Gigi needed, knew it before she knew herself. How could she have doubted him? Shortchanged him? A swell of affection filled her heart as she turned and looked at him, a lump in her throat. Today was their last day in paradise. They weren't galloping away into the sunset, but this was even better.

Rex snapped a photo.

Smiling, she urged Lucy forward.

Chapter 10
ELLEN

Hump Day. Finally, mid-week rolled around. It was too slow, in Ellen's opinion. She glanced at the time on her cell. Another thirty minutes and she'd be out of there. She went back to her stack of papers, staring at the same page. Her mind wandered elsewhere, willing the time to go faster.

The knock on the door made her jump. It announced an unwelcome intrusion. Too late to put on her coat and escape. The door opened before she could invite them in. Only one person would do that.

"What are you working on?"

She looked up, hoping he wouldn't notice how tense she was. "Going over the preliminary reports for our meeting."

"Show me. Let's look over it now," said Andy as he closed the door.

"I don't think that's a good idea, Andy," said Ellen. "I have some more work to do. Will tomorrow morning work?" Ellen stared at him, taking notice of his pressed lips, the slight hint of anger. At her. She wasn't expecting this.

He hadn't given her a deadline.

"What?" snapped Andy as he took a step closer.

"I mean, with all due respect, please let me finish up and fix any errors," said Ellen, lowering her voice until it was barely audible, hoping it would soothe him. "Before wasting your valuable time on it." She didn't need this today. Today was one of the days she *had* to leave on time. Her mother had agreed to take care of Angie, having assumed Ellen had to work late. Ellen let it go at that, for now. She didn't go into the real reason—meeting Brad after work.

Andy stopped, blinking, trying to decide.

Ellen could feel her heart thumping, the beat pulsing through her body. She uttered a silent prayer. Please, please. What had gotten into Andy? This Jekyll and Hyde aspect of his personality was a new reveal. The charming man, the old Andy, was gone. In front of her was a different Andy, one that she didn't know and didn't like. She faked a smile, the most beguiling one she could muster. "I'll have it finished for you tonight. First thing in the morning I'll meet with you."

He stood, glaring at her.

"I'm so sorry I didn't meet your expectations. Please give me a chance."

"Send me the report tonight," said Andy, briskly. His anger and irritation still brewing, although somewhat abated with her apology.

"I'll email it to you," said Ellen, pushing the feeling of dread down, as if she didn't have enough to do tonight, and knowing she'd be spending a sleepless night.

Just as abruptly, he turned and walked out the door. Ellen glanced at the time. It was two minutes after five o'clock.

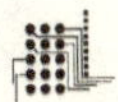

Driving through the rush hour traffic, Ellen breathed a sigh of relief. She wanted to put the unpleasant encounter behind her, not let it spoil the evening. She was meeting Brad for dinner, then expecting to make it home by early evening.

She smiled, her thoughts wandering back to Sunday when Brad came to her house to meet Angie. The next day he had called her, asking if she had time to grab a quick bite after work on Wednesday. He kept his tone neutral, not betraying his thoughts except to say Angie was a beautiful baby.

The diner was on her way home, a convenient stop for both of them. Its menu featured American cuisine, capitalizing on the words 'home-cooked' and 'made from scratch.' Ellen pulled into the parking lot. Getting out from her car, she saw Brad wave, sitting at a table by the window.

Brad rose to his feet, smiling to greet her as she walked in, pulling a chair out.

Ellen sat, grateful for Brad's chivalry, for this change in scenery. A solitary plucked flower in a small glass vase graced the table. The flatware came wrapped in a paper napkin, delivering the promise of an unadorned set and a plain meal. Her glass had water in it, filled with ice. A menu lay next to it. She smiled back.

"Glad you could make it," said Brad.

"Me too," said Ellen, thinking, *you have no idea.*

"Have you eaten here?"

Ellen shook her head. "I've passed by it, but never stopped." She scanned the menu. "Is the food good?"

"If you like a simple meal, the old-fashioned, home-cooked kind."

The waitress appeared. After a quick greeting, she went straight to business. "What'll you have?"

"How's your special today?"

"It's selling out like hotcakes."

I'll have it," said Brad, pushing the menu to her.

She turned to Ellen, showing the name "Maddy" pinned on her blouse.

"Let me have your fish and fries."

"Can't go wrong with that," said Maddy approvingly as she picked up the menus and left.

"Good day today?" said Brad.

"It could have been better," said Ellen, deciding not to get into it. "How's yours?"

"Busy, and productive. I didn't eat lunch today."

"Ooh, do you have a cafeteria?"

"We do, but it closes early. If you miss the hot food, then it's snacks from the vending machine."

"I take it you don't cook and bring your lunch?"

"Are you kidding?" said Brad, laughing. Then he straightened up and turned serious. "I *can* boil an egg."

"Mind telling me how long you boil them?"

"I set my timer to twenty minutes," said Brad in all

earnest. It was the one thing he knew how to do in the kitchen, and he was proud of it.

"You must like your yolks rock solid," said Ellen, a mischievous grin spreading as she teased him.

"Oh yes," he replied solemnly, not catching her drift.

"Well, I boil my eggs for eight minutes, nine minutes tops. You know if you cook them too long, the egg whites will start to get rubbery and the yolk hard," said Ellen.

"You like them soft, and I like them hard—just like they call them—hard-boiled eggs," said Brad, beaming.

"You know there's more than one way to boil an egg?"

"Just saying, if you ever boil them for me, that's how *I* like them."

"Is that an invitation for breakfast?" said Ellen playfully, feeling a strong urge to boil an egg and slowly peel it for him, stripping away the shell bit by bit.

As they chatted, Ellen relaxed in her chair, enjoying the unpretentious hospitality of the place until the meal arrived. Watching Brad dive into his food, seeing how hungry he was, she waited until he had finished before asking, "So Brad, what was it you wanted to talk to me about?"

"Angie," said Brad. "How adorable she is, and you—"

"She's the love of my life. I couldn't be happier."

"I see that. You've done a great job."

Ellen beamed, hearing him gush over her baby. *Their baby.*

"I've been thinking," said Brad. He wiped his mouth with the napkin, then paused to hold her gaze for a moment. "And I don't want you to take it the wrong way." He swallowed, starting over. "I've been thinking about all this, the shock of finding out that I have a daughter, meeting her for the first time, falling in love with her too—"

Ellen nodded.

"I never thought I'd be a father. I was immersed in my career, traveling a lot, and the last thing on my mind was a baby." He drew in a long breath. "When I met you, we had a lot of fun. After you stopped answering my calls, texts, and even the door, I thought that was it. That you didn't want to see me anymore. I had no idea of the real reason."

"I'm sorry to put you through that," said Ellen. "I had to wrestle with it, figure things out. Then, when I decided to go ahead with the pregnancy and keep Angie, I was determined to do it on my own, to become the best mother I could."

"I'm starting to understand that. Meeting Angie has changed my life too." His fingers played with a spoon. "That's what I want to talk to you about." He pushed the spoon away and sat up, meeting her gaze directly. "I want to be part of Angie's life. I wanted to talk to you and see how we can work it out."

Ellen had held her breath, waiting for him to tell her, not sure what he'd say. As she listened to him, she felt warmth expand in the pit of her stomach. She closed her eyes, holding that moment to herself.

"Ellen," said Brad, gently prodding her back to the conversation.

"Baby steps, okay?"

"Yes, one step at a time," said Brad, liking where this was going, looking forward to taking the first step.

"Oh, Brad," said Ellen. "Angie will be six months old next week."

"Her birthday is on the eleventh, right?"

"How about . . ." said Ellen, as an idea started to form, "a little celebration on her six month birthday?"

"Oh, I like that," said Brad, getting excited.

"A little party with cake and ice cream?"

"And presents."

"What about guests? I could invite my mom and dad," said Ellen.

"Mine live out of town, but I will invite them."

"You've told them?"

"Yeah, they were thrilled. My parents asked for a picture of Angie."

"Yes, of course," said Ellen, delighted. "Would they like a framed photo or digital?"

"Either is fine, or both. And I'd like one for myself too."

"Do they like to travel?"

"They are getting on in age and not traveling as much."

"We'll just have a little party this time, then maybe plan for a big one-year celebration?"

"They can't wait to see their first grandchild. I'm sure they would be delighted."

The ideas were churning as they discussed and made plans, and it felt so good to Ellen. So good that she almost forgot the time, that she had to go.

Chapter 11
LILLY

Lilly kicked her shoes off at the door and flung her purse on the table. Barefoot, she walked to the kitchen and grabbed a spritzer from the refrigerator. This day hadn't gone well, and she couldn't wait to get home.

The knock on the door broke the silence. Lilly swiveled, caught by surprise. Who could it be? She wasn't expecting anyone. As if the day could get any worse; now wasn't the time to talk to anyone. She hesitated. The knock persisted, louder this time. Sighing, she opened the door to find a tall, good-looking man with a rugged face standing outside.

"Hello, Mrs. Cooper."

She froze, staring at the same man who had come to question her about Gary, the cab driver who was found dead on the sidewalk outside her home. She was surprised to see him again.

"Do you remember me, Mrs. Cooper?"

"I didn't catch your name—"

"Steve Cosine." He paused politely. "Do you have a few minutes to talk?"

"Now's not a good time."

"This won't take long," said Steve, taking a step forward to look over her shoulder.

"I just got home."

"A few minutes and I'll be out of your hair."

"I've already answered your questions before," said Lilly, irritated.

"If you'll allow me," said Steve in his smooth, deep voice.

Lilly shrugged, resigned to get this over as quickly as possible. She gestured, pointing to the wooden chair in the living room, while she moved to sit on the couch. "What's this about?"

"I have some questions for you about Gary Smith who drove a cab. He was found dead in front of your home the day of the big storm."

"We've already gone over that," snapped Lilly.

"I have a few more. Have you ever been to the warehouse at Peter's Street?"

"No, I don't know the place." Lilly frowned. "What does this have to do with me?"

"We found Gary's fingerprints on a van parked outside the warehouse," said Steve, eyes probing Lilly.

Lilly shook her head.

Steve shifted in his chair. "We traced the warehouse to a Dr. Kite. Do you know him?"

"Kite—" said Lilly, as she stiffened, clenching her jaw. It wasn't the direction she wanted to take.

"Please answer my questions. We have reason to believe Kite is missing, and he may be another link to Gary."

"I'm afraid I can't help you." She stifled a cry, frozen in fear at the mention of Gary's name as it brought back visions of his death, and the reason Steve came to her home to question her that first time.

"Can't—or won't?" said Steve, eyes piercing.

Lilly rubbed her knee, trying to stall, biding her time.

"I ran a check on Kite's credit cards—when he used them, where he went," said Steve. "All activity stopped the day after the storm."

Lilly licked her lips.

"I'm going to ask you again. I advise you to think hard about Kite."

She sighed and spread her hands on her thighs. "Now that I think about it, I did meet Kite, but it was briefly at a restaurant."

"Would that have been at Duggers?"

A sinking feeling came over Lilly as she realized that Steve knew more than she had guessed.

"I met him there once, but it was by accident."

"So you didn't know this Kite before that?"

"No."

"How did this, umm, accident come about?"

"I had already finished the main course when he arrived. I had taken his lucky table, but of course, I had no way of knowing. So when the hostess brought him to his usual table—the table I was sitting at—he was disappointed to see it occupied."

"Then what happened?"

"I invited him to sit with me while I had my dessert."

"Didn't you think it was odd?"

She shook her head. "No. It was a chance meeting, his lucky day, as he said." She added, "He turned out to be a pleasant table companion, gracious and grateful for the kindness."

"And yours? Was it also your lucky day?"

"At the time it felt like it."

Chapter 12
DR. KITE

Watching Tiffany leave, get in her car and drive away, Kite felt let down, his enthusiasm dampened. He felt sure Tiffany was stalling. Kite didn't know why. Still, he was willing to give her some more time to think about it, to make a choice.

He had the two chips left, and that was all he had to offer her. Kite had almost no money, and no wish to continue the trawling for human test subjects. That part of his life seemed a distant past. The shock and trauma of the fire, seeing the blackened remains of his warehouse smoldering under the embers, hastened Kite's decision to close that chapter in his life.

He clenched his fist, gripping it hard. Cursing. It wasn't how things should have turned out, what he had envisioned in his mind. A fantasy, a happily ever after, had slipped between his fingers. How could he have been so wrong? What was he thinking?

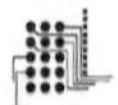

She didn't know where she was going. Tiffany drove aimlessly, on autopilot. Her mind was elsewhere. Overhead, the clouds gathered, drawing a curtain over the day, summoning the night before its time.

It wasn't supposed to be like this. For several months, Tiffany had played the part dutifully, going along with the plan. Kite was a subject, an assignment. No more, no less. She'd let her objectivity slip a little at a time. A chipping away that she hadn't been aware of, or even wanted. She had to remind herself to remain focused, to stay the course, to keep her head on her shoulders. Was she going crazy?

Her car had a mind of its own, taking her down the coast to the pier. Dusk would soon be settling in, and this place was her favorite on the beach. A little pier, now fallen into disuse, the wood on the far end slowly rotting in the water. No longer safe, it still commanded a majestic sight, a runway rising above the water and held up by crisscrosses of thick, long wooden poles.

She could feel the dampness in the air as moisture seeped into her clothes and stuck to her skin. She turned to watch the sunset. The crisp color veiled by the clouds.

Tiffany could smell the ocean, the swell from afar carrying all sorts of sea creatures and shells spilled onto the beach. She could hear the waves, powerful and rhythmic.

The cry of seagulls flying overhead broke the serenity of the moment.

It was a place she escaped to when she wanted to be by herself. One that asked nothing and took nothing. She found peace and acceptance here. She was just a blip in time, a dot on the beach. The vastness of the ocean, the endless stretches of sand, stirred a strong response. Had the beach been there, meeting the seas, for eons? She shivered as the darkness of the night descended, feeling her mortality, her fleeting existence on earth.

And Kite? She understood where his ego, vanity, and determination had taken him. And she glimpsed his remorse and humility.

Chapter 13
GIGI

Packing and leaving, Gigi felt a piece of her would always be there. And she carried with her the memories of the vacation, of Rex, the calm, peaceful feeling, the beauty of the land. Rex had suffered another relapse of his illness after the ranch outing, and he was struggling with his luggage. She walked over to him, placing an arm around his shoulders.

He turned, welcoming her gesture, her caring. "Hey girl," he said, smiling bravely to hide the pain.

"Let me get that," said Gigi as she lifted the suitcase into the trunk of their rental car. "Is this the last one?"

"Yup. Ready to go?" He paused, turning around one last time before leaving. "I'm going to miss this place."

She hooked her arm around his waist, feeling the curve of his hips. "Me too," said Gigi. She had been happy here in their hideaway. Gigi sighed, soon they would be back in the real world. She was worried about Rex. And anxious about what Steve Cosine had to say.

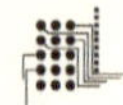

Steve dropped by their apartment Monday afternoon. He was dressed as usual in his frumpy shirt with no tie.

Rex clasped his friend's hand, delighted. "Man, it's good to see you."

Steve looked the same—tall and gangly, big bones that carried his frame effortlessly, the lined, weathered face still handsome. Add a hat and he'd easily pass for a cowboy.

"This retirement has been anything but quiet." He chuckled.

"You've been doing okay?"

"Yeah, exhausted is more like it. The unexpected havoc from the storm created a mess. A lot of cases since I've been recruited back to help." He ran his hand through his thick head of hair, reminded he needed to get it cut, although Steve was thankful he had the good hair genes, like his dad.

"Getting enough sleep?"

"About four to five hours."

"Man, that's not enough."

"It'll do. I don't have the luxury of sleeping longer."

"Hey, you're supposed to be retired. But it sounds like you're busier now than when you worked full-time."

Steve nodded. "The difference being I choose what I want to do, and how much I want to work."

"Would you like something to drink?" Rex headed to the kitchen.

"Sure, what've you got?"

Opening the refrigerator door, Rex pointed to the

bottled drinks. "We quit drinking beer. Got all kinds of juices and non-alcoholic drinks."

"I'll take a root beer," said Steve.

Rex nodded, grabbing a ginger zinger for himself.

They sat down at the kitchen table, waiting for Gigi to join them.

Rex wondered why she had disappeared so quickly after a quick hello to Steve when he'd arrived.

"Hey Gigi," Rex called. "We're in the kitchen. Are you coming?"

"Be there in a minute," said Gigi, as she changed into a comfortable T-shirt. She reached out to the dresser top, steadying herself. The unease Gigi felt since receiving the email from Steve crept back, bringing strong emotions and memories. She had suppressed them, put them out of sight and out of mind, and moved on with her life.

A thought crept up, casting a shadow over her. She shivered. Her secret. She had never told Rex. What if Steve had found out?

Chapter 14
ELLEN

"Angie asleep?" said Ellen as she stepped through her door.

Mrs. Fulbright put her two hands together and bent them, her head resting on top.

"I'm sorry, I ran a little late tonight."

"Problem?"

For once, Ellen didn't mind her mom's curious prying. A gnawing sense of dread, a discomfort. Now that she was home, the last thing she wanted to do was work on the report. The very last. But she had promised Andy.

"Here, come and sit with me," her mom said, patting the couch. "I can tell something is bothering you."

"Mom, Andy's gone weird on me."

"What do you mean?" She frowned. "I thought Andy's been sweet on you. I mean he's your boss, and he's an attractive man."

"He was, but he's changed."

"Changed? How so?"

Ellen gave a nervous laugh. "Like you wouldn't believe. I'm feeling it."

"Okay, now you're frightening me. When did this start?"

"The night of the social, he was charming, sexy, came on to me." She paused. "Then I met Brad and he wanted to talk, so we left the party. I told you about that."

Ellen's mom nodded.

"We went to an empty meeting room to talk." She frowned, trying to remember as she told the story. "We didn't close the door, but at one point in our discussion, I thought I heard something, a cough. I chalked it up to someone walking by in the hallway, although I didn't see anyone." Her hand flew to cover her mouth as her eyes opened wide. "Oh my God. Do you think Andy was lurking outside and listening to our conversation?"

"If he were watching you, he would've seen you leave . . ."

". . . with Brad, and he might have followed us . . ."

"When was the next time you talked to Andy?"

"On Monday morning. When I came to work, the first thing I saw was his short, terse note taped on my door."

"He wasn't in a good mood?"

"Not that day."

"Can you think of anything else that could have upset him that night, anything you said or did?"

Ellen shook her head.

"Then today he barged into my office right before I was getting ready to leave and gave me a hard time on the report that I was working on."

"Did you end up staying late to work?"

"I think that was his intention, but I stalled him, said I'd deliver the report to him tonight and see him first thing tomorrow morning."

Ellen straightened up, eyes sparkling as she clasped her hands. "Brad asked me to meet with him tonight," Ellen added quickly. "I've got exciting news to tell you."

Chapter 15
LILLY

She spent another restless night, tossing and turning. Her plan with Kite wasn't going as smooth as she thought it'd go. She'd lived in fear of another knock on the door. Or rather a pounding at her door, one that could only mean one thing. The police were coming to get her.

The thought of spending time behind bars terrified her.

Tracking Kite down had been easier than anticipated. She was determined to find him. Lilly did the only thing she could do, and luck was on her side. She went back to Duggers, the restaurant where they met.

Lilly sat at his favorite table, his favorite place, and talked to the hostess. Sally was her name. She wasn't wrong. Old habits die hard. Before he left the city, Kite had his last meal there.

According to Sally, he stopped by to say goodbye to all his friends there.

"Did he say why he's leaving?" Lilly asked.

"Something about the storm and his business burned to the ground."

"Was he devastated?"

"Yeah, he was tearing up. He sat there, staring at his plate, slouched in his chair."

"Not his usual self, then."

"Oh no," said Sally, adamantly shaking her head. "I've never seen him like that."

"So he came by to say goodbye?"

"And have the last meal."

Lilly opened up to Sally. "I shared a table with Kite. Do you remember?"

"The only time that happened was a while ago. But that woman—" Sally looked puzzled for a moment. "She looked worn, torn up about something. And a lot older. I mean, that *couldn't* have been you."

Lilly smiled, nodding.

"What? But you look different now."

"Oh, that was the old me, and now you see the new me."

"Wow, I wouldn't have guessed. You, you're like a different person."

"Well, I cut my hair too."

"You sure did."

"Got rid of all my hair and the baggage with it," said Lilly. She leaned back. "And I feel so much lighter."

"Whatever you did, I want to know."

Lilly threw her head back and belted out a throaty laugh. "I want Kite to see me."

"Oh, he should see you. He won't even recognize you."

Lilly said quietly, "Look, I'm worried about Kite. Did he happen to mention where he's going?"

Sally whispered too, acting conspiratorial. "Well, he was headed toward the coast, a little town about twenty miles north of Chas Town."

"Ah, someplace quiet, away from the tourist crowd."

"I just know it's about a couple hours from here, two and a half max," said Sally. "A little hideaway mostly frequented by locals."

"You've been there?"

"A long time ago, as a child. We passed through there once. Stopped to have a meal at the diner." She smiled. "We ate at 'Square Meal.' Who can forget that name?"

Lilly paid for the meal and left a generous tip.

The waitress came back, assuming she wanted the change.

"No, you keep the change," said Lilly, smiling.

Chapter 16
GIGI

If anyone were up to anything fishy, Steve would sniff it out. Sitting in the kitchen with Rex, waiting for Gigi, he thought she should be thrilled about the new lead in her case. *Why wasn't she? Did Gigi have something to hide?*

He got himself into this by doing a favor for Rex, helping him out. He glanced at Rex. He seemed entirely at ease, the same old Rex he'd always known. He checked the time. Eight minutes in the kitchen chatting with Rex and still no Gigi in sight.

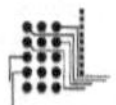

Putting her best face on, Gigi turned on her charm as she walked out to talk to Steve, offering a quick hug.

"You look great," said Steve, scanning her for signs of the accident or scars and finding none.

"So good to see you," said Gigi. "I never got to thank you in person for all that you did."

"No more nightmares?"

"All gone." Gigi smiled.

"Let me get to the point about the new development. You saw the email?"

Gigi nodded.

"The man that we traced the fingerprints to is dead," said Steve.

"Oh no," said Gigi.

"Unfortunately, he died in the storms."

"What was his name?"

"Gary."

"Was he driving the van?"

"When he died, he was driving a taxi."

"Uh . . . what's the connection with the taxi?"

Steve took a swig of his drink and put it down. "Let me explain. After the storm, the van was found parked in front of a warehouse that had burned."

"So Gary—"

"His prints were found on the van."

"So what's with the warehouse?" said Rex.

"We had to do some digging. We found a connection between the warehouse and a Dr. Kite."

"A medical doctor?" asked Rex.

"That is the puzzling part," said Steve, shaking his head. "This Kite, he didn't graduate from medical school or have a license to practice. But as far as we can tell, he was conducting some health-related research and experiments."

"So have you talked to this Kite?" said Rex.

"Not yet, but I have some leads I'm following up on."

Steve fiddled with his bottle, picking it up and turning it. He pretended to study the label as if the number of calories became of utmost importance.

"Gigi, help me understand the connection," said Steve. "The van, you, Gary, the warehouse."

She shook her head.

"Do you know this Gary?"

"No," said Gigi emphatically.

"What about Dr. Kite—Gigi, do you know him?" said Steve, eyeing her intently.

This question was one that Gigi dreaded. The secret she had kept from Rex. Gigi turned to look at him, throwing a smile to disarm any ill-feelings. She sat up, pulling her shoulders back.

"Yes," she whispered.

For a moment there was stunned silence in the room. Steve had toyed with the idea of a possible connection with Gigi, but to hear it was a different story.

Gigi reached over to touch Rex's hand. "I want to tell you something. But before I do, I want to apologize to you."

"I don't think you have to apologize."

"But I do, and I'm relieved to be doing this now," said Gigi. "I've been carrying this secret around."

Rex squeezed her hand.

She turned to him and paused. "I know Dr. Kite. He was my doctor."

Surprised, Rex stopped squeezing her hand.

"Remember when I had that condition, ringing and buzzing in my ears . . . the tinnitus?"

He nodded.

"It had gotten worse, constant, day and night. I couldn't deal with it, and I sought out doctors in search of some relief. I was frantic, out of options, and desperate. So when I heard about this doctor, who was unconventional and secretive, I became curious. The arrangement made was for me to be picked up by a cab driver and taken to see Kite. The first time I was blindfolded and didn't see where I was going."

"The first time? So you saw him more than once?"

"Yes."

"What happened?"

"He implanted a microchip in me," said Gigi. "It cured my illness."

"What kind of microchip?" said Rex. *How could Gigi have kept this from him?*

"It was a prototype, a new chip he had developed after years of research." She smiled. All I know is that he cured me of my disease, and he put me back to perfect working order."

"So can you talk about after that, when you went back the next time?" Steve asked.

"I hadn't thought of him for quite a while until he contacted me again."

"Was there a problem?"

"Not that I'm aware. Kite said he had received a new shipment, an upgraded mind-control microchip, and he wanted me to come in to have it replaced."

"How did you get there this time?"

"I was picked up by a cab driver the second time also."

"But you weren't blindfolded this time?" said Steve.

"This time, I saw where he took me."

Steve rapped the table with his hands. "Let me guess, the warehouse?"

Gigi nodded.

She sat back, relieved the truth had come out. She studied Rex's face to garner his response. She had seen confusion, which turned to anger. Now it was replaced by worried concern.

"Rex," said Gigi. "I'm sorry. Please forgive me. I never meant to keep secrets from you, but Kite swore me to secrecy before the first implant."

"Gigi, I had no idea you went through all this. I see you as a strong woman. And you kept your promise to Kite to keep it secret."

Steve said, "I have a few more questions." He pulled a photo from his pocket and laid it on the table. "This man." He tapped the face. "Do you know him, Gigi?"

She leaned in, studying his features. "Yes."

"Do you know his name?"

She shook her head.

"How do you know him then?"

"He was the cab driver. He took me to see Kite."

"Flip the photo over."

"Gary Smith," said Gigi, as she read the name written on the back.

Chapter 17
LILLY

Naomi repeatedly tried to reach Tiffany. Her previous calls had gone straight to voicemail. It was getting late, and she wanted to try once more before she called it a night.

On the second ring, Tiffany answered. "Hello?"

"Tiffany, I'm so glad I've finally reached you."

"Naomi?"

"Yeah, where have you been? I've been calling. I was worried something's happened to you."

"I took a walk on the beach. There's no cell service there."

"We must talk."

"Shoot, I'm listening."

"No, I mean in person. I'm *here*."

"What?" said Tiffany, surprised. "Why didn't you tell me you're coming?"

"Lilly sent me," said Naomi. "I dropped everything and scrambled to get here."

"Well, you shouldn't have."

"She was worried about you."

"Why, for Pete's sake?"

"Look, why don't we talk about it in person?" said Naomi. "I'm starved. Is there someplace we could grab a bite?"

Hearing a few low rumbles in her stomach, Tiffany was quick to respond. "Square Meal. You know where it is?"

"I passed by it earlier on my way into town."

"See you there in a few," said Tiffany.

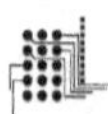

The restaurant stood by itself on the edge of town. The faded wooden sign that said "Square Meal" had seen better days, the cracks in the paint a sad indicator of the disrepair. But it didn't seem to affect its customers, the local crowd that hung out, who trod on its worn floors and embraced the establishment despite its exterior decay.

Naomi was the first to arrive. At this late hour, a wide selection of tables was available. Catching sight of the waitress, she smiled. "Table for two, please."

The waitress nodded and waved her hand. "Hon, just sit anywhere you like."

Naomi slid across the bench seat to sit by the window.

She didn't have long to wait before the waitress came by with the menu and two sets of silverware laid on top of paper napkins. "What'll you have to drink?"

"How's your iced tea?"

"It's good, and not too sweet, if you know what I mean,"

said the waitress. "You know what you want to eat?"

Naomi shook her head. "I haven't decided yet." Looking up from the menu, she added, "My friend will be joining me."

"I'll be back with your drink."

Leaning against the hard back of the seat, Naomi took in the dim interior. An undefined color, some shade between gray and smoke-green, was painted over the washed-out interior. The dim light chased shadows and dark murky streaks on the wall.

"Thank you," said Naomi as the waitress set her drink on the table. Her eyes scanned the wood, marked with scratches, notches, and carved hearts bisected by arrows with initials inside. She wondered, how many couples have sat here carving their initials and they're still together? With her finger, she rubbed the heart in the center of the table, the biggest one she could see, feeling the ridges, following its curves and the crude initials.

"Hey, you made it," said Tiffany, interrupting Naomi's thoughts as she squeezed into the bench across from her.

Throwing her a warm smile, Naomi said, "I was close by."

The waitress appeared and took their order. The menu was sparse. They ordered quickly, and service was fast. Fried catfish and okra for Tiffany. Grilled shrimp and rice for Naomi.

"So how's the program going?"

"We're about to wrap up. Two more days until the end," said Naomi.

"Got some good prospects for round two?"

"Out of the twelve, in the beginning, we lost one. A handful made it this far to achieve a state of cleansing and renewal, both physically and mentally."

Tiffany nodded. "That sounds about right."

"Of course, they find out after they finish the program about the next round," said Naomi, with a slight frown. Lilly had demanded absolute hush on this, and she disagreed with it.

"And it's expected some will go home, having achieved the goals they signed up for," said Tiffany.

"And some will decide to go on as we did," added Naomi.

"Taking on assignments, changing the world one project at a time," said Tiffany, stifling a yawn.

"You got lucky on that one. I had to stay and help Lilly with the next class."

"You've got those superb organization skills," murmured Tiffany, smoothing things over. "Perfect for that job."

"Well, I'm here to help."

Tiffany quickly brought Naomi up to speed. When she got to the part about the two new microchips, Naomi's eyes widened.

"We need to tell Lilly. Have you talked to her?"

Tiffany shook her head. "Not yet."

"Let's do it now. Lilly's worried sick about you."

Tiffany picked up her cell phone and scrolled to Lilly's name.

Lilly picked up on the first ring.

"Hello."

"Naomi is here with me."

"Are you all right?"

"I'm fine. I turned my phone off when I met with Kite and was out of pocket for a while after that."

"So tell me what happened."

"He came to my apartment, you know, to check up on me."

"He was worried after your dizzy spell."

"Yes, and Kite brought groceries. I made coffee, and we chatted for awhile."

"Did you ask him about the warehouse?"

"It burned, everything was gone. But no one was hurt."

"And the chips?" said Lilly eagerly.

"He still has two microchips."

"Wait just a minute. So Kite's chips didn't all get destroyed in the fire?"

"Yes, but these weren't in the warehouse. Kite found them in his laptop carry bag."

"Go on."

"Well, he, um offered me a choice."

"A choice?"

"Between the two chips."

Lilly paused before continuing. "These chips, what do they do?"

"Well, one is a medication tracking chip, so you wouldn't forget to take meds like I did."

"And the other?"

"He mentioned pheromones, something like a love potion," said Tiffany as she looked at Naomi, catching her eye.

"Put Naomi on the phone, will you?"

She handed the cell over to Naomi, mouthing, "She wants to talk to you."

"I'm coming over there."

"But . . . the class isn't over yet."

"We've got two more days. Can you handle it?"

"So you want me to come back?"

"You know the drill."

Naomi gulped. Lilly must have a lot of faith in her to ask her to close the program. "Of course, Lilly."

"I knew I could count on you," said Lilly, relieved. "Oh, and hand the phone back to Tiffany please."

"You want to talk to me?" said Tiffany.

"Have you told Kite when you'd have a decision?"

"No, I just told him I needed time to think."

"Okay, call him and set up a time to meet tomorrow afternoon."

"But what about you?"

"I'll be there—but don't tell him yet."

"You're coming, right?"

"I should be arriving in the morning. I'll go straight to your apartment. See when Kite is available. Be sure to tell him to bring the microchips."

Chapter 18

ELLEN

Barely awake, Ellen dragged her heels getting ready for work. She stayed up way too late last night working on the report. But she finished and sent it in the early hours of the morning.

Suppressing a yawn as she got off the elevator, Ellen headed straight to her office. The door was ajar. Ellen was sure she had closed it the night before. Walking in, she saw a note taped to her computer. It was from Andy, telling her to see him—just like the one he wrote previously. How did he do it? Get here so early, beat her to the office—and he must've read her report. One thing Ellen was sure about that man, he was a workaholic.

She pulled a copy of the report from her briefcase and walked quickly to Andy's office. Better to get it over with— the sooner, the better. She took a second to compose herself, then knocked on his door firmly. She barely gave him time to respond before marching inside.

He met her at the door; he had been expecting her. This

morning he was back to his charming self. All smiles.

"Ellen," he said. His hand lingered on her arm, touching her bare skin as he guided her forward.

She jumped as a little spark of static electricity snapped between them.

"Ouch," said Andy, exaggerating. "That's quite a shock."

"I'm wide awake now."

"I see you stayed up all night."

"I was tired. I crashed on the couch."

"After you delivered the report," said Andy with a smirk.

"You've read it?"

"Sure did."

"So um, what do think?"

"It's good."

Ellen whirled, planning a quick escape.

"By the way, Ellen," said Andy.

Heart thumping, she slowly turned around.

"You need something else, boss?"

Quick as a fox, he moved, sliding up to her, so close his pant legs brushed hers.

She wriggled her foot a few inches away, hoping he wouldn't notice.

But he did. Closing in, Andy was now right on top of her.

Ellen could feel his breath blowing on her cheeks. No wiggle room left, he got her pinned.

Chapter 19
LILLY

She packed light, taking only a duffle bag for the trip. Time to get some sleep. She set her alarm for 5:00 a.m., plenty of time to drive to the coast and meet up with Tiffany. Soon she'd be face-to-face with Kite.

There was one more thing she had to do tonight. Whipping out her cell phone, she scrolled down the contacts list to find Steve Cosine.

Holding the phone to her ear, she got out a pad and scribbled a few words on it, as a reminder of what to say. The call went to voicemail. She left a message and asked Steve to call her that night, saying that it was urgent.

Chapter 20
DR. KITE

He walked along the beach, hoping to calm his mind from the thoughts swirling around. He had to get away to think things through.

She said she needed time to think. Kite had stayed away, not calling her.

If Tiffany didn't respond by tomorrow, he was going to take matters into his own hands. He would, this time.

Taking his shoes off, Kite sunk his toes in the sand, feeling the coolness as he pushed his heels down. He stepped carefully, searching for seashells washed up on the beach from the Atlantic.

He kept his mind preoccupied, focusing on finding the one special shell buried amongst the abundant and common clams, cockles, and periwinkles.

His toe bumped into something. A knobby whelk. A few inches to the left of it, he glimpsed a scotch bonnet, his favorite. "Huh," grunted Kite, as he snatched it up. Blowing the sand off, he scraped the inside with his fingernail, scooping out embedded sand.

Occupied with finding seashells, he lost track of time. Leaving the beach, Kite checked his phone for the bars indicating cell coverage. This time she had called and left a voicemail.

His smile turned into a broad grin as he listened to her message. He wasted no time returning her call.

Chapter 21
LILLY

The harsh sound of her cell phone startled heavy-eyed Lilly from her slumber.

Cursing, she grabbed the phone.

"Hello," said Lilly, groggy from sleep.

"Oh, did I wake you up?" said Steve.

She didn't respond.

"I didn't hear your call earlier when I was in the shower," he continued smoothly.

She listened to the deep, masculine voice on the other end of the line, trying to picture the face of the caller.

"It's Steve Cosine, returning your call."

Oh crap! She clamped her hand over her mouth, glad he couldn't see her expression. "Oh, I did call you, didn't I?"

"Yes, ma'am," said Steve. "Is this too late to call you back?"

"No, tonight is fine." Lilly cleared her throat. "This is Lilly. You came to see me recently and gave me your card."

"Lilly Cooper," said Steve.

"You, um, said to call you if I had information about Dr. Kite."

"Have you heard from him?" asked Steve, his attention sharpened.

"Not exactly. But I found out where Kite is."

Stunned by this unexpected bit of news and Lilly's apparent willingness to work with him, he took out his notepad and a pen, ready to scribble.

"But before I tell you, I want you to promise that you won't do anything rash."

"I can't promise you anything, but I'll take it into consideration."

He could hear her let out a deep breath.

"I have a confession to make," said Lilly. The words slipped out past her lips somehow. Perhaps she felt easier talking to Steve over the phone. Maybe it was something about his voice that was soothing. Whatever the reason, she just wanted to tell him, to come clean. Now.

He waited for her to continue.

"When I met Kite, I was recently divorced. It left its mark on me, and I turned into a bitter, angry woman. That night at Duggers we talked friendly chit-chat at first. Later, before we left, he gave me his card."

"So you had another date?"

"Oh no, nothing of the sort."

"But you called him?" Steve prodded gently.

"Yes, about a medical procedure."

"I don't get it."

"I called and asked him to help me look and feel better,

to recover from the divorce."

"How would he do that?"

"His research. He had developed a prototype mind-control microchip for this. He offered it to me. I thought it over, made my decision, and called him back."

"Where's this chip?"

"He injected it in me."

A chip, inside Lilly. He whistled, letting it sink in—what Lilly just said, and what Gigi said.

"It's in you now?"

"In my arm."

"So you have news about Kite?" said Steve.

"Yes, and I've found him—finally."

"Where?"

"In a little town about twenty miles north of Chas Town."

"That's not too far from here."

"I'm heading out there in the morning," said Lilly, yawning. "That's why I went to sleep early."

Steve thought hard. Things were moving fast now, the pieces all of a sudden falling in place. The van, Gary, the warehouse. Kite, Gigi, Lilly.

"When are you leaving?"

"Five o'clock," said Lilly, adding abruptly, "Look, I've got to go or I'm not going to be able to get up early."

"I'm coming with you," said Steve.

Chapter 22
ELLEN

Her lipstick was smeared. A few strands of hair slipped out from her neat bun. Ellen stared in the bathroom mirror as she let the water run from the faucet. Grabbing a towel and wetting it, she poured soap on it before scrubbing her lips, then her face clean. Devoid of makeup, she got another towel and repeated the same procedure.

Making her way to a stall, she went in and locked the door. Alone, safe, she closed her eyes as she leaned back.

What was he thinking? She had said no. That didn't stop Andy from coming up close, pressing against her, his thighs moving and touching hers, his breath warm on her cheek.

Ellen felt trapped, pinned next to the wall. They were in his office. She didn't dare scream, yet she wanted to. Up close, his attractive face turned ugly. Insistent. She didn't want this. It was all wrong.

Stunned, she froze. Like a frightened rabbit. Her mind trying to process what was happening. To her. In Andy's office.

Then he rubbed on her, his breathing becoming faster.

She wriggled her arm up in front of her chest, wedging a space between them.

With a quick movement, he flung her arm out, his fingernails digging into her, hurting her.

She cried out, "No!"

It angered him. He grabbed Ellen's cheeks and forced her head back, pushing his lips down on hers.

She turned her head, squirming.

It was the loud knock on his office door that saved her.

Chapter 23
GIGI

Rex felt a mixture of emotions about Gigi, what she revealed in the meeting with Steve. At first, he felt blindsided, angry, and upset. Rex blamed her for not telling him. He had trusted her, confided in her. How could she have kept it secret?

But as she revealed why she did it, he started to understand. He knew she was remorseful.

After Steve left, Gigi had cried. All her pent-up emotions from her ordeal, the accident, the nightmares—everything resurfaced.

Hearing her sob broke his heart. Rex moved closer to her on the couch. He wrapped his arms around her, holding her tight. They rocked ever so slightly with each heave of her sobbing.

He held on, not letting Gigi go until her crying subsided and her tears ran dry.

Chapter 24
DR. KITE

He woke up, just like that, without the rude awakening of an alarm. He had slept well. Refreshed, Kite stretched, feeling good. What was it about today? The thought of Tiffany brought on a slow smile. He applauded himself for being patient. Soon he would see her again, in the afternoon.

He busied himself around the apartment, straightening things up. Before noon, he stepped out to walk downtown to look for a new shirt to wear. It was slim pickings at the general store, but he managed to find something.

Keeping alive the hope that flickered, he could hardly wait.

Chapter 25

LILLY

Lilly pulled up along the street, looking for Tiffany's apartment. She glanced at Steve, sitting in the passenger seat, which was tilted back to accommodate his long legs. He looked comfortable, sprawled out like that. "We're almost there."

"We made good time."

It was still morning, early. On impulse, Lilly blurted, "I could do with some coffee now."

"Wouldn't hurt to get something to eat too," said Steve. "I don't know about you, but I'm hungry. We've got some time to spare."

Lilly was already turning down the street.

The only place in town was the Square Meal.

She pointed to a table in the back, leading the way as the waitress hurried to snatch a couple of menus and place settings.

"You folks new in town?" said the waitress.

Lilly glanced at her name tag. "Ruby, is it?"

Ruby nodded.

"Ruby, I'd like some coffee, scrambled eggs, and toast," said Lilly, handing the menu back.

Ruby scribbled on her pad, eager to take the orders.

"And you, sir?"

"Give me some of that bottomless cup of coffee," drawled Steve.

"You want yours black?"

"Any way you got, I'm easy. But if you'll bring me a creamer with some milk, I'd be doubly pleased," said Steve, grinning.

"Would you like some food to go with the coffee, sir?" said Ruby. If she were earning stars on her uniform, she'd be a five-star waitress for a five-star customer.

"Tell you what, just bring me today's special," said Steve.

"All righty," said Ruby, smiling.

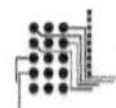

Tiffany got up early. She didn't sleep well. After a restless night, she wasn't looking forward to the day. As if the stress of meeting with Kite wasn't enough, now Lilly was coming, driving from the city.

A long, hot shower was what she needed. She undressed, stepped into the tub, and turned on the water. She stood under the spray, closing her eyes, letting the water flow over her body. She stayed there, not moving, not reaching for the soap.

When she'd looked for an apartment, the shower was a

deal-breaker. She fell in love with another place, freshly painted mint green and cute as a button. A claw-foot tub sat in the middle of a small bathroom. In the end, however, she chose a simple apartment—cheap, clean, no frills, but with a shower.

There was something to be said about showers. They had a calming effect. Today was no different. Tiffany put on a pot of coffee, fried two eggs, toasted a couple of slices of bread, and smacked them together for an egg sandwich.

Chapter 26
LILLY

The caffeine did the work as adrenaline coursed through her veins, sending a jolt. Lilly's sleep had been cut short this morning, and the stress of sudden, last minute changes didn't sit well with her. Steve Cosine had merely said he was coming with her. He didn't ask or plead. He made the statement quietly, in a matter-of-fact manner. It almost didn't sink in when she heard it on the phone.

She knew it was pointless to argue with him. He was a man of quiet authority, who knew when and how to use it, and people respected him.

Sitting across the table from him at the diner, she studied Steve. He was sitting back in his chair, his shirt sleeves rolled up, looking relaxed. She thought, *Intelligent, but not cunning. A man of few words.* Tapping her finger, she smiled.

"Tired from driving?" said Steve.

"A bit, but I'm fine now."

"Good."

"I don't mean to pry," said Lilly, toying with her knife. "Why did you want to come?"

"To talk to Kite."

"Have you met him before?"

"No," said Steve.

"So it's your first time?"

Steve nodded.

"I almost didn't come," said Lilly.

"Why not?"

"I'm running a business, and we're down to the last two days of this session," said Lilly.

"What kind of session?"

"It's a program for women, two weeks of training and endurance."

Steve raised his brow. "How are you able to break away?'

"My assistant. She's a former top graduate, and she'll take care of it."

"You're leaving things in good hands?"

"Yeah, she's good." Lilly shifted in the seat, ready to get going. "Shall we?"

Steve picked up the tab on his way toward the cashier by the door.

By the time they got to Tiffany's place, it was around noon.

Lilly knocked on the door and it swung open immediately.

"Tiffany," said Lilly, smiling in greeting.

Stepping forward, Tiffany gave her a quick hug as her

glance met Steve's.

"I'm Steve Cosine."

"A friend of Lilly?"

He didn't answer.

"He's here to talk to Kite," Lilly explained.

"Oh," said Tiffany, looking at first to Lilly then Steve.

"May we come in?" said Lilly. "We can talk about it."

Tiffany recapped and brought Steve up to date. She didn't see the point of holding anything back since Lilly had brought him here.

Lilly had heard most of this on the phone, but hearing all of it in person gave her more perspective. "So Kite is expecting your decision today on the two microchips?"

"Yes, and he'll be bringing them."

"Have you seen them?"

"He showed me the two injection pens, loaded with the chips," said Tiffany.

Steve cleared his throat. "How does Kite tell them apart?"

"The Number 9 pen has a dot on it," said Tiffany.

"A dot?"

"A black dot. I think he marked it with a magic marker."

"It's a little past one," said Lilly. "He should be here soon."

"Let me know if you have any other questions."

"I do," said Steve.

"Oh?" said Tiffany.

"What is your decision?"

Chapter 27
DR. KITE

He arrived at Tiffany's door at precisely half-past one. He straightened up, felt his clean-shaven cheeks, and sucked his breath in. Finally, he patted his pocket, feeling the reassuring outline of the two injection pens.

Ready at last, he knocked.

Tiffany opened the door, saying welcome as she attempted a smile, her nervousness betrayed by her fingers running through her hair.

Kite felt slightly awkward, sensing a bit of hesitancy in her. "Hello, is this a good time?"

"Oh yes, do come in," said Tiffany as she ushered him through the door.

His eyes pleaded with her for some show of warmth, before alighting on the two people standing farther back in the living room. He gulped. *It wasn't what he'd expected.*

"Let me introduce you all. Lilly Cooper and Steve Cosine."

His eyes traveled to the woman. Lilly, she looked familiar.

Then he remembered. She's the lady at Duggers—Lilly. One of the three women he had implanted mind-control chips.

Steve stepped forward; hand held out. "Steve Cosine."

He shook hands as he sought to find him in his memory banks. "I don't believe I've met you."

"You haven't," said Steve.

"So . . ."

"I'm here to ask you a few questions."

"About what?"

"For starters, your warehouse, Gary, the chips—"

Feeling his palms sweat, Kite started to panic. He thought, *You're busted. So busted.*

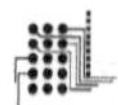

Tiffany spoke. "Kite came to my rescue the other day when I became dizzy at the store. He took me to the doctor and came by to check on me later."

Kite threw her a look of thanks.

She winked at him. At that moment, he relaxed a bit.

"I understand you have something to help her," said Steve.

"Well, yeah," said Kite, wondering how much he knew. What had she told him?

"She's told us," said Steve.

Kite threw a furtive glance at Tiffany.

"You have the chips," said Steve. "Did you bring them?"

A chill settled in his chest. *They know everything!*

Kite was silent. *Should he lie now? He could deny what he told Tiffany.*

He stole another look at Tiffany, noticed the thin line of her compressed lips. He thought, *If he lied, she would know. And he would be a liar to her.*

Kite nodded, resigned. "Yes," he whispered.

"Please bring them out," said Steve.

Kite reached in his pocket, carefully pulling out the two injection pens. He turned to Tiffany. "Have you decided?"

Tiffany was ready. "I'll try the medication tracker chip. I did get dizzy when I forgot my meds."

"Wait," said Lilly. "You're *sure* this is what you want?"

"I'm sure," said Tiffany, offering her arm to Kite.

Kite carefully checked for the mark, looking for the dot, before laying the Number 9 injection pen on the coffee table. He held the medication tracker pen. He nodded to Tiffany, pushing the clicker, preparing to inject the microchip.

Kite desperately wanted to inject the Number 9 chip in Tiffany. He paused, switching the pens, putting down the medication pen and picking up the Number 9 instead. "And this, have you given thought to it?" He approached Tiffany, extending an arm with the Number 9 pen in his hand.

Tiffany's fist slammed into Kite's chin, catching him by surprise, thrusting his head back.

Steve sprang into action, his hand grabbing Kite's wrist, trying to loosen his hold on the Number 9 pen.

They struggled as Kite cried out in alarm, gripping it more tightly. "Please, be careful."

Tiffany ducked under the swinging arms, trying not to get in the way.

"Grab it," yelled Lilly, shouting to her.

Tiffany watched the two men struggle, waiting for her opportunity to reach up and attempt to pull Kite's arm down.

Kite fought hard, as if all his life depended on it, refusing to give up the pen.

Steve exerted pressure, twisting Kite's arm.

Alarmed, Kite relaxed his grip on the injection pen as pain shot through his arm.

In a flash, Lilly snatched the Number 9 pen from his loosened grip.

Kite became outraged, pushing back on Steve, taking Tiffany with him. Tiffany rammed Kite's chest, using her head to push him hard.

Steve let go of him as Kite fell backward with Tiffany collapsing on top of him. They rolled on the floor before coming to a stop. Tiffany caught sight of the other pen that had been knocked off the coffee table onto the floor. She dropped her knee on Kite's chest and arched her back, extending her arm, reaching for the pen with the medication chip.

Across the room, Lilly pounced on Steve. She pushed up his sleeve as she aimed the injection pen on his bicep, clicking to inject the Number 9 chip. Lilly held on to him as skin touched skin, and Steve's pheromones mingled with hers. She kissed him on the lips, sealing his fate. *Their fate.*

Chapter 28
GIGI

She approached Rex's bed, eyes focused on his thin frame curled into a ball. The room was dark, the curtains drawn. She watched his chest rise and fall, listened to his raspy breathing, felt the faint pulse coursing through his vein, knew he was fighting for his life, each labored breath, each flutter of his heart refusing to give up. Sleep no longer provided solace from the pain. It hounded his body day by day, minute by minute. There was no escape. There was no quick end, no merciful death.

"Ah." An involuntary sound escaped her lips as Gigi stifled a cry, watching Rex. The man she loved lay there in bed, fighting for his life. Tears trickled down her cheeks as a wave of sadness overcame her. Gigi would not let him hear her cry. Rex deserved better than that. He hadn't asked for anything, hadn't complained. He was the shadow of a man now, what he used to be had long faded. She ached for the better days, days filled with brightness, laughter, and sunshine. Days where not a thought was given for darkness, for they were in love and on top of the world. They had everything to look forward to, a life together.

Gigi sighed, remembering that day at the cabin when he told her he was sick. She'd tried to suppress the sense of foreboding and fear and put on a brave front, shoving it to the back of her mind, determined to spend those precious few days together in their piece of heaven before coming back to the city, to the reality of life. They'd spoken not a word of his illness for the rest of the days there. Like a pact among friends and lovers, nothing remained to be said then, knowing there would be a time.

"Why?" she called out aloud, seeking an answer. What if she could have given up her foolish youth? If Gigi could have loved him earlier? If she could have more time with Rex? The silent room yielded no answers. She listened to his tortuous breathing, knew he was fighting for life, down to the very last breath. Rex would fight for her and their love.

"Please God, please," said Gigi, unable to hold back the flood of tears as she sank to the floor, sobbing, and for the first time in years begged for forgiveness, for help for someone other than herself, for someone she loved.

At that moment, as she got ready to surrender to the grief, she could feel his pain and the stubborn spark of life. Could she imagine her life without him? Rex, the person who stood by her through thick and thin. As she pleaded for Rex's life, the answer finally came to her.

Epilogue

SIX MONTHS LATER

Chapter 29
ELLEN

Knock, knock.

"Mom and Dad, thanks for coming over this afternoon," said Ellen, opening her door.

"We picked up the balloons on our way here," said her dad, carrying a flotilla of Happy Birthday balloons.

Blowing a puckered kiss in the air, her mom bustled by with a white square box. "Wait until you see this cake! The bakers outdid themselves." She called out to her husband, "Honey, did you remember to bring the matches and the big candle with the number one?"

He winked at Ellen. "Yes, Grandma."

"Hey, you're no spring chicken either. *Grandpa.*"

"Where's Angie?" said Mrs. Fulbright, after she'd unloaded all her stuff.

"She's in her room, getting her diaper changed."

"Brad's here?"

"Yes, he's helping out."

"Nice," said her mom, eyeing the festive party room.

"You did the decorations?"

"I did, with Brad."

"So, how's your new job with the properties sales group?"

"Mom, it's not new anymore. Since I started three and a half months ago, I've sold four units," said Ellen.

"And you have more flexibility in your hours, right?"

"Yes, since I'm a commissioned salesperson. I work from nine to six every day, but my hours are flexible."

"I thought they offered you a staff position?"

"Yeah, if I wanted to be the salesperson for the condo. But I'd have to live in the building until it's all sold."

"You didn't want to move?"

"Nope. I like it here where I'm closer to you and Brad."

"I'm glad you are, dear."

"Yes, it's working out great, Mom," said Ellen. "I show the four different model condos that are available for people to see. It's nice."

"I'm glad. I was getting worried the way your old job was going—you know, with Andy."

Eager to change the subject, Ellen nodded approvingly at her mom's new outfit. "I like what you're wearing—a cute floral dress."

Her mom smiled, touching her arm. "And you look lovely, dear."

She turned to look at Brad as he came out of the bedroom, carrying a freshly diapered Angie. She asked him, "Your parents are coming?"

"This could be them now," said Brad, as another knock sounded.

Ellen rushed to the door and waited for Brad and Angie to catch up before opening it.

"Well hello," said Brad's mom, standing next to his dad, a large gift bag in her hands.

"Hi Mom, Dad," said Brad, leaning forward to greet them.

After a round of hugs, a clamor rose among the grandparents fighting to hold Angie. Ellen smiled as she retreated to the kitchen. Brad quickly followed to get the dishes for the table.

"Let's leave the smash cake in the kitchen until it's time," said Ellen. "You've got your camera?"

"I've got it here," said Brad, smiling as he carefully set it next to the smash cake. "You got a good one, a frosted white cake decorated with a penguin, Angie's favorite stuffed toy."

"Uh, Brad?"

"What?"

"I'm glad you're here."

The party was a success. Angie, smashing the cake with both hands and scooping the penguin—captured on video, in all its glory. They watched the replay, howling with laughter. Angie's first birthday was a hoot.

They sat around chatting for awhile, filled with good food. Ellen finally stood up, bringing the dirty dishes into the kitchen.

Ellen's mom came up behind her. "Let me help you with that."

"No, that's okay, Mom. You go out there and relax," said Ellen. "I'm going to wash and Brad'll dry the dishes."

"How about we take Angie to the park for a few hours, enjoy the day and walk off the calories?"

"Brad's parents?"

"We'll take them. It'll be a lovely walk in the park, especially this time of the day."

"Thanks, Mom," said Ellen.

Fifteen minutes later, she stuck her head back in the kitchen. "I've got Angie's diapers, bottles, and all her stuff. You guys want to meet us grandparents for a birthday dinner? Give you a break from the cooking."

Ellen glanced at Brad.

"Where and when, Mom?" asked Ellen.

"How about the one you guys like so much, you know, with the deep blue sea like stepping into Neptune's world?"

Brad laughed as Ellen squealed with delight.

As the front door shut, she handed a towel to Brad. "Ready to work?"

He rolled up his sleeves. Dipping his hands in the soapy water of the sink, Brad scooped a handful of suds and dabbed it on her nose and cheeks. "Now you look funny."

"Hey, quit that," she said, laughing. "Not fair."

He grabbed his camera and took a picture. Grinning, he said, "I'm holding this for ransom. You'd better be a good girl."

"Oh no, you don't," said Ellen as she tried to catch his arm.

Slipping easily out of her grasp, he laid the camera down in a safe spot.

She was ready for him when he came back, flicking suds on his head.

Brad bent over with laughter as bubbles slid down his hair and wet his shirt. He reached for the hose spray and pointed it straight at her.

She shrieked. "Don't you dare!"

"Watch me," he yelled as he directed a spray of water at her.

She shook her hand, flinging water on the floor as she rushed to wrestle the spray from him.

He was too quick for her and sprayed another one before she could get to him.

They fought over the hand-held sprayer, spraying water on each other.

Finally, out of breath, she was the first to hold her hand up. "Truce."

"You give up?"

"No, we give up at the same time. That's what a truce is."

Brad laughed. "Okay, on the count of three. One, two, three." He put the spray hose back in its slot on the kitchen sink.

"Look at us," said Ellen as water dripped from her head and soaked her top. Looking down, she realized that the wet cotton material was clinging to her breasts, her nipples standing erect.

Brad's eyes followed, staring.

They stood, frozen for a millisecond before bursting out in laughter. Brad held out his arms, pulling her close as he leaned down to kiss her.

She took a step back until she felt the edge of the sink digging in her back.

He moved with her, his lips clinging to hers, not letting go.

She responded to him, the soft probing of his tongue, while the odd sensation of his wet jeans, rough against her bare, smooth legs, filtered through her mind.

They stood there, arms wrapped around each other, and kissed.

When Ellen finally came up for air, she met his eyes and saw the warmth tinged with desire and tenderness. With love.

She glanced at the clock. "We have two hours before dinner . . ."

He laughed. "That's enough time for me to finish *two* desserts."

She led the way down the hall to the bedroom, stopping to grab dry towels from the hall closet.

He patted her with the towel, taking the time to dab her face and hair, then he slowly peeled off her wet shirt and unsnapped her bra before unzipping her skirt. Brad took off his soggy shirt and pants, then lifted Ellen, carrying her to the bed. Unhurried, he dried her from head to toe with slow, tender movements. When he finished, he lay down beside her and let her dry him off.

He watched as she worked, enjoying every minute of it.

She made no effort to hide her body—the telltale signs of weight loss on her flesh, the loose skin, and the striped marks of pregnancy in plain sight.

He saw her, exposed to him, in the light. "You're beautiful, just the way you are."

She caressed his face, tracing her fingers along the muscular contours of his arm. She buried her face in the soft curls of his hairy chest. "I missed you, Brad."

"I've missed you too." He tilted her chin up with his finger and kissed her, surrendering to the softness of her lips.

She murmured, eyes closed, entranced with this moment, one that she had so longed for, one she wanted never to let go. "Can you just hold me, Brad?"

Brad wrapped his arms around her, feeling her quiver as he held her. He pulled his head back to look at her face, into her eyes, and saw the tears. He gently kissed her face and the wetness on her cheeks. "I'm here, Ellen," he said. "I love you."

"I love you," she whispered back.

He kissed her again, tasting the salt of her tears. "Baby, I'm here to stay."

Chapter 30
LILLY

The twelve women sat in a circle, fresh-faced and excited, meeting each other for the first time on day one of the program. Naomi and Tiffany had signed them in, ushered them to the chairs.

A floor-to-ceiling window covered an entire wall of the new warehouse, rebuilt on the grounds of an old one that had been burnt down in a storm—on top of Kite's old warehouse. The sunlight streamed in the room lit only by natural light at this time of the day. The decor was modern and clean-lined. A white leather couch placed along one wall. A vase of cut flowers, its colors vibrant, fresh, welcoming, graced a small whitewashed birch table near the entry.

The door opened. Heads turned.

In strode an elegant woman dressed in a tailored suit. Beside her, an older man with a smooth, relaxed stride, a full head and shoulders taller than her, his weathered face ruggedly handsome,

The air bristled with something akin to sparks. Two people so different, individuals comfortable in their own right, standing together. One tall, one short. One wearing a casual jacket with a cotton shirt and a slightly crooked tie, one well-dressed. A man and a woman, facing them together.

"Ladies, welcome to our program. My name is Lilly Cooper." She turned to the man, touching his hand. "This is my husband, Steve Cosine."

They stood together as if they were one. Steve's eyes on her. Puppy love eyes.

Magnetism emitted from the couple. More refined than animal attraction. Twelve pairs of eyes feasted on them, unable to tear away—power, charm, something they couldn't put their hands on, fascinated them.

Steve joined hands with her, fingers intertwined.

Lilly smiled. *This time it feels right. All of it.*

Chapter 31
GIGI

The hairdresser tucked one more strand into Gigi's fancy coiffure. A work of art the hairdresser took all morning to build. Pleased with the result, she stepped back. Passing the hand-held mirror to Gigi, she swiveled her chair, turning her around until her back was facing the large wall mirror. "Here, have a look."

"Thanks," said Gigi. Holding the mirror, she spun in her chair, viewing her profile, turning to see the back of her hair. She caught sight of her face, seeing the newly etched lines around her eyes, forehead, and mouth. No longer fighting it, but accepting of it. Not only that, the tinnitus had returned, but she'd learn to live with it with the help of supplemental therapies and new treatments. Snatching the tube of pink watermelon lipstick, she touched up her lips, nodding to the hairdresser, ready for the bridal veil. She smiled. *A girl's gotta look good on her special day!*

Walking down the aisle, hearing the sounds of music drifting closer, Gigi focused on Rex, standing there and waiting to start the rest of their lives together. Rex—the love of her life. She quickly blinked a few times, overcome with emotion.

Rex stood tall and straight, sporting a healthy tan and glow, muscles filling out his shirt, full of new energy, his illness cured, his body healed.

His brown eyes locked on her as a smile lit up his face, the boyish grin Gigi knew so well. She saw the love in his eyes spilling out in abundance. Reaching Rex at the altar, she touched him knowingly on his arm, the spot of his implanted microchip—the one extracted from Gigi's arm.

Chapter 32
DR. KITE

People trickled in as the word got out, going to the check stations to find out if they had the microchip implants. It was hard to tell how many had been innocent victims because the warehouse fire destroyed the records. But, starting from a few every night in the beginning, the numbers had increased over a period of a couple of years. So it was possible that a few thousand people may have become unwitting subjects. For the "lucky" ones who had it, it became a prized possession.

Gigi had been the first one to go through this procedure with Rex. It had been simple enough. It took less than the four minutes touted for cataract surgery.

She had come up with the idea and proposed it. Gigi somehow became the poster child—her face and name synonymous with this campaign. A unique opportunity for people willing to donate their microchip. On their applications, they could indicate names of family members or friends who needed the chip. If the name of the recipient was left blank, strangers were matched in the process after an extensive algorithm provided paired names, and face-to-face meetings firmed the decisions. People had to apply and undergo an assessment to ensure no coercion was behind it. The only requirement; it had to be a willing act of unselfishness.

They came out with it in a big way with public announcements on TV, radio, billboard ads, and social media. Gigi became a media darling, synonymous with "Saving Rex," which grew into "Saving Someone."

They filmed the process each step of the way in a documentary. Rex and his illness. Gigi and hers. The filmmakers made sure to include the part about the mind-control chips but stressed that no one had those implanted chips anymore. Kite did not appear in the film except for one clip showing him in prison garb. A brief mention accompanied the clip—Kite had become born-again, and he would be eligible for parole in five years.

The response to the "Saving Someone" campaign turned out better than Gigi had anticipated. Initially, angry outbursts and debates crowded the airwaves. Supporters and detractors had their say. It generated a rowdy response.

Gigi watched the long line of people forming with those arriving well before the early morning opening. There was joviality in the air, laughter sprinkled here and there, a mood of hope and anticipation of what awaited at the end of the line.

Funding from legitimate sources furthered research into Kite's mind-control microchips, yielding some surprising preliminary results. He finally came clean with Gigi, Ellen, and Lilly. When the men brought Gigi to the warehouse after her car accident, Kite had removed the first defective mind-control chip from Gigi's arm. He stored that microchip in the warehouse, but unfortunately the fire destroyed it.

Kite ultimately removed the other two mind-control chips from Ellen and Lilly before serving his prison sentence. Tests on these two chips finally revealed which of the two was the defective microchip—the one he retrieved from Lilly.

Deep within the recesses of the human brain, the battle between the chip and the unconscious mind had raged. It had come down to this. But the tipping point, what Kite did not foresee, was the one thing the mind-control chip could not overcome—the *primal will* to survive.

THE END of the Alterations Trilogy

To my husband, Scott

CONTENTS

CHAPTER 1

My heart was pounding heavily. I tried to urge my hesitant feet to move faster toward my new boss's office, but to no avail. *He'll fire you anyway, so there's nothing to lose* was the mantra repeating in my head.

The faces in the cubicles around me looked like the comedy and tragedy masks. The ones who weren't fired today congregated in happy clusters, each showing off the new tablet they'd received. The ones who were fired wore devastated expressions while packing their cubicles alone. I desperately yearned to be a part of the first group, but I knew that my odds of keeping my job at *Travel Secrets* magazine were close to nil.

I was still berating myself for not jumping at the chance to pitch him my idea at the staff-meeting yesterday. Sometimes I was such a chicken! There was no reason for Ryan Brooks not to fire *that girl who clammed up*. But now that he was our Editor-in-Chief instead of Todd Potts, I had to stay. Working for him would be a stepping-stone to my dream of running my own magazine, the likes of which had never been seen before.

He'll fire you anyway, so there's nothing to lose.

As I reached his office door, a young reporter named Ruth burst out of it, crying. I reached out to pet her shoulder, but she jerked away, her sobbing worsening. I watched her hunched shoulders as she rushed away. I shook my head, breathed deeply, and walked inside.

"Sit down, Rachel," said Ryan, motioning to an office chair in front of him. My throat was too dry to reply, so I just nodded and sat down. A part of me was incredulous and excited at the opportunity of talking to *one of the most successful twenty-something tech-millionaires of our century,* as the media had dubbed him. But my survival instinct was frantically looking for a way to stop the inevitable from happening.

He'll fire you anyway, so there's nothing to lose.

I smiled nervously at Christine Durham, the new Chief Operations Officer and Ryan's right-hand woman. She nodded imperceptibly, remaining expressionless. She sat at a polished, black office table. Both she and Ryan had the signature tablet that he had invented in front of them. I tried to hold Ryan's penetrating glance, but I couldn't do it for long. I looked away, my eyes darting from his black leather swivel chair to his dark blue suit, to his neatly combed, light brown hair, to his clean shaven angular chin, then back to the piercing dots of his green eyes.

"Ms. Moore, there's no sugar coating what's happening here today. I bought this magazine in order to save it, which means cutting costs."

Here it comes, I thought. *He's about to fire you! It's your last chance! Speak now!*

"May I interrupt?" I asked, my voice sounding strained. My hands gripped the steel bottom of my chair tightly as I tried to steady myself. I couldn't let him see my palms shaking. "I... have an idea."

"Please," he said and gestured for me to go on.

"I have urged Mr. Potts a number of times to increase rotation frequency. I'm convinced that sending the same reporters to cover the same places year after year breeds stock reporting." *As is the case for me and the reason you now find me expendable,* I completed the thought in my head.

"And what did your *ex*-Editor-in-Chief say when you suggested it?"

"He said it fosters specialization."

"He told me that, too. He's very fond of his system. However, it hasn't helped produce exciting articles nor increase sales."

Encouraged, I continued. "I agree with him that reporters can become experts on certain places, but a person can only see a place for the first time once. That fresh outlook could bring you the stand out writing you're looking for."

"And who'll be the one bringing this new, rousing, fresh perspective to the magazine - you?" He smiled in amusement, relaxing back in his chair and swiveling from right to left, his fingers steepled at his lips. He seemed thoughtful and dismissive at the same time, as if he was considering my idea despite having sensed this was just a ploy to keep my job. His cavalier attitude angered me. Even his dimples annoyed me. As my vexation grew, so did my determination.

"Yes! I'll bet my job on it!"

"Will you?" he leaned towards me in interest, one eyebrow raised. Oh no! Did he take that literally?

"Ryan," said Christine in a warning tone.

"What?! This is the first time I've had fun this whole, long, miserable day!" This impressive, successful millionaire suddenly seemed like a little boy who was about to unwrap a gift. That was good. He was having fun, and it was thanks to *me*.

"I'm sorry," Christine shook her head, her fingers running over her carefully tied chignon of red hair, her blue eyes turning from Ryan to me. "This sounds illegal," she shrugged, opening her palms to indicate she would like to oblige, but couldn't.

Betting a job I was about to lose didn't matter. "I'll sign whatever papers you wish," I promised Christine, entreating her with my open palms. This whole thing was so unlike me. Normally I was polite and deferential. This was indeed a desperate attempt of a cornered animal to trick her captor to look elsewhere so that she could escape.

He'll fire you anyway, so there's nothing to lose. Ask for what you want most! Go all in!

While Christine was considering my promise, I looked at Ryan daringly and quickly said, "I bet you I can find a scoop in Rio de Janeiro. If I fail, you can fire me then."

"Rio?" he pondered. "Who's covering that right now?"

Before Christine found the answer on her PA, I volunteered, "Kourtney Chapman does. She has been for over three years now."

"While you covered...?"

"Nevada; sir."

"Hmm, anyone would need a change after so long. I had intended to change this stale rotation system, so now it'd just happen ahead of schedule. C'mon Chris!" he urged. "This bet is too good to pass up!" When she shook her head, he turned somber. "If I can come out of this depressing day with the thought that I spared *one* job and gave *one* person a second chance, it would help alleviate this rotten gloom I'm feeling. Find a way, Chris. I want to do this for Ms. Moore."

I realized he was not, as many had referred to him, an evil, rich bastard. He did care about his employees and firing people was hard on him. Suddenly, I thought about him not just as my boss, but as a man. A very attractive man.

"I'll draft the documents," Christine acceded, a tiny hint of a smile hovering over her red lips.

Ryan stood up victoriously and stretched out his hand. "Ms. Moore – you have got yourself a deal!"

No bloody way! I thought in utter astonishment. I was hardly able to stand up and meet Ryan's vigorous grip. "Thank you, Mr. Brooks. I won't let you down."

"To find something new about such a prominent locale will be near impossible. I wish you luck; you're going to need it. And you're going to need *this,* too." He handed me my own new tablet, the personal assistant, or PA for short, which was Ryan's own invention.

"Tha... thank you," my voice quavered. I clutched the white tablet to my chest elatedly, using my body to stabilize the shaking of my palms. I turned to leave.

"Oh, and Rachel." I turned back, an inquiring look on my face. "Have a wonderful time in Rio." He said this with a wink and wide grin, letting me know he knew that, at the end of the day, he was sending an eager gal to a place she was dying to see.

* * *

I felt as if I was floating to my cubicle, where my best friends, Jess and Ashley, were waiting for me. I cleared my throat, and they both looked up from their new tablets. They seemed surprised to see me holding a tablet, too.

"No way!" Jess rose to give me a bear hug.

"OMG!" shrieked Ashley and hugged us both. "And you said there was no chance you were staying!"

After setting down the treasured tablet gingerly on my desk, I joined them in some hushed shrieking and stunted jumps for joy, careful not to overdo it at the office. At least for now, we were all safe from firing. Jess and her popular *Travel Necessities* column were safe, but Ashley's *Women-Only Tours* column was not in demand and may not last.

I perceived Kourtney's disappointed look from the cluster of cubicles across from ours. I stopped hopping. Kourtney grimaced at me, her glare narrowing, her thin lips curved into a hateful smirk. She and her buddies, Deidre and Chad, A.K.A., *The Trio,* have been harassing me since I've started working there. Their dislike of me seemed to grow each day and I had no idea why. It was undoubtedly going to get worse now that I was going to cover Kourtney's locale.

I scowled back at Kourtney. Jess and Ashley followed my gaze. Kourtney flung her sandy, bleached-blond curls aside haughtily and turned her back to us.

"Let's sit down," I said seriously. "There's something I need to tell you."

"What is it?" asked Jess. Her long, brown, curly bangs hid the concern in one of her dark-brown eyes.

"You're not going to believe this. I walked into his office and I just knew he was going to fire me. He started with this speech about cutbacks."

"I got a similar speech," said Ashley, "with a warning I have to do better, or else. He needs to see better numbers, a larger following, or something else to justify continuing with the column. I'm going to need your help coming up with something."

"Of course we'll help," I said, placing my hand on hers and smiling. Ashley's worried blue eyes smiled back.

"*I* didn't get that speech," grinned Jess, our eternal clown, in one of her usual attempts to lighten a serious conversation.

"We know that, you idiot," I scolded Jess. We grinned at each other.

"We'll help you, Ash," she said. "Now, Rach, tell us what happened."

"I knew I had nothing to lose, which, in a weird way, felt so empowering. I asked him to listen to my idea and it turned out he isn't that happy with Todd's system either."

"No wonder he demoted him to editor."

"This is awesome!"

"I went all out and told him I would bet my job on proving that stale system sucks."

"But... how?"

"You bet your job?"

"A job I was about to lose anyway. Quite frankly, when I said I'd bet on it, I didn't literally mean bet, but Brooks got so excited, I realized that was my in. So while Christine was thinking about the legalities of the bet, I announced that if he'd send me to Rio de Janeiro, I'd come home with an exclusive scoop!"

"What?" asked Ashley in astonishment.

"Man," Jess shook her head with a grin, "you *do* have some balls after all, Rach." I grinned back at her. "And I bet you have no idea how to get this scoop."

"Not really. But we have three weeks until carnival."

Ashley still didn't say anything. "I think Ash is in shock," said Jess.

"But..." whispered Ashley, "Rio belongs to Kourtney."

"Oh shit!" said Jess. "I was so excited when I heard about you betting the founder of Brooks Inc., I didn't even think about how pissed Kourtney is going to be when she finds out you stole Rio from under her."

"Rio doesn't *belong* to anyone," I seethed between clenched teeth.

"Just this morning I heard her say how she's looking forward to going to Rio with Chantal Neuchâtel and Kevin Noyes."

"Oh, I'd forgotten she said she was flying there with her model and photographer friends," I recalled. "It's my first time working with either of them."

"I didn't get along with him. He's such a male, chauvinist pig," said Ashley with a scoff. That didn't worry me too much. Ashley thought that about every straight man. "But do you know who Chantal had just started dating?"

"Who?" I asked with interest, letting Ashley enjoy delivering her bit of gossip. Behind her Jess rolled her eyes. I fought the urge to giggle.

"None other than our dear, new boss – Ryan Brooks!"

"Oh, wow," I said in surprise. Chantal is going to have intimate contact with *my* boss?!

"Jeez. If she's Kourtney's friend, I hope she's not going to be too angry you've taken over her buddy's locale," said Jess, looking genuinely worried.

"For the last time, a city does *not* belong to anybody. Besides, she might be nicer than Kourtney."

"You know what? You're absolutely right," smiled Ashley encouragingly.

"Yeah," agreed Jess. "To hell with Kourtney. This is just what she deserves. Besides, who cares how she and The Trio will react? Winning that bet is all that matters."

"Well," I said doubtfully, "you're not the one The Trio gangs up on. They've been making my life miserable ever since I first pitched my idea to Todd." I didn't add that they've been making fun of my weight since I started working there three years ago.

"Of course, because, unlike you, they've got all the awesome, international locales. And you let their bullying stop you from pitching Brooks your idea at the meeting yesterday."

"True," I nodded sadly.

"When are you going to learn to ignore them? You just have to brush it off and go on being awesome," said Jess, hugging my waist.

"I still insist there *is* another alternative," said Ashley.

"Ashley, I've told you many times: I'm not a litigious person."

"But there are harassment laws in New York just for this explicit purpose."

"I've complained to Todd several times."

"And he shrugged it off. 'Office banter' my foot!"

"He did, which is why I was looking for another job."

"Why should *you* have to leave?!"

"Ash," interfered Jess, "we've hashed this out before and Rach said she didn't want to sue. Besides, this is all in the past now. You'll see; everything is going to change now that Brooks has taken over."

Ashley seemed placated. "I hope so," she said. "I hope he will launch a new era for us employees, not just the magazine."

"I desperately want to be here to see what he does with the company," I said, suddenly feeling the pressure of the bet. "I really haven't the faintest idea how I'm going to get a scoop about one of the top tourist destinations in the world."

"Hey," Jess petted my shoulder, "that's OK for now. Three weeks is plenty of time to strategize."

I looked at her with a thankful smile. Recalling my excitement, I said, "this is so awesome. I am finally going to have my Rio dream come true!"

CHAPTER 2

On the red-eye flight to Rio, I was looking at the distant stars glowing through my airplane window with a smile on my face. The passengers seated next to me were already asleep, and I was beginning to drift into unconsciousness, too.

"Excuse me, ma'am," a tired looking flight attendant said. "Miss Chantal Neuchâtel is requesting to see you in first class."

"Thank you," I said uncomfortably. I knew that squeezing past my neighbors would awaken them, but I had no choice. As head of the assignment, I was in charge, and had to do what was needed to succeed in the task, and that included keeping my model and photographer happy. This was doubly so for Chantal who was dating Ryan Brooks and might report back to him. I simply had to get on her good side. I apologized profusely as I squeezed past my fellow passengers. What could Chantal want from me in the middle of the night?

Coach felt more cramped than my tiny New-York apartment. First class felt like a villa in comparison. I took in the drunken familiarity with which Chantal and Kevin were sprawled together on their seats. Her legs were on his; he was massaging her feet. Thanks to Ashley, I knew they used to be an item. I was curious to meet this model, wondering what had attracted Ryan to her. I was hoping there was more to her than the well-publicized, tall, scrawny body, blond hair, and blue eyes.

"You're Rachel, I presume?" she asked in a snippy, inebriated slur.

"I am."

"Why aren't you answering my texts?" she demanded. Chantal and Kevin giggled privately. Their giggles ran a chill down my spine. A sense of foreboding took over me. Surely, they both knew the answer very well and this was just a little game at my expense.

"My phone is on airplane mode. Maybe yours isn't?" I let a scornful tone sneak into my voice despite my basic desire to get on her good side. They giggled again. Chantal sized me up with as much seriousness as she could muster.

"So, you're the one who stole Rio from Kourtney?"

"Rio doesn't belong to the writers, nor any other locale. Not anymore, that is."

"Yea," said Kevin, who was as tipsy as Chantal. "I forgot to tell you that thanks to Rachel here, Brooks is insisting that all writers give her method a go and cover new places."

"Oh, no! Well, maybe I can talk to him about it," Chantal suggested, innuendo in her voice.

"Do you have any idea how pissed everyone is at you?" Kevin asked me angrily.

"Oh, have no doubt I do. Kourtney, Deidre, and Chad let me know very well what they think of this change," I said, my heartbeat increasing. As they both giggled again, I asked: "Was there anything you wanted from me?"

"Did you arrange for the west facing suite I requested?"

"Of course."

"What about the water?"

"Yes. And the flowers, and the beauty products."

"And the healthy shakes?"

"I made sure the chef knows your preferences. Here," I said, producing two neatly printed lists before she got a chance to continue with her incessant questioning. "I have emailed you a detailed list of all requested additions made to the regular hotel care," then I raised my hand and prevented her from speaking, "and since I knew there would be no access to email on board, I've gone ahead and printed a copy for you," I handed her the list, "and a copy for Kevin." He snatched the list from me impatiently and crumpled it in his front seat pocket without looking at it. Chantal followed suit.

"Well," she smiled insincerely, her pale blue eyes remaining cold, "you're quite the busy bee. I'm sure you understand why I had to double check you'd followed my instructions to the letter. I wouldn't want you getting any fresh ideas about *my* routine, like you did with Kourtney."

It took all my self-possession not to look at her seethingly and reply snarkily. I had to give her the benefit of the doubt, because there was a small chance she was just angry about what I did to her friend. After all, they were supposed to travel together, and Chantal is just hurt and is letting it out on me. I simply had to rise above it for the mere chance, slight as it now seemed, of winning her over to my side.

"Oh, I understand completely," I assured her with a genuine smile. Both she and Kevin looked at me with confusion, their expressions saying *if you understand, how come you're smiling genuinely?* Clearly, neither of them was accustomed to dealing with a positive person. Maybe I still stood a chance of befriending them. And wouldn't it be so nice and helpful to actually have my team on *my* side? "My friends are important to me, too." Before they got a chance reply, I merrily added "good night!" and went back to coach.

In the dark of coach, I grinned, happy with myself for rising above, but also at the thought of how their mouths must have hung open after I'd left. To be on the safe side, I instructed the flight attendant not to interrupt me in the name of those two passengers again. Then I begged pardon once more as I squeezed across my row and tried to drift into sleep.

But other, less happy thoughts invaded my mind. Even though I've always faced reality from a benevolent perspective, I had to admit other possibilities to myself, as a safeguard. I knew perfectly well there was a chance Chantal was just a straightforward bitch whom I just made excuses for. And if she really was nothing but a shrew, would her connection with Ryan make her a threat to my job? And how could he *choose* to date someone like that? Or perhaps he was so thick, he couldn't see past her beauty? And how could someone be so addled in his personal life, but be such a success in his business?

There was still so much for me to figure out in this life.

* * *

Walking toward baggage claim, I was eager to meet my two tour guides. It was my idea to hire both a man and a woman to show me around Rio, hoping to increase my chances at a scoop by having the points of view of both sexes. Reaching the airport's welcoming area, my eyes scanned the signs people held up to greet newcomers. My name was written on a sign held by a strikingly beautiful, mulatta woman. Like me, she seemed to be in her mid-twenties. Her body was tall, thin, and shapely. Her tight, yellow Capri pantsuit emphasized both the beauty of her bronze skin and the smallness of her waist. Her full breasts were barely contained in the tight, sleeveless top. Her curvy lips and almond-shaped, brown eyes were adorned with little makeup. Her long mane of brown curls floated freely over her shoulders. I, who was petite and curvy, always envied the taller women on whom a round butt like mine looked more proportional, as it did on her. Of course, she was at least twenty pounds lighter than I was, I thought, critical of myself as usual. Instinctively, I put up my guard. Every beautiful woman I'd met in my life was always a bitch, so I thought it was safer to put up my defenses. I walked toward her and held out my hand, my attitude cool.

"Hi, I'm Rachel. You must be Isabel."

"Yes, I am Isabel. How are you?" She had pronounced her own name Ee-sa-bewoo in a melodious accent. She kissed both my cheeks with the ease of someone who had been through this ritual thousands of times. I recalled reading about the two-kiss greeting and felt an immense relief that Americans settled with a handshake.

"I'm a little tired, but very excited."

"Oh, you look great; not tired at all. Welcome to Rio!" I felt myself warming up a bit to her sunny disposition. She got a porter to collect the bags and we started walking toward the exit. "You know, we don't really pronounce the 'r', 'ch', or 'l' sounds in Portuguese, so your name is pretty much impossible for us to pronounce. How about we just call you *Raquel,* which is a common name here?"

I didn't point out that this name started with an 'r' and ended with an 'l', too. She had pronounced it 'Ha-que-woo', making the name sound exotic and sexy. I smiled and asked her to repeat it and she gladly did.

"I kinda' like it."

"Wonderful! Let me just text the driver that we're coming out." She clicked on her cell as we walked. "He's the other tour-guide you requested."

"Oh; great."

As we exited the air-conditioned airport in mid-morning, we were welcomed by a light blue sky and a blanket of thick, humid heat. My body was surprised by the contrast to the frost of February in New York. I breathed deeply and exhaled slowly. As much as I loved my hometown, I had to smile at the thought of spending two weeks in the Brazilian summer. My smile was gone when I noticed the two smokers dawdling up ahead.

"They're with us," I told Isabel. "Kevin! Chantal!" I yelled and waved my hand, signaling for them to come over. They both walked lazily toward us. I wondered how Chantal was going to react upon seeing how beautiful our tour guide was.

"It's no wonder you're excited," said Isabel. "Carnival is right around the corner, as you Americans say."

"Your English is very good."

"Thank you. After all, a big part of my job is to help tourists understand Portuguese. I took a lot of English classes and I also try to watch a lot of American shows in English without the usual dubbing."

Isabel's sunny smile was unwavering. In New York, her happy-go-lucky temperament would have been mocked as naïve, or her innocence simply an act put on in order to get something. But could this Brazilian be the genuine article?

A van pulled up. I heard the trunk pop and the porter started loading the bags. The van driver got out. He leaned back on the van and lit a cigarette. He took a long drag as he scanned me openly from head to toe with a cocky half-smile. My heart started beating faster. He was one of those guys who dripped both testosterone and a surly attitude. His muscles were chiseled and tanned, and his light brown curls had blond specks of sun in them. His amber eyes had a feral look about them, which insinuated we both knew the sole purpose for which men and women were put on this earth. I forgot everything else and just hoped I wasn't salivating.

"Otavio, this is Raquel," said Isabel.

"*Prazer*," he said in his deep, mesmerizing voice. "That means 'it's my pleasure.'" I extended my hand automatically for a shake, but he used it to pull me closer to him. As he kissed both my cheeks, my resentment of this ritual vanished. He looked deep into my eyes as he said, "Raquel is so much better than the other name Isabel mentioned. It is so much sexier, just like you." Unsure what to think, I looked at Isabel, but she didn't seem to think there was anything inappropriate about this blunt flirting. "This name," he raised one brow, "I can pronounce, *sim?* That means 'yes.'"

"*Sim*," I concurred hoarsely, my throat dry.

"Don't let us interrupt you, Rachel," said Kevin mockingly.

I cleared my throat, saying: "Kevin, Chantal, these are our tour guides, Isabel and Otavio."

"Great. Can we go now?" asked Chantal impatiently.

"Prazer," Kevin said in Portuguese underscored by an American accent. He kissed Isabel's cheeks. "How ya' doing?" he nodded to Otavio. "Kourtney never got *two* tour guides," he said to me accusingly. I decided not to reply.

Otavio held the van's door open for Chantal as she climbed in without granting him one look of acknowledgment. Kevin followed her, then I did, smiling at Otavio nervously. Never in my life had someone so hot flirted with me. In America, no one had ever let me forget I was the overweight, curvy girl, but he acted as if he didn't see it. His confident, crooked smile and the intimate look in his eyes suggested he knew exactly what he was doing and how excited he made me feel. As his hand grabbed mine to help me into the van, my skin prickled and my heart began to race. I slowly sat down and folded my legs, then flung my hair aside with a toss of the head, more aware of my own body and of every movement than I had ever been in my entire life. Was this how a movie star felt when the camera was on her?

"Raquel," Isabel started speaking to me from the front passenger seat, but Kevin cut her off.

"Her name's *Rachel*. She ain't no Raquel."

"Well, Otavio and I are going to call her Raquel," Isabel smiled unperturbed. "It is much easier for us to pronounce."

"Whatever," he shrugged and frowned, inserting his earbuds in his ears. Chantal already had hers on. They leaned over their cell phones. I was relieved to have them both disconnected from our conversation and quiet for a change.

"You were saying?" I asked Isabel.

"Oh, yes. You asked that I introduce you to some of the classic songs about Brazil, so I made a playlist for you."

"That's so sweet of you," I said with a smile.

"I thought you said Raquel needed to find a scoop about Rio, something new and original. She is not going to find it in those old songs," teased Otavio with a half-smile via the rear-view mirror.

I smiled back at him nervously as I realized I'd completely forgotten about my assignment. This guy is going to be trouble.

"I'm trying to absorb the culture: old music, new music; female tour guide's perspective, male tour guide's perspective," I explained, determined to refocus on work.

"Well, you got lucky. You could not find someone better to show you a good time in Rio if you tried!" Otavio bragged.

"You must forgive him," Isabel shook her head. "He *is* the best tour guide in town. The problem is, he knows it." I couldn't help but smile at Otavio, who grinned back at me.

Isabel and I talked about the songs. One song caught my attention. It was called *Happiness,* by *Antônio Carlos Jobim.* It spoke of the happiness of the poor, who work all year for the fleeting dream of Carnival, for a moment in time in which they can wear a costume and pretend to be a king, a pirate, or even just a gardener. It seemed that the happiness of Carnival was underscored by much sadness. The song was playing while we drove past a *favela,* the famous shantytowns of Brazil. It filled the mountains in the distance with small, clay-brick homes that looked dilapidated, unfinished, and sooty. No wonder the poor needed the escape of carnival, I mused.

Isabel told me about the city sectors as we drove through them. I was impressed by the huge port, adorned with the biggest oil rigs and cruise ships I had ever seen. Then came the grimy, graffiti-filled wrecks of old ship yards. The city center was dense with glass-windowed skyscrapers that reflected Gothic church spires. We drove past dense neighborhoods of tall apartment buildings, all overlooking the picturesque Guanabara Bay. The bay view left me gaping in awe. The perfectly still blue water was dotted with sailboats and framed on one side by a beautiful beach and on the other by the famous Sugar Loaf mountain, its cable cars floating peacefully to the top and bottom.

"It's gorgeous!" I said, my nose glued to the window.

Even though they must have heard it many times before, Isabel and Otavio smiled with pleasure. Isabel said: "We can eat lunch at the hotel. Do you feel like you need to rest, or are you ready to see the city?"

"Oh', I'm ready. I napped for a few hours on the plane." I sneaked a resentful look at Chantal, but she was focused on her cell phone and noticed nothing around her.

"Great! Let's start with Sugar Loaf. From the top of the mountain you can see most of the city and get a feel for how big and beautiful it is."

I paused to consider this. Quite probably, no scoop hid in one of the world's most famous tourist sites. But isn't this what I told Ryan in his office – a travel writer needs to see a new place with fresh eyes? "Sure," I concurred.

"And this," Isabel exclaimed proudly, "is Copacabana beach!"

Otavio stopped the car in front of the *Anderson Hotel,* the tallest building in Copacabana. Colorful flags of different countries waved gaily above the hotel's sign. The valet, a black man wearing a gold-trimmed, dark green uniform with an accompanying top hat, opened the van door for us.

"*Obrigada,*" I thanked him, feeling a bit self-conscious about speaking the Portuguese I had tried to learn via an audio course these past three weeks.

"*De Nada,*" he said with a smile.

I stretched my shoulders and took a deep breath of the salty ocean air. It prickled my nostrils, and I instantly felt calmer. That feeling disappeared as soon as I heard Chantal's voice.

"Rachel, as you probably know, I've kept this trip a secret from the media so far." I did not know that, since I hadn't followed

Chantal on social media. I realized it might be a good idea to do that. "I don't want any announcements or tweets or anything of the sort from you. Got it?"

As she spoke to me like a slow-witted underling, it was hard to continue making allowances for her. "Got it," I replied coldly, "as long as you do the shoots I require for my scoop."

She scoffed. "This whole scoop idea is ridiculous. Rio is one of the most publicized cities on the planet. What makes you think *you* can get anything new?"

"She bet *your boyfriend* she'll scoop out Rio," explained Kevin as he got out of the van. I cringed inwardly at the mention of Ryan being Chantal's boyfriend.

"Oh, Kevin. He's not my boyfriend. Not yet anyway."

"Oh, I bet you can charm him into a commitment real soon. Anyway, he bet Rach she either brings a nice, big, original scoop back, or she's out of a job."

"Hilarious," she said smilelessly. They walked toward the hotel arm in arm.

"Is that true?" Isabel asked with a frown. Otavio looked concerned, too. "You're going to lose your job if you don't come up with a scoop?"

"I'm afraid so."

"Well, we'd better get to work!" announced Isabel. I smiled back at her, happy to have an ally.

We all rode the elevator to the thirty-first-floor suite. I was pleased that Kevin and Chantal occupied rooms on a different floor. We said we'd see each other after breakfast, and the elevator door closed on them.

"Oh, I can't wait!" I declared as I walked eagerly down the corridor, Isabel and Otavio following me. I inserted the key card into the door. It was a corner room, as I had requested, and the maid had drawn the heavy, blue curtains open. She must have known the view was the reason the guest, or, in my case, the newspaper, paid exorbitant amounts of money to stay here. I gasped as I neared the window.

Copacabana beach was made up of a long, wide, crescent sandbank, which was encircled by the famous black and white stone pavement patterned to look like waves. To its right was the busy, bustling road called Atlantic Avenue. It was, in turn, framed by a strip of hotels and apartment buildings, all of which were then framed by luscious green foliage growing on the tall, brown, granite mountains around which the city was built. Nestled in this fabulous crescent of contrasts was its focal point: the calm azure waters of the south Atlantic, crowned with clear blue sky. The ocean's waves splashed white foam over the perfect sandy beach in intervals that invoked the peaceful sway of a lazy swing. I fell in love with the city immediately.

"It's just... breathtaking!"

"We call Rio the *Marvelous City*," said Isabel proudly.

"Well, it's no wonder. Let's order some lunch. I'm starving!"

"I'll call room service."

"Mind if I smoke?" Otavio asked, an unlit cigarette already held between his oval lips, his lighter at the ready.

"Hmm, the air conditioner and the smoke make for a nasty combo."

"That's fine. I'll go out to the balcony."

I watched him walk. His sensual gait reminded me of a wild cat, his feet hardly leaving the floor as he advanced forward. He closed the door behind him, lit his cigarette and inhaled deeply, nodding at me with amusement from the other side of the glass. I couldn't help wishing I could join him out there. Instead, I headed to the bedroom to get ready for our forthcoming outing.

CHAPTER 3

I needed this alone time to try and get some control over my muddled mind. But how could anyone focus on a goal when swept away by a tidal wave of emotions? It wasn't just lust that overwhelmed me. It was utter bafflement. I was wanted by a guy that would have been considered way out of my league in America. Hot, muscular men wanted hot, skinny women, or fit ones at least. This was an inexplicable anomaly and I knew I had to find the reasons behind it. But this was the wrong time to ponder that. The real question was, could I still put work first in spite of this?

Naked, I looked into my eyes in the mirror. I will *not* let him distract me from my job, and if he does, I'll fire him! I'm not here for sex; I'm here for my career!

Still, I could not stop thinking about Otavio the entire time I showered. His primal gaze made me very aware of my femininity. Then, faced with the wardrobe I'd brought from home, I couldn't decide what to wear. In the New York business world, I had learned that a woman shouldn't stand out by wearing flashy colors, deep cleavage, or dangling jewelry. Every successful, female exec I had ever seen blended almost seamlessly with the men around her, and I strove to do the same. Ashley was on the same page, hence our wardrobes were full of dark, long slacks, dress shirts in muted color, and dark shoes with sensible heels. But not Jess. She marched to her own beat.

I smiled as I imagined what Jess would say now. "You're on vacation, Rach. Hell, your name's not even Rachel anymore! You wanna be a Raquel? - dress accordingly. Be daring! Enjoy yourself!" And I knew this was what I really wanted to do. So I allowed myself to wear my nightclub clothes; the ones I wore when I tried to attract a man: skinny jeans, a black tank top, and strappy, red-leather slingbacks, which, I reasoned, weren't *that* uncomfortable. I blow-dried my brown hair, enjoying the way my recent blond highlights complimented my dark green eyes. I put on some makeup, hurrying as I heard the knock at the door, knowing the food has arrived.

A room service waiter wearing a maroon uniform unloaded items from his cart onto the table by the window. His cart was covered with a white tablecloth, in its center one tropical flower nestled inside a vase. Isabel, Otavio, and I sat at the table. I signed the check and the waiter beamed, thanked me, and left.

"So, what's the deal with tipping?" I asked, placing a small bite of cheesy eggs in my mouth. Otavio began scarfing down his steak and eggs like I would have if it weren't for their company. My mother, who was very focused on appearances, said that there didn't exist a man who would not be put off by a woman who eats heartily.

"Ten percent is automatically included in restaurant and hotel bills, so there is no need to tip. Americans always leave more, which is why that waiter looked so happy. You want milk and sugar?" Isabel asked as the heavenly aroma of the coffee she poured wafted in my direction.

"Cream and sweetener, please. Yes, now I recall I did read about that. Well, ten percent isn't enough anyway," I said, buttering a warm bun. She handed me a cup. "Hmm, the coffee is wonderful! How's your papaya?"

"Fantastic. Have you ever tried a Brazilian papaya?" asked Isabel.

"I haven't."

"You don't know what you've been missing," said Otavio with a curved smile. He used his own fork to cut a piece off the peeled papaya, which he then extended to me. I didn't want to appear prudish by refusing to eat off his fork, so I tried to take it from him, but he didn't let go. He leaned closer to me and fed me the luscious fruit. I couldn't help letting out a little sigh of pleasure.

"Oh my God! It's delectable!" I licked my lips and proceeded to finish the papaya. Otavio looked at me with pleasure as I ate, then he went out to smoke again.

"Those shoes look great but are you sure you won't be more comfortable in some wedge heels?" asked Isabel.

"Probably, but I don't own any."

"What?! Oh, you must let me take you shopping as soon as possible."

"Hmm. As great as that sounds, I won't feel comfortable doing that until I find a scoop."

"I understand. And you're sure you're not too jet-lagged to go out?"

"I'm fine for now. Maybe I'll take a nap later. Now, let me text my colleagues."

"Are they always so... unsocial?" Isabel asked, careful with her choice of words.

"I don't know them that well," I said noncommittally. My phone buzzed with their reply. "They'll be in the lobby in five minutes."

"OK; let's go then."

In the lobby, I noted Kevin wore jeans and a black shirt just like I did. I wrinkled my nose. His brown hair has been styled with gel and combed upwards in short, messy spikes and his face was unshaven, as usual. His small, wry, brown eyes lit up when he saw Isabel.

"Hello again," he smiled warmly at her. "You must let me take some pictures of you one of these days."

"With pleasure," Isabel smiled back.

"Since when is Chantal Neuchâtel not enough?" asked Chantal, pouting like a pampered little girl.

"Never!" replied Kevin with a lecherous look in his eyes.

"Let's go!" said Otavio impatiently, passing between them as he led the way out. Was he trying to get Chantal's attention? Surely, he did not seem like a guy who was used to being ignored. Kevin and Chantal followed him outside. With high heels Chantal stood close to six feet tall. She was nearly flat chested, had no ass to speak of, and had no fat I could perceive on her body, except for her plump lips. Her cascading blond hair looked natural, and her eyes were light blue, like the color of a wave right before it reached the shore and ebbed away. I grimaced as I recalled reading her disinterested look described as *mysteriously captivating*. I sighed inwardly, unable to understand why aloof was considered sexy.

The valet brought the van. Otavio sat at the wheel, and Kevin loaded his equipment in the trunk. I sat in the back near Isabel, making sure to sit right behind Otavio's rear-view mirror. Kevin climbed onto the long side seat.

"Where's Chantal?" I asked. We all looked out the window to glimpse her red mullet dress. The short front exposed her long, thin legs and the long back trailed widely behind her in the breeze like a matador's cape, enticing its prey. She was flirting with a group of tall, fair-haired, European-looking men, her wedge sandals putting her at even height with most of them. She entered some information on her phone and trotted to the car in her runway gait. She sat near Kevin and said in her usual monotone, "Those Dutch tourists invited us to a party today. Or tomorrow. They said they party every night."

"Awesome," Kevin nodded.

Chantal put in her earbuds and clicked on her phone, rudely cutting herself off from our company. I wasn't displeased that this was becoming her habit.

"So, have you decided where you wanna go first?" asked Otavio, his gaze alternating from Isabel back to me.

"Sugar Loaf mountain," I answered with a smile.

Kevin, who had accompanied Kourtney on her many trips here, felt he had to comment on my choice. "Classic," he said, wearing a derisive know-it-all smirk and nodding. I bit my tongue, wishing I could have taken another photographer with me.

Otavio checked the traffic along with my reaction to Kevin in the rear-view mirror. He seemed pleased with my disdainful look.

Isabel said excitedly: "I think it's time to tell you my idea for your scoop."

"What idea?" I asked with a smile.

"The idea I had when I heard that my new client would be an American reporter looking for a new scoop about the city."

"Which is…?" I asked with interest, pleased to realize hiring Isabel was already paying off.

"You probably know that there are a few ways to do carnival here."

"Yes. There's the people's carnival in the streets, and there's the carnival procession at the Sambadrome, the one we always see on the news in America."

"That's right, but there are a few ways to do carnival at the Sambadrome itself: you can view it from the benches or booths, as most of the tourists do, or you can *participate* in it, as some tourists do. But I want you to participate in the rehearsals, which tourists never do, and if all goes well, we'll convince them to highlight you in the parade, as if you were a real *Carioca!*"

Carioca, I recollected, was a nickname for a person born in the city of Rio.

"And you're positive tourists never do this?" I asked excitedly.

"Most tourists pay to buy a costume and be part of the parade, which is how the samba schools survive. But, what I have in mind is a bit different. If you are a good enough samba dancer, I can try and convince my samba school to put you on top of the allegoric car; you know, the parade float. That honor is usually reserved for Brazilian celebrities. You can be the first American to do it, or at least the first to write about it, which would be a good scoop for you and good international exposure for our school!"

"That's a great idea! Thank you!" I exclaimed, suppressing my urge to hug her. After all, we've only just met. I rubbed my palms together in excitement.

"You're welcome." She grinned. "I spoke to my samba school masters and they've agreed to audition you tomorrow night."

I tensed at the thought. "Oh Good," I said meekly. "Why are they called schools?" I changed the subject, trying to gain time so I could wrap my mind around this idea.

"No real reason, only because the first one that was formed used to meet near a school."

"I see," I chuckled. "Now, do you think that *I* should do the story, you know, to give it a more realistic feel, or should I have Chantal do it? After all, it's why she's here."

"Why don't you both do it?"

"This story ain't gonna be good enough for Brooks," stated Kevin. "Kourtney and I already did it a few years back."

"She took part in the rehearsals of a samba school *and* danced on top of a float?" asked Isabel in surprise.

"Well, no. We didn't attend the rehearsals. What for? It's nothing but a big waste of time. And she didn't dance above a float, but she did participate in the carnival parade, so I don't think this will be different enough for our boss seeing that such similar things have been done in the past. And it will definitely not be enough to win Rachel the bet," he smiled slyly.

"I think you're wrong. It's never been done before, and that's the whole point of the bet," I protested.

"I'm so glad you like the idea! The only remaining question is, how good a dancer *are* you, Raquel?" inquired Isabel.

"I bet *Rachel* has two left feet!" Kevin sneered.

"Hey, paparazzo! Don't *you* also have some music to listen to?" Otavio spat, almost growling at Kevin, as he alluded to Chantal's oblivion of our conversation.

"Whatever," said Kevin. He began playing a game on his phone.

Otavio looked at me through the mirror. He gave me a small reassuring nod of the head. I smiled a small smile and nodded back at him in understanding. I was glad to have him and Isabel on my side.

"To answer your question, I think I'm pretty good," I told Isabel. "I danced jazz for three years, and I take Zumba classes at the gym. My favorite teacher is an amazing dancer who works us very hard. And he's sexy as hell, too," I added, and Isabel and I exchanged grins. Otavio's face fell, so for his benefit I added, "Of course, he's totally gay, but there's no harm in looking." Isabel smiled, and I could sense Otavio relaxing.

"That's great! We'll go to the samba school tomorrow after we practice dancing samba together tonight."

"Oh, I'd sure like to see that!" said Kevin mockingly.

"Me too!" stated Otavio, challenging both Kevin and myself, although in entirely different ways.

"Guys," I said defensively, "I think the first rehearsal should be private." I hated saying it, because I *longed* to dance with Otavio, but I feared my samba dancing was too poor to present.

"You're missing out on an angle, Rachel," said Kevin, serious for a change. "*If* this is going to be the scoop, you need to document it from the very beginning."

"He's right," nodded Isabel. "We should take some pictures and even videos documenting your entire carnival journey." All three of them nodded and I found I had to agree.

"OK, OK," I raised my palms in surrender.

"Otavio should be there, too. He's a great dancer!" added Isabel with a smile.

"Great!" I smiled at him from under my lowered lids, feeling my cheeks redden as he looked at me. *Why* didn't I know how to flirt?

"I don't know what's the big deal about dancing," muttered Kevin and went back to his game. Otavio shook his head at him with pity, and then winked at me.

When we arrived at Sugar Loaf mountain, Otavio hastened to get out and open the door for me. I smiled widely at his old-fashioned chivalry and got out. Kevin mumbled something under his breath in disdain and proceeded to get his equipment. He hung his camera on his neck, then struggled for a moment balancing a large tripod and his heavy bag.

"Need a hand?" asked Otavio, a rough edge to his voice.

"No thanks, man. I got it," answered Kevin. Chantal got out of the car, her earbuds still in her ears, and stretched her long body. Otavio examined her with a smirk and raised an eyebrow. For once, I appreciated her dismissive attitude, since I'd hate to compete against someone like her. When Otavio caught me looking at him, his curved smile returned.

"So how tall is Sugar Loaf mountain?" I craned my neck to look up at the peak.

"Four hundred meters," he answered.

"Or thirteen hundred feet," said Isabel, completing his sentence. They smiled at one another.

"And why do they call it Sugar Loaf?"

"Because it resembles an old loaf of sugar," explained Otavio.

"A *loaf* of sugar?"

"Yes," continued Isabel. "For more than a thousand years, sugar was crystallized in clay containers that looked like cones."

"Just like this conical shaped mountain," I smiled in understanding.

"Exactly!"

"Its name is also a reminder of the importance of the sugar trade in Brazil's history."

"Every tourist has the same questions. And here I was hoping you'd have more original ones," Kevin complained.

"Actually, very few people ask about the name of the mountain," said Otavio in a menacing tone. "As a matter of fact, even most Brazilians don't know the reasons behind the name."

"Well, I've heard it many times before," said Kevin, sounding more submissive this time. Climbing up into the first of two cable car rides, Kevin photographed Chantal's blank stare a few times. I ignored them and let the sheer joy of being in that gorgeous locale sweep over me. Forgetting my desire to attract Otavio, I looked at the view with bubbling excitement. Then I stuck my nose to the glass, mimicking the kid near me, until he finally noticed it and returned my smile. I noticed Otavio's thoughtful gaze on me, as if the silly side of me surprised him. Then he gave me a huge grin, and I responded with one of my own. He kept on watching me as I tuned in to Isabel's commentary of the famous cable car.

When we exited the car at the first mountain stop, Otavio extended his arm to help me. I didn't need it, but I reached for his hand just the same. When our skin touched, I felt currents running up and down my arm. My eyes darted to his, as if to seek an answer to the question "Did you feel that, too?" The flicker in his eyes confirmed it.

I got out of the cable car and we started walking to one of the observation points. I stood in front of the magnificent city, Otavio leaning so close to me, I could feel his breath on my ear.

"Do you remember anything from the car ride between the airport and the hotel?" I turned to him, fighting not to get lost in his bewitching stare. *This cocky bastard thinks he is so amazing, he can make me forget what happened two hours ago?!*

I took a step forward, my hand absently rubbing the warm spot on my ear. "We came from there, right?" I asked and pointed north.

"Very good!" he said with genuine pleasure, disarming me. "So you remember Guanabara Bay."

"How could I forget?" I smiled, looking at the water below.

"The bay was discovered by Portuguese explorers on January 1st 1502, which is why they named it River, or *rio, de Janeiro*, which means of January," said Isabel. Otavio nodded in agreement, and they both activated their 'guide mode,' starting their tale about the city, taking turns as they spoke.

"At first," said Otavio, "people only lived in the historic part of the city center and near Guanabara Bay."

"But then, in the early 20th century," said Isabel, "the first tunnel was carved through the city's mountains, allowing traffic to reach Copacabana."

"A transit system was built, and streetcars began to operate."

"More tunnels were carved inside the mountains and new roads were paved."

"Connecting all parts of the city: *Centro, Zona Norte, Zona Sul* and *Zona Oeste*."

"The city center, the north zone, south zone and west zone," explained Isabel.

"They even filled in part of the bay itself, making it possible to build the road we drove on today," added Otavio.

"Amazing!" I exclaimed.

"The bridge connecting Rio to the city of Niterói was built," said Isabel, pointing to the long bridge and the city on the other side of the lake. "And ferries were added."

"An internal and an international airports were built, and the Metro system."

"And don't forget all the bicycle lanes now available."

I smiled at their seamless alternating. They continued to tell me about the various neighborhoods and landmarks we saw around us while Kevin took snapshots of Chantal. She posed for the camera wearing her trademark disinterested look, a crowd of curious onlookers gathering around her.

"And that's where my samba school is," Isabel pointed to a distant point in the center of town. I smiled and nodded at her, my nerves tightening at the thought of my audition tomorrow.

After the second cable car ride to the top, I found myself alone for a few moments. Standing at the peak of Sugar Loaf mountain, I breathed in the fresh air and decided I was standing atop the most beautiful city in the world. I was amazed at all that human beings had done over the years to transform Rio into such a breath-taking, high-rise-filled city among the hindering mountains, bay and ocean. What kind of genius did it take to come up with the idea of a land reclamation project, basically setting up an embankment that extended the city into the bay, allowing a highway, park, museums, and airport to be built? What did it take to build this port and start the sugar trade? I fanned myself with a brochure I received upon entry. And what kind of fortitude did a man need to continue blasting a tunnel inside a mountain in this scorchingly hot and stiflingly humid city? What kept a man like that going? I pondered.

"Here's the water you asked for," said Isabel, handing me a cold bottle she'd purchased at one of the kiosks. Kevin and Chantal were just joining us by the food stands.

"I feel like moving here and living here forever!" I declared.

"I knew you would let your first assignment get to your head," mocked Kevin.

"This is *not* my first assignment!"

"First one outside the States counts as first one," nagged Kevin, dampening my delightful mood. "It's just like you to fawn over a dangerous, over-crowded town you don't even know, in the middle of this bloody, friggin heat!" he added, wiping his sweat soaked face. Good thing Rio did not have to count on a whining baby like Kevin to build it, otherwise it would not exist, I thought.

"I'm gonna go grab Chantal and me something to drink," said Kevin. "Keep an eye on my equipment, K?"

"Sure, sure," I said, sitting down on the bench next to his tripod to rest. "You can take five."

"Rachel," he said, bending down to my level to stare me in the eyes ominously, "I don't need your permission to take five. You'd know that if it weren't your first assignment." He rose and walked away. Chantal plopped on a distant bench, texting on her phone, ignoring everything around her, including the amazing view.

"This guy is not cool. Want me to talk to him?" suggested Otavio.

"No, but thanks. It's just the way some men talk in the U.S."

"Men or *boys?*"

"Good question," I concurred. "But let's not say anything. I'll just take it; I'm used to it."

"Well, you shouldn't take it."

"I agree," said Isabel.

"I have my own way of dealing with people like him. For instance, when he comes back I think I'll ask him to take a few more dozen pictures under the heat of the midday sun."

They smiled as they understood my little scheme. After Kevin returned, he pouted and whined as he carried his heavy equipment from one lookout to another, photographing Chantal in front of various backgrounds: our hotel and Copacabana beach, the famous statue of Christ atop Corcovado mountain, the Guanabara bay, and more. Isabel took snapshots of me on my cell phone, first grinning with joy, then with a thoughtful faraway look, then with a coquettish, sexy smile. Finally, after making sure Chantal couldn't see me, I did my best to mimic her vacant look. Otavio, who seemed as though he was drinking in my image, finally cracked a half-smile and said: "*You* would *never* make anyone believe you are bored up here." His smile evaporated, and he said seriously, "They should be publishing pictures of you enjoying this place, not of...," he said with a frown as he looked at the hollow expression on Chantal's face. "Are you telling me anyone finds *that* beautiful?" He lit a cigarette and walked away, leaving me to ponder.

When Kevin's shirt was soaked through with sweat and he was too exhausted to complain, I declared we had enough pictures. We took the cable cars down the mountain.

As Isabel and Otavio dropped us off at the hotel, Isabel said to everyone: "So we'll meet at Raquel's room at 9:00 PM for some samba dancing, OK?"

Kevin grumbled and walked away with Chantal. My eyes locked with Otavio's for a charged moment. "See you then," I said with a smile.

CHAPTER 4

A dance rehearsal, I thought with apprehension as I put on my makeup in my hotel room. I have to dance in front of Ms. Gorgeous and Mr. Sex-appeal, who are both probably awesome samba dancers, *and* in front of Mr. Negativity and Ms. Bored. What had I gotten myself into?

I stopped applying my foundation and looked at myself in the mirror. Rachel Moore, this is your career. Just pretend you're taking a samba class at the gym, like you do Zumba classes. There, it had taken me a while to make my way from the back row to the front. Now I danced front and center without inhibitions. It was easier at the gym, since I knew no one would make fun of my weight in Andy's classes. He accepted people as they were. As a result, I felt comfortable expressing myself through dance. Maybe I could pretend I didn't know anyone here, too, just like in Zumba class?

I finished applying my makeup and put on my black exercise tights, sports bra, and red undershirt. I looked at myself in the mirror and sighed, thinking I could look pretty good if I only lost another ten, fifteen pounds. OK; maybe twenty. After all, I was only size twelve, and I could be size ten or maybe even eight if I dieted real hard for a few months. I left my feet bare and gathered my hair atop my head in a very high ponytail, a look that made me look like some sort of a go-getter cheerleader. I smiled at my own reflection.

I looked at some of my teacher's Zumba videos on YouTube. Andy was a phenomenal dancer who enjoyed flaunting his sensuality. I enjoyed seeing him move, and dancing along to the videos was a good, fun warm-up. When I heard a knock at the door, I quickly closed YouTube. I had no doubt my tormentors would pounce on my gay Zumba teacher the moment they laid eyes on him.

"Hello, Raquel," Isabel smiled and kissed my cheeks. She wore a fuchsia mini dress that enveloped her body and exposed her long, tanned legs. Her feet were adorned with four-inch golden heels. *Was she going to dance with those?* I wondered, feeling a mix of trepidation, jealously and excitement.

"*Olá*, Raquel," Otavio placed a box on the floor, then took long strides toward me. His smile widened as he detected my nervousness. He put both his hands on my waist, causing shivers to run up and down my spine. As his lips lingered on my cheeks for a kiss, I breathed in the refreshing scent of his cologne, my hands resting on the strong muscles I felt through his gray T-shirt. I knew I must have seemed like easy prey to him, since I didn't conceal my excitement at his interest, but I had no idea how to conceal it or how to play hard to get. "Your bartender for the night took care of everything you might... what's the word? In Portuguese we say *desejo.*" I was entranced by the exotic sound and by the way his full lips rounded to finish the word, as they would if he laid them on my mouth to kiss.

"Desire," answered Isabel with a smile.

"Desire," he said with a sultry, meaningful look and gazed into my eyes. I swallowed. He smirked.

"We found those two at the bar," Isabel nodded toward the hallway.

"Yo," was all Kevin said to me as he walked inside. He wore torn jeans and a sleeveless T-shirt, showing off the spiderweb tattoo on his shoulder. He carried his tripod, his camera hanging off his neck. Chantal followed him, barely avoiding the furniture as she texted on her phone. She wore a silver, sequined mini dress.

"I love your dress!" Isabel exclaimed.

"Oh this? I just threw on the first thing I found," said Chantal lethargically. Maybe the secret to playing it hard to get was to act disinterested, I wondered. Didn't I repeatedly read in magazines that men go crazy over the one woman who's out of their reach? But it made no sense to me. Why approach a woman who is sure to reject you? "Rachel, you couldn't find a dress that fit you?" Chantal asked, narrowing her eyes at me. Kevin smiled at this vicious remark, but one look from Otavio erased the smile off his face.

Otavio bent over to grab the box and placed it on the table. He proceeded to show me: "*Cachaça,* vodka, limes, and sugar – the perfect ingredients for a *Caipirinha* or a *Caipivodka.*"

"Awesome! I've been meaning to try drinking Cachaça!" I smiled. My expression changed when I noticed Kevin's face. I thought I was able to read his disdainful thoughts: *Of course you want to try Cachaça, Rachel. You have to go by the book and say and do what every other tourist ever says or does in Rio.* I was surprised when he said nothing, until I noticed the fleeting deferential look he gave Otavio, who was looking at him with a menacing frown. I wondered what had transpired between the two. Whatever it was, at the moment, I was thankful for it.

Isabel and Otavio raided the suite. They found five glasses and an ice bucket, which Isabel proceeded to fill while Otavio sliced the limes with his pocket knife. I had a feeling they had done this for other tourists before.

"Just sit down and relax," said Otavio. I smiled somewhat nervously as I sat on the couch. I watched him as he started preparing the drinks, my eyes drawn to his strong hands and thick, powerful fingers. He put the lime quarters in all five glasses and then he took out a mortar from the box. As he deftly crushed the limes, he explained, "Caipirinhas are our national drink, made from this sugar cane rum, known as cachaça, lots of limes, and sugar. We also brought vodka, since Caipivodkas are preferred by tourists," he added, glancing at Kevin and Chantal.

"Oh, yea!" said Kevin. "Cachaça sucks. Only Caipivodkas for me... er, please," he added politely.

"Me, too," said Chantal as she continued to text.

"I'm glad we were able to predict what you would like," Isabel smiled at them as she returned with the ice bucket. She sounded like the perfect hostess, but when she gazed at me, she winked. I smiled in return.

Kevin busied himself playing a game on his phone. I looked back at Otavio as he dug a spoon into the sugar bag repeatedly for each of the glasses. He added lots of ice cubes, and only then did he open the bottle of Cachaça and poured generously over the sugared pulpy limes and ice cubes in three of the glasses. He stirred the cocktails and finally handed me one, crouching down to my level.

"This looks yummy!" I smiled.

"Try it!" he urged. I took one sip of the drink and grimaced miserably. Otavio and Isabel laughed, and Kevin and Chantal peeked at me over their phones.

"You don't like it?" asked Otavio, frowning.

"No, I *do* like it! It's just that you made it so strong!" He grinned.

"Hey, what about me? All I get to do is bring you ice, waiter?" teased Isabel.

"It's bartender," corrected Otavio and bowed in mock deference.

"Get me my drink, bartender!" commanded Isabel playfully.

"Can we get on with photographing? Chantal and I have a party to get to," glowered Kevin.

"So I guess you don't want this?" smiled Isabel as she poured vodka over the remaining two glasses. Kevin smiled at her and accepted the drink, which seemed to shut him up for a while.

I have to dance in front of this asshole in a little bit, I thought. I swallowed the rest of my drink and handed Otavio the empty glass. "One more, please, bartender."

"Already?" he asked, looking pleased.

"Yup. If I'm going to strut my stuff in front of all of you, I'd better have another."

Isabel lounged near me on the couch and we sipped our drinks as we discussed New York, which she had visited a couple of times before and which we both adored. I was always delighted to speak about the beautiful skyscrapers visible from my small apartment's window, the busy streets I enjoyed navigating on my way to work, and the nature of my job at a travel magazine. When I felt I had postponed the inevitable long enough, I downed my second drink and got to my feet. "Let's get started," I said.

"Did you download the songs I told you about?" Isabel asked.

"Yes," I said and started the samba, placing my phone in the small docking station I'd brought from home, which amplified the sound. I started doing some stretches, jumping in place at times as the upbeat music took over me. Isabel got up to stretch with me. I smiled at her, happy not to be the center of attention. I gathered up my courage and spoke to Chantal: "Chantal. You're going to have to dance at the samba school tomorrow with me, and at the carnival parade if they let us, so you'd better join us."

"Should I tell her?" she asked Kevin lethargically.

"Tell me what?"

"Save it for later," Kevin told her. "You can dance tonight and tomorrow night, can't you?"

"Fine," she acquiesced.

"Tell me what?!" I demanded.

"You'll know in time," was all Kevin said. I frowned angrily.

Chantal got up and asked, "Is this the song we're dancing to?"

"Before you start," Otavio said to Kevin, "help me move the sofa out of the way." Kevin mumbled something but helped move the three seat sectional to the end of the room. He then situated himself near his tripod and camera, waiting to photograph us. Otavio cleared the table and lamp out of our way, too, and finally, the round carpet. The center of my hotel room was now empty, the parquet floor ready for dancing.

I used to be too shy to go out dancing, feeling it was safer to stay home or go out to a bar instead of risking the kind of rejections I had gotten at middle school and high school dances. But the variety of dance classes I'd taken over the years helped increase my confidence. My dancing style was a mishmash of jazz, salsa, Zumba, and samba movements. Still nervous, I decided to change my perspective. Think of it as a chance to make up for all the times you declined to go out dancing, I told myself. This time you said yes. Embrace it!

The next song began with high-speed notes. It was as if the song writer dared you not to dance to his gripping music. My determinations lined up in my mind like bullets: *Ignore Kevin! Forget Chantal! Don't look at Otavio! Don't even look at Isabel! Just try to keep up with the beat!*

I started dancing, moving toward the center of the empty space. I gave the dance my all, flinging my arms up, gyrating my hips, my feet moving in rapid, complex patterns. *It's all or nothing, baby!* And it felt great!

From the corner of my eye I could perceive Isabel's fuchsia dress moving swiftly as she gyrated her bum to the samba beat, two flashes of golden pumps tapping at breakneck speed on the floor. And was Chantal trying to do the tough girl Hip Hop she did for her new perfume ad with *this* rapid song?

She looked ridiculous. Even though I'd let myself glance at them, I did not allow myself to look at Kevin. I ignored his camera's flashes, but I was determined not to look at him, knowing his cantankerous attitude could take the wind out of my sails.

I fought the urge to look at Otavio, knowing there was a chance he might not like my dancing, and I just couldn't risk his reaction damaging my fragile confidence. Besides, if he liked it, I'd probably start dancing differently, dancing *for* him. And that would change something important. So I continued to ignore everyone and dance for myself until the song ended.

Kevin and Otavio clapped and whistled loudly. Chantal plonked on the sofa chair near Kevin, who got up, stood behind her and started rubbing her shoulders.

"Wow!" said Isabel, panting for air, "Is this girl good or what?!"

"Not bad, Rachel," agreed Kevin smilelessly.

"She's marvelous!" declared Otavio, his eyes piercing mine approvingly.

"Thank you," I said, feeling the blush rise on my cheeks. "I love dancing."

"It's evident," he said. Then he looked at me enticingly: "Now you are going to dance with me!"

"Dance with you?!" I repeated, somewhat stupefied.

"Of course. What did you expect?"

I smiled awkwardly, not saying that it was exactly what I had both longed for and feared. I could count on one hand the times I'd danced with a guy before and never with someone like him. But there was no denying that the closer we got, the more he threatened to come in the way of my work.

"If you're going to dance on top of a float, we need to work on your samba step. Yours, too, Chantal," said Isabel amiably.

"This has gone on long enough," she said impatiently. "Rachel, I'll do whatever shoot you want me to do, but I won't be able to dance in the parade on Monday. I'm having surgery on Sunday."

"What?!"

"She's finally having her breasts done!" boasted Kevin, placing the hands that massaged her shoulders a moment ago on Chantal's small mounds of breasts.

"Kevin, you're such a beast!" grinned Chantal pleasurably, unfazed by his gesture of intimacy.

I found it hard to compute all this information. Yes, they used to date, but she was with Ryan now. Then again, models were often close to their photographers, and even if it was a betrayal of Ryan, it was none of my business. *My* business with her was that she was here to do my shoots, and the most important one was dancing in the carnival. And now she was just sitting there, like the uncaring, unfeeling bitch she apparently was, oblivious to the fact that she had scheduled her damn vanity surgery at the worst time for me, oblivious to my needs and to the fact that her timing might take my career down!

I felt my hands starting to shake with anger. I curled my fingers into fists and asked as politely as I could, "Can't you have it done *after* the parade? After all, we're here for a week and a half after it ends."

"Impossible. The doctor who did Claudia has already agreed to postpone his vacation until Monday for me, not to mention operate on the weekend."

"Then why the hell did you take the job?!" my stupefaction obliterated any remains of shyness.

"To get the surgery done, like I said. And I'm doing it all on the company's dime. Well, all but the surgery itself. Not bad, eh?" she smiled at Kevin, who beamed at her cunning.

"Ryan *should* pay for the surgery," insisted Kevin with a sly grin. "After all, he's the one who's going to reap the benefits."

"I'm not sure that relationship's gonna last," she said nonchalantly, looking down at her nails.

"Oh?" he asked, looking very interested.

"Never you mind! The point is, with my perfume sales skyrocketing, pretty soon I won't need anyone to pay for anything. Brooks might prove too much of a pain in my ass. Too serious."

"Why don't I call Ryan Brooks and tell him everything you've been up to, ha? What will you do then?" I challenged her, grabbing my phone off its docking station and sitting on the sofa across from her. I stared at Chantal. Isabel sat next to me, her hand petting my arm soothingly. Otavio shoved an unlit cigarette in his mouth but did not move toward the balcony. We all wanted to hear her answer.

"Rachel, Rachel, Rachel," she shook her head at me as if I were a slow-witted child. "Think ahead, past your little parade. *This* is the scoop every newspaper and magazine would kill for! There is not a man in existence, nor a woman for that matter, who will give up the chance to see these new babies bigger!" she jiggled her breasts, arching her back forward and smirking. "The truth is, I don't care if you tell him. *I* don't need your little story. But when Ryan rejects your scoop, I have no doubt you'll be able to convince him that my augmentation is a big enough scoop." She turned to Kevin. "Get it? A big scoop?"

"Yea, yea; I got it," he grinned lasciviously. "Let's get out of here, then. Let 'Her Majesty' here mull over what you said. She'll see that you're right and realize how much she needs you."

Desperate to save my job, I pleaded, even though I knew it was useless. "Chantal, I need you to model at the parade! Don't you care that you're completely screwing me over?"

She stood up and towered over me. "Darling, there are two kinds of people in this world: the kind that screw others and the kind that get screwed. Now be a resourceful little girl, like you were when you screwed Kourtney, and find a different solution, like using a local model, for instance. Or use your pretty friend here," she nodded in Isabel's direction. "But remember, if you tell Ryan anything, the new boob scoop goes to somebody else!"

"I know keeping your mouth shut is not one of your strong suits, Rach," Kevin said, "but believe me, this time it'll be in your best interest."

Kevin picked up his things and they both headed for the door. I wanted to yell or throw something. I hardly managed to hold back the tears of anger. I felt a horrible despair, like I used to feel when I was bullied in school. I clenched my hands into fists and asked, "Are you going to come with us to the samba school tomorrow? After all, it was your idea to document all the steps."

"Sure; we'll be there," Kevin said. When Chantal looked like she was about to protest, he whispered something in her ear, which seemed to appease her.

"Fine. We'll be there. It'll be good for my image," she smirked. "I'll start tweeting it right now: *Chantal Neuchâtel in touch with the poor, Brazilian masses.* Remind me to bring a case of my perfume, K?" she told Kevin.

Yea, because perfumes is just what these poor folks need! I thought in frustrated anger.

"But that perfume isn't sold in Brazil yet," frowned Isabel, trying but failing to cover up her eagerness. She sneaked a furtive, apologetic look at me.

"I believe the perfume's release date in Brazil is set for June," Chantal clicked on her phone rapidly. "Yes. Right before Lovers' Day. But *you* can buy a whole case from me right now!" she smiled magnanimously.

"Thank you," Isabel said to their departing backs as they left the suite. I looked at her grimly. "Sorry, dear. I couldn't resist it.

I'll get to have it before anyone else. Do you have *any* idea how my girlfriends and I are dying to try *Climax*?!"

"Come sit outside and breathe some fresh air, Raquel," said Otavio, clearly eager to have his smoke. "It will calm you down."

"Alright," I acquiesced, trying to process everything Chantal and Kevin had said. "Coming?" I asked Isabel, who was texting with a smile.

"You go and relax. We'll continue practicing when you come back."

CHAPTER 5

I breathed deeply before stepping on the balcony's tiles. They were warm, just like the evening air. I stood near the guardrail, taking in the beauty of the city at night. The beach was illuminated by powerful projectors, so it was visible at night, too. The busy avenue sparkled with lights from hundreds of apartments, hotel rooms, street and traffic lights. The restaurants and kiosks were all full of people.

"I think a good way to get back at that idiot is for you to dance in the parade yourself," Otavio said.

"Hmm, I think both Chantal and I should dance. This way I could have two versions, one with a model, and one without. Some readers prefer the latter, since they seem more authentic. The good magazines and sites have both kinds."

"So?" he smiled widely.

"There's a reason why I chose a life behind a desk, and not one in front of the camera."

"Oh, and why is that?" He slowly approached me, an alluring look in his eyes.

Did I have to explicitly state that which was so painfully obvious? "Think about the women you see in magazines, or on TV. I'm not exactly built like any of them, am I? I'm too..." what word should I use? Round? Fat? "Curvy," I said.

"That may be the case in America. But if you open a magazine or watch TV over here, you'll find that things are a bit different. Over here, a curvy woman is a goddess!" he announced, his eyes slowly roaming about my body, his mouth curved into a suggestive smile.

What kind of a guy uses such blatant lies to seduce a woman? My eyes shot up angrily at him. And why would a hot guy like that waste his time on me, when he could have any smoking-hot girl around? What was he up to?

"I'll never figure American women out! You give them a compliment and they get angry." He seemed genuinely perplexed, so I didn't pursue the matter. "Come on! Let's dance!"

Back in the room, he dimmed the lights and started to play music on his cell phone. Wordlessly, he grabbed my hand and started guiding me, twirling me into him for a long moment, then away from him, repeating the movements in different variations, while singing along to the samba song. His eyes did not leave mine, except for the times he enveloped his body behind mine for one, electrifying second, during which my mind melted and my heart thudded. I struggled to follow his lead, to move in unison or to contra move, all while bubbling with confusion at his flirtation and with the kind of passion I had never felt before.

Afraid of getting distracted from my assignment by lust, I wondered if I should try to resist his lead and try to lead myself? I'd done that once with a nice guy before, and he just let me share the lead with a goofy smile on his face. Besides, wasn't it important to show the guy he wasn't the boss? So I tried to resist one of his spins, hoping to spin him instead, or acquire an edge in another way. Otavio simply grinned at me and dipped me backwards, very low, grabbing me with both of his strong arms, then flung me back up, following with another inward, then outward spin. He left me with no choice but to submit. And I found I enjoyed every single second. By the end of the song, I was smiling widely, intoxicated by the experience.

He let me go and quickly demonstrated some complex samba moves. I tried to mimic his steps, but I didn't do very well.

"Stop, stop, stop the music," he said. I smiled in some embarrassment and stopped moving, my breath a bit labored. Isabel paused the music. She came and stood next to me, and she and Otavio tried to teach me how to improve my samba steps in a slower manner. After a while, we ordered some appetizers and Otavio made some more drinks.

"So what do you think?" asked Isabel, she and I sprawled lazily on the couch. "Are you ready to dance in front of everyone at the samba school tomorrow?"

"I don't know if I would ever be *ready* to dance in front of samba experts, but I'll do it anyway." Anything for the sake of my dream, I had vowed to myself way back when I was a teen.

"Will you give me a ride home, Otavio?" asked Isabel.

"Sure," he replied, emptying his glass with one gulp.

"You guys are leaving?" I asked with some disappointment, not sure what I expected would take place next.

"Yes. My fiancé, Tiago, is back from a business trip to São Paulo and he will be waiting for me."

I glanced at my cell and saw it was nearly midnight. "Oh, I didn't realize it was so late! I guess I'll see you guys tomorrow."

Isabel smiled and kissed both my cheeks before she turned to go. Otavio did the same, his smile as seductive as before.

Left alone, I was struck by how silent the room now was. I decided to play some Bossa Nova, hoping the delicate sounds would relax me and prepare me for sleep. My body was more than ready for it. But, despite the alcohol and fatigue, my mind still raced with the many images, thoughts, and feelings of my first day in Rio. I changed into my comfy, red shorts and white camisole. I pushed the armchair to the window and proceeded to lounge on it, my feet dangling from the arm. Most of the lights in the hotel rooms and apartments ahead of me were out, but the beach and the street were still brightly illuminated. Thoughts raced through my mind: Isabel, Rio, the bet, Kevin, Chantal. Underlining all those thoughts, like a sweeping ocean current, was one thought: Could it possibly be that Otavio was sincere about my appeal? I was so conditioned to think I was flawed, I could hardly acknowledge the possibility. But... what if he was?

The knock on the door nearly made me jump out of my skin. What the hell? I walked to the door and asked: "Who is it?" And, remembering I was in a Brazilian hotel, I added, *"Quem é?"*

"It's Otavio."

My heart pounded rapidly as I opened the door. He stood there with his teasing half-smile, a pint of ice cream in his right hand, and a bottle of Champagne cradled in his left.

"Wow! How did you know how much I wanted something sweet?" I asked as I let Otavio in and grabbed the ice-cream from him as I led him inside.

"I could sense it," he smiled as he picked up all the empty sugar wrappers near my coffee cup and showed them to me. We both smiled. "Champagne?"

"Sure!" I squeaked nervously.

He grabbed the ice bucket. "I'll be right back," he grabbed my key card off the console table at the entryway.

"I'll be outside," I smiled, taking the ice cream and the spoons with me. As I sank into the beach chaise, thoughts passed through my head a mile a minute. Drinking this Champagne at this hour, alone with *this* guy, all equaled zero resistance. And I'd just met him! Jess would say *Go for it!* while Ashley would put down Otavio and all playboys of his kind as the type of men who just took advantage of women.

But what did *I* want to do? Even though I knew this could distract me from my work, I had to ask myself: wasn't this a rare chance for me to be with a hot guy who, in America, would be considered way out of my league; a guy for whom *I* was somehow a foreign beauty? Didn't I owe it to myself to enjoy this moment?

I released my hair from its imprisoning rubber band, shaking my head as I helped the soft ocean breeze muss my locks. My gaze met Otavio's stare as he came back from his ice run and stood in the room, reminding me that I was not only being watched, but also evaluated, appreciated, and desired. I rearranged my legs in a more elegant, seductive pose.

I devoured a big spoonful of ice-cream. I closed my eyes as the sweet, velvety flavor of creme-caramel filled my mouth, wondering in the back of my mind if Otavio was devouring my look of pleasure. I heard the cork pop loudly. I opened my eyes and smiled at him. He joined me on the balcony with two tall glasses and the bottle, which was immersed inside the ice bucket. He pushed the second chaise next to mine and lay in it. He handed me a glass and we clinked.

"*Saúde!*" he said. "That means to your health."

"Saúde!" I replied, and we both sipped from our glasses.

"How's your first Brazilian Champagne?" he asked, his eyes delving into mine.

"It's sweet, just the way I like it."

"I did not want to get a dry one, not with ice cream. Is it good?"

"Try some," I answered huskily, and fed him a teaspoon. He opened his mouth and closed his eyes as I let the slightly-melting ice-cream descend onto his extended tongue. I felt my mouth water. He swallowed, then opened his eyes only half way, a sensual look in his eyes. "Delicious!" Yes, indeed, I thought, but found I couldn't speak. I took another long sip of the Champagne. "I wanted to show you something. Here," he said, and searched for something on his phone, "check this out." He leaned close to me and revealed a photo of a voluptuous, beautiful woman, with an hourglass figure.

"This is Rafaela. She is Brazil's hottest model. She drives all the men crazy!" I looked at the photo more closely. I knew that despite her bewitching, dark beauty, and despite the popularity of curvy women with some American men, most would find her too round, too padded, or simply too fat.

"Why are you showing me this?" I asked, inhaling a whiff of his cologne. My heart thumped so loudly, I wondered if he could hear it.

"Because I *know* how much you need to see this," he said softly, his gaze interlocking with mine. He couldn't know! Could he? But how? How could he possibly know? I asked myself. "You see," he continued, "I've been watching you all day. I've watched you take crap from those idiots so many times, and you didn't say anything, almost as if you thought they were right, or that you deserved to be treated that way." His fingertips started tracing my bare leg up my thigh, paralyzing me while simultaneously giving me goosebumps. "Then when you, with your exquisite figure, said you belong behind a desk, I just knew you needed, more than anything, someone to show you how beautiful you are."

I could have wept. My deepest wounds, the ones that formed the calluses of my soul, devoured his words like a life-giving balm. I leaned forward, my face nearing his, my eyes closing, lips parting. He pressed his lips on mine and drew me into a passionate kiss. This was not a tentative, timid, or awkward kiss. It wasn't too eager or hurried, the kind where the lips don't align together, or the noses bump. This was the kind of kiss I'd always dreamed about, like a kiss from the Golden Age of Hollywood, where the strong male lead knew what he was doing. And like the women in those black and white movies, I let myself surrender to him.

He clutched my back and pulled me onto his chaise, so we both laid on it. He kissed my mouth, then made his way to my earlobe, making me squirm with delight. Then we kissed again, his hands delving into my hair, down my arms, then under my shirt on the small of my back. How far was I willing to let him take this tonight?

He opened his eyes and so did I. We looked at one another. He leaned on one elbow, then reached out for my face. His ran the back of his fingers on my cheek tenderly, as if he were trying to reassure me I had nothing to worry about.

"There are so many things I want to share with you, to teach you," he said while caressing me. "But it's getting late, and I should probably go."

That sounded more like a question than a statement. Clearly, he was letting me dictate what happened next. Knowing he was willing to wait made me more impatient to have him. But I couldn't; not yet anyway. Not before I'd made headway on my scoop.

A quick glance at the large clock and temperature gauge posted on a tall lamppost across the street showed it was past 2:00 AM. He *had* to leave if I were to get any work done tomorrow. "Is that going to be OK with you?" I asked.

"I can stop now, but it'll be a lot harder if we go any further," he smirked, his fingers running up my thigh.

"Let's wait then," I said.

"Hmm, that's not going to be easy," he said and kissed me again, a hungrier kiss that made me feel as though he wanted to consume me, tonight. He was hoping I'd change my mind!

"You are an amazing kisser!" I declared, tearing myself away from him and standing up. He grinned in understanding and rose to his feet. We had one last, lustful kiss at the door.

"See you tomorrow, beautiful!" he said with a smile and a wink.

"See you tomorrow," I smiled back.

CHAPTER 6

I woke at noon. I got up and moaned, clutching my head. Stupid hangover! I dragged myself to the bathroom, got a couple of Ibuprofen and downed them with an entire bottle of water. When I dared peek in the mirror, I snarled grumpily at my reflection, a bedraggled apparition of wild hair and smudged mascara. Before I took a shower, I ordered some breakfast. How was I going to survive until the coffee got here? And why on earth don't they have a coffee kettle in the room?

I felt more human after showering and dressing in fresh clothes. I stood out on the balcony, shading my eyes. I took in the crowded beach dotted with dozens of red parasols, the blue waves of the Atlantic, and the sunny sky. People were sunbathing, swimming, playing various sports, or just hanging out in the kiosks. I yearned to join them. But first, I had to focus on work.

I checked my cell phone. There was a message from Isabel. *Want to have breakfast together?* It was a couple of hours old. I texted back. *Sure! But I'm only having mine now...*

Her reply came in quickly. *I already ate. We're on our way. Be there soon! :-)*

I made sure to have my makeup on before she and Otavio arrived. I felt nervous, unsure whether or not to hide what happened last night from Isabel. I'd have to let Otavio take the lead.

While waiting for breakfast, I perused my personalized PA Gazette. The fact that all of Ryan's companies were connected on his staffs' personalized PAs enabled a seamless and efficient running of the Brooks enterprise worldwide. The efficiency of the complex search algorithm was renowned in the tech industry, and Jess claimed many competitors had tried to decipher and copy it. The personalized PA's of Brooks Inc. have revolutionized entire companies. It had been proven that supplying all of one's employees with PA's, albeit an expensive move, improved a company's productivity by thirty percent or more. All I knew was that its search results were always unique, and that its gazette had carried not-to-be-missed news. I loved that every employee could insert some personal news of his latest career achievement in the gazette. What a great way for Ryan to recognize the hard work of his employees. I was eager to publish my scoop when the time came.

I Skyped Jess and filled her in on everything that happened.

"It's almost 1:00 PM over there. Why are you yawning so much?" she asked.

"I was up late last night, and the coffee isn't here yet."

"What? I would have thought you'd be working like crazy and getting adequate sleep like the responsible person that you are," she teased.

I had to tell her. "Check this out," I texted her a photo of Otavio.

"Oh, baby! Who's *that?!*"

"*That* is my tour guide and the reason I was up late last night."

"No! Wait, let me get Ash."

"Don't. She's just going to criticize me. I'll tell her when I'm good and ready." Ashley, a declared feminist, was so critical, we often left her out of conversations likes these, inevitably bringing me and Jess closer together than Ashley and I were.

"You're right. If she hears you hooked up with a Brazilian hottie your first night there, she'll flip!"

"We didn't hook up. We just kissed."

"How was it?"

"It was so good, I don't know how I had the strength not to go any further."

"What for? Why not let yourself have fun? After all, you're only there for two weeks."

"I know, but even that was too fast for my taste."

"I guess it was, ha? Anyway, I'm proud of you for getting that far. He is just to die for!"

"He is. And he's drooling over me like I'm the hottest girl in town. I just don't know what to make of it."

"That you've finally found a guy with good taste, who can appreciate you! That's what you should be thinking!"

"Thanks, sweetie," I inclined my head. I knew that it was hard for Jess, our amateur comedian, to say serious things like that. "Now, I have to tell you about the scoop idea Isabel, the other tour guide, had." I filled her in.

"This idea seems great, hon. But listen, I've gotta go. Lon and I are conferencing with the international tech team." Ayalon "Lon" Ryder was Ryan's Chief Information Officer and known as an Israeli tech wizard. Jess, who incorporated the latest tech gadgets into her column, was very excited to work with him. He was famous for having developed the PA alongside Ryan.

"Sounds cool. But do you have just one more minute? I have to tell you what Chantal did to me."

"Sure, I can spare a few more minutes." Jess's ears got red with anger as I told her about Chantal's impending surgery. "I can't believe that bitch won't be able to dance in the parade," she spat. Then she added tenderly, "well, honey, you're just going to have to be brave and do it by yourself."

"I know. It won't be easy, but I'll do it."

"And Rach, I hate to say this, but you've got to try and stay nice to her. She's right that you're better off using her story than telling on her if it comes down to it. Man, she's good!"

"You're probably right."

"Have you seen her video promoting her new perfume, *Climax?*" Presently, Jess sent me a link and we watched it together. The video showed Chantal entering a nightclub alone to the sound of a wild, techno beat. Colorful lights flashed on her pale blue eyes and dirty blond hair, then highlighted her tanned, skinny body, which was draped in a very revealing satin slip dress that looked more like sexy lingerie. Several handsome, muscular men danced around her, and she gyrated with them. Then the music and light-flashes grew more frantic, the camera flashing from one sweaty body part to another. The ad ended with a sexual, female sigh, and the female announcer saying in a sexy voice: "Climax. Get her what she wants!"

"My God! I need a cigarette!"

"Right?" agreed Jess. "She knows sex sells and she's not ashamed to take advantage of that."

"Listen, don't tell Ashley about any of this 'cause she's bound to let it slip." Like she told everyone in the office about the bet, I recalled bitterly. Ashley had apologized for the slip, but the memory of the weeks of torture by The Trio prior to the trip were still fresh and painful. I felt no remorse for *swiping* Rio from under Kourtney, as she termed it, since she and the others had made fun of me covering Nevada for the past three years. Three long, boring years. But now *I* was here, I reminded myself.

"I won't tell her. Let's talk tomorrow, OK? Or before that, if something else happens with the hottie."

"Nothing's gonna happen before tomorrow. I have work to do!"

"You never know," she grinned wickedly at me.

"Bye," I said, shaking my head. We blew air kisses at each other and hung up.

By the time Isabel and Otavio arrived, I was already done eating and elbow deep in work.

"*Boa Tarde*," said Isabel. "That means good afternoon." She kissed my cheeks and looked about her for a place to hang the dress she'd brought. She hung it in the entry closet.

Otavio looked freshened up too, and even sexier than I'd remembered, if that were at all possible. "Hi," I whispered with a smile.

"*Oi*," he smiled back and gently kissed me on the lips. I turned to see Isabel's reaction.

"*Oba!*" smiled Isabel. "I felt there was something between you two last night. *Que beleza!*" To my baffled look she translated, "It means how great." I looked for hidden signs of scorn or judgment but found none. It puzzled me.

"I love how easy it is to surprise her," Otavio told Isabel. He stood behind me and weaved his hands around my waist, hugging me to him. "What did you think Isabel would say?"

The gamut of my thoughts wasn't wide. I was certain Isabel would think I was easy. But, in my darkest, most ridiculous thoughts, I imagined she and Otavio smoking stubby cigars and laughing at me like partners in crime, talking about how easy it was to bag this tourist, especially after telling her exactly what they both decided was needed in order to score. Never in my life had I imagined her response to be as laid back, as nonjudgmental, and as sweet as it was.

"Otavio, you're making the woman blush," smiled Isabel, sitting in one of the chairs near the table, arranging the short skirt of her orange, cotton dress around herself.

Otavio looked at me with a grin, kissed my lips again, then let me go. I smiled awkwardly and signaled to him to take a place at the table as I sat between them, facing my computer.

"Well, you saw what kind of people I'm surrounded with. If they saw you kiss me a day after we met, I'd be branded as a slut in a second!"

"That is just wrong," Isabel said and they both shook their heads. "You see, over here sex is not treated like I've seen it treated in American movies. Yes, married women are expected to remain loyal, but before they get into a committed relationship, they are free to enjoy sex, to enjoy men and to enjoy themselves. No one will judge them for it, call them names, or expect anything less. That is what our bodies are for: to make us *feel* life; to make us enjoy life."

"That sounds wonderful," I said longingly, "so simple and open. I wish it was like that in America, too."

"Who's that?" asked Isabel, pointing at the image on my PA. It was a picture of Kourtney in a clown costume walking in the Sambadrome carnival procession that was part of my research of her past assignments. I showed them the rest of the photos. There was a tandem hang glide in São Conrado, sailing a day-boat in Guanabara Bay, stirring Caipivodkas in a nightclub in Lapa, doing Capoeira with some kids on the multicolored tiled steps of Santa Teresa, and playing *futevólei*, or foot volleyball, on Ipanema beach. When I finished scrolling the images, I was back at the clown photo. Kourtney's body of work made me doubt the strength of my scoop and wonder whether I should continue to look for a different story.

"Oh boy. These are some of the other ideas I had for a scoop," said Isabel. Noticing my frown, she added, "don't worry. She didn't ride the float or attended rehearsals. That story is all yours."

"You're right," I smiled resolutely, my doubts allayed. "And thanks again for coming up with ideas for scoops."

"My pleasure," she smiled warmly.

"Are you ready for a break?" asked Otavio. "You haven't been to the beach, yet." He smiled and winked in invitation.

"Oh my goodness. If you only knew how I'm dying for some sun or a dip in the ocean. It snowed all week before I left!"

"I wouldn't mind being in the snow for a week or two," said Isabel.

"At least you've seen snow before," Otavio said to her. "I never have."

As he stepped out for a smoke, I replied to him before he closed the balcony's door, "Believe me, it gets old fast. Oh, how I've missed the sun!"

"Then what are we waiting for?" asked Isabel. "Put on your bathing suit."

"But what about work?" I asked, temptation weakening my resolve.

"There's not much left to do before the samba school tonight."

"But shouldn't we practice my samba moves some more?"

"You'll do well enough. I've been meaning to explain something to you. You see, in exchange for a small role on their float, my school will get exposure in one of Millionaire Ryan

Brooks' magazines." My heart sank. Was this the reason she suggested this scoop in the first place? But it couldn't be; not if she had other scoops lined up. I really didn't want to believe her motives were less than pure. "Unless you fall flat on your face, you're in the parade!" she declared happily.

"So if I trip and mess up, I'm out?"

"I'm afraid so. Every school parading in the carnival is rated by a few judges, and the competition is very close. They can't afford to have clumsy people on their floats." At my worried expression, she added warmly, "judging by what I saw yesterday, you're going to do great."

"You really think so?" I asked hopefully.

"Absolutely! Now go get changed."

"O.K. Do you have your bathing suit on already?" I asked, getting up.

"Underneath. Now go!"

Excited, I rushed to get ready.

* * *

It was a Saturday afternoon and the beach was crowded. My first sensation was utter joy at the sun permeating my pores. My second was utter shock at what the Brazilians wore, or more precisely, didn't wear, at the beach. The men wore small, form-fitting, spandex bathing suits, instead of the boardshorts I was used to. And the women, almost without exception, wore thongs. I looked around, overwhelmed by all the exposed butts I saw: flat butts, curvy butts, small butts, big butts; most with cellulite, some without; and all very, very tanned.

Isabel peeled off her dress and tossed it on the sand. Her long, bronzed legs were topped by a beautiful curve of the butt, which was completely exposed, the tiny, white, thong triangle covering an area of about two square inches. The two meager triangles of her top barely covered her nipples, leaving very little of her round breasts to the imagination. On her back, peeking from under her cascading curls, were four tattoos of colorful butterflies hovering around a rose.

"*That* is the tiniest bikini I've ever seen in my life!" I exclaimed.

"It's a micro-bikini. It gets me the best tan possible."

"I bet it does," I grinned at her.

She spread a colorful sarong on the sand, lay on its corner and invited us to join her. I sat near her and smiled, running my hands through the sand, wondering for how long I could postpone taking off my clothes.

Otavio's crooked grin widened. He spread a brown towel near our sarong, took his shirt off and threw it on the towel. I gulped at the sight of his strong looking torso and arms. He took off his jeans, exposing tight, green, spandex bathing suit, which left very little to the imagination. I couldn't believe the degree of physical exposure they were both completely comfortable with.

"Need any help with that?" Otavio motioned at my shirt.

"No; I got it," I said, wishing Isabel weren't here, so he could help me peel off my clothes. That would have been so hot, I imagined, forgetting to get undressed.

"She's in another world, *querido*," said Isabel.

"What's that?" I asked, awakened from my reverie.

"It means 'dear'."

"How do you say it?"

"Que-ri-do, for a man, or *querida*, for a woman."

I repeated those sounds as I took off my navy-blue T-shirt. My modest, black, one-piece suit was the dreary opposite of Isabel's bikini. I took off my black shorts while sitting, struggling not to show too much. Otavio looked amused as he smoked his cigarette, his eyes letting me know he knew he'd end up seeing all of me sooner or later, so my attempts at hiding my body didn't matter.

"Oh, that's no good," said Isabel. "How are you ever going to get a tan with that bathing suit?"

"I have news for you: tanning is passé!" I announced, slathering on some sunblock.

"That news made it to Brazil, too. But some sun is good for you."

"But it's really strong right now."

"Hmm," she muttered. "You're right. Ready for a quick dip?"

"Not yet," I said, dreading getting up and parading in front of Otavio.

"Are you sure you'd rather stay here with this guy?" she joked, motioning to Otavio, who grinned at her in return. I didn't know what to say.

"She'll be alright," he looked deeply into my eyes.

Isabel smiled and ran to the water. She crossed her hands over her head and dove into a wave right before it crashed on her. I'd always wanted to do that! I thought wistfully. Isabel resurfaced and started to swim.

Otavio buried the cigarette butt in the sand and moved over in my direction. "Give me that," he said. I handed him the cream.

"You're sure you want to put this on before going in the water?" he asked. I nodded. Otavio rubbed his palms together with the cream, then started lathering my shoulders and neck in massage-like strokes. The nimble fingers forced me to let my guard down, close my eyes, and focus on the relaxing sensation. "You like it?"

"Mmm," I said, almost purring.

"You don't relax much, do you?"

I smiled a small smile, not wishing to reply. I knew that most people lived for such moments of relaxation, for the weekends, for letting go of work and the stress related to it. I was certain that if I tried to explain to him that I actually liked working, he wouldn't be able to understand.

He freed my hair from its imprisoning rubber band. "That's better," he said, and ran his hands through my hair. I smiled. "If Isabel weren't here, I'd cover you with a towel and we would make love right here on the beach," he said with eyes half-closed. He'd better be kidding! "Let's join her. I need to cool down."

We started walking toward the water. The hot sand prompted me to speed up until I reached the first wave. My reaction was immediate retreat, my toes curling from the shock. Despite the sweltering heat, the water of the Atlantic Ocean was cold. I decided to advance slowly, letting each body part get numb as I got used to the temperature.

"That's not the way to do it!" Otavio declared. Before I had a chance to realize what he was about to do, he lifted me, carrying me in his muscular arms as he hurried into the next exploding wave - and boom! I yelped as the wave swelled over both our heads, pulling me from Otavio's grip.

"Argh! I can't believe you just did that!" I exclaimed, feeling helpless. Otavio's huge grin was boyish and so sweet, I couldn't stifle my smile. I splashed him, and he cowered in response.

"Ever do it in the ocean?" he asked, his eyes darkening and his eyebrows rising suggestively as he approached me.

"Get away from me! Isabel is coming over. I thought we got in the water to cool off."

"I can't help it," he claimed, making puppy eyes at me. I grinned, shaking my head.

"Isn't the water great?" beamed Isabel.

"I was freezing before, until *someone* threw me in the water. I'm pretty used to it by now," I said, swimming a little.

"You are such an *idiota,* Otavio! Pay attention, Raquel. Idiot is idiota in Portuguese."

"Thanks. I'll try and remember that," I grinned in Otavio's direction.

"Damn," he said with a smile and shook his head.

"So, how do you like our beach?" asked Isabel.

"Seriously? It is the prettiest place I've ever seen." They smiled contentedly.

I started floating on the water, letting them chat amongst themselves in Portuguese. I took in the blue sky above, the lull of the waves, the long, sunny beach, ending in a brown and green mountaintop. I felt I couldn't have asked for anything more. For a moment, there was no deadline, no bet, nothing to deliver, nothing to hide. It was just me, and my ability to let go and enjoy the moment. I breathed deeply through my nose and let the air slowly out of my mouth.

Otavio appeared, blocking the sun above me, holding my floating body. I tensed. "Your sighs are making it harder to keep my hands off you," he said seriously.

I noted that Isabel was making her way back to the beach. I stood up and did what I wanted to do since I'd laid eyes on him today. I kissed him fervently, my hands running all over his sinewy back. He answered me hungrily, his rugged hands roaming over my back and waist.

I felt like teasing him. Perhaps I'd wrap my legs around him and nibble on his ear, like he'd taught me? Afterward, I could tease him when he had to wait to get out of the water. But that wasn't me. Or was it?

I severed our kiss and smiled at him. I could tell that my kiss had inadvertently already achieved what I thought I was too shy to do. I slowly backed away from him, my smile widening to a grin.

"What are you smiling about?" he shouted, pretending to be angry. My smile only grew wider. Here I was, on this gorgeous beach, with a guy like him, with this sexy, new name, acting like I'd only ever dreamed about. I felt naughty, carefree, and full of life. There was no way they were going to refuse me tonight at the samba school!

CHAPTER 7

Back at the hotel, we practiced the samba and had fun laughing at this and that. I felt very comfortable with both of them. As the sun started descending, Otavio excused himself.

"I need to go home and change."

"How about you Isabel?"

"No, I brought a dress. In fact, I brought a dress for you, too, from my mother's store. I can't wait to see how it looks on you."

"Wow, I don't know what to say. Thank you!"

Once Otavio left, she showed me the dress. "Now go get ready so we can see it on you," she urged.

My mind wandered to Otavio as I showered. Then I recalled Ashley, with whom I hadn't spoken since I left. She would say that he was too big of a distraction and that I should focus exclusively on work. A part of me knew she was right. But I also knew I couldn't let him go. I got out of the shower, cleaned the steam off the mirror, and looked at myself resolutely.

The attentions of a guy like Otavio presented a wonderful opportunity, the kind I'd never had before, and might never have again. I vowed to myself to pursue my scoop vigorously while still enjoying everything this man had to offer, even if it meant not getting any sleep until I got home in a couple of weeks.

I looked at my stomach. It was flat, but not ripped by any stretch of the imagination. Still, to my delight, a line had appeared in the middle of it since I started exercising. Along with a pair of lovely, perky breasts, not too big nor too small, I thought I looked pretty good from the front when naked. Maybe I should get the fat sucked out of my butt while I was here? After all, didn't many Americans, Chantal included, come here for the purpose of getting plastic surgery for the fraction of what they cost in the U.S.?

That thought lingered while I applied some makeup, donned the dress, and looked at myself in the full-length mirror. The one-shoulder, dark-green dress was short and tight, and had a frilly black bottom. Its color complimented my green eyes. I put on the black dancing shoes Isabel had brought me, which were *only* three inches tall, as she put it. I surveyed the result. I actually looked more like a Raquel now, than a Rachel. I stepped out to the living room, allowing myself the hint of a strut.

"Wow!" declared Isabel. "You look fantastic! I just knew that dress was the right size! How do you feel?"

"Petrified!"

"Don't be! You'll do great, and besides, I'll dance with you."

I felt like hugging her but stopped myself. She didn't have such qualms. She pulled me in for a warm embrace, which I reciprocated, wondering if all Brazilians were so affable and sweet.

* * *

We rode toward the samba school in a van with Kevin and Chantal. Otavio checked me out in the rear-view mirror occasionally as he drove. I smiled at him but focused on trying to memorize the lyrics to the song of the samba school, which, Isabel said, wouldn't hurt me to know. I put on my headphones and listened to the pure samba rhythm over and over again.

I looked out my window at the glorious Guanabara Bay lit up by lamp posts. I loved the fact that the Brazilians flooded their beaches with lights at night, ostentatiously letting passersby know of their beauty at all times of the day. Traffic flowed rapidly at night. Thirty minutes later, we arrived.

"Is this the school?" I asked, motioning to a large building as Otavio parked the car.

"Yes. How are you doing?" asked Isabel as we all got out of the van.

"Nervous," I replied, breathing deeply in an attempt to relax.

"Don't worry," said Isabel with ease. "They'll love you."

"I agree," said Otavio as he slowly scanned me from top to bottom. "You have nothing to worry about."

"Rachel, Rachel," Kevin shook his head as he lifted his equipment bag to his shoulder, "you have a lot to be worried about. You're going to samba with pros and ask them to offer you a benefit only locals and celebrities are allowed."

"But I *have* a celebrity with me," I protested, motioning to Chantal. "We just won't tell them she won't actually do the dancing on Monday, and that it's going to be only me parading."

"And me," said Isabel with a reassuring smile.

"And me," added Otavio, looking at Kevin with a challenging look.

"Whatever. I'm just here to document your failure," he said with a smirk.

"Hey, asshole! Why don't you keep your opinions to yourself!" Otavio said, standing in front of Kevin with a menacing expression on his face.

"Yes," Isabel showed her support, too. "I think she's going to do just great!"

Kevin grunted in answer and began walking toward the school with Chantal.

"I don't know how she takes that guy. *Ele me enche o saco!*" declared Otavio.

"He is getting on my nerves, too," agreed Isabel.

"I've had a lifetime of practice with idiots like that, and believe me, he's not even the worst. I'm not sure why, but usually girls are the worst. If you're even slightly different than the mainstream, they will come after you. But it means a lot to me that you two are on my side. It's a rare experience to have anyone but my friends, Jess and Ashley, stand up for me."

This remark seemed to make Otavio pensive, and Isabel sad. She grabbed my hand and said: "Let's get out there and get the best scoop ever, so that you can go home a winner and become the boss of your magazine and fire all the idiots who work there, OK?!" I laughed, and we started following Kevin and Chantal in the direction of the open-air hall. Isabel added: "By the way, I love how that dress hangs on you."

"It's too short," I protested with a smile.

"And what have you got to hide?"

"This!" I exclaimed and punched my own behind.

"You're wrong! Your *bumbum* is pretty. Look how it curves and sticks out beautifully."

"Exactly! In America, they treat me like I have a hump!"

"People with smaller, flatter butts here get plastic surgery to get a bumbum like yours," added Isabel.

"Didn't you notice all those butt implant at the beach?" asked Otavio, pinching my behind. My surprised jump made him grin with satisfaction.

"Plastic surgery *to look like me?!*" I asked incredulously. I stopped and stood in front of them both. "Do you guys have any idea what you're doing? You just took a lifetime of abuse, curses, rhymes, judgment, and tears, and turned it all upside down! It'll take me a long time to digest this. I'm in shock!"

"And I thought *I* had a hard time growing up in the *favela*," said Otavio with a shake of his head, sympathy in his eyes. I recalled the crowded mountain dwellings I had been seeing all over town. I knew he was exaggerating, but I valued the fact that he understood that people had to go through different battles to survive, physically or spiritually.

"I hope this knowledge will make it easier for you to dance in front of the samba masters tonight," said Isabel.

"What can I say? You two just gave me the best pep talk of my entire life. I'll try to focus on that and forget my nerves." I pondered this brand-new perspective. My whole life I'd accepted the view point that I had something to hide, not something to flaunt. Now I was in a country whose ideal of beauty was diametrically opposed to that. Could it be that what I grew up to believe was ideal feminine beauty was only subjective to north America, or perhaps just to the prejudices of a few?

Otavio and Isabel were quickly surrounded by dozens of people who seemed delighted to see them. Everyone hugged and chatted in Portuguese. I felt the love in the air, even between Isabel and some of the other beautiful women. There wasn't a trace of hostility, and it gave me a warm feeling inside.

Then the chatter subsided. All eyes rested on Chantal, Kevin, and me. No one spoke English, and I could only assume Isabel and Otavio were explaining our plan to them. They pointed at me occasionally, and at Chantal, who was hauling a box of perfumes. The older members of the group seemed to consider the proposition, chatting amongst themselves. Finally, a chubby, white-haired black man in a colorful carnival shirt invited us to follow him and we all proceeded into the large, open-air assembly area.

Chantal looked ill at ease, probably because nobody seemed to recognize her. She urged Isabel to explain who she was, and quickly began handing out small bottles of *Climax*. In no time, the air smelled like cloying roses. Was that smell supposed to attract guys? The women seemed delighted however and looked at Chantal reverently.

We joined the members of the samba school at the long tables and I was introduced to Brazil's famous traditional dish, *Feijoada.* The main dish was made up of black beans cooked for hours with both fresh and cured meats, which lent the beans and the thick black sauce a rich, savory flavor. The side dishes ranged from rice and cassava meal, to salads and fried bananas.

I enjoyed feasting under the stars to the sound of samba music and melodious Portuguese chatter. The quiet samba was calming, the strumming of the guitar strings lending the evening an enchanted air, which filled me with a feeling of bliss. I sipped on a Caipirinha, sensing my defenses dropping in the face of the camaraderie around me.

When most of the food bowls were empty, somebody grabbed a tambourine and spun it high in the air. This seemed to be a signal that we would now be moving on to the performance part of the evening. I watched the commotion of the band setting up and of the women cleaning up the tables. Isabel approached me. "They are ready to see you and Chantal dance," she said simply.

I looked at the men and women who gathered around the musicians and singers. Each of them performed a complex series of steps without a second thought, as if they were born to do this. But they *were* born to do this and I wasn't! White people don't have rhythm! Suddenly, I felt paralyzed with fear and self-doubt. What made me think Chantal and I would ever be accepted as their float dancers?!

But another thought surfaced, its rationale calming: *You're just panicking! You're forgetting Britney, Madonna, Fred Astaire and Ginger Rogers! Get a grip!*

"Sure," I told Isabel. "Just let me use the facilities first, OK?"

When I was far enough away so no one could see nor hear me, I Skyped Jess. Waiting for her to answer, I leaned back on a wall for support, breathing heavily.

"What's up? Your email said you won't be able to talk tonight because it's the big night at the samba school."

"Jess..." I tried to speak but could say no more.

Luckily, I didn't have to. "Oh, sweetie! It's just a dance! It's going to be alright."

"Easy for you to say. I'm surrounded by people who dance for a living every day of their lives. They're all nice, but I'm an expert at detecting mockery. I'll see it, under their smiles, and I'll know..."

"Darling, you gotta stop! You're talking crazy."

"No, I'm not. I'm not going to do it. I'm going to get another job when I get back home, simple as that. I'll find a place without Todd's crappy office politics or bullies like The Trio. I'll... I'll find a mature place of work!"

"Sweetie, do you really think a place like that exists?"

I had no answer. I knew she was right, of course. No place of work is ever flawless. If an employee chooses to stay in a certain job, then the only choice he has is to accept it – or to fight for the change he wants to see.

"You wouldn't believe what my tour guides told me today," I changed the subject, trying to gain some more time.

"What?"

"They said a lot of people here get butt implants so they can look like me."

"O-M-G! That's the opposite of here! I mean, I know the popularity of big butts in songs is growing, but I don't see a lot of guys around changing their attitude, or a lot of girls for that matter. That's awesome, darling!"

"Jess," I finally let the feeling out, "I'm scared."

"So? You love to dance!" I stayed silent. "Tell me this," she continued, "what's the worst you can imagine happening?"

"I stumble trying to perform a super complicated move, and I fall flat on my face with my skirt up, exposing myself to everyone as the big fraud Kevin insinuated that I am!"

"So?"

"What do you mean *so?* You need more?"

"So what if you trip and fall?" She waited, but I didn't know what to say. "Rach," she continued softly, "you're calling to ask me to encourage you, but don't you know that everything I've learned about courage I learned from you?" I said nothing, so she continued. "When I see how things or people are, I make fun of them, but I accept them. But when you see how they are, you fight to change them."

"I saw you get off the couch last year and start going to the gym, which is something you've never done before. It wasn't easy, but you stuck to it, and now you love it. Me, I stick to the couch, where it's nice and safe and where no one can judge the way

I move. You, my dear, have asked for each and every one of the things that are about to happen tonight. And baby, you're ready! Now go kick some butt!"

As she spoke, my eyes filled with tears. "Jess, I always knew you were a big softy underneath the gruff exterior. I love you."

"Aww, I knew you were going to become all sappy!"

"Gotta go shake it now."

"You go girl! I wanna hear all about it tomorrow."

Jess was right. I was here because of a series of actions *I enacted.* Well, now it was time to reap the results. I went back and stood next to Isabel, who looked at me with worry. I nodded, my lips sealed decisively. Chantal stood beside Isabel, looking bored and impatient. Kevin was ready to photograph everything.

Isabel motioned to the white-haired man. He got up and faced the crowd. "Amigos," he started talking, and Isabel whispered the translation in my ear, "Friends, tonight we have a special treat for you! An American reporter from New York has flown all the way down here to be a part of our carnival with her fellow model. She has prepared a special dance for us, so please clap your hands for," he paused. Otavio whispered something in his ear and he continued, botching both our names with his pronunciation, "Chantawoo e Raquewoo!"

Five men and one woman all grabbed their microphones and started singing this year's samba song of their school. The rapid beat of the samba swept me away. I stepped in front of the band and started dancing, adhering to the beat and pushing away all shyness and all reservations. The youngest and prettiest girls joined me, including Isabel, the ruffles of her red dress mingling with mine. I smiled at her and increased the speed of my foot work as much as I could in an attempt to match hers. Despite her four-inch heels, she was impossible to keep up with, but the other women seemed to have no trouble matching her steps in similar heels. I could tell she herself was working hard to keep up with the best dancer in the group, a tiny woman with a braided Afro, crooked teeth and a devilish smile who had probably danced the samba from infancy.

Isabel grabbed both of Chantal's hands and pulled her into our circle. Chantal danced as badly as she did last night. I understood why she chose to wear only a black mini skirt and a tube top not much wider than a bra. She was trying to distract people from her dancing. I felt really foolish about my cold feet before. After all, I *knew* I was a good dancer!

Otavio joined us, as promised, along with a few other men. We all danced together merrily. The samba school band, which was called a *bateria*, beat their crazy rhythm repeatedly. After we finished the song for the first time, I felt many pats on my back. Everyone else joined us, and the upbeat song was repeated. I noted Kevin took a video, too, and I made a mental note to share it with Jess tomorrow.

After twenty minutes of rapid dancing, I took a break. I sat on the bench, feeling parched. A chilled bottle miraculously appeared, handed to me by a smiling, young, black boy wearing tattered clothes and with a missing front tooth.

"*Obrigada,*" I thanked him with a smile, opened the bottle and gulped the water quickly. The boy grinned. Isabel joined me and handed him a blue note of two Reals, which seemed to please him. He took it and ran away. I handed the half-empty bottle to her, and she drank the rest of it. I was pleased to see I was not the only one whose breathing was labored.

"You're in!" declared Isabel.

"I'm in?! Oh, my goodness!" I shrieked and hugged her.

She smiled broadly at me. "I had no doubt you could do it! Now, I talked to the seamstress and she said she will have our costumes ready on time, even though it is so last minute."

"Remind me to give her a handsome tip, OK?"

"Of course. Now listen, you must pace yourself. The parade takes over an hour to complete."

"An hour?!"

"Actually more. The samba schools have to finish their parades in no less than seventy-five minutes, and no more than eighty-two minutes. They will be judged for that, and for many other, how do you say, judging *critérios*."

"Criteria," I provided.

"Yes."

"Tell me more about this competition."

"Every year, about fifteen samba school compete in the Sambadrome. Each school chooses a theme, composes a song, builds five floats, and designs costumes to tell the story of the theme. The theme could be a Brazilian artist, or a passage from the bible, etc. Our school's theme this year is Brazilian Women Who Shine."

"Cool!"

Before Isabel could elaborate, the peaceful evening was interrupted.

CHAPTER 8

A sudden ruckus began. A gang of young men and women, all wearing black and sporting wild tattoos and spiky hair-dos, walked into the building with a menacing gait. The loud Brazilian Hip-Hop music emanating from their boom box filled the air. The samba music and dancing stopped, as though a paralyzing agent had now engulfed everyone but the gang. My heart started beating faster. The man who appeared to be their leader nodded at people, greeting them loudly and smirking at their timid responses. I could see guns peeking out of pockets, jackets, and pants. There were a lot of vacant stares among them, the red, unfocused eyes of people on drugs. Isabel's hand squeezed mine. I was petrified.

The gang situated itself on the bleachers in the back of the building. Their leader arrived at the seat of the old man, who managed to maintain his look of dignity and authority as he got up to face him.

"*Sente-se, senta!*" ordered the gangster. The old man sat down. The gangster put a hand on the old man's shoulder and continued to speak.

"What did he say?" I whispered to Isabel.

"He said they're just here to watch the rehearsals."

I frowned in alarm when I noticed that Otavio was approaching the head of the gang not meekly or with good will, but with a withering, mocking stare.

"What is he doing?!" I whispered. Before Isabel could answer, Otavio pressed a button on the Ghetto blaster and the hip hop music stopped. In the dead silence that followed, only the cicadas were heard. I held my breath in terror, whispering to Isabel: "I can't believe he just did that!"

"Don't worry. The head of the gang is his big brother, Bastiao. He's in charge of the favela they grew up in. When they show up at these events it's to remind people who's the boss and to sell their filthy drugs. But don't worry. Otavio knows how to take care of him."

That's his brother? I thought in shock. Sympathy toward Otavio and the life he must have led inundated me.

As Bastiao talked to Otavio, his baby brother, his tough manner seemed mellower. Isabel translated, explaining that Otavio had demanded his brother not cause any problems, and that Bastiao had replied that he was just there to enjoy the music. Otavio walked away, his facade still menacing. Samba music resumed as Isabel and I made our way toward Otavio. I noticed Kevin approaching him from another direction.

"Wow, man!" Kevin said, trying to muster a feeling of camaraderie between him and Otavio. "You know that guy?"

"That man," uttered Otavio, pronouncing the word *man* disdainfully, "is my brother."

"Awesome!" exclaimed Kevin and patted Otavio's shoulder. "I had a feeling someone would be selling here. Hook me up, bro. You know, nothing big, just some grass."

My surprise was short lived. Now it all made sense. I finally realized why Kevin and Chantal had agreed to come here tonight, despite the fact she wasn't going to dance in the parade at all. Kevin had correctly assumed that in a gathering like this, someone would be selling drugs. I couldn't believe I was so naïve even for a second to think they came here to help me.

"*I* don't do drugs and I am *not* your bro!" spat Otavio between clenched teeth, positioning himself in another combative stance. He managed to look menacing in front of Kevin, who was taller.

"C'mon man! I'm not talking PCP or Cocaine here. Just a bit of pot. What's the big deal?"

"If it's no big deal, go get it yourself."

Kevin stared at the gang timidly, shifting his weight from one foot to another uncomfortably. "Look man, he's *your* brother and *you* work for *us*. So why don't you get off your high horse and stop pretending like marijuana is some sort of major drug and get us some." He motioned to Isabel and me, as if insinuating the pot was for us, too.

"Speak for yourself! I don't want any!" I exclaimed.

"Me neither," added Isabel.

"Of course!" he said, facing me with a wide, challenging stance. "I should have known Miss Goody-two-shoes wouldn't want to have a good time! What the hell is wrong with you?!" He was about to continue putting me down when Otavio stepped between him and me and said calmly: "Don't worry man. I'll get you a bit of *Maconha*. First time, as you Americans say, is on the house."

"Awesome! You see? That wasn't so hard, right? Oh, and get some for Chantal, too. And don't be too stingy," he winked. He left to tell Chantal the news. Isabel put her hand on Otavio's shoulder to stop him from leaving, looked closely into his eyes and quietly asked: "*Querido*, what are you going to do?"

He removed her hand from his shoulder with ease and said: "Don't worry. He won't get hurt," he smiled slyly, "but he won't forget this night, either." He started walking toward the gang. Isabel sighed.

"What do you think he's gonna do?" I asked.

"Oh, he'll get the pot all right, but it won't be just pot."

"You mean he'll lace it with something else? Jesus!"

"He won't hurt anyone. Come on," she said, and grabbed my hand, "let's go dancing."

We joined a woman who was teaching the others some samba steps. As I worked on mimicking her, my eyes roamed about on occasion to watch the events develop. Otavio talked to his brother, then proceeded to Kevin, handing him something. He then walked toward me, his gait confident, a cocky half-smile on his face, his eyes still staring ahead ruthlessly. He grabbed my arm, spun me around rapidly, guiding my spin so I would end up close to him. I could feel his breath on my lips as he declared: "No one talks to you that way! Not when I'm around!"

I smiled, enjoying his nearness for the first time since our ocean kiss. I took in his masculine scent, his rugged hands, the cocky, sexy look in his eyes. I'd never had a protector in my life nor thought I'd needed one, but it sure felt nice to have one now.

The music stopped, and people clapped. The sound of the cicadas was heard again. Otavio still held me. I breathed in, waiting to see what would happen next. Then, a new kind of music flooded the hall. To my surprise, it sounded like tango.

I had no idea how to dance this music. Once, I had a date with a guy who took me ballroom dancing. He said I followed him well, despite my inexperience. I loved the dancing, but the guy, not so much. I wondered if the fact I desired Otavio very much would help me dance this sensual dance better.

When couples around us started dancing, I was relieved we weren't going to be the center of attention. In fact, unlike some of the men, Otavio kept his moves simple and easy to follow. He held my outstretched left hand with his right and led me with long, sexy strides forward, our cheeks close together. Then he stopped me and twirled me out, then into him. When I stopped, his body alongside mine, he dipped me, then brought me back up so we could face each other. He guided my leg, until I wrapped it around his, as I saw the women around me do. I felt his warm breath on my ear as he swayed me close to him. Our feet intertwined, our cheeks touched, our pelvises gyrated *Dirty Dancing* style. The Brazilian tango had notes of samba in it, too, and of some old European style music that I didn't recognize. It was proud, sultry, and full of yearning.

The open roof allowed for a lovely breeze; the view of the star-studded sky infused the evening with unforgettable charm. Couples, some young, some old, danced sensually with each other.

I felt a sense of togetherness emanating from the Brazilian people. It enveloped me, too, in these strangers' instant acceptance tonight, in Isabel's friendship, in Otavio's embrace.

I noticed Kevin rushing past us, Chantal keeping pace with him.

"Are we leaving already?" I frowned.

"I don't think those two will be able to leave for quite a while," Otavio said, a suspiciously innocent expression on his face. Isabel approached us, looking somewhat angry.

"Otavio, really!" she said reproachfully. "He put a laxative in the pot," she explained to me. "Thanks to you, they'll be in the bathroom for the rest of the night."

Otavio grinned. "Tell me you don't think they totally deserved it!"

Neither Isabel nor I could suppress our smiles. "But... how did you do it?" I asked incredulously.

"A couple of eye drops is all you need."

"What?! You swiped the eye drops from my room?!" I asked in shock.

"Nah, they took that stuff out of American eye drops years ago, as I learned from my brother. He gave me the eye drops I used on those assholes. Don't look so worried. They'll be fine by tomorrow."

"Just a little dehydrated," grinned Isabel.

"And a little pooped!" I added, and we all burst out laughing. I knew it was low, but I couldn't really blame Otavio for doing it to Kevin after he treated him as if he were a servile idiot, nor to Chantal, after the way she'd treated me last night. I weaved one arm around Otavio's and one around Isabel's. "Let's go? I think Kevin and Chantal can take a taxi."

After laughing some more in the car, we finally calmed down. Otavio drove us back to the hotel.

"So, what do we do tomorrow?" I asked Isabel.

"You mean today?" she smiled. "It's three in the morning!"

"Wow!" I glanced at my cell automatically to confirm. "So what do we do today then?" Now that I was admitted into the parade, I felt I could finally relax about work.

"Well, a few things happen in Rio on Sunday, especially during the weekend before the carnival. Every Sunday they close one side of Atlantic Avenue, the long street parallel to the beach. People bike, kids play, some roller skate, or just walk along the road. It's lovely and relaxing. Now, because it's carnival season, there will be *blocos* passing all over the city."

"That's the free street carnival with the different blocks."

"Exactly! There are hundreds of groups of musicians and dancers who simply walk around the streets of Rio and make music. There is always a huge crowd, sometimes even a few million people."

"A few *million* people?"

"Yes. It's the reason so many locals leave the city during carnival."

"*Leave the city?* I thought everyone loved carnival."

"With this many people coming to celebrate from all over the world, with the traffic, the noise, the mess, the trash, many of the locals leave. Anyway, I want to take you to see one of the best blocos tomorrow. It's in Ipanema, so we can rent a bike near your hotel and bike there, then hop to the Hippie Fair, then go dance with the bloco."

"Hippie Fair? I don't know if that kind of thing is for me..."

"They have amazing leather purses and belts, cheap souvenirs and so many other things. You'll love it!"

"It actually sounds perfect. I do need to buy some gifts for the poor chumps who stayed back home. Are you going to come with us, Otavio?"

"I can't. I have to go help my mom with something, but I'll meet you at the bloco in the evening."

"Good," said Isabel. "We can dance on top of their bus. It'll be good practice for you."

"Yea," I smiled meekly, feeling tired of my pursuit to re-invent myself. I just need a good night's sleep, I told myself.

"The bloco's parade starts at seven, so I'll come to your hotel around noon. We'll have a late lunch after the fair, OK?"

"Sounds like a plan."

We arrived at my hotel. "Thanks for dancing with me tonight," I said and parted from Isabel with a hug. I felt a kinship with this woman who had repeatedly helped me, sometimes without even being asked. "And you," I said to Otavio, shaking my head, "I don't know if I should kiss you or kick your ass for what you did to my stupid coworkers." He smiled with satisfaction, and I grinned back at him. At that moment, I couldn't care less about possible repercussions.

"Don't worry," teased Isabel, "all women feel that way about him."

I kissed Otavio quickly on the lips, and went back into my hotel, Isabel's words forming a pang of jealousy in my heart.

CHAPTER 9

A persistent noise interrupted my sleep. When I realized someone was knocking at the door, I rose quickly to open it, noting it was almost eleven already. The waiter set the breakfast I had ordered last night on the table. I caught a glimpse of him checking me out when I bent over to get his cash tip from my wallet. I smiled furtively to myself, handed him the money, and he left. As I ate, I checked my personal and professional social media and email accounts.

I was Facebook friends with a few of girls in my Wednesday Zumba class. They were outraged that Andy's class, which was our favorite, has been moved to Friday evening, a time slot in which the gym was mostly empty because most single people went out. But why? I wondered if it had anything to do with the fact that his class was rather salacious, or rated X, as he jokingly called it. Recalling it made me realize Andy's sensual routines were the reason I loved his class, and why I had no intention of missing his classes, even if they were moved to this crummy time slot.

On the company's Facebook wall I saw a picture of Chantal on top of Sugar Loaf mountain, with an accompanying comment: "Don't miss our April issue with exclusive tips about Rio de Janeiro!" I cringed at her flat expression and at the reminder of my deadline. I ate faster, feeling the urgency to start my day.

The first thing I did was email Ryan about me dancing at the samba school yesterday, and on the float tomorrow, feeling certain he'd love this scoop. I felt so proud of the samba school's acceptance of me, I couldn't wait to dance in the parade tomorrow and to see the winning photos published in the magazine.

Jess beeped me. I opened Skype and saw her and Ashley, each holding a Mimosa. They were having brunch in one of our favorite restaurants. Jess explained that Ashley was already caught up on Chantal's rotten behavior and on my anxiety about dancing last night.

"So how did it go?" asked Ashley.

"It was awesome! I'll send you the video later. So, I'm in the parade, on a float, which is a brand-new story that hasn't been done before."

"Told ya you had it in you!" Jess smiled knowingly. I told them about Otavio's brother and his gang.

"Who's Otavio?" asked Ashley, sipping on a Mimosa.

"He's the male tour guide. He and Isabel are teaching me how to samba." When Ashley wasn't looking, I winked at Jess and she nodded back at me. I appreciated her discretion.

I told them how Kevin tried to bully Otavio, and about Otavio's sweet revenge. My two tipsy gals couldn't stop laughing when I described the looks on Kevin's and Chantal's faces as they ran to the bathroom.

"OK, I admit that it's funny," said Ashley, "but that could have been dangerous."

"Nonsense!" declared Jess. "It was just a harmless prank. Not everybody simply takes abuse like Rachel does. Some people stand up for themselves, in one way or another." She caught herself and looked at me placatingly, but it was too late to spare my feelings. "Sorry, Rach." When I didn't reply, she added, "you know I didn't mean that!"

"I know sometimes it seems like I'm a coward, but I tried complaining with Todd when he was Editor-in-Chief and it got me nowhere."

"I know you did, sweetie. I'm sorry. Forgive me?"

"Fine, you're forgiven. Hey, Ashley, sorry we've been missing one another. Got any new ideas for the women-only column?"

"Not yet, but not for lack of trying."

"Don't worry; you'll get there. Jess and I will do whatever we can to help."

"Thanks."

We talked a while longer. Before I hung up, I showed them my balcony view.

"OMG! You're so evil for rubbing it in our faces!" said Jess.

"Show her our snow. Make her jealous, too!" joked a very tipsy Ashley, who didn't handle alcohol very well. I smiled as Jess reflected the snow-covered court surrounding the glass-enclosed restaurant with her phone.

"Well, at least you're chillin'. I gotta go back to work!" When they heard what I had lined up for that day, they scoffed at my idea of work. We parted, blowing kisses to one another.

I continued working until Isabel showed up, nearly an hour late. "People here are always late," she shrugged. "I'm giving you a real example of what life is like in Brazil," she joked, her peals of laughter flooding the quiet suite.

I smiled and decided there was really no point in fussing, as I would undoubtedly have done in America. "It's OK," I said, and we exchanged kisses.

"That's all you're wearing?!" I exclaimed, referring to the frilly, pink bikini top she had on instead of a shirt, and to the iridescent mini-skirt.

She grinned. "It's going to be another really hot day and we're going to be outdoors the whole time. There's no need for anything more."

"What about the restaurant? You'll freeze in the air conditioning over there."

"There's no air conditioning where I'm taking you."

"Humph. Oh well, I think I'll survive."

"Oh, you will," she smiled. "And remember to wear shoes you can bike in, walk in all day, *and* dance in." I looked down at her wedges skeptically. "They're really comfortable!" she exclaimed with a defensive smile.

"In my experience, wedges only *look* comfortable." I looked down at my own clothes: faded jean shorts, a black tank top, and comfortable tennis shoes. I grimaced and looked pleadingly at Isabel, "No good, eh?"

"It's a street carnival and most tourists will dress exactly like that. Or we could get you a bathing suit top at the beach."

"Who would buy a bathing suit at the beach, where you can't try it on?"

"Tons of women do. They hide behind a towel. And the guys go nuts, waiting for something to slip and show," she grinned mischievously.

"Hmm, I think I'm good. But maybe I will change my shoes."

"What else do you have that's comfortable?" she asked and peered over my shoulder as I started searching my messy suitcase.

"I really have to organize everything in the drawers, hang some things on the hangers. But... my clothes don't really go with the fashion here."

"You must have brought something magnificent. I've been waiting to check out your New York fashion since you got here!"

"I'm afraid I'm going to have to disappoint you."

"Can I take a look anyway?"

"Sure, knock yourself out." Isabel went over my clothes, organizing them neatly in the drawers and closet, commenting to herself in Portuguese as she worked.

"I don't know how you can live without more colors in your wardrobe," lamented Isabel.

"Once I started working at the magazine and pursuing my journalism career, I'd realized that women at the top never draw too much attention to their femininity. They wear muted colors, reserved clothing, and little jewelry, so they can better blend with the men. As a result, they're taken more seriously. So I gave up on colors years ago. Besides, that's what everyone wears when they go out: all black, and sometimes jeans."

"Impossible! It seems better in TV shows."

"That's TV. Plus, it matters what job you have and where you want to get in life. Still," I sighed, "now that I'm here I feel some sort of urgency to go and buy clothes of all the colors in the world!"

"Great! You can get lots of those at the Hippie Fair, and some pretty, flat shoes, too."

"Awesome! But these kinds of clothes won't fit in an American office. How do women dress for the office here?"

"I'll show you when I take you to my mother's store. She has one in Leblon, which is the neighborhood where we live, but I'll take you to her downtown store, which has the same clothes for half the price!" We exchanged smiles.

I ended up wearing the sneakers anyway, since I had no other pair of shoes I could comfortably wear for an entire day. We took the elevator down to the noisy street. Not far from the hotel's exit, a couple of orange bicycles were docked at a long, orange rental station.

"Oh, we got lucky!" exclaimed Isabel. "We won't have to wait for someone to return the bicycles." Isabel dialed a number, which released the bikes. I was impressed to hear that the bike rental cost only five dollars a month, so I decided to tweet that on the magazine's feed, with a photo of Isabel on the bike, the pretty beach behind her.

"By the way," she asked, "where are Kevin and Chantal?"

"After what happened yesterday, I decided not to get in touch with them today. My guess is they're resting and rehydrating and are probably very angry at Otavio. Besides, she has her surgery this afternoon, and I wouldn't be surprised if he chose to accompany her there instead of documenting the bloco tonight."

"Are they a couple or not? I heard them mention she's dating your boss."

"She is dating him. Really, I have no idea what's going on between them. I heard they used to date. Maybe they've just remained close."

"Maybe," echoed Isabel, looking as doubtful as I felt. "Who cares? The best part is that we get to spend a whole day without them!"

"Woo-hoo!" I exclaimed and grinned at her.

We climbed on our bikes and cycled across Atlantic Avenue, along Copacabana beach. The heat of the sun was welcome after all those hours in the air-conditioned room. As I put on my sunglasses, Isabel cycled near me and warned, "Remember: Watch out for pedestrians. Many tourists are distracted and don't realize they have to look right and left before crossing the bike lane. And today is worse, because half the street is closed."

I nodded, feeling pretty distracted myself. I took in the gorgeous sights of the beach on this cloudless, sunny day. To our left, the sand was speckled with red umbrellas, makeshift stalls, and tanned men and women playing *futevólei,* volleyball played only with the feet, chest and head. The black and white pavement of Copacabana was studded with Kiosks, all laden with green coconuts. The smell of fried food wafted from inside the huts, the plastic chairs around them were all occupied with beer drinking patrons. I pedaled on with a smile.

We arrived at the famous *Copacabana Palace* Hotel. Isabel pointed to it as she slowed down and fell back next to me. "Want to take a picture?"

"Another time." I smiled back at her, and we continued to pedal.

The busy road was inundated with people of all ages. I noticed a child on a toy car nearly running over an old lady with a cane; an older man jogging shirtless toward us, his sagging chest still retaining some of its former mass; two fit, young girls skating with skill as a middle-aged man was trying to keep up with them but was incapable of generating enough speed. I saw impressive sandcastles, massage beach-huts, and a four-man band singing in front of a restaurant for some money. We kept on biking, a smile fixed on my face. Everything delighted me. I felt surrounded by such beauty and relaxation, I had to wonder why the whole world didn't move here.

"Did you notice these numbered towers?" asked Isabel, pointing to a white tower that boasted the number four on it as she fell back to bike near me again.

"I did. What are they?"

"They're the lifeguard towers, and they are exactly one kilometer apart."

"Lifeguards," I grinned. "Now that's worth slowing down for." Isabel grinned back. "So we've biked four kilometers so far?"

"Pretty much. Want to stop for a coconut?"

"Later. Let's keep going!"

"OK," she said and sped up a bit to gain the lead again. Her long brown curls flew freely, and every man who saw us stared at her. Inspired, I freed my hair of its elastic band, hoping to get some looks of appreciation, too. I bet I would get just as many looks as Isabel did if I wore as little as she was wearing. Well, I smiled to myself, maybe not *quite* as many. I shook my head right and left, letting the breeze flow in, inadvertently shaking off the remaining staleness of a cold, confining winter, and of cynical, bitter colleagues still clinging to me.

At the end of Copacabana was a large gathering of people. We stopped near some rocks, then climbed on them to peer into the crowd. A cheerful melody and a sense of expectancy suffused the air, as we all waited to see what would come out from behind the small, red curtain that was set up near a temporary stall.

"This song is my childhood favorite!" exclaimed Isabel. The jolly guitar and flute sounds accompanied her sweet voice as she continued, "It's called *The Band* by *Chico Boarque*. It talks about how the town's people all put their suffering or what they are doing aside to watch the band pass. The serious man who counted money stopped; the sad girl smiled; the closed rose opened; the hidden moon emerged, all to hear the band sing a song of love. For those few moments, everything was positive, everyone was happy, all was peaceful."

As I listened to what she said, her words came to life around me. The curtain swung open, and a procession of the most adorable toddlers began to march. Their flamboyant costumes and head ornaments boasted all the colors of the rainbow, although their tender feet had barely mastered walking. The previously serious, distracted crowd was transformed. Everyone, young and old, sang the song with a smile, moving their feet to the happy melody. They each gasped when a tiny, tutu-clad beauty tripped, only to be rescued by a slightly older, dashing boy. As the toddlers continued to march, people's smiles grew bigger and the singing got louder. The significance of the carnival became apparent. For this one week, the entire country of Brazil lets go of the daily tensions of life and relaxed in order to see the bands pass. That thought filled me with joy.

I smiled at Isabel. "Everything here is so wonderful!"

"Wait until you see the Hippie Fair and Ipanema," she answered with a smile.

When we turned our bikes toward lifeguard tower number eight and onto Ipanema Beach, the atmosphere seemed to change. I saw a lot more tourists and many tanned, lean teenagers with surfboards. I barely had enough time to take in the towering, brown mountain peaks at the end of the long stretch of beach when Isabel stopped biking.

"The Hippie market is there," she said and pointed inland. "We'll come back to the beach when it's time for the bloco," she added, seeing my disappointed expression.

I followed Isabel as we cycled the busy streets until we got to the bicycle docking station near the Hippie Fair. As we returned our bikes, my senses were overloaded with the sights, sounds and smells. I felt a bit overwhelmed. Isabel put her hand in mine and turned me to face her, "Let's not get separated, OK?" she asked as my eyes focused on hers.

"Good idea. I could use some water."

"*Agua de coco,* or coconut water, is better. It gives back the minerals to the body."

"Cool; let's get some."

"Turn your backpack to the front. It's safer that way."

"Grr," I growled, "that would make my front sweaty and make me look fat."

"It's the safest thing to do in a busy market like this one." I noticed her small purse was hanging on her hip in front of her.

After some adjustments, we stopped at a kiosk and ordered two coconuts. I marveled at the sight of the huge, tent-filled square, overloaded with colorful merchandise, vendors and buyers. My eyes jumped from leather bags to mementos of Rio to stalls of clothes to towels and hats with emblems of Brazil – and back to Isabel.

"This is so cool!"

"Right?!" she smiled with pleasure. "I bet we can find some nicer flat shoes for you here, and some souvenirs for everyone back home."

"Awesome!"

I was entranced by the short, black, female vendor who procured a cleaver and competently hit my coconut in three precise movements, producing a small triangle, then motioning to the straws on the counter.

"Wow! I'd be scared I'd chop my own hand off!"

"Me, too," agreed Isabel and handed me a straw.

The coconut water had a subtle sweetness to it. At first, I thought it was boring and not sweet enough, but I quickly sipped the rest of it. The refreshing sensation spreading through my warm body made me change my mind. "De-licious!" I declared with a smile.

CHAPTER 10

After a couple hours of asking for prices, trying things on, and giggling with pleasure, our experience was complete. I was now wearing a new, red bathing suit top underneath my black tank top and new, red, ballet flats, which were very popular here. Isabel dissuaded me from buying too many things, reminding me there was a long night of walking and dancing ahead of me. She also explained that other, smaller markets were open all week long. By now it was past five and I was hungry. The heat felt stifling. Luckily, the restaurant was only two blocks away. How could they not have air conditioning? I wondered again with irritation.

We got to the long line of people waiting to eat at the famous *Girl from Ipanema* restaurant, where *Vinicius de Moraes* and *Tom Jobim* wrote their famous song. Luckily, they knew Isabel well, since she brought a lot of tourists to eat there, so we were able to skip the line. I glanced around self-consciously, but people didn't seem to mind. Either the heat had gotten to them, or they just found it too hard to complain in a foreign language.

The restaurant was very crowded, with not much room to maneuver between the tables and chairs. We were seated at a small table for two, which was situated on the outer perimeter of the open, windowless restaurant.

"That steak smells great!" I said, deeply inhaling the beef smell emanating from a griddle plate on a nearby table.

"It's what I always get. Let's share that and some fries, OK?"

"Mmm," I concurred, salivating, "and some juice, too, OK?"

"Just juice or juice with cachaça in it?" she grinned suggestively.

"Alcohol in this heat? Oh, that's gotta be something."

"Why not? It's carnival!"

"You twisted my rubber arm," I smiled. We debated which drinks to get. When the haggard, gray-haired waiter finally arrived, we ordered two caipirinhas, one with passion fruit and one with pineapple. We waited for a long time for him to deliver them, and when he finally did, Isabel ordered our food, asking the waiter to wait until we sipped our drinks.

"Yummy!" I declared.

"Order two more?"

"Absolutely!"

She did. "What's *Alcatra*?" I asked when the waiter left.

"Sirloin."

I nodded and sipped my pineapple drink, then her tart passion fruit drink, then mine again. We drank both very quickly. The heat and my empty stomach were a perfect recipe for getting drunk fast. I sat back in my seat with satisfaction and glanced at the wall, where a black shirt hung encased behind glass, white music notes printed on it, boasting the famous song the restaurant was named after.

"I want one of those!"

"They sell them here. And here's a little scoop for you: they sell them for half the price at the Hippie Fair," she grinned and winked at me. I smiled widely at her. She checked her text messages. I checked mine, too, seeing the tweet replies and shares of my bike photo. I showed Isabel how many compliments she got. Afterward, I decide to ignore my phone and relax, switching into people-watching mode. When the large steak finally arrived on a sizzling, cast-iron plate, accompanied by a towering plate of fries, I asked the waiter for ketchup. He nodded, disappeared, and never brought it. I cut into my meat, approving of its red center. I savored the flavor of the juicy, salty steak, and dipped crispy fries in its meat-flavored oils.

After I was done, the waiter showed up with the ketchup, apologizing in Portuguese. It no longer mattered, so we sent him away with our empty plates and our espresso orders.

"Dessert?" asked Isabel.

"I don't think so. I don't want to spoil the taste of umami in my mouth."

"What's that?"

"The savory taste, which is not the same as salty. They call it the fifth taste, which you usually get from meats or mushrooms."

"Interesting. I've never heard of that."

"I learned that from a cooking show." I leaned back in my seat, full and content.

A passerby handed us some fliers. The headline said *Jogos Humanos,* and the rest seemed like the lyrics to a song. "That's our block, *Human Games,*" said Isabel.

"Interesting name. Why did you choose this block out of all the others?"

"One reason is their singer is so dreamy," she smiled.

"I thought you were engaged, lady!"

"I am, but it doesn't mean I can't enjoy what I see. Their song is interesting, too. Here, let me translate some of it: "When I lust, she snubs me; when I ignore, she chases me. If we continue to play, when would we kiss? Human games, push and pull, strut, dance, run, but stay in one place. Stop disguising your *yes* with a *no.* Even peacocks let the sun warm their backs."

"Even peacocks let the sun warm their backs?!" I said with emphasis, feeling the giggles rise within me.

Isabel grinned back at me, pouring sugar into her espresso. "They're just being poetic."

"Does the writer mean he's the sun," I asked in a playful tone, which made Isabel laugh, "and that he wanted to warm her back?" Our laughter grew. "And does he mean she's the peacock?" Isabel's body trembled with laughter, her tiny cup clinking on the plate she held. We both laughed uncontrollably, garnering a few stares and smiles from the diners around us and from the occasional passersby.

"Seriously, about the rest of the song," I attempted to regain my self-control as I wiped a laughter-tear from the corner of my eye, "who acts that way nowadays? Maybe women used to say *no* when they meant *yes*, but not anymore they don't."

"Really? Are you sure?"

"Yes! They don't need to play games like that where I come from. Things are more open and clear."

"Are they?" Isabel asked, her raised eyebrows and secretive smile raising doubts within me. "I know from American movies and shows that they do."

"What do you mean?" I frowned, grimacing at the wonderfully bitter espresso.

"You have your rules of the game. And, as I see over and over again, when a woman does *not* follow the rules, she will drive the man crazy!"

"For example?" I asked, curious to hear Isabel's secrets to driving men crazy.

"In America, at least if TV shows and movies are correct, you have this rule that the third date is the one where the man 'gets lucky'," she said, using air-quotes. "But where is the fun in that? Where is the anticipation, the surprise? A woman must be enticing, mysterious, inconsistent. *That's* what drives men crazy!"

Perhaps it was true for someone as beautiful as her. I felt it was perfectly fine to postpone having sex until you felt you were ready, but to wait three dates just to convince yourself that you are chaste was rather silly. But wasn't that what I was doing with Otavio? Suddenly, the whole idea of waiting to please society's standards felt ridiculous, but so did Isabel's suggestion to be capricious purely for inconsistency's sake.

"I'll think about it," was all I said.

She asked for the check, and I put on the black dancing shoes she gave me, storing the red flats in my backpack along with my sneakers. I sat back, enjoying the sight of the crowds. We saw many people dressed up in costumes and heard a lot of firecrackers exploding. At some point, a four-man band showed up on the pavement and played *The Girl from Ipanema* for us. I placed some money in their donation cup and thanked them. They moved on.

I bought the shirt from our aging, sweaty waiter. Feeling sorry for him, I left him a handsome tip, despite the slow, mediocre service. We started walking toward the ocean among thousands and thousands of people. The beach road was closed to traffic and there was very little room to move within the dense crowd. Isabel stopped, turned to me and looked into my eyes, grabbing my arm, "Stay close, OK? It's very easy to get lost."

"I can see that," I said with trepidation.

"Hey! We're here to dance and have fun. Don't worry; I won't lose you! But if I do, just make your way back to the hotel or to my house, which is closer. Here," she said and rapidly texted on her phone, "I texted you the address. The maid, Bach-bada, is at home."

"Who?" I grinned sheepishly, trying to get her to repeat the funny pronunciation of Barbara.

"Bach-bada," she repeated, then shook her head dismissively with a smile when she understood I was joking. Brazilians really could not pronounce the letter R.

We walked toward the towering mountain peaks in the distance, the setting sun aflame behind them in a dazzling spectrum of yellow, orange and red, the ocean waves appearing silvery to our left. We were nearly hugging one another on our huddled walk, struggling to navigate the sea of hot, sweaty bodies in our progress toward a blue bus that boasted a small band and a couple of singers above it. They all wore white shirts with red and blue stripes on them, the colors of their bloco. The closer we got, the louder the music was. How were we ever going to find Otavio?

It was easier than I thought, since he was the one driving the bus at a rate that must have been about two miles per hour. When he saw us, he gestured to a guy who walked near the bus to replace him. He jumped out of the bus, kissed Isabel's cheeks, then kissed my lips, pulling my waist closer to him. He motioned to the top of the bus, and we both nodded. Isabel climbed up first. I was shocked to see nothing but a thong underneath her mini skirt. A few men ogled her butt as she climbed up, some nudging their friends to look also. Otavio turned behind me, grabbed my waist, and lifted me onto the ladder. I smiled and started climbing. He was following me very closely. I was relieved I'd worn pants.

It felt less confined to tower above the masses of sweaty bodies, but even on top of the bus, there was not the slightest of breezes. Isabel mingled with some people she knew. Otavio was all mine, I thought happily. He must have been as happy as I was, since he kissed me hungrily, his hands running all over my back, as mine were on his. Then we looked at each other with a smile.

"Hello," I smiled.

"Hello. Want a beer?"

An ice-cold beer seemed perfect. "Sure!" I watched him fetch two, cold, Brazilian beers from a cooler. The muscles of his legs were visible underneath the long, frayed jeans, his carnival T-shirt stuck to his chest and back from the heat. My mouth was watering. We sat down, facing the sunset on the bus's roof side benches. Otavio sat behind me, his body burrowing into mine, his hand hugging my stomach. We clinked our bottles together and sipped. I could not recall a beer ever being this good in my entire life. I smiled happily.

The band progressed slowly from Ipanema toward Leblon neighborhood, endlessly repeating their carnival song. A few people danced on top of the bus. The setting sun was replaced by dark purples and blues, but the suppressing heat of the day was not much relieved. There seemed to be something primal about the heat of summer and the beat of the music, a feeling which magnified my lust for Otavio.

Otavio ran his cold beer bottle over my forehead, savoring my look of joy. He trailed up the hand that was on my stomach underneath my shirt, while simultaneously lowering the cold bottle toward my chest and kissing my ear lobe. I was flooded with various sensations of pleasure. I closed my eyes and my lips parted in yearning, just letting myself feel.

When his hands approached my breasts, I stopped him.

"Urgh," he grunted in my ear, kissing my neck deftly.

"Not here," I said.

"Then where? Down there?" he pointed to the water. "Just you and me in the cool water. Doesn't that sound like heaven?"

"Actually, it does," I said, an admission that only encouraged his roaming hands and skillful lips. I had to stop this from going further at once! I turned around to face him, my body disconnecting from his. "Maybe on a quiet, solitary night you could persuade me to do it, not with thousands of people around."

Isabel must have heard me. "I read online there are over two million people here tonight," she said, approaching us.

"What?!" It was hard to imagine that many people.

"Uh-huh. Look at these pictures." Some aerial photos taken before the sunset showed the most crowded beach and streets I'd ever seen. "Listen, let's not even try to go back to your hotel tonight. That could take hours! You can sleep over at my place, OK? My home is right there." She pointed to a nearby building.

"But I don't have anything with me."

"I'll take care of all that. Now, do you want to stay on the bus and do some dancing, or go up and rest? We can watch the whole thing from the balcony."

"Yes, let's do that," I said, knowing Otavio wouldn't try anything up there. He'd simply have to wait until we were alone. Besides, I was getting tired of the heat and the repetitive song. We got off the bus and pushed our way through the crowd to get to the gate of the tall building. The doorman spotted Isabel and buzzed us in, greeting us with a smile and wishing us a good evening. We responded in kind and took the elevator to her parents' penthouse apartment.

In the elevator, Otavio showed us the angry texts he'd gotten from Kevin earlier that day and his replies. He managed to pacify Kevin and convince him it was just a bad batch of pot. Isabel shook her head with a smile.

"Do you really think that trick was worth it?" I asked. "He said he wanted to have you fired, and I bet he could have done it, too."

"He wanted to have me fired from this assignment, not fired from my job. And was it worth it? Sure, but not just to see him and that bitch suffer. It was worth it because he'll never mess with me again!"

I nodded in understanding and was reminded of Jess's words. Maybe I *was* too much of a wimp? Maybe, if I were half as tough as Otavio, my co-workers would lay off me?

Isabel's parents were traveling abroad to avoid the carnival and the apartment was softly lit and cool, apart from a small light emanating from behind the kitchen.

"That's Barbara's room," explained Isabel as she grabbed us some cold sodas from the fridge. The maid's door opened, and a thin, average height woman came out of a minuscule room. Her gray hair was short, her white T-shirt and Bermuda shorts nearly glowing on her dark, brown skin. Isabel introduced me, and the expressionless maid nodded. Her eyes lit when she noticed Otavio, who seemed very happy to see her, too. He kissed her cheeks, and said he'd stay with her in the kitchen to fix himself a snack. She insisted on making it for him, but he stayed there to keep her company.

"They know each other from the favela," said Isabel. "I guess she's known both of us since we were babies, because she was my nanny."

"You had a nanny?!" I asked in astonishment, unaccustomed to such things.

"Yes. They are very common here. And she's the housekeeper, too. She introduced me to Otavio a few years ago, asking me if he could work for the tour agency. I had so many doubts about him when we first met," she smiled, reminiscing. "In comes this tough guy who acts like a rebel, almost as if he knows everything better than you. You know how cocky he can be." I beamed in agreement, admitting to myself how sexy I found that. Isabel continued, "I didn't expect a *muleque*, a brat, from the *favela*, to speak English as well as he does, or to have his brains or his manners. You should see how he treats the rich ladies who hire us. His arrogant charm is something they can never resist, and his tips are always amazing!" I felt a pinch of jealousy in my heart, wondering with how many of his clients he had been intimate. "He told me it was his dream to be a tour guide, and I was happy to play a part in helping him realize that dream. We've been good friends ever since. I even introduced his mother, who lives in the favela, to my friend, Maristela, who's a wonderful public defender. She's representing the favela against the government in a big eviction lawsuit. So... how about it? Say you'll stay for breakfast! The cook is on vacation, but Barbara makes a wonderful *cafe da manha*, which means breakfast. I'll get you something to sleep in, and we have some extra toothbrushes.

"Sure, I'll stay."

"Great! Now let's go watch the parade."

"In a minute. I want to wash up a bit."

In my few minutes of solitude, I digested what Isabel had said about Otavio. I knew Brazilians felt sex was something natural to enjoy, and I just had to accept the fact that I wasn't Otavio's first, nor last, nor was he mine. But could I respect that lame dream of his? As if a tour guide's job was something to yearn for or make big plans to achieve. It was just a regular, easy job.

I looked in the bathroom mirror. Stop being so petty and judgmental! I told myself. After all, not every dream had to be a career.

I washed my hands and sprayed some rejuvenating water on my face. I've never told anybody about my dream of starting a new kind of magazine, not even Jess and Ashley. I kept it a secret, dreading what I expected others to say, including my best friends: *It's been done to death! What makes you think you can do anything new and original? Where will you ever get the capital or the investor who would listen to you?* But I knew those problems could be solved. What I had to determine first was the nature of the spirit behind the magazine. I knew very well what I *didn't* want it to be, but I was still figuring out what it *would* be.

We went out to the balcony to watch the block's procession. From high above, one could really grasp the quantity of people filling the streets.

"Oh my God! I can't believe how many people are there!"

"The whole city is full of blocos tonight and will be so until Wednesday."

"Amazing." Now I could now glean why so many people chose to leave town.

Otavio emerged to the balcony with Barbara. "I told her you're going to parade for her samba school tomorrow," he said, "so she wants to see your samba." He grinned, but the old maid looked dead serious. Otavio made some room on the balcony by moving some of the outdoor furniture, and Barbara played the song we danced to last night.

"What did I get myself into?" I shook my head. I gestured to Isabel to join me.

"I'm tired," she pouted.

"What's the big deal? C'mon!" said Otavio, pulling me to the center of the balcony, and we started doing the steps he'd taught me side by side. Barbara watched for a minute, then stepped in, moved me aside, and started correcting *his* steps. Isabel and I laughed at his incredulous expression. Before too long, we were all dancing together amicably. Barbara, clearly a samba master, was correcting everyone, especially me. My reluctance turned into appreciation. By the end of that night, I felt ready for the procession tomorrow.

CHAPTER 11

I paced nervously in my hotel room, glancing at my cell from time to time. The hour of the evening parade was approaching. I'd already changed into my African slave costume, a primitive looking, knee-length dress, made of rough, saffron-colored canvas, with two big holes for arms. I wore imitation golden chains around my wrists and neck. My hair was in a high ponytail atop my head, the long, blond hair extensions weaving throughout it making it look like a horse's tail. As I applied my makeup, I thought of what Jess had said earlier, which was the only thing that calmed my nerves: I would be sharing the stage with thousands of others, which meant I wouldn't be the center of attention, so there really wasn't a cause for nerves. She also reminded me how well I did at the samba school, and that knowledge helped.

Otavio and Isabel showed up. The material of his pants was the same as my dress's. He wore chains around his neck and wrists, too, and his tanned chest was bare. He wore a golden, African head ornament. His flat, square, tan boots were similar to mine. I was relieved I didn't have to dance in heels the entire eighty minutes.

"Here's my little slave!" he declared, kissing my lips. We grinned at one another.

"Where's your costume?" I demanded of Isabel. She was supposed to wear the same costume as mine.

"There's been a change of plans."

"What do you mean?" I asked, crestfallen.

"Oh, I'm still parading."

"She's been promoted due to someone else's accident," explained Otavio as he headed to the balcony for a smoke.

"One of the main *passistas,* the professional carnival dancers, just had a severe back spasm and won't be able to perform. So they asked me to do her part."

"But you're *not* a professional dancer."

"No, but I was in training for many years before I met Tiago. He's not going to like it, but I decided to do it anyway. He's not going to be there, and I simply have to help my school."

I've decided now wasn't the time to ask what Tiago has against her dancing with the samba school, and if she was OK with his attitude. "So what's your new costume?"

"I'm not sure. It's waiting for me at the Sambadrome, which is why we have to leave earlier than planned. It's a good thing you're ready."

"I am, but I'm not sure about Kevin and Chantal."

"I texted them from the car, telling them to meet us here, and that we're leaving right away. I hope you don't mind."

"Not at all."

"If they can't make it now, they'll have to take a taxi and meet us there," added Isabel.

I heard a knock and went to open the door. They were both there. Kevin smirked at my costume. "It's about time somebody put you in chains, Rachel."

Chantal raised an eyebrow as she studied my outfit on her way in. In return, I scanned hers, recalling she had the surgery yesterday. Her shirt seemed very, very tight. She caught my glance. "Silly me, I haven't gotten a chance to buy bigger shirts yet," she pouted in a mock self-conscious tease. Through the glass door, I noted Otavio's eyes roaming over her chest. When he saw me, he rolled his eyes and winked at me. I smiled but felt a pang of jealousy nonetheless.

"We should leave now," said Isabel.

The suite's phone rang. "Hold on," I said, and answered the phone. The voice on the other side paralyzed me.

"Rachel? It's Ryan Brooks. Listen, I'm down here in the lobby, trying to reach Chantal, but there's no answer in her room. Does she happen to be with you at the moment? She doesn't know I'm here. Hello? Rachel?"

I swallowed and answered: "Yes, she's here with me. Room 1810. Yes, I'll see you in a bit." I hung up.

"What's the matter, Raquel?" asked Isabel worriedly.

"Yea, Rach, you look like you've seen a ghost," said Kevin.

"Raquel?" asked Otavio as he came back inside the suit. Everyone looked at me expectantly.

"Our boss is on his way up!" I declared, looking at Chantal.

"What?!" she jumped off the sofa. "Damn! That hurt!" she cursed and hugged her breasts. "I'm not supposed to jump or do any sudden movements like that yet." She seethed at me, as if any of this was my fault.

"Don't look at me. He's here to see *you!*" I said defensively.

"What do I do?" she whined, looking at Kevin. "He'll know I'm not here to work, and he'll be angry I didn't tell him about the surgery!"

"Go out to the balcony and wait for him there!" he ordered, closing the curtains overlooking the balcony. "It'll give you a couple more minutes to think about what you're going to say. Can't you open a few more buttons on that shirt?"

"I've already told you the bandages have to stay on until tomorrow."

"Yea; sorry."

There was a knock at the door. She looked anxious. "Go wait outside!" ordered Kevin, to which she quickly obeyed. He made a move toward the suite's door.

"That's alright," I said and stood in his path, "I'll get it." I walked toward the small hallway and opened the door, hoping my expression wouldn't betray the rapid beating of my heart.

Ryan smiled widely when he looked at me, his lively, green eyes examining my costume. "Oh, Rachel. If you're willing to work as my slave, I won't have to fire you at all!"

"Hilarious," I murmured.

Ryan grinned widely, his eyes twinkling. Happy to see him, I smiled back and gestured for him to come in. I tried to hide the turmoil of emotions raging within me. I didn't want to lose my job with one of the most successful, brilliant, up-and-coming businessman of our time; he could help me get far. But that was only if he would recognize something brilliant within *me*, too, something I felt I had, but only at times.

Ryan placed his bag on the floor and walked inside. I found his commanding manner uplifting. His sense of purpose seemed to envelop the room. The part of me that strove for excellence and self-improvement felt inspired - and guilty. Hadn't I acted mostly like a tourist so far? I'd hardly done any work since I had arrived in Rio!

I made the introductions. "Ryan Brooks, this is Otavio, our tour guide."

"*É um prazer te conhecer,*" said Ryan and stretched out his hand with a smile.

"It's a pleasure to meet you, too. We can speak English, but I have to say, your Portuguese is excellent!" Otavio shook Ryan's hand, appreciation radiating through his cocky smile.

"As is your English. Seeing you and Rachel in these costumes reminds me of studying Brazilian history." Ryan looked at Kevin and nodded. "Kevin."

"Ryan." They said nothing more. I wondered if I detected a bit of tension between those two. Did Ryan know of Chantal's and Kevin's history as a couple?

"And this is Isabel, our second tour guide," I said.

"The pleasure is all mine," said Ryan with a charming smile, kissing Isabel's cheeks. "You are not going to parade tonight?" he asked, noting she didn't wear a costume.

"I am, but there's been a last-minute change, and I have to do a fitting for someone else's costume at the Sambadrome."

"Oh, wow," he said, looking at his watch, "then we should be leaving soon."

So he's here to watch the parade, I realized, feeling the pressure mount.

"Yes," concurred Isabel, looking relieved. "And, if I may make a suggestion, you should leave that watch at the hotel, and all other valuables."

"Thank you for the reminder. I'll do that. I wanted to leave my bag in Chantal's room. Where is she?"

"She's waiting for you on the balcony," I said, and gestured toward the glass door. Ryan rolled the door aside, then closed it behind him. The shut curtains afforded them the privacy they needed.

Isabel moved beside me. "And he thought he'd surprise her?"

"Yes," was all I said. I wanted to tell Isabel how much I yearned to tell Ryan my suspicions that Chantal and Kevin were still sleeping together, but Kevin was listening keenly to everything that was being said.

"Shh!" he admonished.

We stayed quiet, listening to the muffled voices outside. Otavio came near me and tried to hold my hand. I squeezed his palm, then let it go. I dreaded what Ryan would think if he saw us being intimate. Otavio frowned as he looked at me.

The balcony door opened. "Darlings," said Chantal, her carefree tone trying to mask the worry in her voice, "we're going up to my room for a little while, so that Ryan can freshen up and relax after his long flight." Her hands ran over his shoulders and back as she said that. I tried to glean Ryan's state of mind. He didn't look happy, as one might expect when reuniting with a new love interest. He looked serious and drawn. "We'll have to take a cab later and join you there."

"Yes," Ryan added coldly, "and since Chantal is *not* dancing in the parade, there's no need for her to leave quite yet."

"Oh, darling," said Chantal as she slid her body along his in a failing attempt to be sexy, her folded arms protecting her breasts. "Don't you dare be upset! After all, *you're* the one who ruined *my* surprise."

Otavio and Isabel looked as surprised as I was by Chantal's spin on the events. Kevin smirked a bit and nodded faintly at her.

"But you're here to model for Rachel's scoop. I'm paying your agency for that!"

"I told you that your magazine will get to scoop my new boobs story, which will draw a lot more attention than Rachel's little parade, that's for sure!"

That fucking bitch! was all I could think, rage and worry flooding me. Isabel's hand petted my tight fist. I couldn't look away from Ryan and Chantal, nor react. I had to absorb every little thing about Ryan's reaction to what Chantal said.

"None of my magazines is *that* kind of magazine," Ryan said impatiently.

"Well, perhaps you should reconsider that, since you'll lose a fortune. However, I take my bandages off tomorrow, so I'll be able to model for Rachel again — as long as it's not in a pool, hot tub, or the ocean. That'll take a month."

"Miss Moore and I have a wager, which I plan on honoring. Because of you, her odds will be diminished." Chantal opened her mouth, no doubt to speak ill of me again, but then she closed it, probably in deference to the respect Ryan showed me. She's not stupid, I thought, as we both exchanged hateful looks. Ryan turned to me and said gently, "Rachel, I apologize for Miss Neuchâtel's unprofessional behavior. You're just going to have to make this an autobiographical piece. Those fly off the shelves, at times."

My intense relief made me want to cry. "Thank you, Mr. Brooks. I'll do that."

"Good. I'll be out there in the crowd tonight, cheering you on," he added with his charming smile. The smile was gone as he said to Chantal, "Let's go."

After they left, I wanted to linger back in the suite, perhaps have a drink, or breathe some fresh air on the balcony. Ryan made me feel safe, for now anyway. But there was no time to waste.

"Come on! I don't want to be late!" urged Isabel.

CHAPTER 12

I didn't have a purse, so I placed my cell in my pocket. "I hope you don't plan on using your phone during the parade! That's all we need for the judges to see a slave check a text message or take a selfie!"

"Got it. But how do people keep track of the time during the parade? You said they have to complete it within a certain time frame."

"There are clocks everywhere on the avenue."

The Sambadrome avenue used to be a regular road. In the 80s, it was converted into a permanent stadium specifically for carnival. The 700-meter stadium now had bleachers on each side for spectators. We were headed to the staging area in the back.

After the heads of the samba school fawned all over Isabel, expressing their gratitude I imagined, they started fitting her for the costume. Isabel's maid, Barbara, was there, too, dressed up as a lady from Brazil's state of Bahia. Being backstage was fascinating, watching makeup being done, seeing flimsy bras being glued to breasts, and shimmer being applied to long, exquisite legs.

Kevin was not allowed to take pictures back there, so he went to set up his equipment on the avenue. Otavio went to lend a hand with last minute adjustments to our float. I sat on a tall stool, my feet moving back and forth with a nervous tick to the contagious samba rhythm played by one of the schools ahead of us, which was already parading in the large, open-air avenue.

Isabel was dressed in a bejeweled thong, its matching bra connecting to an elaborate neck ornament encrusted with pearls and crystals. The expensive designer heels made for her predecessor fit her closely enough, their thick, bejeweled straps extending up to her knees. The black feathers protruding from the heels' backs matched the long, feather-covered wings at the back of her bra. Her body and face glittered with shimmer, and her makeup highlighted the blue contact lenses they put in her eyes. She, too, wore chains around her wrists, but hers were silver and shinier than Otavio's and mine. On her head was a large, sparkling tiara, which emphasized both Isabel's high forehead and her fabulous mane of hair, which emerged from it like a cascading waterfall. The inexplicable addition of a pearl-encrusted, muzzle-like device was connected from the back of her head to her neck ornament. A small, wiry man speaking in rapid Portuguese demonstrated how it could be closed and reopened with ease. Isabel nodded. He gave her a four inch, metallic-looking object to hold, and she was ready.

"I have a ton of questions!" I declared with a smile after the little man left, snapping a few pictures of her.

"I'm sure," she smiled back at me, "but I have to go over my new routine now, then have some pictures taken. We'll talk afterward," she said and hugged me.

I hugged her back gently, mindful of her wings. I whispered in her ear, "You look absolutely stunning."

She smiled warmly at me, her eyes penetrating mine. "Nervous?"

"How could I not be? And, on top of everything I worried about before, now my boss is here, too!"

"Oh, yes. He and 'the model who can't model' will be in my friends' private box." Seats in the Sambadrome ranged from cheap ones on rows of concrete, to exclusive private boxes complete with buffet, waiters, private bathroom, etc.

"That's nice," I murmured, feeling distracted by my nerves.

"You know what my friends said when they heard about you parading tonight? They were so impressed."

"Oh, you're just trying to make me feel better," I protested.

"Seriously! Half of them said they'd always wanted to parade in the carnival, but never did, and absolutely everyone agreed that you're incredibly courageous to have come here from abroad and dance in front of the school masters like you did on Saturday, when the focus was only on you. Really, today shouldn't be half as scary, even if your boss is out there." She smiled at me, her gaze showing me she knew she was winning me over. "And you know what else they said when I told them about your job and your bet with your boss?"

"What?"

"They said you're absolutely awesome!"

I worried some tears might spring out of my eyes and ruin my makeup, but instead I just laughed in relief. "Really?"

"Really. And they're all dying to meet you, which is why I insist you come to my bachelorette party on Friday."

"Oh, stop it! You're gonna make me cry!" I laughed again.

"There can be no tears this evening. Tonight is a celebration! It's that one day a year we Brazilians dream about, remember?! Now, go be wonderful!" We smiled at each other. "Oh, and don't you and Otavio dare make out during the parade! It'll cost us points!"

I grinned at her. "Guess we'll have to save it for later, then."

"I guess so," she grinned. "And don't worry about me. I have about twenty friends here tonight and I can catch a ride home with any one of them if you two happen to… disappear," We both giggled at her implication, and she went to get her photo taken.

It was past 11:00 PM. Different schools would parade until roughly 5:00 AM. I was happy that our school was next, and not one of the ones due to begin at two or three in the morning. Otavio found me, and offered me a sip of his cold beer, which I happily accepted.

He discarded the empty bottle, kissed me, then grinned and said, "Let's go!" I followed him to our float, which was as big as a four-story building. It looked like a huge, green tiered cake; the tiers acting as dancing platforms. Six enormous statues of the upper bodies of black slaves with blue eyes protruded from the sides of the float. Its top was a little, round, elevated stage, beautifully decorated with over six feet of white and golden plumes arranged in a large oval. Otavio caught my gaze and explained, "That's where Princess Isabel will dance."

"*Our* Isabel?"

"No!" he laughed good-naturedly. "*Princesa Isabel,* the one who signed the emancipation of slaves more than a hundred years ago. Some slave you are!" he shook his head and beamed at me. Then he opened a green door for me at the side of the float, a door I couldn't detect until then. *So that's how we get in there!* I mused, following him inside. We climbed a couple of ladders, then stepped out to our tier. Our semi-circular, earth-toned tier surrounded the entire back of the float. It was decorated with golden straw and lots of bamboo and encircled by a bamboo railing.

We were the only ones there. "You are the prettiest slave I've ever seen," said Otavio, hugging me from behind as he nuzzled my neck, his arms fondling my stomach over the coarse fabric of my dress. I was too charged with excitement and tension to relax. He turned me around to face him. "You're not still nervous about dancing, are you? Because if you could dance with an old, expert *sambista* dancer like Barbara, you can dance in front of anyone!"

"It's not just that."

"Your boss? He'll love it, too. But, in case this story is not enough for you to keep your job, I'll help you find something else. So let your worries go. Tonight we celebrate. Tonight is for us!"

I smiled at him. Just when he was about to kiss me again, more people arrived on our shelf. We exchanged greetings with the newcomers. Their costumes matched ours, their excitement evident. Everyone seemed eager to get started. Finally, someone's head peeped in through the door, his black eyes seeming intensely nervous. "*Dois minutos!*" he announced, then disappeared.

"Two minutes," Otavio translated. "Ready?"

"Ready! But where is Isabel? I have to see her dance!"

"Sorry, but we won't be able to see her from here, since she's walking in front of our car and we're facing the back of the parade. You'll have to wait and see her on television." I knew Isabel was recording the parade for us to watch together later, which was good, since the more I saw, the more questions I had.

We heard the name of our samba school being announced on the speakers, followed by the loud cheers from the crowd. My heart started beating faster. For one quick moment, Otavio's hand closed over mine in reassurance and he winked at me. Our school's song started playing. It was the kind of samba you simply had to dance to, the fast rhythm of the numerous drums and other percussion instruments creating a sort of an inner turmoil, an urgent call to dance that no one could resist. We all sang the song, despite the float not yet having moved from our spot at the back of the Sambadrome. I knew we were the third float out of five, and every float was preceded by many different sections, with participants dressed in different costumes, and by the *bateria*, the large musical percussion section.

Our float started advancing slowly toward the other side of the Sambadrome. Everyone on our shelf danced and sang as we emerged into the long avenue. Stadium lights illuminated the iridescent costumes of the paraders and their excited faces. Any lingering regret I felt of not being able to see Isabel or face the front of the parade was completely gone. I was utterly swept away by a feeling of elation so strong, it was like nothing I'd ever felt before. After all, tens of thousands of people would see *me* dance. These projectors were here to highlight *me*. These television cameras and audience cell phones were filming *me*. I danced my heart out, sweat dripping down my back, a huge grin broadened on my face. Tonight, I was a star!

We passed row upon row of concrete bleachers, where people sang and danced. I felt the love and excitement emanating from the audience. Their enthusiasm kept me going happily, despite the oppressive humid heat, which was magnified by the bright lights flooding the avenue. The coarse fabric of my costume seemed to trap my body heat inside it, making me feel even sorrier for slaves than I had ever felt before.

We passed the many private booths from which I could perceive some masked faces and some hands holding Champagne glasses. Otavio motioned toward one of the booths. Hanging from it was a long, rectangular sign: "*Vai* Isabel! Go Raquel! Vai Otavio!" Isabel's friends must have made that sign for us. I grinned at Otavio, who winked at me. I felt that primal lust for him again, like I had at the block party, the combination of the intensive heat and the percussive sounds underscoring his sex appeal and the thumping of my heart. I felt near to drooling over the sight of the sweat glistening down his tanned, exposed chest and over his chiseled arms. The thought that tonight could be *the night* underscored my rapid heartbeat with a heavier thud of anticipation.

I tried but couldn't make out Ryan in the booth. I wanted him to see me as I was now, glorious in my accomplishment. At that moment I felt so empowered that I didn't care if he thought I wasn't good enough for his magazine. If that was the case, he could take his job and shove it! There were plenty of other jobs in this world. I smiled and put the thought of him out of my head.

Other than the slave costumes around me, I saw the section of the kids dressed as clowns, the men dressed in outfits decorated in piano keys, and the woman dressed as the famous Brazilian singer, *Carmen Miranda.* She wore Miranda's trademark hat covered in faux fruit and was surrounded by men dancing around her with huge, cardboard bananas. The rest of the sections were too far away for me to see.

By the end of the hour, I was beat. My legs hurt from dancing, my arms hurt from swinging high in the air, and even my cheeks hurt from smiling. I felt relieved when our car finally turned away from the avenue to park at the side of the covered rest area. The dancing on our tier came to a stop. The others began leaving, happy smiles still on their faces. I, too, felt euphoric.

"You did it!" declared Otavio. He spun me up in the air victoriously, then put me down very close to him.

"I did it!" I answered and kissed him ardently. When he looked into my eyes, he found the confirmation he was looking for. After the dance lessons, the rehearsals, the parade, and especially he always taking my side, I felt that our initial desire was now cemented by a unique bond. I was ready.

Hugging each other's waists, we made our way to the van.

"Let's go to my hotel?" I asked with a suggestive smile as we sat in the van.

"I have another idea," he said mysteriously and started the engine. He must have seen the disappointment on my face, since he laughed and said, "I'm glad to see we both have the same thing on our minds," he winked, helping me relax a little. "I want to take you to a special place."

"Sounds great. But why tonight?" I asked, caressing his thigh.

"Patience, *querida*. You'll understand when we get there."

"You're not going to tell me anything else?!"

"No."

"But I have to know!"

"I promise that it'll be more fun if you see it first," he grinned and said no more. He started some Bossa Nova music, lit a cigarette and started driving. The soft caress of the deep, soulful saxophone notes washed away the tribal carnival beat, reprogramming my mind and soul with mellower sensuality. I increased the flow of the air conditioner and sighed happily. "Help me get this off," he said, pointing to the head ornament, which the roof of the car bent awkwardly.

"Sure." I reached over and slowly undid the ornament from the many pins fastening it to his hair. When I was done, I tossed it in the back seat. I felt too shy to just reach over and play with his curls, as I longed to do, so I focused on removing my own hair extensions instead. When my hair was finally free, I shook my head side to side, bringing a lustful smile to Otavio's lips.

CHAPTER 13

Otavio drove inside the gate of what looked like a small apartment building. He stopped at a drive-through kiosk to contemplate a chart of prices on the wall, which was labeled *Vênus* Motel. The prices were for *apartamento* or *suite*. Why pay for a dinky motel room when we could have gone to my hotel room? I wondered. Otavio made his decision and the incurious attendant handed him a numbered key. He moved aside to let Otavio snap a photo of the price chart, which puzzled me further. Then he lifted the gate arm and we drove inside. We parked inside a private garage and Otavio lowered the automatic door behind us.

"A motel?" I asked incredulously. "Why on earth would you bring me to a motel when we could have gone to my hotel room?"

"Come. You'll see."

I had to push aside the creepy feeling motels gave me and remind myself I trusted Otavio. I held his hand and followed him up the stairs. He unlocked a door. We stepped into a small corridor, which had two other doors. He jiggled the handle on the right, nodding when he found it locked, then unlocked the door on the left. It opened to a small, enclosed area, with a small dining table, two chairs, and a mini-fridge.

We stepped inside the suite. The enormous room was painted light green and white. It boasted a red leather couch, a glass coffee table, and a potted palm. It had a white jacuzzi and a large black bed, topped with white sheets and surrounded by mirrors.

I didn't know what to think. Yes, we came here for a specific reason, but being intimate on a bed raised on an elevated platform, while our bodies were well lit by numerous lights, our every pose and intimate part displayed so clinically in the mirrors' reflections, didn't seem romantic at all. But maybe it could be? Maybe he'll agree to dim the lights, or perhaps even turn them off altogether?

"Welcome to Vênus Motel!" he smiled and gestured to the elegant room as if he were showing me a house to buy. "And this is not all," he added and tried to lead me toward the balcony.

"Give me a minute," I said and headed to the back of the suit. The large bathroom impressed me. It had a spacious shower, an enormous bath with jets, and even a steam room. There were two plush, white robes and matching slippers on the granite countertop. I felt like taking my costume off and letting myself be more comfortable in one of those robes, but I wasn't sure yet if I was staying or not. What on earth was Otavio thinking bringing me here?

My intent to reprove him was replaced with astonishment as I came out of the bathroom. My jaw dropped. I couldn't believe my eyes. Otavio had opened all the curtains, revealing the gorgeous, intimately lit pool we had on our balcony. Our own pool!

Otavio stood outside, smoking and drinking from a bottle of an American vodka cooler. He smiled at me, ran his fingers over my dress's collar and asked, "Don't they have robes back there?"

"And how would you know?" I asked, trying to sound coquettish, but feeling a pinch in my heart as I wondered how many women he'd brought here before me. I continued, speaking quickly before he had a chance to answer, "I don't get this place. Motels usually creep me out, but this room is like a country club crammed into one room. The only thing missing is a tennis court!"

"Here," he said and handed me a bottle. I took a long sip. He turned me around to face the black expanse in front of us while he undid the chain around my neck. "Wait 'till you see the ocean in the morning. The sunrise is only a few hours away." He let my chain fall on the stone tiles with a clink. He caressed my arm as he spoke, trying to relax me. "Can you undo my chain, too?"

As I undid the clasp on his chain, I asked, "But how is it you're able to afford a room like this with not only a sauna and a jacuzzi, but an ocean view and a private pool *too*?"

"How much do you think it costs?"

"Why, a hotel room on the coast with all these amenities could run all the way up to three grand a night. It won't be less than 2K, I can tell you that!"

"I had a feeling you were going to ask, which is why I took a photo of the prices."

I looked at the photo he showed me. "I can't believe it! It didn't even cost a hundred dollars!"

"For ninety dollars we get the whole place to ourselves for six hours," he whispered into my ear.

"You… you brought me to a by-the-hour motel?!" I asked, flabbergasted.

"Raquel, no *estrangeiros* come to these motels, I mean no foreigners, because they usually already have a hotel room."

"I know. That's why I don't get why you brought me here."

"You said over and over again that you wanted to do things tourists usually don't do, so I thought I'd surprise you and bring you here. You don't like it?"

"You know what? You're right. I'm going to shut up and enjoy this amazing value. Hell, if this wasn't sex-related, I could have used it as a scoop! But you've got to at least let me pay for half of it."

He placed one arm around my waist and pulled me to him while inserting his other palm under my hair, pulling my face to his. He looked firmly into my eyes as he replied, *"Absolutely not!"* Then he kissed me, shutting me up. I kissed him back, my heart beating excitedly with the expectation of things to come.

Until that moment, sex was something I'd thought of as rather pleasant, but not much more. I had had a few short-term relationships, but as I looked back on them I knew I was never really in love, nor even in lust before. Not like I was with Otavio. I finally understood what people meant when they talked about earth-shattering sex. It wasn't just two hot bodies moving in blind lust. I felt we were connected not just by my quest for a winning scoop, but also by the hardships we both knew, which allowed him to empathize with me. To sleep with someone who had shared an important part of your life's journey, someone caring with whom you shared a victorious moment, significantly elevated the experience.

Added to our spiritual connection was Otavio's expertise. He seemed to speak the body's language fluently. As I lay in bed passively, as was my custom, I expected what I'd experienced before: for him to lay on top of me, unite with me for a few, brief moments, and that's it. But Otavio had other plans. He took his time kissing every inch of me thoroughly, sending chills up and down my spine, taking me by surprise repeatedly as I discovered new sensual points in unexpected places. He told me how beautiful my body was again and again, aiding me to relax completely in bed, until the softly-lit mirrors above us did not distress me anymore. As my inner defensive walls crumbled, so did the tension of self-consciousness. For the first time in my life, I heard myself sighing pleasurably out loud. This was another surprise, since I didn't know I had it in me. My sighs seemed to spur Otavio on. The exploration of his lustful lips intensified. My ecstasy mounted higher and higher like a storm gathering momentum to turn into a tornado until a final yell escaped my lips, the inner vibrations of my body achieving the final, orgasmic peak.

I looked down to see my hands trembling in the aftershock of the most intense physical pleasure of my life. "You'd better get used to that," said Otavio hoarsely. His cocky smile was hardly perceptible and the look in his eyes was dead serious. I wanted to answer playfully *don't make any promises you can't keep!* But even if I did have the courage to say it, I found I couldn't speak. I hoped he could see the gratitude and amazement in my eyes. I pulled him toward me and kissed him ravenously. Then he continued to make good on his promise.

We didn't waste precious time sleeping that night. From the bed we proceeded to relax in the bubble-filled jacuzzi. Then we had some breakfast, which was brought in by a waiter who used the discreet side door. We sat back on the long balcony chaise. Otavio's body encircled mine. We watched the colors of the sunrise banish the dark of night just as Otavio had expelled the crippling inhibitions from my soul. Then he sat beside me and fed me chunks of papaya and mango. When their luscious fruit juices ran down my breasts, he slowly licked them clean. Our sensual dip in the pool ended up leading us back to bed. By the end of the six-hour time-frame, we were spent.

"I guess we have to leave," I yawned, feeling sleepy, but saddened at the thought of leaving.

"No one says we can't sleep here," he answered. "We can stay as long as you like, then pay the total when we leave. Or we can continue, eh, 'researching' other motels."

"I love that idea, but I have to work," I said and forced myself to get up. I had to find out if Ryan had accepted the parade as a winning scoop.

"I'm glad *I* don't have to work," he smiled. I smacked his arm. "Ouch!" he laughed. "Let's go. I'll take you back to your hotel." I snapped a few pictures of the suite and the stunning view before we headed back to Copacabana.

* * *

After dropping me off, Otavio went back to his place to catch up on some sleep. I was eager to contact Ryan but allowed myself a long nap first, setting my alarm for noon. After hitting the snooze button repeatedly, I finally woke up. I grabbed a caffeinated soda from the mini fridge and ordered some food and coffee. I showered, my mind filling with thoughts as its fogginess lifted. The biggest question on my mind was whether or not the parade scoop was going to cut it with Ryan.

Soaping my body made me remember why it had to be cleaned, which brought back the ecstasy I had experienced last night. I looked down at my palms, recalling their tremor last night. For a moment, I wished I was just here on vacation, so I could devote myself entirely to surrendering to my lover's expertise.

I smiled at that and got out of the shower. As tempting as that thought was, I knew that the nature and urgency of my assignment in Brazil made our whole relationship a lot more exciting. Heck, it was making my life more exciting!

I emailed Ryan a brief message:

Dear Ryan, I hope you enjoyed watching the parade last night. I feel certain the unique manner in which I've covered the parade will suffice in order to win our bet. Looking forward to hearing from you, Rachel."

Jovially, I pressed Send. Then I Skyped Jess over breakfast.

"Hey Sweetie," she said.

"Hello dear," I smiled.

"You had sex!" she proclaimed.

"Jess!" I said, trying to sound reproving.

"Say that without a smile," she dared.

"I really can't. And I don't really want to. I'm so full of joy, I'm ecstatic."

"Oh my God! You have to tell me all about it!"

"What can I say? He took his time and it was awesome. *He* was awesome."

"Oh, c'mon! I want some juicy details." Since I smiled but said nothing, she added, "If you don't tell me more, I won't tell you about it after I sleep with Lon!"

"What?!"

"We're going on a date tomorrow night."

"Oh, honey, that's wonderful! I'm so happy for you."

"Thanks," she smiled, almost shyly. "Dating a tech god like Lon Ryder is like a dream."

"Oh, yea?" I smiled at her, not stating the obvious. Lon was so different from the bad boys she usually dated. I realized the type she usually went for resembled Otavio. "You have to tell me all about it afterward."

"Oh, like you told me anything about your Latin lover boy? C'mon! Fill me in on some raunchy stuff!"

"I said he was phenomenal and that's enough."

"You're such a prude!"

"From my experience, people who brag about sex are not getting any. Or the sex was so awful, they're shouting to the world it was great."

"So according to your logic, keeping quiet means it was..." her voice trailed off.

"Wondrous," I finished her sentence, my eyes trailing off to the distance as I remembered.

"I get it," she said, smiling and nodding in understanding. "So, how did the parade go?"

"It was amazing. What an experience! I'll send you some pictures. But wait, you wouldn't believe what happened before the parade. Who do you think showed up at my hotel room yesterday with no advanced notice? Ryan!"

"No!"

"Yes!" I quickly filled her in on his visit.

"Wow," she said when I was done. "I get the feeling he and Chantal won't last long."

"Me too."

"By the way, I had an idea," said Jess. "I'm thinking of asking for Lon's help in digging some dirt on Chantal; you know, something you could use as leverage."

"Hmm," I frowned. "I don't know about that. Technically, he's our boss. Are you two even allowed to date?"

"Luckily, there's no rule against it at Brooks Inc. And I'll only ask him if I feel I can trust him, OK?"

"I guess so. What made you think about it?"

"She just pissed me off when she risked your scoop like that. I just think that, for once, it's time for you to gain the upper hand."

"That *would* be a nice change."

"So, did Ryan say anything about the scoop? Who won the bet?"

"No, we didn't get a chance to talk about it. I've emailed him now with the same question. But I'm not worried."

"That's great, sweetie. Let us know when you hear from him."

"Where is Ashley anyway?"

"She had a deadline."

"Oh, OK. Send her my love, but don't tell her about Otavio yet. I'll do that when I talk to her."

"No problem. Enjoy your hot, Brazilian love-affair," she said with a mock sexy look.

"I will," I answered with a similar look and sway of my chest and shoulders. We grinned at one another, blew air-kisses, and hung up.

I looked over the polished parade photos Kevin had sent me. I enjoyed the sight of the colorful, festive parade, taking special joy in the photos of myself and of Otavio. These are our *before* pics, I grinned to myself. Would our new intimacy be visible if new photos were taken now? I smiled at the thought.

I texted Isabel about coming over tonight to view the parade, as we had discussed before. She replied succinctly, saying merely that 7:00 o'clock would be fine with her. She added she would not be serving dinner, but that snacks would be available. I replied *it sounded great* and added a smiley face. She replied with a dry *OK; see you then*. I could not help wondering if something was wrong.

CHAPTER 14

Ihaven't heard from Ryan all day. I was disappointed Otavio wasn't able to get to my hotel earlier than 6:30, due to a family situation he didn't elaborate upon. It gave me some time to do a bit of shopping. I bought a few colorful summer dresses, the likes of which I'd never owned before. For that evening I picked the fuchsia dress with the black trim. I smiled happily at the feminine, softer image of me in this vivid, bold color. *Who cares I have more weight to lose, if a guy like Otavio can't have enough of me?!* I put on some black slingbacks, applied some light makeup and went downstairs.

Otavio picked me up in a small sedan. "Oh, wow! You look great!" he said enthusiastically.

Faintly smiling, I looked deeply into his eyes, wishing to remind him of our intimacy the previous night. He smiled back, his sexy half-smile more proprietary than ever before. He pulled me to him and kissed me deeply. When he let me go, I looked up at him breathlessly, marveling at how easily he made me feel faint, something I'd never felt before.

"Careful. If you keep on looking at me like that, there is no way I'm taking you to Isabel's to watch TV, especially when your hotel room is right up there." I smiled at him, not trying to hide the pleasure his remark gave me. "Ay, yai, yai!" he said, pushed me back into my seat and buckled me in. "I wish we could stay, but..."

"Watching this parade is actually part of my work," I reminded him. "It'll make it easier for me to write about the experience."

"Sure. Also, Isabel is upset. I'm hoping we can cheer her up."

He's such a good friend, I thought and inquired, "What happened?"

"Take a look at the newspapers on the back seat," he said as he started weaving through traffic.

"Oh!" I squealed with delight. The front page showed a fantastic photo of Isabel in her costume.

"I thought you only made those noises for me," he joked, his hand caressing my leg for an instant, then going back to the gear shift.

I grinned at him. "Do you think Isabel saw this?" I asked, wanting to pet his leg, too, but force of habit stopped me. *You're being silly!* I told myself. Alas, the habit of reticence was not an easy one to break.

"Do you think Barbara would go to sleep before buying the morning papers after a parade? Never!"

"So, do we know who won already? It'd be such a perfect scoop if our school wins."

"More schools are parading today, so we'll only find out tomorrow. But, yes, Isabel saw it, and so did the rest of the world."

"So what's the problem?"

"Her stupid fiancé is furious with her."

"Oh-o."

"Exactly. I always knew he was an idiot, but she loves him. They've been together for years, even before I've met her." I was happy to hear that, since it allayed my fears they might have been intimate in the past. "I'll let her tell you all about it, but, between you and me, I think he's just being a *hipócrita.*"

"A hypocrite?"

"Yes."

"I don't get it. How can anyone not like it? She looks amazing!"

"Oh, he liked it alright. But that doesn't mean he wanted the rest of the world to see her like that."

"Hmm. I know it might sound phony, but some people are obsessed about privacy."

"He's obsessed about his public image. Hand me a cigarette, will you?" I placed a cigarette between his lips and lit it for him, remembering similar scenes form old movies. He took a deep drag and continued to drive and smoke while I browsed through the papers. Occasionally, I glanced up to look at him and at the view, and to ponder Isabel's relationship with Tiago.

Barbara's eyes lit up as she opened the door and saw Otavio. They fell into a quick discussion in Portuguese while we walked into the apartment. I was relieved that the cheek kisses custom did not apply to the staff, wondering if Barbara was relieved, too. When the dejected Isabel showed up, I wished her kisses were more emphatic. She wore no makeup and her eyes looked swollen and red from crying. Still, even in a frumpy white T-shirt and jean cut-offs she looked beautiful.

Someone I haven't met stood beside her. "Raquel, meet one of my very best friends, Maristela."

"Ola Raquel!" she said, and we traded kisses. "I've heard so many wonderful things about you!"

I smiled at her sweet, direct manner. Maristela's short, blond hair framed a pretty face with blue eyes. She wore a beaded blue dress and big, emerald jewelry. The effect was an intellectual, yet slightly Bohemian look. Her warm smile seemed sincere and inviting. We entered the living room, which was furnished with a long, black, leather couch facing a big screen TV. Isabel and I sat in the center, Otavio to my right, and Maristela near Isabel. Barbara disappeared into the kitchen.

I turned to Isabel. "What's going on?"

"This!" she stressed and pointed to the top paper on the pile of newspapers Otavio had set on the coffee table.

"What about that? Of all the women in the multiple parades last night, they chose *you* to be on their cover. How is that a bad thing?"

"Tiago was so angry."

"I thought you said he's in São Paulo for work."

"He is."

"So how did he find out?"

"Last night, he took out these very important, very rich clients to have dinner at a fancy restaurant. Of course, the carnival was on TV," she explained, her puffy eyes alternating between Otavio and me. "He's a regular there, so everyone knows him – *and* me. Everything was going great until he saw me on the screen. He said he went insane with fury when he had to sit there and listen to the American clients talk about what they'd like to do to the hot babe on the screen. Then came their waiter and declared right in front of everybody, *Isn't that your fiancé?* The sheikhs, who enjoyed seeing all the exposed bodies until then, started complaining about the immodesty of my costume and how they were sorry but were going to have to leave earlier than they realized. He said he lost the deal and that he was never so humiliated and angry in his entire life."

"Was he angry you were so exposed on TV, or that he lost the deal, or both?"

"Thankfully, he's mostly angry about losing the deal. He's not crazy about me dressing up as a famous slave and wearing so little on TV, but, on the other hand, he does like the way I looked."

"Of course he loved the way you looked! He's got a hot fiancée, and everyone knows it!" I said, trying to make her feel better.

"They sure do!" concurred Otavio.

"He's just angry because he lost a lot of money, but that won't last," I added.

"Raquel is right," Maristela chimed in. "And you know how possessive he can be. Your body is his, period. He likes when people stare at it on the beach, but hearing other men talk about your sexy body might take a little longer to forget."

"He said he's too angry to talk and will call me tomorrow."

"Don't you see?" I smiled. "It means he's not so angry at you for doing it, but more at the fact you were seen by clients who canceled a deal. Just give him some time. I bet he'll call you later or tomorrow at the latest."

"You really think so?" she smiled meekly, her tears drying.

"I'm sure of it!"

Isabel smiled, measuring Otavio and me. "So... where did you two disappear to last night? You look fabulous in that dress, by the way."

"Thanks, darling."

"So?" she asked.

"I'm going to leave you to fill in the ladies," he said. He kissed Isabel's forehead, making her smile. Then he turned to me and kissed me on the mouth, his lips lingering on mine for a long moment. Then he grinned crookedly, put a cigarette in his mouth and proceeded to the balcony.

Isabel and Maristela looked at me with expectant smiles. Even if I was thinking of keeping our intimacy private, Otavio's kiss had made that quite impossible. I turned to Maristela and explained, "I'm sorry, but I feel strange talking about it even with my best friends."

"Oh, she's so shy, isn't she?" said Isabel, pulling me to her. "Remember what I told you, Raquel. We look at sexuality as a wonderful thing to celebrate."

"That's right," nodded Maristela with a warm smile.

"So if I tell you he... took me to a motel last night?"

"We'll say that's great!" declared Isabel.

"And ask which one?" grinned Maristela. She and Isabel laughed.

"Vênus motel."

"Oh, that's a good one," said Maristela, she and Isabel nodding approvingly. "We should write you some recommendations." I was surprised. Maristela was older than we were and wore a wedding ring. I realized motels here weren't only for young, single people.

"Great idea! Let's write down some of our favorites, including the best theme rooms," said Isabel.

"Hilarious. Otavio did suggest we continue our 'research'," I said using air-quotes, "of motels tonight. I didn't know there were theme rooms."

"As they say in the movies: Girl, you don't know the half of it! Can I use this?" Isabel asked, pointing at my PA.

"Yes, let me show you how."

"What is that?" asked Maristela.

"It's the tablet my boss invented. In many ways, it acts as a personal assistant, so that's what he calls it, or PA for short. I *do* hope my scoop lets me keep my job, so I can keep this baby," I said, hugging the PA. I'd gotten quite attached to it over the past few days. It was the first time I'd taken it out of my hotel room, and I felt I had to be very vigilant about it. I gave them a quick tutorial. Then I opened a web folder, and quickly dragged and dropped the motels' links they'd opened, including the specific theme rooms they'd mentioned, into it. They were duly impressed by the device.

"So? How was it?" Isabel nudged me with a coquettish smile.

Right then, Otavio came back from the balcony. Sashaying his way to the kitchen he said with sass, "Don't worry, I'm just passing. You can keep on talking about me." We sheepishly grinned at him, and he shook his head as he disappeared into the kitchen.

"C'mon! Tell us before he comes back!" urged Isabel.

"What can I say? He's amazing."

Isabel smiled dreamily. "How?"

"So amazing I don't know why I'm wasting my time visiting you when I can be alone with him!"

"Then why *are* you here?" she teased.

"I have to work *sometimes*," I smiled widely. "After all, covering the parade is my job."

"Does this mean Ryan accepted it as your scoop?" she asked sanguinely.

"I'm waiting to hear from him."

Barbara and Otavio brought out plates of snacks and drinks and set them on the coffee table in front of us, Otavio discreetly removing the newspapers. I smiled at him, pleased to see he was concerned about Isabel and with helping the maid. "Maristela, *a gente tem que falar*." I looked at him inquisitively. "Sorry, Raquel. Maristela, Barbara, and I have to talk for a bit before we start the show. Maristela is representing Barbara, my mother, and the entire *favela* in a lawsuit." I looked at Maristela expectantly.

"I'm a public defender and I'm representing them in a gentrification, or displacement lawsuit against the government. You see, they're living on some prime real estate, and the government wants them out, so they and the developers connected with them can start building their own buildings and charge a hefty rent. But these people have lived there their whole lives. They can't just be forced out or bought out. They want to stay in their homes, near their families."

I nodded in understanding. "Sure, you guys go ahead and talk." Otavio, Maristela, and Barbara sat at the dining table to talk. Isabel and I talked quietly.

"Barbara lives in the same favela where Otavio grew up. She was their neighbor and she used to help his mother when his father beat her. That was years ago, before Otavio's big brother beat their father so forcefully, he never came back to bother them. Otavio loves Barbara very much. She helped him get away from that life, referring him to our tour agency. And when she and his mom and their neighbors needed legal help, I asked Maristela to help them, and she was happy to help. She lives for these cases, even though the pay might be very low."

I nodded sadly at the thought of Otavio's mother being beaten by his father, wondering if Otavio was beaten, too. Perhaps this was part of the reason his brother had a chosen a life of crime? Still, how come Otavio turned out to be the exact opposite?

When they were done talking, Otavio brought Barbara a chair and placed it near his seat on the sofa. Isabel clicked on the remote control, and the recording of the parade started to play.

"The reporter said our school is about to start parading," translated Isabel.

"Thanks. I never really understood the special significance behind your carnival. This time, I want to understand everything, so I can do a good job writing about it."

"I hope it won't take too long," Otavio whispered in my ear, his breath sending chills all over my body. I smiled at him, feeling awkward because of the others. Why did I always feel I had to hide the fact I was a sexual being?

The name of our school was *Vai-Vai* or *Go-Go*. The first group to parade[1] was an incongruous looking group of women, with different outfits, professions and statuses from all ages: A superwoman, a ballerina, a nurse, a maid, a whore, a slave, and a Victorian lady. They danced, smiled and waved to the crowd as they slowly progressed forward.

"Who are they?" I asked, reaching for my diet *Guarana*, a popular Brazilian soda.

"The first group to walk is called *Comissáo de frente*," explained Isabel.

I keyed it in my PA's translator. "Front liners," I read aloud.

"This particular group is called *Shocking Pink*. They introduce the theme of this year's parade, which is the female force

---

[1] The parade described can be viewed on YouTube: https://tinyurl.com/sharparade

in the country's cultural and social progress," explained Maristela with an enthusiastic gleam in her eyes.

Next was a couple dressed in the most ostentatious outfits I'd ever seen in my life. "Wow! Who are they?"

"The master of the room and the flag carrier. She carries the flag of the samba school and twirls around from the beginning to the end of the Sambadrome. He dances around her, calling attention to her and to the flag. Their backs are never supposed to face one another, or they will lose points."

"I just can't get over how fantastic their costumes are!" I exclaimed. The lady who carried the school flag wore an ornate Crinoline gown, those enormous old-fashioned rigid skirts, with steel supports holding layers of dark purple, black and white fabric, with hundreds of black feathers at the bottom and hundreds of purple feathers at the back, finished with a bejeweled front cleavage. She wore a crown of matching colors and feathers and held the *Vai-Vai* black and white flag in her hand. The room-master wore a costume of the same colors and feathers, a white cape behind him and a matching crown on his head.

"Now comes Barbara's group, the *Baianas*, who are the African-Brazilian ladies from Bahia."

"Like the ladies we saw selling fried shrimp sandwiches at the Hippie market; those with the head turbans and white, layered skirts?"

"That's right. There's Barbara!" Everyone was very excited to see her on TV, and the rapid Portuguese chatter ensued. Barbara's look of pride was unmistakable.

"You look beautiful, Barbara," I said to her with a smile. Otavio translated and Barbara nodded at me with a small smile.

More groups continued to appear and parade, each group consisting of dozens of people wearing identical costumes, each paying homage to an important figure or idea related to the school's theme. The first allegoric car was slowly making its way ahead, the giant, white letters illuminating the school's name.

"You don't have to tell me what *that* is. It's the Garden of Eden. Look at that giant, silver snake! Those huge female statue heads look like they're glowing. And there's naked women under those trees!"

"Nudity is officially not allowed..." Isabel started explaining.

I cut her off excitedly, grabbing her wrist, "Look at that! A white Eve with a black Adam! No way! And Oh my God!" I paused, my hand jerking to cover my mouth. A moment lapsed before I could talk again, "They actually have God up there? Could it be?"

"Oh, it could," grinned Otavio, clearly entertained by my reaction.

"Oh, the Brazilians," I shook my head, grinning. "I can't believe what they come up with. A black Adam *and* a black God! Something like this would make a lot of people in America very angry."

Barbara asked Otavio something and he explained. Isabel said, "She wants to know what you said and if you like it or not."

"It's so awesome, *so* grandiose. Tell her I love it, OK?" She did, and Barbara seemed pleased. The camera view changed to bird's-eye view and we could see the entire Sambadrome. "Wow! I had no idea of the sheer enormity of the parade – and I was *there* yesterday!"

Isabel, Maristela, and Otavio smiled at me, then at one another. Barbara said something to Otavio.

"She's asking if you tried cheese bread before," he translated, motioning to a plate of golden, round puffs. I smiled at Barbara and tried one.

"Hmm. That's unusual."

"It's made of tapioca flour," explained Isabel.

"Nice," I said and took another. "Here, you have one."

"I'm not really hungry," she said, sipping her diet drink. "Besides, I'm hoping to lose a few more kilograms before the wedding next week."

"*Absurdo!*" exclaimed Maristela.

"I agree; it *is* absurd," I said, my eyes locking with Maristela's with mutual approval. "You look great. And you gotta eat something." She accepted the cheese bread, holding it in her palm, but not eating it. I grabbed another piece for myself.

"Who's *Maria Quitéria?*" I asked with my mouth full, reading the subtitles preceding the next section.

"A Brazilian Lieutenant who served in the Brazilian war of independence in 1822 dressed as a man," said Maristela.

"Awesome!" I clicked some of the details on my PA.

The band, consisting of more than a hundred members, marched backwards to a hidden enclosure in the middle of the Sambadrome in an organized formation. They were to stay there and play until the rest of the school passed. A few male singers in white suits stood near the band, repeatedly singing their school song with undiminished enthusiasm. I recognized many of them.

The second car was preceded by two large statues of golden horses and two of golden dragons. The top podium displayed an older lady in an ornate golden costume, a regal looking crown on her head and red rubies highlighting her fanciful garb. The subtitles on the screen described her as *Leopoldina, a Majestade Imperatriz*.

"That is the Austrian empress, Maria Leopoldina, who helped issue our declaration of independence from Portugal along with her husband, *Emperor Dom Pedro*," illuminated Maristela.

"Fantastic! This is like the best history lesson ever! And who's this *Titila a Bela?*" I asked, indicating the second podium, on which danced a lady in an ornate red ball gown with golden embellishments.

"She was Dom Pedro's mistress."

"That's awful!" I declared and searched it on the PA. "Ugh! Dom Pedro forced Leopoldina to accept his mistress as her lady-in-waiting, which is a sort servant," I explained. "Poor woman." I shook my head, thinking of the empress, married to a pig she probably didn't choose, and subjected to this kind of humiliation. I felt angry at the evil mistress, but then I thought better of it. The things women needed to do in order to survive were a lot different back then. Who says it was any better for the mistress?

Just when I was getting impatient to see us in the parade, a gorgeous single dancer appeared on the screen holding a pyrotechnic wand, the size of a dynamite stick. Fiery flames burst from its top and landed at her feet but did not break her confident long strides. Everyone in front of her backed away in a hurry. She twirled the stick in front her as she danced her fast, complicated samba moves.

"O-M-G! It's you!" I called excitedly and hugged Isabel's waist. She hugged me back. I couldn't stop my exclamations, "Look at those phenomenal legs! Look at you dance! How can you do those samba moves with those heels?! Girl, *you* are so hot! You're nothing short of perfection!" Isabel smiled gratefully, shyly hiding what I suspected was a bud of pride. I could tell that my comments touched Maristela and Otavio, too, and maybe even Barbara, who didn't understand what I was saying, but the tone was unmistakable.

"She's right, *querida*," nodded Otavio with a warm smile. "Best and hottest *passista* I ever saw!" I was glad he encouraged her. Maybe she would stop this crazy wedding dieting now. She was already thin and losing more weight would make her look emaciated. I hoped she didn't have an eating disorder.

"And that bejeweled two-piece suit with that fantastic crown - what an amazing costume!" I continued. "And what's up with the face mask? You never did explain it to me."

Isabel paused the parade, freezing her own image on the screen, a gorgeous beauty with wild hair escaping her glittering stone-studded crown, a round mask of pearls and white stones over her mouth, a silver chain attaching it to the back of her head, like the chains on her wrists. She asked Barbara something in Portuguese. Barbara started speaking, her look pensive and distant. We all listened respectfully, Maristela translating quietly.

"Isabel is dressed as the child slave, *Anastacia*. She was born nearly 300 years ago, to an African slave who was raped by her white master. She was the first black girl who was born with blue eyes in the whole of Brazil. All the white women were jealous of her exotic beauty, so they demanded the son of the man who raped her mother to put an iron mask on her face, the kind they put on slaves in mines to prevent them from swallowing diamonds. His son, whose advances Anastacia repeatedly rejected, raped the poor girl and put the horrid mask on her face, ordering it to be removed only once a day for feedings. Slowly, the metal seeped through her skin and into her bloodstream. A few years later, she died of metal poisoning."

I was enveloped with sorrow, my cheeks wet. Then I felt Otavio's hand in mine, jolting me back to the present. His eyes were comforting. My eyes rested on his, gripping his hand tightly.

Barbara extended a frayed, wallet-size photo of a statue of a black girl with sad blue eyes and an iron mask on her face. I reached for it with a trembling hand. I looked at it as Barbara continued her tale. "Anastacia is revered and remembered by many people, not only for her immense suffering, but for her ability to forgive her tormentors. We believe God saw this and granted her the ability to heal and perform miracles."

As I handed the photo back to Barbara, our eyes met. I nodded gravely, a single tear falling from my cheek onto my dress. We were all quiet for a few moments. Otavio looked grim. Isabel and Maristela shed a few tears.

Then Otavio pressed *play*, jolting us from our morbid reverie back to the joyous parade. It was jarring, but I was grateful for the distraction, which helped me let go of this horrifying story. The image of Isabel unfroze, and she lowered her mask, smiling victoriously as she danced and twirled the fireworks baton. I reached for a napkin and dried my cheeks, sniffling.

"Hey!" said Otavio with an encouraging smile, "it's our turn next!"

I smiled back and turned to Isabel, "You look so glamorous, you don't make me think of slavery or suffering at all."

"Oh no; that's not what my character is there for. I'm supposed to implore people not to stay silent as others suffer; to speak up and to defend the weak."

"And to demonstrate the power of the black woman!" Maristela added ardently. She and Isabel exchanged smiles.

"Well, you're doing an amazing job of it all," I declared. I held myself back from saying that if Tiago was angry at her for portraying *this* character, then he was just a jerk.

"That's our car!" stressed Otavio with a smile.

Our car's name was *Seeds of Liberty*. Atop it was *Princess Isabel*. I read from the PA: "Princess Isabel signed the *Golden Law* in 1888, bringing an end to hundreds of years of slavery."

The woman who posed as Princess Isabel on our car wore a white gown studded with golden embellishments, white gloves, and a golden crown. She, too, towered in a high feather-encircled podium, with two huge torsos of black men with blue eyes revolving underneath her, their right hands extended upward in a wave. I remembered seeing them last night. I understood their significance better now.

Suddenly, there I was on the big screen, along with Otavio and the rest of the paraders on our bamboo-laden shelf. Isabel, Maristela, and I shrieked while Otavio and Barbara smiled warmly at one another. The image on the big screen showed us dancing, our hands circling our bodies up high, back down, then sideways. Unfortunately, the camera only focused on us for about ten seconds before turning to bird's-eye view of our car. We weren't satisfied until Otavio rewound the recording a few times for us to watch again, laughing gaily at the fact we were on TV. Barbara was saying something to Otavio.

"What did she say?"

"She says our *quilombo* looks beautiful, and so do we," said Otavio.

"What is qui...?" I stumbled.

"The *quilombo* was the place built by the slaves who managed to escape. It was their own little place, built mostly of bamboo," Maristela explained.

"Oh, that explains all the bamboo. Man, I wish they showed us a while longer. You and I," I dramatically told Otavio, "we managed to run free and hide from our masters!" He smiled widely at my enthusiasm. "Tell Barbara she taught me how to samba well."

He did, and then translated her answer: "She says you danced very well."

I smiled widely at her. We continued watching, eating and chatting. More sections passed that celebrated famous women aid workers, novelists, composers, etc. I got tired and stopped asking about every specific group or costume. I felt as though the important ones had passed, and that I had more than enough material to write about. Barbara retired to the kitchen.

"So what do you think are our chances to win?" I asked after the parade was over.

"Not great," winced Isabel. "One of the cars knocked down one of the clocks."

"No!"

"Uh-huh.

"But everything else looked fantastic!"

"I think it did, too," said Maristela. "But we haven't seen the competing parades."

"True. Is it available on DVD?"

"Sure," said Isabel. "I'll get it for you." I noticed her eyes looked melancholy again.

"Don't worry," I rubbed her arm, "Tiago will call soon and all will be well again."

"That's right. He probably just has to figure out how to appease his clients, or deal with the fact he lost them," added Maristela.

"I think so, too," I nodded. "Now, what time is the bachelorette party on Friday?" I didn't dare ask if it was still on.

"It's at 8:00 o'clock in a hotel in this area. I'll text you the details. As a matter of fact, some of the girls are coming over soon. Do you want to stay and meet them? They're all dying to meet you!"

"Really? That's nice. But I think I prefer to do some more *research* tonight," I grinned.

"That's right," declared Otavio, who just came back from a smoke, putting his arm around me possessively. Isabel and Maristela smiled widely at us.

"Where's Barbara? I wanted to thank her."

"She's in the kitchen," he said and turned to lead the way.

"Did I tell you that Barbara used to skip meals and other necessities to afford her carnival costume?" asked Isabel. "She did that for years, like so many of Brazil's poor. In recent years, I started giving her an additional bonus out of my own money, just to pay for her costume. You should see the joy in her eyes every time. I'm thankful to Maristela for giving me the idea."

"What a lovely, sentimental custom," I beamed at Maristela.

She smiled widely at me. "Well, their salary is ridiculously low, about five hundred dollars a month. So I pay my maid and nanny more, help with medical expenses, etc. And when my favorite maid wanted to leave, I even sent her to college, in the condition that she stayed working for me, of course."

"Did she?"

"She did, but now she charges five times more!" everyone laughed. "It doesn't matter. She's like family." What a wonderful way to treat the help, I thought.

"Help me tell Barbara in Portuguese that the food was really good."

My attempt to speak her language seemed to please Barbara. "She's glad you liked it," said Otavio. He kissed Barbara, then Isabel and Maristela walked me and him to the door.

"It was so wonderful getting to know you, Raquel," Maristela said warmly as she kissed my cheeks.

"Thank you for coming," Isabel said to me. "It was wonderful watching the parade with you. You made me notice so many details and appreciate all over again how amazing and complex our carnival really is."

"And I'm so glad you let me experience it with you; the parade itself *and* the private tutorial about it," I said, nodding at Maristela with a smile to acknowledge her contributions. "It was a wonderful experience." I kissed Isabel's cheeks and smiled. I couldn't think of anything else I could do to cheer her up. Otavio kissed her cheeks and said a few more things in Portuguese.

Left alone, he hugged me from behind and whispered in my ear, "Ready for some more research?"

"Ready!"

CHAPTER 15

A few nights later, I was alone in my hotel room, working. I had a couple of hours before I had to leave for Isabel's bachelorette party. I opened my inbox then stared at it, immobile. An email from Ryan entitled *Your Parade Scoop* was waiting to be read. My livelihood, my future, and my career depended on the content of that email. I took a deep breath and clicked.

Dear Rachel, I really enjoyed watching you dance in the parade and seeing the photos and video of you dancing in the samba school rehearsal. It looks like our bet is guiding you to pursue some fun assignments and I just love seeing that. Unfortunately, I don't think that such a well-televised event as the carnival qualifies as a new scoop, as I'm sure you'll agree. I hope you will find a new scoop, proving yourself to be a valuable addition to the company. Sincerely, Ryan Brooks.

I sat still for a long time, tears trickling down my face. Tracing back my actions in Rio up to now made me feel like a fool. I'd accepted the first idea suggested to me and did very little to come up with anything else. And I had allowed myself to be cocky, feeling so sure I'd win that damn bet. The thought that Kevin was right had disgusted me, but there was no denying he was. At the next thought, I felt an anxious thud of a heartbeat. Did Ryan already know he was going to reject my scoop when he came to visit?

The memories were painful to recall. Ryan's joke about my costume; Ryan admonishing Chantal for endangering my scoop; me dancing with extra vigor as we passed the booth in which Ryan sat and watched us. And all along he must have known it was a losing story. And I couldn't really resent him for any of that, because, when I tried to see it from his perspective, his motivation became clear. He couldn't tell me when he saw me, standing at the doorway in my slave's costume, not when he knew it would ruin the entire experience for me, which it would have done. He let me have that one, brilliant night. How could I feel anything but grateful to him for that?

I sighed a deep sigh, my chest inflating, then deflating like an airless, flightless balloon, a balloon which once flew high and mighty, but was now deflated. How could I regain my strength and fly again?

My cell buzzed, rousing me out of my contemplation. I reached for it, seeing the time and the reminder that Isabel's party was in less than an hour. I hadn't even showered yet. Maybe Isabel and her friends could help me come up with something new? Or should I continue to surf the web, even though I'd found nothing so far? I not only felt conflicted, but also angry at myself for resting on my laurels since I'd gotten here. I wondered if Jess could help me configure the PA in a way that would optimize my research even more. Thankfully, I had looked for a story three whole weeks before I left home to fly here, so at least I could credit myself for that.

As I debated what to do, I automatically clicked on some of my saved links on the PA. Looking at *Travel Secrets'* web edition, I came face to face with Kevin's carnival photos. I smiled at the photo of me and Isabel dancing in the samba school, then of Otavio and me dancing at the parade, and then of Isabel holding her pyrotechnic baton. It didn't matter to me that the school only came in third place; to my mind, we were the best. I was pleased Chantal did not end up being a part of this merry piece. My article got many hits, Likes, and shares. Why couldn't *this* be the measure for winning the bet?

I broke down and started to sob. Who the hell was I kidding? There was nothing in this city that wasn't already online. This stupid bet was impossible. Goodbye job and goodbye career! It's all gone down the toilet. I'm only deluding myself further with the hope that Isabel's friends would be able to help me when even *she,* a travel agent who knew all there was to know inside and out, couldn't come up with anything new.

I inclined my head, my tongue feeling the salt of the tears. Some tour guides I'd got, I thought dismally, my negativity evaporating all the good with its poison. But the moment I tried to think of Otavio as a lousy tour guide, my head shot up. A thought that, up to now, was hanging at the outer periphery of my consciousness, had now boastfully declared itself: Otavio *did* get me something new!

I stopped crying as my head swam with the implications of my recollections: Otavio saying *no foreigners come to these motels,* which is why he brought me there, to *surprise me with something new.*

I seized my PA for a quick inquiry. A few minutes of surfing came up with absolutely no entries in English for Brazilian motels, with only one exception, which was a short review on a travel site, written by a Brazilian. *Oh my God! This is it!*

But can it be? Could I really pitch my boss a by-the-hour motel?

I started pacing the room with thoughts, ideas, and questions zooming through my mind. Time was short, and I had to act. I realized I still had Chantal, Kevin, and my spending budget at my disposal. And she must be feeling better by now, especially since she had these few days to rest. I grabbed my cell and called Kevin, asking him to meet me at my suite for a new assignment. I heard Chantal giggling in the background, so I asked him to pass the message along to her. I ignored his tone of annoyance, said I'd be waiting, and hung up.

I paced the room again, my body restless as my mind raced. I would spend my remaining few days in Rio collecting new information and new images that would make it impossible for Ryan to say no to me. I would use whatever resources I had to make it the best damn travel article series he'd seen in a long time.

They arrived together. Were those two having an affair, and if not, wouldn't covering motels make it easier for them to have one? Chantal sprawled on the couch and Kevin took the single sofa seat. Each of them held a cell phone at hand. I knew I had about five minutes before they lost focus.

"I have a new assignment for you both. I found a new scoop I'd like you both to shoot."

Chantal perked up, probably recalculating the income she thought she'd lost when Ryan found out she wasn't here to work.

Kevin's expression was amused. "What *new* scoop is it this time? The colorful steps of Santa Theresa? The new ice bar in Barra? Or perhaps a visit to Corcovado?" he mocked me, naming some of the most famous tour options in Rio.

"I guess I had that coming after thinking the carnival was going to cut it. But tell me this, have you ever been to a Brazilian motel?"

"Oh, so you finally got some?" he leered. "That's right, I forgot; Brazilians are nuts for big butts."

"Then they must be absolutely crazy for you," said Chantal. They exchanged self-satisfied, idiotic grins.

"Just answer the question!" I demanded impatiently.

He frowned. "I've been to plenty of hotels, pousadas, and even a couple of hostels in town, but no, I've never been to a motel. What's the big deal?"

Despite my aversion, I smiled widely at him. "I'll send you to one now and you'll see for yourself. And since it's my intended scoop, you both need to remember you're vowed to secrecy until the magazine publishes the articles."

"Don't worry; we won't say a word or share a photo without your OK," Chantal agreed grumpily.

"Great! I'll arrange everything ahead of time. It shouldn't take more than a couple of hours. Otavio will contact you with the arrangements."

"It could take a week for all I care, as long as I'm back on the payroll," smiled Chantal.

"This had better be good, Rach. For your sake, I think I'll Google it before we go."

"Be my guest. You won't find anything – in English, that is." I smiled victoriously. As they headed for the door, they'd already started Googling it, skeptical looks on their faces.

I called Otavio. "Hey," he said softly. "I thought you were leaving me all by myself tonight to party with the girls."

"Unfortunately, I am. But I need you for something else."

"Sure, anything."

"First, you need to know that Ryan has rejected my scoop."

"I'm sorry. That really sucks!"

"It sure does. But I remembered something you said about the motels, that no foreigners ever visit them."

"That's right."

"So I did a little research and discovered you're right. All internet entries about Brazilian motels are in Portuguese, which means they are indeed unknown in the U.S. In short, I'm going to go all out to convince Ryan they're the scoop of the century!"

"Alright!"

"This is where you come in. I'm sending Chantal and Kevin to cover Vênus motel's honeymoon package. I decided to photograph Chantal with a local male model in the fanciest setting I could find. I want to blow Ryan's mind, so he won't even think of saying no to this concept."

"Great idea. So what do you need from me?"

"I need you to reserve the motel's fanciest suite and all special add-ons, to find and pick up a local model, then pick up Chantal and Kevin and drive them all there. See if they need help at check-in. After that, you can leave. Kevin will pay for it all with his company card. How long do you think it'll take?"

"Let me make a few phone calls. Meanwhile, aren't you supposed to be getting ready for the bachelorette party?"

I looked at the time. "Oh my God, you're right. I have to run! But I want you to keep me posted all evening. Kevin and Chantal will be ready to go when they hear from you."

"Don't worry. My company has hired models in the past, and I'm sure I can get someone fast. The rest is easy. Go get ready and have a wonderful time tonight."

"I will. And Otavio, *thank you!*"

"Anytime," he said.

I hung up, feeling incredibly fortunate to have his help. I quickly got ready for the party, eager to ask the ladies more about the local motels.

* * *

"Wow, Raquel! Let me look at you!" said Isabel as she spun me around. "You look great! I love this teal dress. New?" I nodded. "Beautiful! Don't forget, we still have to get you a new dress for my wedding next week."

"Oh? I didn't know I was invited," I smiled as I kissed her cheeks.

"Of course you are! You'll still be here next Wednesday, won't you?"

"It's my last day here," I said, feeling a pang of sadness.

"Perfect. Why do you look so sad, querida? Is it because you're leaving, or is there another reason?"

"Ryan didn't accept the parade scoop."

"Oh no!" she frowned, looking concerned. Then she resolved, "We'll just have to find something else. We can even ask the girls tonight. All of them put together know everything there is to know about what's new in Rio."

"Thanks, dear. I'd love that," I replied. I didn't mention the motel idea, since I kept on going back and forth on it and I wanted a break from those thoughts. "Your dress is so lovely," I told Isabel. Her strapless cocktail dress was a light Champagne pink. The top was a luxurious, bedazzled satin, the bottom ruched layers of airy organza that fluffed around her at the slightest movement. She complimented this sweetheart look with her carefully stylized mane of curls, and contrasted it with four-inch, black pumps. She had a tiara over her head and a sash that said *noiva*, meaning bride. "You look absolutely wonderful, my friend."

"Thank you dear," she said with a glowing smile. We proceeded toward a large pack of women. "Introduce them slowly," I whispered in her ear, "and tell me what they do for a living. Maybe it'll make it easier to remember all their names."

"Oh, we don't want to talk about work today!" she said in a girly tone. We approached the gathering of very short, colorful cocktail dresses, tanned legs in slingback heels, flowing long hairdos, and tantalizing scents. "Girls, meet the famous Raquel!"

Squeals of excitement were heard. Isabel and I passed from one woman to the next, me wondering how on earth I would look after all those heavy-lipstick kisses.

"Raquel, this is Priscila, our party planner."

I smiled at the blue-eyed, red-headed woman wearing a dark blue mini dress. We traded kisses, then she handed me an elegant Champagne flute.

"Did you plan all this?" I asked, gesturing at the decorated room.

"Yes. This room is my work," she said proudly.

"Oh, are there more rooms?"

"Yes," answered a lean, muscular, petite woman in stilettos.

"Raquel, meet Maria Flor," said Isabel. "She's in charge of what you'd call the *after party*," they traded naughty smiles, piquing my curiosity. This was my first bachelorette party, but I had a pretty good idea what went on in American ones thanks to the movies and TV. I wondered if Brazilian ones were similar.

Maria Flor kissed my cheeks. Her little black dress was cut nearly down to her navel, the kind that made flat chested women like her able to display two tiny mounds in a very tempting way. The black makeup around her small, green eyes made them stand out in her pretty, round face. "*I* decorated the other room. We will move there later." If that room was anything like this one, we were in for a special treat, I thought.

This elegant party room had heart-shaped decals on the walls and red satin heart-shaped pillows on the sofas. Heart-shaped balloons and matching confetti were strewn about the room, and a big sign hung across the space from wall to wall, saying *"Cha de lingerie de Isabel."* I guessed it meant lingerie tea. But the brass serving-trolley under the sign was loaded with alcoholic beverages. I smiled. I supposed calling it a tea was just an expression. I eyed the dessert table hungrily. It had black and white chocolate balls, chocolate-covered strawberries, and an elegant, vanilla layer cake shaped like a wedding dress with *Felizes Para Sempre*, or happily ever after, written on it.

Open doors led to the wrap-around balcony, letting in the light evening breeze and the beautiful view of the lit stretch of beach. The balcony was filled with couches, lounge chairs, and some tables. A few TV screens flickered with scenes from a soap-opera.

"Well, *this* room looks unbelievable!" I declared, and everyone laughed gaily.

"Here," said Isabel and handed me a shot glass with a clear liquid in the bottom and a frothy, pinkish top layer.

"What is it?"

"Bico do Peito Manteiguinha."

"Which mean?"

"In English it is called Buttery Nipple," someone answered.

"Ah," I said, and downed it in one gulp. Everyone cheered. I smacked my lips. "That's awesome! It tastes like cake!" I got a few more smiles and giggles, and Isabel continued to introduce me to the women. There were lawyers, doctors, businesswomen, office managers. I said to Isabel, "I can't believe you have so many friends!"

"This is not even everybody. I have two, close, religious friends who would never dare set foot in a party like this. You will meet them at the wedding."

"Well, I think they're missing out."

"Alright," declared Isabel, wringing her hands decidedly, "it's time to start the makeup class."

CHAPTER 16

Everyone proceeded to sit in the professional makeup chairs that were strewn about the large room. A staff of makeup experts in black uniforms swarmed the floor. They placed square, light-bulb surrounded mirrors in front of each of us while making jubilant chit chat. The multiple televisions were quieted, and the volume of the music lowered. I was excited to get a professional makeup session for the first time in my life. I followed everyone's example, cleaning my face with the provided cleansing cream, then allowed someone to tie a white band around my face to hold the hair back. Isabel and I exchanged smiles. As I'd suspected, she still looked beautiful, even without makeup.

A plain woman with way too much makeup on stood in front of Isabel and explained the first step to us. Our rep began to demonstrate on Isabel's face. Isabel took advantages of her pauses to translate: "There are three types of concealers and two types of base, and we need them all." A few more reps now swarmed to each guest, concealing all blemishes and spots and banishing all dark circles off every face. My rep persisted in speaking to me, despite repeated explanations that I did not speak Portuguese. As she put makeup on me, I picked a warm puff pastry and a cocktail from the many passing trays of food and drink.

"Good?" asked Isabel with a smile as I wolfed down a savory snack.

"So good. I was starving!"

"Well, you're in the right place!" exclaimed a woman with short brown hair and a friendly smile. "This is the best catering company in town."

"Wow! A catering company, a makeup class, and a party planner? Not to mention this fancy hotel. It must have cost a fortune!" I said. Then I introduced myself, "Hi, I'm..." I was about to say 'Rachel,' but I caught myself and said, "Raquel."

"I'm Carolina."

"She's our banker," Isabel said.

"Tiago's family comes from old money. They own one of the biggest oil companies in Brazil," said a tall, slim woman, with a gorgeous red cocktail dress and expensive looking highlights. She freely dipped her appetizer in an accompanying sauce. "I'm Elisete," she added, then daintily bit her food.

"*Prazer*," I retorted. "What do you do, Elisete?"

"I'm a divorce lawyer."

"As Isabel probably told you, I'm a travel writer. Tell me, what's that you're eating there?"

"It's called *bolinho de bacalhau*, which means codfish balls. You mix the fish with some potato and eggs and cover it with bread crumbs. Then you deep fry them and you get these wonderful little balls."

"And that?" I gestured to her dip bowl.

"Olive oil and hot sauce. It makes them even tastier!"

"I better try it then." I smiled.

Elisete prompted a waiter to bring me a sampler tray of appetizers and proceeded to explain them to me. She ordered side plates of olive oil and mayonnaise, and I started to worry about calorie intake. As the makeup instructor struggled to continue applying our base, rouge, and the multistage eye makeup around our eating and chattering, I continued to sample appetizers and sip my drink. I praised the food but tried to pace myself. "How do you eat like this and stay so skinny?" I asked Elisete, watching as another mayo covered French Fry made its way into her mouth.

"It's easy!" she declared with a self-satisfied laugh. "Anyone can do it!"

"Stop getting on my nerves, Elisete!" said Maria Flor with an impatient scowl. "Tell her the truth."

"I would call it *internal* plastic surgery," said Carolina. I looked at her questioningly. "You know, some of us get surgeries to improve the outside of our bodies. My husband and I, for example, hate exercising, so we get a surgery each year. Last year I got my breasts done; this year I got my calves done, etc." I was shocked by the matter-of-fact way in which she described such private affairs. "Well, Elisete did an internal surgery to help with the outside of her body."

I looked at Elisete expectantly. She drew out the moment, nibbling the end of another catfish ball. "You see, Raquel, my mother is a chef. She cooks amazing delicacies. So, in order to keep on being able to eat her food and stay thin, me, my brothers, my sisters, and my dad, all got our stomachs... how do you say it?"

"Stapled?" I asked, aghast.

"Yes!" she retorted triumphantly. "Stapled!"

"Oh," was all I allowed myself to say, the alcohol making it easier to smear a fake smile on my face. "Now I understand." I did not dare tell a complete stranger and one of Isabel's friends that I thought she was absolutely insane to undergo a dangerous surgery just for the sake of satisfying her own gluttony.

"I can eat whatever I want. The secret is to keep it all in small doses," she smiled and ate another fry.

I turned to Carolina, hoping to change the subject, "You said that your husband had some plastic surgery, too?"

"Yes," Carolina smiled. "He had a chest muscle surgery... eh..." she searched for the words.

"He had a pectoral implant?" I asked incredulously.

"Yes. And he had calf implants, too. And we both get *lipo* once a year, you know, to suck out the fat."

"Liposuction?"

"Yes. It's so easy."

Someone else asked something in Portuguese. An argument broke out.

"What are they talking about?"

"This year's *Globeleza*, which is the *Globo* channel carnival muse." Isabel pointed at the TV screen. A young black girl, who could not be more than eighteen, was expertly dancing samba in crystal-studded heels, wearing nothing but a few scant colorful stripes of body paint, her firm body completely hairless. I was surprised to see something so provocative on the nation's most popular television channel.

The makeup expert said something about her and everybody seemed impressed. Isabel explained, "He said it took eleven hours to do her body makeup. Anyhow, every year *Globo* has girls from all over the country compete to win the great honor of being their carnival beauty, which is what *beleza* means. The girls are arguing whether or not she had plastic surgery. Some say she's all natural. Others say she had butt and calf implants and someone even said she had some ribs taken out."

"That's crazy!" I said, unable to accustom myself to the ease with which Brazilians spoke of and admitted to having undergone plastic surgery.

"That's nothing. One of the past winners of the *Miss Bumbum* contest," to my incredulous look, Carolina added, "yes, there is such a thing here as the Miss Butt contest. Anyway, her fat grafting surgery went wrong, and now her legs are rotting."

"Ugh!"

"Yes, it's very sad. She said she is being punished for her vanity. But we all want to look perfect, don't we?"

"I guess," I acceded, thinking that the word perfect could be very dangerous. "I didn't realize plastic surgeries were this popular here." I could not understand why anyone would get plastic surgery in a country that is so accepting of any body type or perceived physical flaws.

"Oh, everyone gets them," someone said.

"And complications like that are rare," said Elisete casually. "Yes, sometimes they look worse afterward, and sometimes there is damage, but not often."

"My little niece just had surgery last week," said Carolina.

"What?! Why would a kid need plastic surgery?"

"She's been teased her whole life because her ears stick out. So, for her tenth birthday, she asked to correct that. I think it's wonderful we have the option to save her from being teased for the rest of her life, wouldn't you agree?"

I nodded pensively. I suppose I could have been spared all the heartache of my youth had I asked my parents for a butt reduction when I was younger. I looked searchingly into the eyes reflected in the mirror. Despite it being my source of much self-criticism, it was also a source of self-love. Skinny or not, I loved the person I saw there, a person who was largely shaped by that harassment. A different body would have produced someone different, and, perhaps, not as likable; someone insensitive to others, like Chantal. I shuddered at the thought.

I looked at the carnival's muse again, trying to detect if the suspicions of surgery were correct or not. "I can't tell if she had surgery or not," I said. "She seems all natural to me."

"And who cares anyway?" smiled Isabel. "She looks amazing. I wish I had a body like hers!"

For a minute I thought I'd heard wrong. How could it be that the prettiest girl in the world coveted someone else's body? Then the sad truth hit me: no woman was ever completely pleased with her body. I placed both my palms on hers and said, looking deeply into her eyes, "You, my dear, are nothing short of gorgeous.

You're stunning! Here, have a snack," I said, nodding to the closest food tray.

"You're sweet, but I'm still trying to lose a bit more weight before the big day."

"You're crazy! I insist you pig out tonight, since *I* think you need to gain weight!"

She smiled and hesitantly reached for an appetizer. She ate it so quickly, I had no doubt she was starved. However, apart from a couple of bites of cake, I did not see her eating anything more after that.

The chatter stopped as the instructors demonstrated the many steps of the complicated eye makeup, which included no less than seven products. I was delighted to see how the dark green of my eyes popped in the black makeup frame, accentuated by the gold and copper shades I'd chosen. As I debated a shade of red for my lipstick, Isabel and Carolina worked on puffing my hair, saying it was too flat. When they were done, and my Burgundy lipstick applied, I looked very glamorous indeed. My straight hair was raised, and for once, it had some body to it. Pleased, I smiled at my reflection, then looked at Isabel. "Meet – Raquel!" I said and pouted haughtily. She grinned widely at me. "This was so much fun. I can't wait to see what comes next," I added.

Maristela showed up, hurrying to kiss Isabel. "Finally!" Isabel said.

"I'm so sorry I'm late. I got held up in court." She turned to me. "Raquel, you look wonderful!" she said as she kissed my cheeks. Her turquoise, Boho-Chic, maxi dress looked beautiful on her, complementing her blond hair, the beaded belt highlighting her waist.

"I'm afraid you're too late for the makeup class," said Isabel. "But you haven't missed the juicy part!" Everyone exchanged meaningful looks; some giggled.

A waiter brought a fresh plate of appetizers for Maristela, who ate heartily, explaining some of the finger foods to me with gusto, and insisting I try what I hadn't tasted yet. She was the only one who, like me, wasn't thin, which made me feel more comfortable around her.

My phone buzzed. "It's a message from Otavio," I told Maristela.

"Oh? Where is he?"

"He's actually in a motel nearby, doing a favor for me."

"Huh?" her brow furrowed. "You're sending him to a motel *without* you?"

I didn't think Maristela had realized how loudly she said that. All the heads curiously turned toward me, each woman waiting for an answer. My natural desire to keep intimate matters private was not going to withstand the night.

I breathed deeply, reminding myself that sex was viewed differently here, so the deriding comments a woman might expect for a physical relationship in America were unlikely imminent. "It's somewhat of a long story, but the gist of it is that I have to bring a brilliant scoop about Rio for my boss or I lose my job. I thought of using Brazilian motels, which are very different than American ones. I have no idea if my boss will accept it for our travel magazine, but it's the only thing I've got right now. I was actually thinking of asking everyone what they think about the idea, and if they have any further tips on motels themselves, or any other fresh leads."

An enthusiastic discussion arose in both English and Portuguese, bringing a smile to my face. Everyone had something to say and wanted to help. They were all surprised that their motels were not frequented by tourists and all thought it was a completely valid tip for a travel magazine. I was still unsure. The makeup class was ending, and the conversation was interrupted as everyone started to mingle.

"So Otavio is helping you? He is such a wonderful guy," Maristela said to me, sipping from a glass of white wine.

"He *is* great. Just a couple of hours ago, I asked him to take my annoying photographer and model to a motel, hire another model, make all the arrangements, and he's just texted it's all done. He even sent me a picture of Kevin's incredulous look when he first walked into the motel. Check it out, Isabel." I showed her the photo of the shocked expression on Kevin's face. She grinned. "I sent them to the best motel room and asked for the honeymoon special. He says they both refused to believe the low price!" Their shock made me feel more confident about the scoop. I wanted to squeeze Otavio with all my might for sending me that picture.

"OK, girls; time for cake!" declared Priscila.

We all posed for pictures near the cake, then took pictures of cutting and of eating it. More champagne was served. A man in uniform stood in the corner, waiting to be acknowledged. He was holding the biggest flower basket I'd ever seen. Maristela spotted him and alerted the others. Isabel stood on the tips of her toes to smell the gorgeous Stargazer lilies and pink roses. She smiled, and everyone sighed in longing. Tiago's name was mentioned numerous times. I buried my nose in the intoxicating smell of the Lilies. Isabel's eyes beamed with happiness as she laughed and rubbed some pollen off my nose. She pulled out a note from among the flowers' stems.

"He says he loves me, and that he hopes we have a lot of fun tonight *and...* that he paid for a room for each and every one of you for the night!" She kissed the note and threw her hands up in the air in victory. The women shrieked, jumped, and hugged each other in a girly fashion. I was so happy that Isabel and Tiago were able to make up and to forget their post-carnival feud.

"I've arranged it so when you get your memento bag from the party people at the end of the party, they'll give you your room key, too," explained Priscila. "The rooms are all on this floor, which is now all ours!" The ladies cheered.

Maria Flor announced with a mysterious look and a crooked smile, "And now, to the real *Cha de lingerie!* But first, a cigarette!" Most everyone headed to the balcony.

"You're sleeping over, right?" Isabel weaved one arm in mine, and the other with Maristela's as we sauntered in their direction.

"I don't have pajamas, or anything else I need."

"Don't worry. Tiago has taken care of all that," explained Priscila.

"Who is this mysterious man you're marrying, Isabel?"

She laughed. "You will meet him at the wedding. He is not mysterious at all, just very, very rich. He likes to show it, and *I* don't mind at all," she raised her eye brows coquettishly.

"Well, he sure knows how to make an impression."

We joined the others outside. Some of the ladies smoked, some drank, some clicked their cell phones. I leaned on the railing, breathing in the sea air. I was spellbound by the magnificent view of the brightly lit Leblon and Ipanema beaches. I smiled widely at Isabel.

"You seem to be doing better," she smiled back.

"How can anyone feel anything but wonder when faced with the beauty of Rio?" A few ladies nodded in agreement; some looked at me approvingly. "As for my scoop, I can't help but worry. Americans are more conservative than Brazilians or at least that's what they outwardly claim. The association between motels and extramarital affairs is pretty strong."

"That's a shame," said Maristela. "You know what my first association with motels is?"

"Tell me," I said with a smile, and we all sat down. I was eager to listen to her story.

"I think back to the time before I got married. As is the custom here, I still lived at home while dating my Leonides. It took a long time until we finally had enough money saved up to buy our own place."

"Excuse me, but why didn't you just rent an apartment?"

"Those can be very expensive and usually come with absolutely no furniture or appliances in them. So, what is a young, loving couple to do when they want to... you know, express their love to one another?" everyone smiled widely at this.

"Go to a motel," I said, realizing that motels meant freedom and independence here.

"You guessed it. We told our parents we were going to the beach," everyone smiled at this, "which was not a lie!" she added, wagging her finger and smiling widely. "But after a quick, romantic dip in the ocean, we'd head to a nearby motel to make love." Her eyes became distant as she remembered. Then she added, "I think that, to most of us, motels are a symbol of a few hours of freedom to be alone and connect with your loved one." Nods of confirmation abounded.

"For me, it was more about figuring out what sex was all about," said Maria Flor with a fiendish smile as she blew cigarette smoke out her mouth and nostrils. More nodding and some uttering of *sim* or *yes* were heard.

"Kind of like you were doing with Otavio, no?" grinned Carolina, garnering some laughter and murmurs of assent all around. I hoped they were not able to see me blush in the soft evening light.

"Puxa, Carolina. Raquel might not want to talk about it," Isabel came to my rescue.

"But I want to know what's he like in bed," someone said, garnering a few whistles.

Elisete came to my rescue. "What I want to know is where you shop for haute couture bargains in New York," she said.

"Yes!" said Carolina, which some of the ladies echoed.

I looked at Isabel and Elisete gratefully and started telling them what I knew. Everyone was excited to ask questions about New York, which most of them had visited. They were still eager for tips, especially on shopping. I ended up benefiting from their knowledge of New York just as much as they did from mine. They were particularly excited about the specialized shopping tours I mentioned.

They had all tried to help me come up with new scoop ideas. Despite our failure, I greatly appreciated their help. Everyone had promised to keep on thinking about it. Finally, it was time to move to the second party area.

CHAPTER 17

That large room was darker; the music louder and mostly American. In the center of the room were chairs draped with red satin covers. A modeling runway platform, decorated with black, satin lingerie, featured a stripper pole in its center. Behind it was a black curtain. The windows were covered with black lace, and dim, red lights replaced the regular ones. Instead of a champagne tower, the table exhibited a unique centerpiece tower of Italian leather high-heels, which I thought was very original and beautiful. I examined it up close. All the heels were from the most expensive Italian designers. I imagined just this tower had likely cost Tiago a small fortune. I snapped a few pictures of it. Near it lay a beautiful, red and black corset cake. The walls were decorated with black and red lingerie, garter belts, feather boas, etc.

The chairs were covered with fancy, red antimacassars, and were filling up fast. I sat on one of them. Waiters passed by with more food and drink trays. I opted for another Buttery Nipple. I was curious, so I looked up its ingredients online. It had Irish

Cream, Butterscotch, coffee liqueur, and vodka. No wonder it was so tasty. I found something funny about its description, and looked around me, wanting to share the joke.

"Hey!" I waved at Isabel, Maristela, and Carolina, who were coming back from the powder room. They came over and sat near me.

"Oh! I'll have another Buttery Nipple, too!" declared Carolina.

"Me too!" said Isabel.

"Me three!" joked Maristela. A waiter passed by and they each got one.

"Guess what they call it in English, other than Buttery Nipple."

"What?" all three of them asked.

"Sucking Cowboy!"

They all laughed. "Oh, what an image!" declared Isabel.

"To Isabel and Tiago!" Carolina raised her shot glass.

"Isabel and Tiago," Maristela and I echoed, and the four of us downed our shots.

"What's that table in the corner?" I pointed at a table covered with a black table-cloth and a long, white, scroll-like paper.

"A suggestion-box."

"Why do you need a suggestion box at a bachelorette party?"

"It's full of suggestions," said Carolina, lowering her forehead and raising her eyebrows meaningfully, "for the groom."

"Oh!" I grinned crookedly as I comprehended. "For example?"

Carolina brought the scroll over and read dramatically. "First, it says *I, Tiago Ferreira Monte da Silva, promise to* and then we insert our suggestion of what we think a man should promise when he marries a woman. For instance, someone wrote *kiss Isabel every day.*" This made Isabel smile.

Maristela read one, *"Tell her you love her every day."*

"Aww," we all said in unison.

"Give her flowers every week," Carolina continued.

"Give her an orgasm at least three times a week!" exclaimed a tipsy Maristela and we all laughed.

"Bathe her all over with soap and," continued Carolina, before Isabel cut her off.

"Thanks, but that's enough. I don't think I am brave enough to read the whole list at the moment." She whispered in my ear, "I don't know if I'll ever muster the courage to give it to Tiago. He only knows about the makeup class portion of the evening!" We grinned at one another.

Once it seemed like all the women were there, the music was turned down as Priscila went up on the little stage. The chatter stopped. "Ladies, the time has come to open presents."

"Presents?" I asked in alarm. "But I didn't bring anything!"

"Don't worry, querida!" Isabel assured me sweetly.

I promised myself I would buy her something before I got back to New York. A couple of party people carried a burgundy, velvet-covered stand with the gifts on top and placed it at Isabel's feet. She opened the first gift, which was a very small, black silk nightie, that garnered many oohs and aahs from the ladies. There was a faded picture of a little girl inside the gift box. Priscila, who now sat near us, explained, "Instead of writing a note, Carolina and I found this cute idea on the internet."

"We added photos of ourselves as little girls and Isabel has to guess who's it from!" exclaimed Carolina with a grin.

"Oh! What a sweet idea for a shower game!" I smiled. Isabel continued to open gifts and to guess who the giver was, getting it wrong half the time, to howls of laughter from the crowd. Most of the gifts were sexy lingerie items. The exception was a pair of ugly, boxy, granny-pants that was received with hysterical laughter.

"Now, I must know who gave me this." she looked at the picture and said immediately "I should have known it's from you, Carolina!"

"It's for when you're not in the mood!" Carolina exclaimed, and the room shuddered anew with waves of laughter. Other gifts were a coupon for a dancing pole lesson, garter belts, and furry, high-heeled slippers.

When all the gifts were opened, the party staff loaded them back onto the ornate bench and removed the gift wraps. More food and drink trays appeared. I chose a chocolate martini this time. The lights dimmed, and a few spotlights now focused on the runway. I wondered with excitement what would happen next. The incessant whispering and furtive smiles made me suspect it would be something big. I was just about to ask Carolina, when Maria Flor stepped out from behind the black curtain with a dramatic flair. She stood near a microphone, a long, black, silk robe covering everything but her black, crisscross, strappy platforms:

She signaled to one of the party people, and traditional, burlesque music came out of the speakers. The long, lazy notes of trumpet and trombone brought images of a French can-can dancer, slowly exposing her leg from under heavy petticoats with a tempting smile. Maria Flor's voice carried over the music: "As you all know, I was in charge of the more... naughty part of the evening," she said and exposed a well-toned, fishnet-stocking-covered leg out of her long robe. We whooped and clapped, photographing her with our cells. "So I decided that just having a stripper was not enough. Most of you gave Isabel beautiful, new lingerie that, I am sure, will make Tiago very happy," she paused for laughter. "In return, we wanted to give everyone something special to remember this night by. And so," she raised her voice, pointing to the two, heavily-draped garment racks that were wheeled on stage by two of the party people, "if you want to keep this fantastic, *imported* lingerie, you first have to... model it for us!"

Whistles and applauds flooded the room. All the party people stepped out of the room. The girls rushed to the stage to choose their costumes, their butts swaying to *Pussycat Dolls'* sultry song, *Buttons*. I, on the other hand, was rooted in place. *We* were going to be the runway models?! And these women, these respected businesswomen, wives, and mothers, were *happy* about it?! I, who'd never even stripped in front of a man in private, would now go up on stage to strip in front of all these women and their camera phones?!

I went up on stage and whispered in Isabel's ear. "I think I'll sit this part out."

"What?! No! You *have* to participate!"

The moment the others heard I was hesitant about performing, they all started cajoling me. Each of them was even willing to part with her choice of undergarments if it was going to help sway me. I chose one of the outfits offered to me, a cute corset whose matching underwear was *not* a thong, and they all laid off. The ladies chatted gaily as they undressed freely without any sign of embarrassment, drinking more Champagne or cocktails, helping one another zip up a figure-hugging corset or hook a tight bra. Isabel, who was getting undressed, noticed I wasn't following suit.

"Help me with the zipper," she said and turned. I unzipped her dress and watched her get completely naked, then put on her chosen lingerie. "Why aren't you getting ready, querida?"

"I'm still not sure I wanna do it," I explained, clutching the lingerie to my chest clumsily. "I'm not a model. I've never stripped in my life. Some people never do."

"Think of it as your opportunity," she smiled suggestively, then tightened a white satin robe around her body. She looked pensive for a moment, then asked, "Would it, how shall I put this... add to your motivation if Otavio were here?" I must have blushed, because she laughed gently. "Why don't you imagine him sitting in the crowd?" I didn't respond. "Seriously, Raquel, you're a mystery to me. A part of you can be so shy, but another part is very bold. It isn't easy to see how they're both part of the same person." I thought about this. "I don't see how the shy Raquel made the bet with her boss or danced in front of our samba school masters." Maybe, I thought, that's because I'm not really Raquel, but still a shy wallflower named Rachel. The name Raquel, in my mind, belonged to a more daring, open, sexy woman.

"I don't know," I replied. "I have lots of ideas, but I don't always act on them. I bet Ryan because it was either that or be fired. Then I danced in front of the masters because I needed the scoop, and because Jess asked me a simple, but insightful, question: *What's the worst that could happen?"*

"Your friend sounds very wise. What would she say about you stripping tonight?"

"She'd tell me to do it if I felt like it, and not let my fears hold me back."

"So, what are you afraid of? We're all friends here. No one is going to make fun of you."

"I don't know... I guess I'm afraid I won't know how to do it. I have no idea how to dance like that, you know, touch myself suggestively, not to mention use a pole!"

"Oh, please! Most of us don't know how to use it. It's there mainly for Maria Flor to show off what she's learned in her pole dancing lessons. As for the other part, once the music starts, the sexy beat will be your guide. Listen, why don't you change, just in case you feel like stripping after you see us do it? And if you don't, it's an opportunity missed, but not the end of the world. OK?"

"You're right," I smiled. "But I'll go change in the ladies' room."

"OK," she smiled and shook her head.

Yes, I thought, I'm too shy to completely undress in front of a bunch of strangers. Maybe if I had known the others for more than a one evening, I wouldn't have minded. After all, they were all very amiable and, unlike some caustic American women I knew, did not seem judgmental at all.

Thinking about these women's sweetness made me feel bad at the judgmental way I'd just looked at them, the way I'd learned from my mother over the years. I'd scanned their naked bodies like *The Terminator*, noting any little flaw, like cellulite or acne, in some sort of an inventory in my mind, all to be filed in the feel-good folder called *Nobody's Perfect*. Isabel didn't qualify in that file, and I was relieved I didn't resent her for it, like I resented Chantal.

I got into the tiny stall and changed. I quickly regretted not changing with everyone else when I saw how hard it was to get into the tight corset by myself. Never having worn one, I did not foresee this difficulty. After much struggle, I managed to tie it at the front and wiggle it backwards. When I was done I tried to draw in a deep breath of relief, but the restrictive garment didn't allow it. How could corsets ever have been the norm?

I wore the red, satin robe over my lingerie, then fixed the old-fashioned back seam on my skin-toned stockings. I sneaked a furtive look at my image in the full-length bathroom mirror. Here, under the harsh lights, it wasn't easy to not be critical. The big, puffy hair looked slutty, not glamorous, the makeup looked whorish, not fancy, the lingerie seemed raunchy, not seductive. Besides, I was only here for work; wasn't I?

I have news for you, I told myself. You're here to have fun, too, and to grow as a person beyond what's safe and comfortable. This makeup is for going out dancing in dark places, and so is this hairdo, so stop fussing about what you look like under florescent lights. As for the lingerie... well, they're all going to strip, so you can do it, too. And, if not, no harm done.

I got back to the room with nothing but undergarments and a silk robe separating me from the others. I felt exposed. But they all wore nothing but silk robes and heels. I sat near Isabel, who hugged me in a gleeful, tipsy state. I responded in kind, and we downed some penis-shaped jello shots with a hoot, the rest of the girls joining us.

The inevitable striptease song, *You Can Leave Your Hat On,* sang by *Joe Cocker,* began, the seductive notes of the trumpet and saxophone interspersed with the Andante tempo of the piano. Maria Flor was the first to strip. I thought her brave, then quickly realized she was quite at home and itching to perform. The black fedora atop her raven black hair was the perfect prop. She lowered her negligee inch by inch. Then she tossed it in the air and exposed a black thong, which was connected to black, silk stockings with a garter belt. She spun around, her gold boa around the stripper pole. I guessed her black bra was an add-a-size bra, since she looked bustier than before.

Her striptease garnered much applause thanks to the variety of tricks and poses she performed with the stripper pole. Those classes sure were useful, I concluded with some jealousy as she clung upside down from the top of the pole with her legs, threw them apart in a perfect, straight spread, and sexily let her body slide down the pole. We all took dozens of photos with our cell phones. We cheered enthusiastically when she finished. She bowed, then kissed her own shoulder and said to the microphone, her head flung high in a winning attitude, *"Eu sou poderosa!"*

"What does that mean?"

"It means *I am powerful!"* grinned Maristela.

"I like it," I smiled in return, repeating the words in my head. Maria Flor was not the only one who announced her own strength with a self-kiss that evening. Some of the others posed their undergarments more quickly, walking the cat walk and pausing at its end, being photographed by friends' cell phones, then turning back to descend from the stage. Their simpler routines put me more at ease. Others danced to entire songs. Perhaps, with the right song, I could strip, too? But what song? Isabel explained to me I could choose a song from the playlist backstage or use a song on my cell, which could be connected to the sound system. I started scrolling through my music app.

Most of the ladies had tattoos, including the lawyers and bankers. They posed in chemises, baby dolls, and camisoles of all colors and patterns, to which they added feather boas, satin gloves, and stockings. Some trod carefully on their platform heels, others plowed forward with confidence. Each tried to let her inner model shine through. Some dared using the pole while others didn't, each ending up without her negligee and with a smile plastered on her face. Most women seemed very much in touch with their femininity, which I greatly admired. I recalled the women I knew back home and thought most of them were too tense and worried about correctness to allow their femininity to show. I sipped some champagne, reminding myself not to drink too much lest I slip and fall on the catwalk.

Maristela modeled a white, satin, wedding night peignoir, with matching burlesque corset and garter belts, and black feather boa. She danced to the sound of *Etta James's I Just Want to Make Love to You.* I adored the way the song pit low notes versus high notes, raunchy versus vestal. The sweeping melody begged for a swaying of the hips, the tenor sax's call luring you in. Maristela's dance was playful, with subtle hints of sexiness shining through. She smiled most of the dance, and I sensed that I'd do the same once I got on stage, projecting my friendly side to the ladies, with just a bit of sensuality. Whatever else I had in me would stay carefully guarded within.

Carolina was the last to strip besides me and Isabel, who was supposed to go on last. Her choice of *Shania Twain's* song, *Honey, I'm Home!* brought a smile to my face. As the violins accompanied the beat of the drums in Shania's signature, upbeat, country and pop mixture, Carolina went on stage, still in her sienna cocktail dress. The smile on my face grew, then turned to laughter at Carolina's comedy act. She tossed her dress and exposed an old-fashioned, white Pantaloon with a frilly bottom and matching white camisole. She gyrated her Pantalooned butt in front of us, hugging the pole and doing some lewd, ridiculous movements. She grabbed her pantaloons, then took them off with one pull and tossed them to us, exposing the ugliest, striped granny-pants I'd ever seen. Then she took off the camisole, and we saw that the huge undies were held in place by matching suspenders, which she snapped, then pretended it hurt her breasts, which were perked up by a horrid, matching bra. The laughter shook the room. I wiped a few laughter-tears away. Carolina continued with hilarious pole tricks, and I saw many hands shaking with laughter as we all tried to capture her show on camera. I wondered why she was a banker and not a stand-up comic. We clapped and whistled for a few minutes afterwards.

When the laughter died down, it occurred to me that, despite the many surgeries that gave her perky butt and boobs, Carolina was the least feminine of the bunch. She was cute, but not seductive at all. I suppose self-deprecating humor decreased anyone's sexuality, and the wall many people erected with their jokes had the same effect. Nevertheless, we all lauded her, one of the girls even wolf-whistling loudly.

Isabel loaned me her mirror to fix my makeup. Now it came down to me and her.

"I know it's your big day, but maybe I could go last?" I asked hopefully.

"Well, it's not my big day yet," she replied while texting, "so, sure. If it means you're going to do it, I don't mind not going last."

"Thanks. You're the best!"

"Wait 'till you see the surprise I've arranged for you," Isabel said.

"What surprise? No, no! What if I'm not comfortable with it?" A few horrifying scenarios ran though my head, the worst being having to perform with one of the strippers Maria Flor had mentioned earlier.

"Stop worrying. It's nothing bad." And with this she headed for the stage, a mysterious smile on her face.

Damn! Curiosity was eating me up. But I had no time to dwell on it. The husky, soulful voice of *Ella Fitzgerald* flooded the auditorium with the song *Whatever Lola Wants*. I smiled and focused on Isabel's performance.

She wore a white, heart-shaped corset with black, lacy frills at the top, underscoring her deep cleavage, tiny waist, and mocha-colored skin. She wore a white thong, white satin gloves, and black feather boa and heels. The lyrics may as well have been changed to *Whatever Isabel wants, Isabel gets*. Her rare feminine beauty, a combination of her joyous demeanor and natural beauty resulted in a sexy dance reminiscent of an ostentatious feline. She swayed around the pole slinkily, avoiding some of the lewd movements normally used, simply using it to highlight her limber physique, using the twinkling of the piano and the blasting of the trumpets to her advantage. She was a delight to watch.

She finished her dance with one hand on her hips, the other gloved hand stretched to us as its forefinger commanded us to *give in*. We all clapped enthusiastically. Maria Flor and Carolina climbed on stage and put the bridal sash and tiara back on her. Maria Flor stood at the microphone, saying, "Now wasn't that fun, ladies?! But before we move on, we have one more performance from our shy American reporter, Raquel!" Everyone clapped and cheered as I proceeded toward the stage. Isabel whispered something to Maria Flor, who added, "She'll be ready in just a few minutes. Meanwhile, keep on drinking, everybody."

CHAPTER 18

Everyone got off the stage. I crossed paths with Isabel on my way backstage. "If you don't like my surprise," she said, "remember, I meant well, and don't be angry at me, OK?" I frowned. "And don't worry about saying goodnight to me afterwards either," she said and smiled mysteriously. I was more mystified than ever. It sounded like Isabel had invited Otavio over, but that would mean she broke her ardent rule of *absolutely no men allowed* at her bachelorette party. "Now go! I know you'll do great! Remember what Jess asked: *What's the worst that could happen?*"

The thought of Jess made me smile. She would never do something like this in a million years. But, if she were here, she would tell me to ignore my fears and just strut my stuff and have fun with it. I wanted so to go out there and do just that, but then the truth that lay beneath my excuses struck me. Exposing my body was not the issue, because that's not what stripping was about. It was about seduction. And I just didn't see myself as a seductress. I sighed, wishing I knew how to smash through these barriers.

Behind the black curtain, I connected my cell phone to the stage sound. I put on the strappy, black heels Isabel had loaned me. I decided to think of this strip more casually, and if I smiled a lot, like Maristela did, that would have to be OK. And, perhaps, I'd think of Otavio occasionally, as motivation.

"Hey," said a husky voice behind me. A pair of strong arms hugged me from behind, and a pair of lips stroked my earlobe.

"Oh my God!" I turned to face Otavio, his arms circling me in an intimate hug. "What are you doing here? Isabel said it's women only!"

"Well, it was *she* who texted me. She said you didn't think you could do the striptease that all the other girls were doing at her party and wondered if I could help." He hovered very near me, his lips close to mine. "I was all done with the motel errand, and I was sitting in my apartment, missing you, so I came over to see what I could do. I'm so glad I did. You look fantastic!"

He ran his hands over my robe. I dropped my head back to answer his hungry kiss. My satin clad body trembled at his touch. The amiable reserve with which I'd conducted myself with the women was a jarring contrast to what was becoming my natural state with Otavio. With him, I not only wanted to open up, I wanted to surrender completely to his demanding masculinity, to feel the kind of abandon I'd never allowed myself to feel before we'd met.

Then I noted something was different about him tonight. I felt he was getting aroused much more quickly than usual. His cocky self-control was replaced by the kind of urgency I'd never personally seen in a man before. I realized that something about my appearance tonight was making him lose control.

This realization felt like I'd flipped a switch. Up to that point, whenever he told me how sexy and beautiful I was, I smiled, but only half believed it. After all, he was an experienced, sexy man trying to make me feel better about myself. But now, seeing the uncontrollable passion *I* had ignited within *him* was akin to seeing the proof of those claims. I thought, I *am* beautiful. I *am* sexy. I *am* powerful. And with that, all the doubts and hesitation were gone.

I tore myself from him. We were both breathless. "If it weren't my turn to strip, we could have done it right here, right now," I said smilelessly, not letting him know if I was joking or not. I looked at him wantonly, then grinned crookedly at the torment on his face. I sashayed away, the feeling of sexual power flooding me. I slowly fixed my lipstick, enjoying the sight of Otavio's mouth hanging open. I grabbed the red feather boa from the rack, looked at him one last time from under lowered lashes, pressed play on the title of my chosen song, and emerged from behind the curtain.

The sultry drums and finger snapping notes of *Fever*, sung by *Peggy Lee*, flooded the large party room. The ladies clapped and whistled. The stage-lights made it nearly impossible to see the crowd, but it no longer mattered to me if I saw them or not. From the corner of my eye, I could see Otavio walking toward the dimly lit back of the room. I was pleased he didn't sit with the girls, so his whole attention would be focused on me. Ha! As if he had any choice in the matter!

My every move was motivated by the desire to show Otavio the hold I had just realized I had over him. Singing and snapping my gloved fingers, I slowly strutted forward on the stage. I danced around, gyrating my hips, flinging my hands up high, then slowly running my palms over the red satin robe and down my body. I imagined Otavio's heart-rate increasing as I slowly undid my belt and took off the robe, exposing the red corset with black-lace trim and matching underwear. I flung the robe to the enthusiastic ladies. I continued to dance, letting my red satin gloved hands trail all over the luxurious feel of my corset, then on my arms, then down to my stockings. As I moved the soft and airy boa around myself in a serpentine manner, I hoped Otavio was suffering. I wanted *him*, the master of seduction, to feel the kind of torment I felt when he made my hands shake and brought me to ecstasy.

I put my boa around the pole and held on to it with one hand, throwing my head backwards. Then I circled the pole seductively. The cheering got louder. I used a pause in the music to look in Otavio's direction alluringly and snap the strap of my garter belt. The whooping got louder, and I imagined Otavio's jaw dropping even lower. Finally, I threw the feathers at the girls and ended my show by striking a confident pose, kissing my shoulder and saying into the microphone, *"Eu sou poderosa!"*

The applause was intense, the whistles deafening. Isabel extended my red satin robe, belt, and boa back to me. "I can't believe you didn't want to do it. You were sensational!" She said and hugged me.

"Thanks. Your surprise *really* helped," I said, looking into her eyes meaningfully.

"I'm so glad. I was worried you'd be angry I invited him."

"I don't think I've ever been more grateful to anyone in my entire life."

She beamed. Before she could come forward to hug me, Maria Flor dragged her up on stage, where dozens of black and white balloons and glittering confetti fell from the ceiling. Three very muscular, tattooed men in skimpy, silvery shorts swept in and started dancing with Isabel to the merry sounds of *It's Raining Men*, sung by the *Weather Girls*. Everyone cheered and started to dance, the ladies gyrating with the men, some in their robes, some in their undergarments. I was relieved they'd be too distracted to notice Otavio, or to see us leave.

Not bothering to put the robe on quite yet, I sashayed slowly to where he was sitting, my eyes not leaving his. He didn't get up. When I got there, I towered close to him, planting my stocking-covered leg on the chair nearest him with confidence.

"Torture," he said, his fingers trailing down my silk-covered leg, "pure torture. I thought I was coming here to help you. Instead, I created a tormentor."

When he looked at me, I half-smiled at him. "I'm *sure* you'll be pleased you did."

This was too much for him. He got up resolutely, bent me backwards and kissed me ravenously. I felt aroused, ecstatic, breathless. "Let's get out of here," he said throatily. "There's a motel not too far off."

I breathed hotly on his earlobe as I explained, "Let's go out and get my favor bag. In it is a key to one of the suits in this hotel, all paid for, courtesy of the bride and groom to be."

"That's great," he said, hugging me from behind as we progressed toward the exit, his head buried in my puffy hair, "because I lied. I was going to have my way with you in the back stairs. No way I could have waited 'til the motel."

I was pleased. Every word and gesture of Otavio's reaffirmed the birth of my inner goddess. I put on my robe while he got my things, along with a purple, velvet, favor bag, upon which was embroidered *Despedida de solteira de Isabel,* or *Isabel's Bachelorette Party.* As Otavio led the way to our room, I brought the bag near my lips and furtively kissed it. This will be a party I will never forget.

When we got into the suite, Otavio, for the first time since we'd met, displayed the kind of urgency often seen in modern movies and TV shows. He, who always took his time to progress and made sure to pleasure me first, now frenziedly undid his pants. I was extremely aroused, too, and was eager to succumb. But every action of his disclosed that the tables were now turned, and, drunk on my new power, I had to make him wait, in answer to all the times he'd made me wait.

I arrested his wrists in my hands. "You said waiting is better, didn't you? You said torture makes the climax more pleasurable."

"I said orgasm," he said from between clenched teeth. "Afraid to say it?"

"Orgasm," I said, then flung him backwards onto the bed.

This time was very different. I no longer lay on my back passively, letting him do all the work while reassuring me about my appeal. My newfound confidence let me do the things I'd previously only fantasized about doing but was always too shy to do. I focused on pleasuring him for a change, instead of on my own pleasure. I kissed his whole body, taking my time, advancing slowly from one body part to the next. When I climbed atop him, I was determined to be the one guiding the rhythm of our bodies, watching for Otavio's reactions, for once, instead of closing my eyes. I felt proud when I made him plead to hurry up, until he finally cried out in ecstasy, as did I.

He closed his eyes and seemed to drift away, but I wasn't ready for sleep yet. I gently turned away from him, lay on my side, and looked at the white squares of light the moon had created as it shone through the wooden blinds. I'd never felt more content in my entire life. I recalled hearing people say that it's impossible for a person to change, but I'd succeeded in doing just that tonight. I vowed to myself then and there never to let anyone take away or tamper with this glowing feeling of achievement, nor let it ebb away only to be forgotten.

"What are you smiling about?" asked Otavio, spooning me from behind, his head buried in my hair. My smile grew.

"It felt good to do the striptease; it was empowering."

"No kidding. I hardly recognized you." He pulled his body away. "I'm going out for a smoke. Come out with me."

He stood on the balcony, smoking. Nothing but the moonlight illuminated his naked body, his curls, his sexy mouth. I thought he looked beautiful, and I was happy he kept his body natural, sans tattoos or piercing. I wore my satin robe over my naked body. I felt like marking this unique night by having one, single cigarette. I lit it and inhaled. Otavio seemed surprised and baffled. I leaned over the balcony rail, taking in the beauty of the lit, deserted beach. "I don't get it. One moment, Isabel's calling me because you needed help. A moment later, you go on stage, looking in control, sexy, daring. I've never seen anybody change so fast. And now you're smoking?! I mean, where's the sweet, shy girl I met last week?"

I looked out into the dark expanse of night as I explained it to him, and to myself. "She was always here, letting her bashful side take control, and her doubts slow her down, if not stop her. She believed in the hurtful words of others, that her fuller figure was a curse, a hump, a growth. But then she came here, to this wonderful country, where curves are welcome, where people get surgeries to look like her, and where she met you, the hot guy who was 'out of her league', but still interested. She nodded and smiled when you said she was beautiful, but, deep down inside, she didn't believe you. Not until you looked at her the way you did tonight."

He put his arms around me from behind, kissing my neck. "Why? How did I look at you?"

"You looked at me like you were seeing me for the first time, but you didn't just see me, you saw the feminine entity within me," I grinned and turned to face him, squeezing my body to his, "a sexy, erotic temptress." I could sense I was arousing him again. I decided not to tell him it was his lack of control that most helped me over the hump, since I didn't want him to see it as an offense to his masculinity, which I did not. I knew that the smartest thing now was to let him take control and just surrender to his wishes. And it felt wonderful.

CHAPTER 19

It was Saturday morning, after a very exciting, sleepless night. Otavio went to catch a nap at his apartment, saying he couldn't possibly nap next to me. I grinned flirtatiously but felt relieved. I had some work to do and the thought of a nap sounded like heaven, but both were things which would be much more easily achieved without him around. Now that I was here, alone in my suite, I couldn't stop the inevitable thought: we only had five more days together. I felt a pinch in my heart which scared me. One thing must not happen no matter what: I could *not* let myself fall in love with a guy who lived a continent away. Besides, who knew how many tourists he'd dated before me. I could be just a fling for him, just as he probably suspected he was to me.

I also knew it was time to face facts. I was probably *not* going to find a different scoop than the motels in the short time I had remaining here. I had to charge ahead with what I did have, or all was lost.

I sent an email to Kevin, detailing which motels he, Chantal, and the model should go to next. I sent them to the fanciest places Isabel's friends had recommended. I noted the theme rooms or specialty add-ons I'd like them to use. Then, just to be on the safe side, I texted him to read the email. He texted back *Props for the motels find.* This was a rare show of respect from Kevin. I smirked and moved on.

I jotted down the remaining things I really wanted to do before leaving Rio. I had to go up to Corcovado, the tallest mountain in the city, where the huge statue of Christ stood. Of course, a couple more ocean dips were a must, and Isabel wanted to take me shopping. The wedding was on Wednesday, my last day in town. I was pleased I'd be able to see Isabel's friends again, not to mention finally meet Tiago. And what about special things to do with Otavio? Should I go out of my way to visit the favela he grew up in?

I decided against it. I told myself the short time I had left in Rio should be devoted to those activities I most wanted to do and to some more motel research. But deep inside I knew I had another reason. Meeting Otavio's family and seeing his hometown might bring me even closer to him; that was something I feared. It was going to be hard enough to say goodbye at it was.

I gave one last, loving look to Copacabana beach, which was quickly filling with people, and marched myself over to bed. The moment my body hit the sheets, I was asleep.

I woke up a few hours later to the sound of my phone buzzing repeatedly. Damn! Why didn't I put it on the night dresser next to me? I dragged myself to the living room, where the midday sun brightly illuminated the room. I growled and shaded my eyes. I plopped on the couch with my cell. Isabel had sent me numerous texts, three of which included videos of my strip. I knew Otavio would love to see them, and so did I, as a matter-of-fact. She wanted to know if I was up for going shopping this afternoon, and what my plans were for the rest of my time here. Other texts were from Jess and Ashley, who were both dying to talk to me and hear what was happening in Rio.

I ordered coffee and a large brunch. Then Isabel and I made plans to go shopping. After a reviving shower, I called my girlfriends and told them all about the bachelorette party. Ashley was shocked. She couldn't believe any of it, the way I behaved abroad, the lewd scoop I thought of pitching Mr. Brooks, and the kind of guy I was sleeping with.

"But... he has no staying potential," she lamented, her forehead wrinkled as she struggled to understand my motives. I knew she was miles away from being able to understand the reasons for my romance with Otavio. Ashley lived her own life *by the book*. She'd only date American guys who seemed like they were *husband material.* This meant, of course, a steady job with good income and potential for promotion, which usually implied a background of higher education. To her, the words *stability* and *security* connoted love. My affair with a lowly travel guide, as she referred to Otavio, a guy who lived on a different continent, was completely useless in her point of view, and therefore, salacious and injudicious.

"Oh, come on Ash!" objected Jess. "Just look at his picture!" She showed Ashley the photo of Otavio at the beach that I had sent her.

"Yes, yes. I can see the physical appeal. But sex without the possibility of marriage has no appeal to me." Jess rolled her eyes, and I just listened respectfully, wishing the coffee would get here already. "I'm only thinking of you," continued Ashley. "What if you develop real feelings for each other? Wouldn't it be really difficult for you to leave him? And did you think about *him?* What if he falls in love with *you?*"

This struck a nerve. I knew I was rapidly developing feelings for Otavio, and I suspected the same was true for him. When she was finally done listing her objections, I answered, my eyes looking gravely at hers. "Whatever happens, whatever heartache ensues, whatever long, lonely nights I have to look forward to back home, I wouldn't trade my time here with him for anything in the world."

Ashley looked uneasy, probably because I never really voiced a reply to her objections before. Jess beamed proudly. "He's that good, huh?" She grinned lasciviously.

"He is," I answered seriously. Jess, who probably expected me to blush in embarrassment, looked surprised. "But that's not why. He helped me realize myself and come out of my shell. And don't try to diminish it by making a dirty joke." I pointed a warning finger at her, and her mouth closed. Then I added with a coquettish smile, "Unless you don't want to see my striptease video."

"Oh, no! No jokes, I promise!"

"Ashley, if you're uncomfortable, Jess and I can watch it without you. But I'd love it if you see it." I wanted to shock Ashley out of her cozy existence. Maybe I could do her some good and show her what other ways were possible in this world.

"First, you're going to pitch a by-the-hour motel to our boss and now this?"

"C'mon, Ash! Have some fun," urged Jess. "Send the video already!" I did, and we watched it simultaneously. Seeing myself strip felt naughty, shocking - and wonderful. Jess paused the video, looking at me and saying, "Who's that? I... I don't recognize her at all!" I grinned at her, and she grinned back, sealing our unspoken understanding. She, too, thought it was awesome. Ashley looked pale but said nothing.

We finished watching it. "What did you say at the end?" asked Jess excitedly.

"It means *I am powerful!*"

"That's so cool!"

"Yes. It's something they do here. I love it; it's so self-affirming!"

"Well, here's something else to affirm yourself: I *loved* it. You were great! It's hard to believe you had all this inside you all along, but you did." I smiled proudly. "But I'm afraid you've shocked Ash."

"Nonsense," Ashley said and shrugged with a slight pout. "It's just that I'm all about women's lib, the fight for our rights, and for complete equality. *This* represents the opposite of all that, and the same goes for your scoop. I'm sorry, Rachel. You know I love you, right?"

"Of course," I smiled back at her worried expression. I didn't express the question on my mind: why was celebrating your femininity considered anti-feminist?

"Speaking about scoops," Jess said, changing the subject, "I had a crazy idea. You all know how the press has tried to find the truth about Chantal's background for years, finding nothing?"

"Sure," I said. "Ashley told us that once."

"Uh-huh," nodded Ashley. "Not one reporter found one scrap of information."

"Maybe what was needed was a tech expert, not a reporter," said Jess mysteriously.

"What are saying?" Ashley asked excitedly.

"Well, I've spent the evening with Lon the other day and her perfume ad was online. I said I couldn't believe our boss was dating such a bitch. Lon was interested to hear some more about her."

"Oh, Jess; you didn't!" I said.

"Oh, I did," she smiled.

"You're nuts! This woman could end up marrying my boss, and then where will I be?"

"Nonsense! Lon told me neither he nor Ryan ever intend on getting married." Ashley and I both looked at her with puzzlement. "Lon's against it and he says Ryan's is, too. Anyway, I told him she's treating you poorly and I just happened to mention her mysterious past. So we started digging. It was so much fun; we were like detectives. Anyhoo, Lon and I found some awesome dirt on a certain Chantal Neuchâtel, or should I say Shirley-Ann Newcastle?!" She grinned.

"No way!" I said in disbelief.

"I knew that Neuchâtel sounded fake!" exclaimed Ashley victoriously.

"We were so high with our sleuthing success, we tore each other's clothes off. It was so hot!" Jess grinned broadly.

"And on their first date, too!" said Ashley in admonishment.

"What can I say?" Jess shrugged. "Seeing the smooth way he used the PA for two hours was all this gal needed to get her juices going." Jess and I giggled.

"But it was not very wise," continued Ashley. "How are you going to work together? And if something goes wrong and you break up, he's the boss's right-hand man, and you're way down on the totem pole."

"Let it go, Ashley. It was a chance worth taking. He's the hottest guy I know."

I smiled widely at this, recalling Lon's nerdy look. I was happy Jess was able to look past his appearance. "What else did you two uncover?"

"Yes, anyway, afterwards I felt I could confide in him about her breast surgery."

"You weren't supposed to tell anyone about that!"

"Ryan's already told him about it. Lon said he's already warned Ryan about 'that gold digger,' but that Ryan thinks he's wrong and is giving her another chance." We shook our heads in unison, and Jess rolled her eyes. "I know; go figure. Turns out little Shirley-Ann is poor white trash." I wrinkled my nose in distaste at the expression. "She changed her name and moved around a lot to keep her indigent past hidden. Until now, that is." Jess grinned victoriously. She waited. "Well. Say something."

"I kinda feel sorry for her now."

"Aw! C'mon Rach! Don't you see? *This* is the scoop! You can sell this to any tabloid and make a fortune! Then none of the other stuff is going to matter. Your job, your boss, the bullies – it'd all be irrelevant. Let Shirley-Ann Newcastle set you free!" She said the last bit with a southern accent and an evangelical manner. Ashley and I smiled.

"I'm sure Rachel wants nothing to do with tabloids," said Ashley. "I wonder if there is a way to use it at *Travel Secrets*, but it's not even travel related."

"Hmm... maybe it'd fit as a medical tourism piece?" I pondered. "After all, they're cheaper here, so for the price of the surgery in the U.S., a person can also get a trip to South America."

"But most people already know that," said Ashley.

"I got it!" Jess said excitedly. "You can call it *Photoshopped in Real Life.*"

"I don't think so. Besides, using Chantal's background scoop just feels wrong," I said, shaking my head.

"Do you think she would hesitate for a minute to spill the beans if she had something on you?"

"I'm sure she wouldn't. But then again, she's not me, and I'm definitely not her."

"Grr, you're so stubborn. Ashley? Wouldn't you agree this scoop is Rachel's ticket to freedom?"

"Sorry, Jess, but I'm with Rachel on this one," said Ashley, her eyes locking with mine. We exchanged understanding smiles.

"Why am I not surprised?"

"It's one thing hating her when you think she grew up like pampered royalty. But she must have suffered quite a bit," I said.

"So? Does that entitle her to be such a bitch? This after all the horrible things she did and said to you, Rachel!"

"You're right. It doesn't excuse them." But it did shed light on her twisted personality, I thought. "Still, I'm not going to reveal this."

"Oh, c'mon Rach. You have the power to destroy her career once and for all! Remember what she said to you? Screw or be screwed."

"I remember. And I was furious – then. And now... I don't know. When I heard this, the anger just petered out. I can see how she struggled for a better life, just like the rest of us."

"You," she shook her head and shrugged, "the queen of empathy."

"Which is what you love most about me," I smiled with a beseeching head tilt.

"Of course it is," Ashley smiled.

"Yes, of course," Jess reluctantly concurred. "It's just that *I'm* still mad at her for the way she treated you."

"Listen, how about this? Neither of you says a word about this, and I'll have the upper hand next time something happens with Chantal. OK?"

"My lips are sealed," promised Jess. "It's Ms. Chatterbox here you have to worry about."

Ashley elbowed Jess, who grinned in return. "I can keep a secret!" Neither of us said anything. "Really, I can! I swear!" The resounding silence continued. "You guys; I'm serious! This is Rachel's secret and I vow not to say anything. Say something!"

"Oh, OK," smiled Jess.

"We believe you," I smiled reassuringly.

"Is it finally time for *my* news?" asked Ashley in impatient eagerness.

"Of course! What news?" I asked.

"Well, it's not exactly news. Just something Lon told Jess. He suspects that Ryan is not a big fan of my tours for women-only column because there isn't a parallel market for men-only tours."

"Well, there are. They're called gay tours," Jess joked and we both grinned.

"I thought of making the exact crack when he and I talked about it, but luckily I held my tongue," continued Ashley. "I did say women who travel alone need protection from men and that's the main reason behind the emergence of this market. Ryan says that's fine, but that the interest isn't big enough to justify the existence of my column. Then he added that he's interested in finding the male equivalent. I don't see it myself, but Ryan seriously thinks there's an untapped market there for men-only tours. Anyway, he hasn't done anything about it so far, or about my column, which is doing worse than ever. I had tried to get him to send me abroad for an exclusive women-only tour in France, which is sure to boost readership. You should have seen his face when I pitched that."

"Happy?" I asked hopefully.

"Not at all. He said he can't spend this kind of money on a failing column. I don't know, I feel so stuck. Got any ideas?"

"Not really, but I'll definitely think about it."

"OK," she answered forlornly.

"Don't worry. Between the three of us, and with Lon's help, we'll think of something," I smiled. "Tell us more about this trip to France you've pitched. You know I've always wanted to go there, but it's just so darn expensive."

Ashley's face lit. "It is an amazing, high-end tour. You get to stay in a chateau with the crème de la crème of French socialites. You get to visit their ancient, family vineyards. There's luxury meals, area tours, and even a traditional masquerade ball!"

"Wow! That sounds fantastic! But how can they have a ball with no men?"

"That's the brilliant part. The day tours are for women-only, but in the evenings there is a choice between a women-only activity and a mixed company one."

"Fabulous! I want to go there, too!" I declared, and Ashley smiled at me warmly. "Listen, I've got a good distraction for you. I'm permanently changing my name to Raquel!"

"What?!" they both exclaimed simultaneously.

"Yes. That name changed me, and I vowed to myself to remain true to that change."

"Oh," Jess shook her head worriedly, "that's not going to be easy to do at work."

"No, it isn't. But I plan to give those jerks a good fight when I get back."

"And we'll stand by you!" promised Ashley resolutely. Jess nodded in agreement.

"Thanks, darlings. Now, before I dash away, tell me more about your date with Lon." Jess filled me in on the lovely evening she'd had with Lon, saying how happy she was that Ryan Brooks allowed dating within the office.

"You're asking for trouble dating him," Ashley persisted. "What if something goes wrong, and then he's too uncomfortable working with you? Who's going to leave? I assure you, it's not Lon!"

"I'm sure they're both mature enough to continue working together if they separate. Besides, what if it *does* work?" I asked. "What if he's her soul mate?"

"She doesn't even believe there is such a thing," argued Ashley, "so why mention it? She says she doesn't want to get married or have any kids. So she's just going to date him forever? I really don't get it." Jess's different life ambitions were incomprehensible to Ashley, who was sure wanting a family and a career were the only sensible choices.

"OK, OK, I have to go before you guys have me married and pregnant," joked Jess. "And if I don't talk to you before then, have fun until we see you Thursday, Rach. Oh, I mean Raquel. Oh boy. That's not going to be easy to get used to."

"I still can't believe you're going to your tour guide's wedding. You two just met last week!" said Ashley.

"Isabel and I got really close, really fast. In fact, most of the people I met were very warm and sweet-natured. It's hard to explain the Brazilian mentality. You've just gotta come for a visit." I shrugged with a smile. "OK dears, I don't know if I'll get a chance to talk, but I'll send a ton of pics. And now, sink or swim; it's time for me to pitch Ryan the motels." He's *got* to accept it, I thought. Otherwise, I won't be able to continue working with my two best friends.

"Good luck, baby!" Jess said, locking her eyes with mine. "You've got this!"

"Yes, good luck! And let us know the moment you hear back from him!" added Ashley.

"I will."

We hung up. Over breakfast I'd composed my email to Ryan:

Dear Ryan, since we last met, I've uncovered something huge — and brand new: Local by-the-hour motels, currently frequented only by Brazilians, made up of lavish, but inexpensive rooms, many with private Jacuzzis, saunas, pools, etc., some with fantastic themed rooms. I've already begun outlining a series entitled Rio motels: Affordable Luxury in the Marvelous City. I'd like your OK to move forward. Yours, Rachel Moore.

For a moment, I was tempted to sign Raquel Moore. I grinned at the idea, but thought it was too soon, so I did not change the signature. I added a few motel links to the draft. Now I needed to choose a few photos to add to the email. I looked through the various photos I'd accumulated from the past few motel visits with Otavio, wondering which ones were appropriate to email Ryan. Of course, I only picked photos with neither of us in them, just of the rooms themselves. I chose one from the red Japanese room with the enormous silk fans spread on the wall, and oriental statues framing red couches with satin pillows. I chose another from the Amazon room, which I dubbed the Tiki room, decorated with fake coconuts, palm trees, and a small waterfall, which ran directly into the Jacuzzi. The third photo was of the first motel room we visited, the one I took from the living room just before we left, which included the Jacuzzi, the pool, and the sun rising over the Atlantic. I added those to the draft, which I now considered ready.

I got up and paced, wondering whether or not Ryan would deem the scoop too risqué for Travel Secrets. But trying to second-guess what he'd say was nerve wracking. I sat back down, breathed deeply, and pressed Send. The screen showed the familiar notice *your message has been sent.*

* * *

After eating, I met Isabel at the entrance to my hotel.

"I've emailed Ryan about the motels," I said nervously.

"Good," she smiled, petting my arm. "He'll love it, I'm sure."

"Thanks. Should we take the Metro downtown?"

"The Metro is perfect when the traffic is heavy, which isn't the case right now. You'd miss the view. Let's take a taxi."

City center during midday reminded me of New York, which made my heart ache with longing for the first time since I'd left home. Skyscrapers shaded the crowded streets. People in business clothes rushed to and fro. Corner kiosks were full of diners, the scents of fried food and cigarette smoke filling the air.

When we reached her mom's store, the peppy, young salesgirls immediately rushed to fawn over Isabel, their words pouring out quickly. Isabel said a few things, pointing at me. The chatter continued. Some of them left to continue helping the other customers. Isabel and a few of the girls continued speaking. When they left, she explained, "they're going to get you some dresses to try on for the wedding from our store next door. This one is for bathing suits and lingerie. Now go on, pick something." I looked around and picked a couple of bikinis I liked. "The girls will get you the size you need."

The two bikinis arrived in medium size. "Oh no," I told Isabel, who was trying on bathing suits in the stall next door. "This will barely cover anything."

"Try it on. Remember the new and daring you from last night. She'd try them on!"

I tried one on. Most of my breasts were exposed. As for my butt, it was less than thirty percent covered. No, no, no! These three triangles of fabric were way too small. This was very frustrating, since medium usually fit me in America. This didn't make holding on to last night's feeling of success any easier.

"I need the next size up."

"Are you sure? Show me!"

"Eh, no!"

"C'mon! I bet it looks great."

I extended both bikinis over the stall to the girl. "Even if I did somehow dare to wear them in Rio, there is no way on earth I'll wear them anywhere else. Please, tell her to bring the large."

From their conversation, I gathered that large was *grande*. For some reason, *grande* sounded like *huge* to me. Before I knew it, the sales girls yelled to one another, trying to get the stock girls on the second floor to check inventory and throw down the same bottoms in a size which now, thanks to their idiotic system, all the other customers in the store had the privilege of knowing. No one seemed to notice or care, but I did. It should be my business alone! I hugged my naked body tightly, fuming with anger and embarrassment. When the *huge* bikinis were delivered to me above the stall's door, I tried on my favorite one, but I still didn't think it covered quite enough skin. But if this was large, and I wasn't that heavy, what size did the significantly overweight women on the beach wear? But then I recalled that they weren't trying to cover their butts at all.

"Can I at least see one?" implored Isabel. I opened the door a crack. "Why do you look so upset?"

"How would you feel if someone yelled grande about your butt?"

"You shouldn't mind. That's how they always do things here, and no one cares."

"Well, I think it's rude. Whatever happened to discretion? Anyhow, It's still too small. I'm thinking of getting a larger bottom."

"A *grande-grande*?"

"You're kidding me!"

"What?" she smiled.

"You see, to me that just sounds like *huge-huge*. I don't know whether to laugh or cry." But my goofy side won, and I grinned. "Huge-huge; that's hilarious."

"I'm glad you're able to joke about it. Now, come on, show me."

I opened the door and her eyes lit. "Raquel! You look fantastic!" The pricey bathing suit was indeed beautiful, and it hung perfectly on me. The layers of light greens, purples, blues, and off-whites were interspersed with delicate shadow impressions of palm trees and waves, all blending together harmoniously. "Turn around!" ordered Isabel. I obeyed. "C'mon! You know you look great!"

"I won't deny it," I smiled. It just took some getting used to being so exposed in public. I didn't tell Isabel I was buying this suit mainly for Brazil. Who knew where I'd go next, and if I'd ever use it again. But I'd be a sexy, beach diva for the next five days with Otavio. And that's all I wanted.

"You have to get the matching bag and beach shirt, too!"

"The cover-up? I can't afford it. Don't even mention the bag."

"Nonsense. You'll get my discount, which is 100%," she grinned.

"Absolutely not!"

"OK, how about a 50% discount and you declare it a business expense?"

"Now you're talking!" I laughed. I knew I wouldn't claim it, but the price was no longer out of my reach.

I looked at myself in the mirror, sporting the sensational matching cover-up and beach bag, wearing bejeweled, wedge flip-flops. Isabel placed a large pair of sunglasses on my nose and declared, "You look like a model!" We laughed.

After that, we proceeded to the neighboring formal dress and business attire store, also owned by Isabel's parents. I got a gown with matching heels and accessories, for which Isabel insisted on paying, saying that Tiago promised to pay for everything that had to do with the wedding. Then came a few more dresses and work clothes, all brighter and more colorful than anything I'd ever owned, all of which I paid for. When we were finally done shopping, we were two very happy, very exhausted girls.

We sat in a corner kiosk. Men in white aprons worked behind a counter. The shelves behind them were laden with piles and piles of fresh bananas, avocados, mangoes, pineapples, melons, and oranges. The fresh, fruit juice was reviving on such a hot day. I ate my ham and cheese pastry, and Isabel nibbled on hers. "You know," I said, "you could make a career out of your fashion sense and knowledge."

"What for? I saw how stressed your job made you numerous times; when you had to find a story, or deal with your nasty co-workers, or worry about the opinion of your boss. And you know what I thought all along? - I was relieved that after I marry Tiago I'll never have to work again. I will be set for life without having to lift a finger, which is all I ever wanted. No offense, OK?"

"None taken," I assured her, and went back to eating and people watching. If she was only interested in material welfare and safety, I knew there was no point in talking about the thrill or the self-fulfillment a career could provide. And, whatever happens at the end, this trip will still have been a thrill that I wouldn't have missed for anything in the world.

"I think I'll call the company and get one of the drivers to drive us up to Corcovado mountain," said Isabel.

"What about Otavio? He can't still be asleep!" It was past 4:00 PM.

"You tired him out," she smiled coquettishly.

"I'm going to text him." *Awake yet? Isabel and I want to go with you to Corcovado.*

His reply came in quickly. *Sorry, querida, but I'm in the favela now. My mother will need my help understanding legal stuff when Maristela arrives later.*

That sucks.

I know. I'll come over later, if it's not too late.

I told Isabel what he said. "Do you think I should go see him there?"

"To be honest, even though we provide favela tours, neither I nor most of my friends have ever visited a favela. The question is, why do you want to go there?"

"I'm not sure why myself," I said, silencing my previous inner objections to visiting Otavio's hometown. "All I know is I have this need to see where he comes from. As a writer, I feel as if this is an opportunity to learn about the other facet of Brazil, the one most tourists know nothing about. Also, Maristela's work intrigues me."

"You know, Otavio's mom is the head plaintiff in their gentrification case."

"Wow! Now I'm even more interested. Do you think Maristela would take me with her today?"

"There's only one way to find out." Isabel began to text.

"Wait! We should probably ask Otavio first. He might not appreciate a surprise visit."

"But what if he says no?"

"Then I'll have to respect his wishes."

"Maristela says she's leaving her office in a few minutes to go there. It's a quick walk from here."

"Tell her to wait for us. First, let me text him."

"Fine. I'll sext Tiago in the meanwhile," she said in a naughty look and winked at me.

I smiled, then focused on phrasing my request to visit. *I have to see you, so please don't say no. I'm hitching a ride over there with Maristela. OK?*

I waited for his reply for what seemed like an eternity, wondering if perhaps he was too embarrassed to show me the humble place where he grew up or for me to meet his family. Perhaps he didn't want his family to meet me for some reason. Finally, all he said was *OK.*

CHAPTER 20

Isabel took a taxi home with all our shopping bags, promising to drop mine off at my hotel. Maristela was as supportive as Isabel had been when I told her about emailing Ryan the scoop. "Your courage in betting your job is so inspiring," she said, smiling warmly at me. I smiled gratefully, feeling warmed inside by her comment. She continued navigating rush-hour traffic toward the west side of town. "If this didn't have to be signed today, I would have gone tomorrow afternoon, when the roads are emptier, but this document cannot wait."

"Tell me more about this lawsuit."

"Well, some big developers have been dying to get their hands on the prime piece of land this enormous favela occupies. I represent the tenants who insist they're not moving out of their homes, regardless of whether their measly compensation offer ever goes up. It's been their home for generations, and they're here to stay. But the people who want the land are well connected with our government officials, many of whom are as corrupt as your biggest crime lord."

"That sounds awful."

"It is, and it keeps on getting worse. But as long as there are people like Otavio's mom who are willing to stand up to bullies, the world is going to be OK."

"And people like you, too," I smiled.

"Oh, I don't know," she smiled modestly. "I'm only doing my job."

We chatted some more as she drove on the busy highway. After a while, she got off the main road and said, "Now you're going to see the difference between the city and the favela."

The main road turned into a pothole ridden asphalt. Then the asphalt disappeared, making way for the worst dirt road I had ever seen. I reached for the grab handle to steady myself against all the jumping as Maristela navigated the road and the huge, muddy puddles. We saw a van stuck in the mud in a nearby street.

"The rainy season is early this year," she remarked.

"This is bullshit! A little more rain and people won't be able to leave their houses!"

"No one outside the favela cares about their flooded roads or flooded houses. When the brilliant planners and workers finally made this dirt road, they compressed it on a higher level than the houses, so *if* the water drains, it drains into the houses! But they don't care. The only thing they do care about is that this road is marked as paved in the city plans."

"What?!"

"They took our tax money, claimed they paved the road, then pocketed the money instead. It happens all the time in Brazil. Even when a job is done, it usually costs five times more than it should have cost. Everyone likes a bribe, right?" The bitterness in her voice was so palpable, it made me swallow the bad taste in my mouth.

"I had heard that there was a lot of corruption here, but I didn't know what it meant," I said quietly.

I noticed she was headed dead center to an especially large puddle, avoiding the soft, gooey mud on the sides of the road, which looked like the ideal trap for a car. "Say a little prayer," she winked and drove inside. There was no way of knowing how deep or soft it was in the center. When we made it through, I let out the breath I hadn't realized I was holding. "And you have to vote for these assholes, too. If you don't vote, you get a fine or end up in jail!"

"No Way!"

We kept on driving in silence, passing one clay brick house after another. Most were unpainted and had no windows, just gaping holes in a rain-beaten facade. The few that were painted had long ago ceased to be white. I saw a woman sweeping the water out of her flooded house with a coarse broom. We passed some kids wearing school uniforms, the lucky ones wearing rain boots.

"What's that sign?" I asked, pointing to a plaque someone placed in the middle of a large, mucky puddle.

"It says *our taxes go here.*" We passed the puddle and Maristela read the other side of the sign, *"Our friend will come back soon to ask for votes.* This is part of some demonstrations that are taking place around the entire country."

"Cool!"

"I was more hopeful when they began, but so far they haven't achieved anything except to break some store windows, steal things, start fires, and get arrested."

"I wouldn't exactly call those achievements either," I muttered. "But maybe they'll be heard by the good politicians nonetheless?"

"I wouldn't count on it. The good ones are few and must oppose so much corruption that by the time they're done dealing with one thing, five others pop up. To the people, it seems like nothing is getting done, while expenses and taxes go up."

We rode together in companionable silence until we reached the heart of the favela. Here, houses were very crowded and stacked one atop another. Most of the exteriors were very dirty and graffiti-laced. Some blessed souls painted their houses in gay yellows, pinks, and blues, bringing beauty to this dilapidated place. Crooked electricity poles held enormous tangles of wires. Long stretches of uneven, narrow stairs reached all around us, extending up to the mountains and down to the south side like tentacles. One set of stairs seemed better maintained and was sprayed with colorful graffiti. A few kids sat on them, making rhythmic sounds with sticks on empty plastic pails while two men danced *Capoeira* to the beat. I knew that slaves had come up with Capoeira, a dance designed to hide their practice of martial arts from the authorities.

Maristela parked the car and nodded toward the men. My heart started beating faster when I realized one of them was Otavio. I was transfixed. "Have you seen Capoeira before?" she asked.

"Only on TV. Hey, would you mind taking a video for me?" I handed her my phone. "I want to focus on this."

"Sure."

We walked toward the group and watched from up close. This martial arts technique was more like a dance. It was full of various spins and kicks flying over and under your opponent, but never touching him. I was a little worried, fearing Otavio might get hurt, but no such thing happened. I realized both men knew what they were doing. I took in the agile, speeding image of Otavio as he avoided a kick, then extended his leg to kick his opponent, who avoided it gracefully, too. Then his eyes met mine, and he raised his hand in the air. The drumming stopped, and the dance was over.

Just for a moment, I saw an intimate look of recognition in his eyes. Then he walked over to us with his usual swagger and half-smile on his face. He traded kisses with Maristela, saying, "Excuse my being so sweaty. I haven't been exercising a lot lately, so I jumped at the opportunity."

"No problem," she smiled, still holding on to my cell, patiently waiting for us to greet one another.

"Raquel," was all he said to me as he kissed my cheeks. My senses overflowed. His deep voice, his musky scent, the rugged hands he laid on my arms as he kissed me. I also sensed the different way he acted around me now that we were in his hometown. Not that I expected him to betray our intimacy or to let others know about our affair. Still, after all that had happened between us, it hurt to be treated as nothing more than a friend.

"Cigarette?" he offered me the box and winked. At least here was an admission of our intimacy.

"No, thank you," I shook my head with a smile.

"You don't smoke, do you, Raquel?" asked Maristela.

"I don't."

"Only on special occasions," Otavio whispered in my ear, sending shivers down my spine.

Maristela spoke to the kids, then handed them an assortment of candy. They gathered around her happily, reaching up to catch the goods. Most of the kids were shoeless and shirtless.

"I wish I had something to give them too," I murmured.

"Here," said Maristela, and proffered me a bag of candy. The kids surrounded us both now, and I smiled at their happy little faces as they accumulated more sweets.

Otavio watched me as he lit a cigarette. Then he said a few things to the kids, and we were off. He started for one of the staircases with one of the little girls on his shoulders, a beautiful thing with huge brown eyes, disheveled golden-brown curls, and full, pink lips. We started climbing, the little girl chatting happily in Portuguese, three other boys following us.

"These are my sisters' kids," he explained. The kids giggled and looked at me with curiosity. "They think me speaking English is hilarious," he added, and the kids laughed again. I smiled at them. We passed a few stray cats, a skinny, apathetic dog, and some clucking chickens. The call of a confused rooster was heard, even though it was twilight. It mingled with the sounds of motorcycles, cars, and the chatter of the kids, Otavio, and Maristela. The musty air smelled of fried food, beer, cigarettes, and marijuana. I noticed many eyes on me, some hidden behind walls and corners, some staring openly; some were friendly, some were suspicious. I was a stranger here.

Otavio flung the little one off his shoulders as we entered his mother's home. The kids rushed in, yelling. A woman yelled back at them, then came out waddling toward us. She appeared to be about thirty, heavily pregnant, and looked like a mix between Otavio and the little girl. Otavio introduced us. "Raquel, this is my sister, Ana Maria. I've explained to them you're my friend from America and that you don't speak Portuguese."

I nodded, feeling the sting of the word *friend.* At least he didn't introduce me as a client.

"*Prazer*," she nodded, and we traded kisses. Then she greeted Maristela and invited us to sit. I sat between Maristela and Otavio, taking in the simple surroundings: The shabby, gray, wool couch, the yellow, plastic flowers in a chipped glass vase, the faded, wooden crucifix on the peeling wall. The TV was on, and the kids alternated between watching the animated show and glancing at me from time to time.

A tray of drinks sat on the scuffed, wooden coffee table. "Raquel, have you tried *Mate* before?" asked Maristela. "It's our version of iced-tea."

I took a sip and grimaced. It was the strongest tea I had ever had in my life! The kids giggled happily, and I smiled back at them.

An older woman showed up, wearing a small, silver crucifix on her neck. Even though she seemed only about fifty years old, her hair was already completely white. I recalled Otavio's father was an abusive man and wondered if the old scars near her right eye were a result of his powerful fist. Her thin, wiry body was slightly hunched forward, but she moved energetically. Her brown eyes seemed observant and hard. Otavio rose quickly, and I followed suit.

"Raquel, this is my mother, Ana Angelica."

"Prazer," I nodded, and stepped forward to kiss her. She accepted my kisses coldly without reciprocating.

"*Bem vinda*," she said.

"That means *welcome*," explained Maristela with a wide smile, getting up to kiss and hug her. Ana Angelica's eyes lit up, and she smiled and hugged Maristela eagerly. Since she was clearly capable of warm emotions, that could only have meant one thing: she had a problem with me. I breathed in deeply. It was going to be a long evening.

She ordered the kids to do something, and they swiftly disappeared, then reappeared with a variety of plates full of snack food. She looked at me smilelessly and said something, gesturing to the food. "My mom is inviting you to eat," Otavio explained. His mom sat on a side chair. Everyone started eating and chatting.

"Raquel, please excuse us while we talk amongst ourselves," said Maristela.

"Of course."

Maristela spoke for a while, then there was some back and forth with the others. I snacked on the food, watching cartoons with the kids. The boys ate chips and Japanese peanuts and bugged one another occasionally, but no one bothered Pilar, the little girl. I smiled whenever one of them cleaned her face or tickled her. When the three of them started a fight, Otavio stopped them with one word. I wondered exactly how much help he was to his mom and sister, and how often he visited.

I thought of checking my phone, but decided against it, just in case Otavio's mom considered it rude. I sneaked a peak at Pilar and winked. She grinned at me and generously gave me her doll. I looked at the ragged Barbie, pondering the far reaches of this skinny, blond, American doll. I smiled at Pilar and nodded gratefully. Maybe I could send her a new doll when I got home? I pretended to brush Barbie's hair. Before I knew it, I was presented with a tiny toy brush and a child's brush. I let the pleased Pilar brush the Barbie's frayed hair as I worked on untangling her soft curls. Otavio, his sister, and Maristela looked at me approvingly, but his mom remained expressionless.

After a while, Otavio followed his mom to the kitchen. In response to their exchange, which got louder by the minute, Ana Maria increased the TV's volume. Her own head was buried in her phone. Maristela clasped her hand on mine and smiled in invitation. "Let's go out to the balcony before we miss the sunset, OK?"

"Sure!"

We went out to the crumbling, makeshift balcony.

"Wow!" I exclaimed with surprise and joy. "This favela is huge! And it's got the best view ever; better than the rich people have in *Zona Sul!*" Zona Sul was the south side, an area which extended from Copacabana to Leblon and beyond. From where we stood, we could see the ocean, the pointy mountaintops called Two Brothers Hill, and most of the densely-built buildings of the south side. The yellow, orange, and red sunset blazed over the metropolis as if it were on fire.

"This is the view the developers are coveting," she said meaningfully. I nodded in understanding.

"Maristela, did I make a mistake in coming? I have a feeling my presence is making Ana Angelica mad, but I don't know why."

"I want to explain something to you before Otavio comes searching for us. Ever since he left the favela, he has hardly ever dated local girls. Once he told Isabel and me that they don't really understand him, and I get that. He's worked hard to improve himself, learn a second language, get a job everyone here envies. That allows him to live in Copacabana *and* support his family. So he started dating American women, saying he finds them more interesting." She paused and looked into my eyes, "I hope none of this is hurting your feelings."

"Not at all. Please continue."

"His mother is not angry with you at all. She's angry at him for having only short-term relationships with foreigners who are bound to go back to their homes. She wants him to settle down, get married, start his own family. So that's what they're arguing about. I guess I should have realized this would happen if you came. It's just that I've never seen them fight before. Usually, they are a loving and devoted mother and son."

"I shouldn't have come," I murmured.

"Don't tell *him* that! He's bound to suspect you'd say that for different reasons. Maybe he'll think you look down on his family and the home he came from."

"I shouldn't have come because it's causing him to argue with the mother that he loves. I don't want him to experience pain because of me." Maristela squeezed my arm and nodded in understanding.

Otavio stepped out on the balcony, looking haggard. "Otavio, you didn't tell me the favela was such a beautiful place," I said with a smile, motioning to the view.

"Beautiful," he scoffed. "Ha! I bet you didn't even notice those armed snipers up there?" he asked and turned me around, pointing to a few locations.

I froze, my smile gone. Men in black clothes and ski masks were partially hidden on a few strategically located rooftops, each holding a rifle in his hand.

"You can breathe, querida. They're part of the family," he said bitterly. "They're my brother's men." He lit a cigarette and inhaled. "They're here to defend my mom, Maristela," he looked at her meaningfully, then at me, "and you."

"Defend – against what?"

Maristela must have noticed my alarm. "Let's talk inside, OK?" she said gently. She held my trembling arm and guided me back into the house. She explained that both Ana Angelica and she had received threats because of the lawsuit, but that Otavio's brother's gang was the most powerful in town, so she believed no one would dare make a move against them. All I could do while she was talking was panic and wonder if the house itself was safer than the balcony. What I really wanted to do was leave as fast as possible – and never come back.

Her serene voice and Otavio's presence helped me stop shaking. I hugged myself tightly, my arms underneath my breasts. "Don't you think you should have told me about all this before bringing me here?" I said in more of a plea than an accusation.

"I'm sorry, Raquel. You really wanted to come, and I really wanted to show you that there's another side to Rio, a side most tourists don't see. The threats are very recent, and none of us thinks they'll act on them."

"I don't get how those snipers just stand there, in the open, with rifles, in... in broad daylight!"

"It's the norm over here," said Otavio. "Unless the government is doing another one of its pacification projects. But those are only for show and would not last, I can guarantee you that."

"I saw those on the news in America. They looked impressive."

"Sure, that's why they did them - *para Ingles ver!* For the English to see. It's not beyond them to pass laws they won't act on, just to appear more civilized to foreigners."

"Get outta of here! Who would do that?"

"Brazilians!" he scoffed.

"I'll give you an example," said Maristela. "You might remember from watching the parade that slavery was abolished in 1888."

"Yes," I nodded.

"Well, the law was there since 1833, but they had no intention of enforcing it. The English put the pressure on us to abolish slavery, but the big businessmen whose businesses relied on slavery resisted. So what did the government do to appease the English bankers and lawmakers?"

"Draft a law... only for show?" I whispered, still refusing to believe it.

"Exactly! That's where the expression comes from."

What kind of country is this? I wondered in shock. And how could it be that life in the city down the hill, not far at all, was *that* different? I had no doubt that had I not come up here today, I would have left Brazil completely unaware of its darker facets. Maybe that would have been for the best, I wondered bitterly, still frightened.

"Lucky for you, it's time to go," said Otavio, the rancor in his voice evident. We parted with his family, then with Maristela, and drove away in Otavio's sedan. I'd wanted to assure him the visit wasn't that bad, but I couldn't. All I felt was tremendous relief that it was over.

CHAPTER 21

We rode silently in the car. I felt it was up to me to break the silence, to show Otavio that the awkward experience at his family home wouldn't change things between us. I petted his shoulder.

He smirked and sized me up. "Want to take a dip in the ocean?"

"Sure. Or we can just sit on the beach and talk. Whatever you feel like doing." I didn't want him to feel he had to *perform* tonight, or that sex was all I was after. Besides, right now it was the furthest thing from my mind. We drove along the ocean. Near a stretch of deserted beach, he improvised a parking spot. We got out of the car, Otavio grabbing a couple of towels from the trunk.

I took off my ballet flats. My feet dove into the pliable sand which still stored the heat of the sunshine. Something within me rekindled, and I started feeling that maybe it *was* possible to shake off the gloom of the favela tonight after all. I did not want much at the moment. I just needed to feed my mind with some positive thoughts and images before it was time to go to sleep tonight. I needed to have my world back.

This deserted beach was different than the flattened, urban beaches of the south side. There were some boulders scattered about, some on the sand, some protruding between the waves. The only illumination came from the highway's lighting poles and from the full moon. Otavio guided me to a stretch of sand that looked like a half cave hiding behind seven-foot rocks on the side that faced the highway but allowing us full view of the ocean from the front. We sat on one of the towels; the evening breeze gently fluttered my ponytail. Otavio offered me a cigarette, which I accepted, hoping to relieve my stress. We smoked in companionable silence, the peaceful sound of the waves untangling the knot of my nerves.

"Your mom is a very courageous woman. I'm sorry if my visit upset her."

"She was really angry, wasn't she?" He shook his head and exhaled some smoke out of his mouth and nostrils. "She's got two sons, neither one of whom is married, or has kids, so she's disappointed. The fact that Ana Maria is about to have her fifth child doesn't seem to matter."

"When you say she's disappointed with you and your brother, you make it sound as though you're the same. But he's a drug dealing mobster, a violent man who takes after your father. And you," I paused, thinking, remembering. His dream, which I judged as small, was in fact huge. I now realized it took a hero to change those circumstances and accomplish it.

"Yes?" he asked, trying to hide his curiosity with an amused half-smile.

I looked into his eyes and spoke passionately, gesticulating with my hand for emphasis, "You're the opposite of him! You've worked so hard to leave that life of poverty and crime and to get to where you are now. You're honest, determined, smart, not to mention kind and generous. *You* got out of a hopeless world, while your brother is making it worse! I'm sure your mother can also see that."

His smile was now sincere and full of pride. "She does. It's just that she wants me to date only Brazilians, you know, find a girl to marry, but she knows I date mostly foreign women."

"Why is that?" I frowned.

He ran his hand over my back and said suggestively, "I don't know. I guess I'm attracted to everything American." I smiled, stopping myself in the nick of time from asking whether or not he was interested in a long-term relationship. I knew he had to have had a reason for choosing affairs over amour, and I was intent upon thinking about that later. But, since I was in the middle of one of these affairs, and one that was sure to end soon, I was determined to enjoy it until the very last minute, not complicate things with deep questions. "Anyhow," he continued, "this was the first time she'd ever met someone I'm dating, so it wasn't easy on her."

"The first time?" I asked incredulously.

"The first time."

Then I *am* special to him, which is why he allowed me to visit. It felt so good to know that. I looked deeply into his eyes, wanting so much to tell him what he meant to me, but the words just didn't come out. His eyes delved into mine, then he bent down to kiss me. He laid me down on the sand, his kiss firm and lustful. I kissed him hungrily, my hands pulling him to me passionately.

He disconnected himself from me, stood and reached down to me. "You said you've never done it in the ocean. Let's go!"

I smiled and grabbed his outstretched hand. We undressed each other and ran naked into the cool water. When the water reached my hips, Otavio hugged me, then let our bodies go under an oncoming wave. Emerging still in his arms, I coughed salt water. Otavio was grinning. "You bastard!" I smacked his chest, grinning back.

Then he kissed me again, and it was no longer funny. My legs clung to him. Making love in the ocean was a new, wonderful experience. I felt light as Otavio held me in his arms, kissing my mouth, my neck, and my breasts as I arched back in delight, the salty water enveloping us. The moon beams danced on the waves and reflected in his darkening eyes. Being so free outdoors felt better than any hotel *or* motel room. The heaviness in my heart was long forgotten.

We went back to the open cave, our bodies dripping with water. We got dressed and headed back to my hotel. In the car Otavio said, "Lock your door and roll up your window. It's not safe otherwise." I wanted to enjoy the night air, but I obeyed him instead.

The first time he ran a red light, I clung to him. "We don't stop on red at night. Too dangerous. If someone points a gun at you, it won't matter that your window is closed. You'll have to give him what he wants."

So here it was, the reality of living in Rio, smack dab in your face even at the south side. I leaned back in my seat, pointed the air conditioning vent at my face, and looked out at the magnificent beaches. I felt as though Rio's beaches were the stunning makeup on a deeply scarred and sorrowful lady.

* * *

I recalled this feeling a couple of days later, when Otavio, Isabel, and I visited Corcovado, the mountain with the enormous statue of Christ on top. As I looked at the marvelous city spread at my feet, I felt that so many things made sense now. No wonder the song about happiness as ephemeral and sadness as eternal was so popular. It rang true for many people here, who undoubtedly felt trapped.

"What are you thinking about?" asked Otavio, his arm around me.

"Wondering how beauty can ache."

He looked into my eyes, then hugged me close to him. I wanted to tell him I'd miss him, but it was not time yet. I sensed he wanted to say something, too, but stopped himself.

"Hey, you guys. Stop necking every two minutes," said Isabel, who finally got off the phone. We separated, both of us smiling at her. "Sorry; I had to take that call."

"No problem. Your wedding is tomorrow!" I said.

"I'm getting married tomorrow!" She and I shrieked happily and started jumping, our hands intertwined.

"*Garotas*," Otavio shook his head with a smile and lit a cigarette.

"Girls are the best!" declared Isabel goofily. I grinned. "Let's walk around a bit."

Corcovado seemed to encompass even more of Rio's beautiful vistas than Sugar Loaf mountain, which was now to our left. To our right were the peaks of Two Brothers Hill, patches of brown rock interspersed with lush, green foliage, surrounded by high rises. I imagined the long, lit tunnels within those mountains bustling with evening traffic. At our feet lay a beautiful, serene lagoon, surrounded by tall buildings, parks, and a yacht club. Framing this fantastic megalopolis was the sapphire blue of the Atlantic Ocean, crowned with the pale azure of the twilight sky.

As I saw the planes taking off from the airport my heart ached, knowing I would be on a plane shortly. The only way I knew to combat this feeling was to take a ton of photos of us and of the city. I photographed downtown, the Niterói bridge, and Sugar Loaf mountain. I breathed deeply, wishing there was a way to bottle Rio's sweet scent, so I could take it with me. I photographed the vivid sunset. Splashes of rose and orange were interspersed with purple and blue, the glinting remains of yellow making the glow of the city's lights appear brighter. The projectors that illuminated the statue of Christ every night were turned on. They were strong enough to make it visible for miles and miles.

"Guys, you'll have to excuse me once more," Isabel said as she accepted another call. She started speaking Portuguese. Otavio smiled at me. "Let's take our own tour, OK?"

We walked toward the vista of Copacabana, where my hotel towered over other buildings. Otavio hugged me from behind and spoke softly in my ear. "Your hotel reminds me of our first dance together, how we practiced the samba..."

"Our first kiss..."

"Yes. And over there," we walked toward downtown, still hugging, "the samba school reminds me how you danced bravely in front of the school masters."

"And how you told me how beautiful my body is."

"And you didn't believe me."

"No. I didn't – then."

"Then we danced on the allegoric car in the Sambadrome," he said, pointing towards it.

"Two chained slaves," I smiled.

"Until we freed one another," he nibbled on my ear, directing me toward the west vista of town. "I took your chains off at the motel."

"Giving a me the scoop of a lifetime," I smiled, pushing aside the nagging worry over the fact that the only thing Ryan had said was that he wasn't sure yet whether he could use my scoop, and that he needed more time to decide.

"Is that all you got at the motel?" he whispered in my ear, his hands roaming over my stomach.

"That, and the best sex I've ever had." I caught his smile from the corner of my eye. I smiled back. His favela, which was also visible from here, marred those happy memories. I couldn't help but worry for him, for his family and the favela dwellers, and for Maristela.

"I don't know," he said, turning me around to face him, "that time after your striptease may have actually been better."

"Or that time in the ocean."

"Hmm, so hard to choose," we smiled at one another and kissed. But the desperation seeping into our kiss superseded the casual lightness we were attempting to interject into the evening. We were going to part in two days, and neither of us liked that. Enumerating all we'd done together illustrated without a doubt how important Otavio had become to me. I sensed the same was true for him, too.

"You're taking me to the wedding, right?" I asked, my face close to his.

"Oh, sorry, I'm going with someone else."

"Very funny."

"Of course I'm taking you. Although it's not exactly how I'd like to spend our last night together."

"We'll leave as early as possible and spend the rest of the night together," I promised.

We nodded at one another, then headed back to find Isabel. I gave a last glance at the beloved view, breathing deeply in and out. One more night to soak it all up, I thought. Just one more night.

CHAPTER 22

S till nothing from your boss?" asked Otavio. We were having breakfast at my hotel. He was changing channels on the muted TV while I checked my PA.

"Not yet. Jess and Ashley told me about all the projects he's busy with, but, I swear, I feel like he's trying to get out of losing the bet!"

"C'mon; that's crazy!"

"I know. That's what they said, too. I guess I just have to be patient," I sighed.

"So," he turned off the TV and moved his chair next to mine, his hand roaming up my thighs, "as great as this thing is," he pointed to the PA, "*it* didn't tell you about motels."

"No," I smiled and put away the tablet, my hands reaching for him. "For that I needed you. I can't believe I ever thought hanging out with you was in the way of my work." And the same was true about Isabel. All the things I did together with both of them had led me here, to this wonderful, new place in my life.

Otavio kissed me ravenously. I met his intensity. Last day together, was all I could think about. After a last dip in the ocean, we spent most of the day in bed. Then we started getting ready for the wedding, Otavio having brought his three-piece suit with him the night before.

When I got a moment to myself, I attempted to ease the pain of the next day's separation by concentrating on Otavio's faults. He came from a different world, he was not well read, he had only rudimentary education, he had no interest in old movies, etc. But it didn't work. The only thing that put me off was the fact that he slept around. I was certain it showed a need for self-validation through sexual conquest, which, of course, was impossible to achieve. I'm better off without him, I told myself.

But, when he emerged from the bedroom, wearing a dark gray suit, a crisp white shirt, and a golden vest and tie, my heart started beating faster. In my head, a voice shouted in reply to the only real flaw I could find, *maybe if we stay together, that will change?* I fought back the tears.

"Wow! You're a *gatinha*! A hottie," he explained as he walked toward me. I wore the strapless, burgundy, knee-length taffeta dress Isabel had helped me pick out. I wore my hair up in a French twist, and wore some makeup and jewelry, which wasn't usually the case when I was with Otavio. "Everything OK?" he frowned.

"Yes, yes. It's just that I've never seen you in a suit before."

"This is only for one night, so don't get used to it," he joked and put his arms around me. But neither of us smiled. One night was all we had.

The wedding was held at the Copacabana Palace. We strolled on the beautiful, black and white pavement with its wavy pattern, the light breeze fluttering my skirt and the palm trees. My heels clicked as I sauntered along. Passersby in bathing suits or summer clothes smiled at our evening attire, or perhaps at our displays of intimacy. I felt giddy and light, as one would feel on a summer night, full of love and promise.

It was called a palace for a reason. The ceremony hall's marble floor shined, squares of brown-on-white. Rows of benches were covered in white silk and were already mostly filled with guests. Large arrangements of white and pink flowers hung at the end of each bench. The chandeliers' reflection glowed in the tall windows, their white curtains half open, bringing in the sight of the diminishing moon as it started its ascent over the dark sky. In front of the rows of benches sparkled another chandelier, its electric candles illuminating a sparse metal cross, a wooden podium, and a Persian rug.

We made our way toward the group of a dozen burgundy-clad women. Quite the bridesmaids' entourage, I thought with a smile, and then frowned to myself. Isabel must have realized people might mistake me for a bridesmaid with this dress. Maybe that was her intention all along when she helped me pick it out? If so, I would be deeply honored.

I was enveloped with kisses and hugs and the rapid chit chat of English and Portuguese. Everyone seemed happy to see us.

Otavio was about to excuse himself and head for the groomsmen group, when Maristela came in, some bruises on her face, the white sling on her right arm standing out next to her burgundy, chiffon dress.

"What happened?" Otavio and I rushed over to her, followed by many others.

"Someone jumped on me from a rooftop in the favela. I fell on the steps and fractured my arm."

Others spoke Portuguese, probably failing to understand what she was saying. She spoke to them. Otavio asked something. All I could understand was his brother's name. Then he translated. "One of Bastiao's men is supposed to guard her when I'm not around. I can't believe that idiot let this happen!"

"When he saw I was not badly injured, he ran after my attacker. I heard some shooting, then he limped back with a bullet hole in his leg!"

"You can't go back there!" I said, clutching her good hand for emphasis.

Everyone looked indignant, and very, very worried. A bald man in a light blue suit and a dark blue bow-tie put his arm around Maristela's shoulders. "Don't worry," he said in English. "She won't need to."

"Raquel, meet my husband, Leonides."

"It's a pleasure to meet you," he said with a wide smile. "I've heard so much about you."

"Prazer," I smiled in return. "Do you mean they've won the case?"

"Not yet," said Maristela. "But I told Ana Angelica that we'll speak on Skype for now, at least until my arm heals."

"Querida, I love you too much to take the risk of you going back there," said her husband.

"I agree," said Otavio vehemently. "Things are bound to escalate some more now that one of Bastiao's men was injured."

"Is there any way the attack was about something else?" I asked hopefully. "Maybe someone was just trying to rob her or something?"

"No way," Maristela shook her head. "They left a note, threatening that if I don't drop the case, I, Ana Angelica, and her entire family will regret it." She looked at Otavio, who seemed enraged, his eyes moving rapidly as he calculated something. I felt anxious with worry, for him, for his family, and for Maristela. "Dear Raquel," she said and hugged me with her good arm, "beautiful, brave Raquel. I'm sorry I ever took you over there and involved you in any of this. To us, it's a way of life. I've been threatened before and will be again. But for you, this whole thing must be terrifying."

"Yes," I whispered, soaking up the warmth of her hug.

"Don't worry. Otavio's sister and her children are going to stay with an aunt in another state for a while. And, as usual, Ana Angelica is absolutely refusing to give in to fear. She's a real heroine."

"She's an amazing woman. Still, I wish she would give up the lawsuit," I said.

"We talked about it, but she refuses to surrender. And if she's brave enough to continue, I'll just have to conquer my fears and continue representing her."

"But how can she continue living there when her life is in danger?"

"That's why she's letting her son move back in for protection."

"*Which* son?" I asked between clenched teeth, terrified of the answer. I slowly turned to face Otavio.

"Don't worry. I meant Bastiao. He'll move in with a couple of his men until the trial is over."

"And do you think I will just continue showing tourists around and living the good life in Copacabana until this is over?" asked Otavio, the derision in his voice a feeble attempt to hide the shame he must have felt for no longer being there for his mom on a daily basis.

"No; I expect you to stay where you are, so, if we need to move your mom to your place for a while, we'll still have that option," stressed Maristela. Otavio nodded, his lips sealed in determination.

Festive organ music began to play. "Oh my God! Has Isabel seen you like this?" I asked, worried the long-awaited ceremony would be interrupted because of Maristela's injuries. It seemed a bit petty at the moment, but I knew how important it was to Isabel, and I felt sure no bride would want this pall overshadowing her wedding.

"I held up telling her anything about the threats for as long as I could, but she does know by now." Maristela smiled and gestured for us to take our places.

Maria Flor and Carolina quickly directed all the groomsmen to the left and all the bridesmaids to the right. I had no idea whether or not to stand with the group, so I made my way toward the benches. Both Carolina and Maria Flor stopped me and directed me to stand with the rest of the bridesmaids, who'd made room for me to stand among them. I smiled gratefully and took my place.

I looked at Otavio, who stood near all the similarly clad men, acting as one of Tiago's groomsmen at Isabel's request. Maristela squeezed my hand, bringing me back to the fact that it was Isabel's special moment. We smiled at each other excitedly.

As the wedding march began, everyone stood up and looked back. Isabel was preceded by two maids of honor I didn't recognize, probably the two close friends who were too devout to come to the bachelorette party. A rare case in which the name Maid of Honor actually applied, I thought. The bride paced forward ceremoniously on her father's arm. I could hear gasps and snivels from the audience. She wore a white, satin, strapless wedding dress, its fitted, ruched pleats elegantly accentuating her full breasts, narrow waist and round hips. The rich silk flared below her knees, giving her the appearance of a mermaid. Her delicate veil flowed around her like lace-trimmed cake tiers, extending all the way around to the train of her dress. Her makeup was delicate and flawless. Exquisite diamond earrings and necklace finished her ensemble. My vivacious, mulatta friend seemed transformed into a sort of European princess. The whimsical weave she allowed in her fancy updo was the only reminder of her sweet buoyancy. I smiled widely, enchanted by the beauty she radiated within and without.

Her father delivered her to a brown-haired man with a narrow, unshaven face and small eyes. I instinctively resented him for not having shaved for the big day, even though I knew it was the damn fashion right now. I thawed a bit as I saw the love in his eyes as he lifted Isabel's veil. A catholic priest in an ornate white and gold cloak began the ceremony. Understanding nothing, my thoughts drifted.

What a special way to end my spectacular trip, I thought, as my eyes scanned the faces around me. Seeing Barbara in her Sunday best reminded me of how she taught me some samba steps to help me perform in the carnival procession. Looking at the bridesmaids reminded me not only of the fun we'd had together at the bachelorette party, but of how they welcomed me into their group with warmth and enthusiasm. Feeling Maristela's uninjured hand squeeze mine, reminded me of her courage and integrity.

Did I dare look at Otavio in this precious moment when Isabel and Tiago were exchanging vows, something so universal, I understood it in spite of the language barrier? I couldn't help myself. And neither could he. We looked at one another seriously. I wondered what it would be like if we stayed together. Was he wondering the same thing? The only thing I knew for certain was that this man undimmed the mirror of life I held up to myself. With his aid, I now saw myself clearly, and for that I'd be eternally grateful.

Would I leave an indelible mark on him, too? I recalled what I'd said to him about the difference between him and his brother that night at the beach, and hoped it was something he would hold on to long after I was gone. But I decided to say one more important thing to him before I left.

After a fancy dinner, the married couple took the floor for their first dance as man and wife. Isabel radiated joy. I watched them dance until others were invited to join them. I asked Otavio to dance with me. He gave me the usual cocky half-smile, but by now I could spot the many conflicting emotions behind his guarded eyes. They weren't as reserved now as they once were. I could see the pain and uncertainty in them, as well as the strength and confidence. He stood, held me in his arms, and we slow-danced across the floor. I absorbed his manly scent, the feel of his rough hands, the feel of his strong body near mine.

I wanted to tell him what he meant to me, and to urge him to find someone local to love and build a relationship with – but I couldn't. His mom already did that on a regular basis, and the realization that something as beautiful as what we had could happen for him here, with a local girl, could only come from within. There was a reason he chose only doomed relationships, and that was for him to figure out and change. Besides, there was the very real possibility that *I* was a lot more special to him than his other romances, and that he loved me, and not any one of them. Therefore, telling him to go find someone else felt like selling myself short. So I just looked at him as the romantic violin music swept the air, and simply said, "You mean so much to me."

He didn't answer. He only smiled a small smile, a tinge of sadness in his amber eyes, and said, "Let's get out of here."

Isabel demanded we stay a bit longer, so we could dance together. Her white dress stood out in the sea of burgundy dresses as we all danced wildly to one of *Michael Jackson's* upbeat songs. After they cut the cake, she finally agreed to let us go. It took a while to part with everyone I knew.

Maristela and I promised to stay in touch. "You're my hero," I told her, my eyes becoming misty.

"And you're mine," she smiled back in tears.

"Good luck with the lawsuit. And please don't go back there."

"I won't." We embraced each other.

Isabel walked both of us to the entrance, where we could have an uninterrupted moment.

"I'll miss you," she said gloomily.

"I'll miss you, too."

We hugged, and the tears started to fall. "Never in my life did I imagine a tour guide would become the kind of amazing friend you've turned out to be."

"Never in my life did I imagine a client would become such an inspiring, wonderful friend as you've turned out to be. Right, Otavio?"

He didn't answer, just nodded imperceptibly, his face expressionless.

"Don't cry," I laughed. "Your makeup will run."

She laughed in return, and I thought how much more marvelous the peal of her laughter made the world. As we parted, I promised myself to call her once in a while, so that I could hear its sweet ringing once more.

Otavio and I walked toward my hotel. We kissed under a palm tree. I gazed into his eyes. "Where to? My hotel? A motel?"

"How about… my apartment?" he asked seriously. I realized I hadn't seen his place yet. Perhaps no woman ever did. This, I understood, was his way of answering my words of intimacy.

"Sounds great," I smiled.

CHAPTER 23

W hat would you like to drink?" asked the smiling flight attendant.

"Do you have diet Guarana?" I asked without smiling back, too worn out with fatigue to be polite, too melancholy to care.

"Of course!" She popped a fresh can and poured it over some ice for me.

"Thanks," I said, and sipped. The artificial sweeteners felt sickly sweet. I rescheduled my red-eye back home to a day flight, so that I could spend a final evening with Otavio after the wedding. Now the bright sun blinded my dry, tired eyes. I chose the last row because it was empty and afforded me more room and privacy. The airplane felt cold and I was happy to have my winter gear close at hand inside my carry-on. I still wore my new, marine blue summer suit, stubbornly refusing to surrender to the cold and accept the fact I had left summer behind. I knew there was not much point in trying to sleep before the meals were delivered, but I pulled the fleece blanket up to my chin and tried anyway. Every time I closed my eyes, heart-wrenching images of Otavio appeared before me.

I recalled his small, messy, bachelor's apartment. Its sparse furnishings included a few photos of his family, including one of Pilar smiling from her perch over his shoulders.

I recollected us making love on his couch, on his bed, in his shower, urgently at first, then leisurely. I didn't picture us as a couple but was instead transported back into my own mind at the time, into the sensations I felt during lovemaking: my back arching with pleasure, my fingers clawing, grabbing, scratching. I could almost feel the sensation of the water falling on me from the shower head as I moaned, groping Otavio in the tiny shower stall. I could not decide which torture was worse: trying to escape these snippets, or reliving them again and again, knowing none of it would ever happen again.

My fatigue and hunger were making me cold and so was my light suit. I decided to grab a jacket and another blanket before the approaching stewards made their way to my row with the food cart. The various body aches I felt when I stood up brought a faint smile to my lips. I was like a soldier back from a wonderful battle, happily reliving the memories of the cause of each and every ache. I was terrified of the day when they would all be gone, replaced by nothing but fading images and memories of his touch, his voice, his scent.

I slid my black, fleece-lined sports jacket gingerly over my back, remembering. I was the one who scratched him first, and he, as if in understanding, mimicked me, running his nails on my back, each of us leaving a mark on the other. But even these marks would fade.

I spotted Isabel's wedding-favor gift-bag in my carry-on, which I had yet to open. I sat down and browsed inside the black organza bag with the burgundy damask stamping, the words *Isabel and Tiago* and yesterday's date printed on its side. The same was stamped on the bottom of an elegant Champagne flute with an ivory base and on a votive candle holder studded with pink and white roses. I pulled out the small, burgundy box of artisan chocolates and stashed it in the front seat pocket. I poured some of the golden Guarana into the Champagne glass then toasted it in the air, conjuring Isabel's image in my mind as she looked yesterday. The stewardess smiled when she saw this but said nothing, handing me my meal with the perfunctory, "Enjoy your meal."

I ate quietly, absently flipping through the pages of a magazine on my PA. But my heart and mind were not really in either activity. I nibbled at my food, then laid it on the tray near me, happy to have the extra space. I opened the chocolate box and placed one of the chocolate brigadiers on my tongue. Isabel had introduced me to these little Portuguese truffles before. I began to chew, the flavor of chocolate fudge replacing the taste of the boring airplane meal. It did not lighten the heaviness in my heart.

I flipped through the few images I had taken of Otavio on my phone, a scarcity caused by his grumpiness at being photographed, and by the fact that whenever I saw him, I was often too busy being with him to be taking photographs. I would have to think of a way to ask Kevin for all his pictures of Otavio without receiving too much grief in return. He and Chantal stayed behind, maintaining their availability until we got word from Ryan about my motel series. I hadn't heard from him in a few days, and now that I'd parted with Rio and my wonderful Brazilian friends, I felt the tension mounting.

But I resisted those thoughts for now. There would be plenty of time for them later. I smiled at the photo Otavio's sister sent him of Pilar clutching the new doll I'd gotten her. It was a beautiful doll, with a body not skinny, nor overweight. She wore a purple, sequined dress, headband, and boots. When I gave it to Isabel, to pass on to Barbara and to Ana Maria, I saw a twinkle of emotion in her eyes. She rushed to her room, then came back out, her arms full of dolls, toys, and decorative pillows to add to my gift.

"You'll make her day," I said.

"No; *you'll* make her day! If it weren't for you, I'd never have thought about it. I have been holding on to too many things for far too long. Pilar would make far better use of them."

I put my phone away and I closed my eyes. The image of Otavio crept into my mind, as he looked during our last dance to a song he played in his apartment. We danced naked, our bodies wrapped around each other, the half-moon partially lighting Otavio's face. The singer's low voice sang a song whose sad chords spoke of longing. The singer's audience started accompanying her, and Otavio started to sing, too, his deep voice sending chills down my spine. His sensual pronunciation of the exotic, musical language, his encompassing embrace, and the magnetizing gaze in his eyes were all I could perceive. I was wholly rapt by his existence.

Later, when I'd had a moment alone, I'd looked up the song online and downloaded a video of it with English subtitles onto the PA. Now, alone on a cold plane, I watched the romantic ballad video called *Negue,* or *Deny,* sung by Maria Bethânia. Seeing the hard-featured singer, my heart thudded anxiously. I knew I was headed back to country full of people that would reject someone like her because of her looks, thus missing out on her remarkably powerful voice. And as much as I loved my home, a part of me dreaded going back to working in the company of such shallow beings.

As I read the lyrics to the song Otavio had chosen for our last dance, I started to weep. It was about the mourning of a jilted lover who reminded her beloved that her lips were still wet with his kiss. Until I'd read those lyrics, all I'd had to prove he loved me was the look in his eyes and the way he touched me. Now I knew it with absolute certainty.

I recalled the way we parted at the airport. Otavio stood close to me, his hand on my waist. "Don't ever forget..." he said, then paused, his eyes delving into mine, as if he wanted to say something, but couldn't bring himself to do it. Finally, he smiled and said, "Don't ever forget how beautiful you are."

He hugged me firmly. I returned his embrace, whispering, "I'll never forget – *anything!*"

He desperately closed his lips on mine, so hard, as if he were trying to scorch them with an indelible mark. I was sure he, too, could taste my salty tears.

"Don't cry," he smiled tenderly. "It'll ruin your smile."

I laughed a little, rubbing my eyes. I wanted so much to say I wished I could stay, but a part of me wanted to go back to New York City, my first love, and to my career, my ambitions, and my dreams. So instead I said, "If you're ever in New York..."

"I'll look you up," he nodded with a smile. I turned around and walked away, feeling I'd left a part of me behind.

* * *

"Oh my God!" Jess squeezed me in her arms. "You're finally back. And you look great!"

"Nice summer suit," concurred Ashley before she hugged me. "It's still too cold for it, but I'll turn the heat up in the car if you need it."

"It's OK. I'll just put my coat on."

"What's that on your neck?" asked Jess, her voice insinuating something naughty.

"Just a love bite," I smiled. We started walking toward the exit.

"I bet there are more bites where we can't see," she grinned.

"Maybe," I smiled back, realizing how much I'd missed her goofiness.

"Wow. Do you miss him terribly? I bet she just misses him to bits," she told Ashley.

I knew I had to nip this in the bud. I stopped walking, as did they. I looked seriously into Jess's eyes. "I miss him so much, it hurts. Happy?"

"Not really. Sorry," she inclined her head.

"It's fine."

She put her arm around me as we continued walking. "I missed you, Rach."

"Did you find a new nickname for Raquel?" I subtly reminded her.

"My first thought was Raq, but that sucks. Then I thought maybe Quelle. But then it hit me: Raquel can be shortened to Rocky!"

"Rocky," I smiled and wrinkled my nose at the same time, unsure. "It kinda beats the whole point of having a new, more exotic, feminine name." Jess looked at me with a sad, puppy-dog look. I came around, knowing only she would call me that. "You know what? - it's perfect! It's a champion's name, after all." She grinned at me.

"Are you nervous about introducing yourself as Raquel at the office?" asked Ashley as we buckled up in her car.

"Honestly, I haven't thought about it much."

"What?! The old Rachel would have fussed about it for ages," said Jess from the back seat. "Actually, she wouldn't have changed her name to begin with."

"When I made up my mind to live up to this name for the rest of my life, I was vowing something important to myself: to try and be the kind of person I can admire. Those idiots mean nothing to me."

"Nice to see you're so Zen about it," smiled Ashley.

"I can't get over how much you've changed in just a couple of weeks!" declared Jess.

"Otavio said the same thing," I smiled, my eyes staring into the distance as I evoked that memory. "He said he's never seen anyone change overnight, like I did after the striptease. So I told him he happened to be there the moment things clicked for me, but that it was in the works for years and years, just like it took him over twenty years to leave the shantytown he grew up in, which is a rare achievement."

"I was so relieved that you didn't end up visiting it. I heard it could be dangerous," said Ashley, as she navigated the heavy traffic.

"You heard right, and I did go there. I didn't tell you because I didn't want you guys to worry."

"Oh my God! And something happened, right? I can feel it!"

"Nothing happened. Not during my visit, anyway. I'll tell you about it another time. I'm so tired." I savored the skyline of the city as we drove toward it. "Tell me about you. Have you dated anyone recently?"

"No one of significance. All the good ones are either gay or married, right?" answered Ashley.

I smiled but didn't answer. How could I, when I knew how wrong she was? "And how are things with you and Lon?" I asked Jess.

"Well, you're not the only one with a love bite," she grinned, and pulled down her shaggy, iridescent scarf to boast a purplish mark on her neck.

"I don't know why she's bragging about those," remonstrated Ashley. "All they do is have sex. What are they going to do when that gets old, I just don't know."

"Can't you just let us enjoy ourselves?" Jess rolled her eyes.

"Ever heard of giving away the milk for free?" Ashley asked.

"So, in this scenario, I'm the cow?" asked Jess. The laughter started to bubble up within me.

"You know what I mean. You should have had the decency to wait, at least until the third date."

"Point taken. A good, chaste cow must wait three dates before exposing her rear hind to a suitor." The laughter burst from all three of us.

"Thanks Jess, I didn't think I'd laugh again quite so soon."

"Everything is a joke with her," admonished Ashley.

"Ash, you know that this cow, or this gal, isn't interested in marriage. Lon and I have an awesome connection. If I'm not worried about where it's going, why should you?"

"You're right. I just worry you'll end up alone."

"Well, don't. I can always get a guy. What I really need is you two."

"Aww," Ashley and I both said in unison.

Ashley sighed. "Sometimes I wish *I* could stop obsessing over finding someone," she admitted.

"Maybe if you weren't too busy pretending to be someone you're not on the first date, you'd stand a better chance."

"Oh, come on, Jess. That's mean," I said.

"She's the one who said that that's the recipe for success!"

"It's true, I said that. If you don't hide your flaws, how are you going to find anyone who's worthwhile?"

"Are you saying that only a loser would find the real you attractive?" I asked. "That's crazy, Ashley. You have so much to give and you have so many wonderful traits. You should focus on bringing those out, instead of fussing over hiding some perceived flaws."

"That's right," agreed Jess. "I bet then you'll get some more action. Do you know how long it's been for her?" she asked me.

"I see you guys got really close when I was away," I smiled.

"Not everybody's as... how shall I put it? As uninhibited as Jess is," Ashley seethed.

"She means slutty," Jess explained in feigned earnestness, and I repressed my giggle.

"That's not what I mean! Did you ever think that maybe the reason I can't sleep with just anyone is because I attach so much importance to sex?"

"No!" answered Jess. "C'mon Ash! Sex means nothing. It's just a *really pleasurable* sport. It's the only sport I'm willing to do, that's for sure," she grinned at me.

"*Now* who's exaggerating! Admit Lon means something to you!" I said heatedly.

"He's fun to hang around, that's for sure."

"She's hopeless," Ashley shook her head.

Jess grinned proudly. "Are you up for some more of this witty banter, Rach? Urgh, I mean Rocky? Or are you too tired for company?"

"I *am* too tired. I'll just see you tomorrow morning at work."

"No problem."

I took in the beautiful sights of the skyscrapers all around us. We were almost at my building, and I had to ask something important before they dropped me off. "Did Ryan say anything to you about approving my scoop?"

"Nothing," they both said and shook their heads. I was grateful to Ashley that, for once, she didn't say how much she disliked my scoop.

"He didn't say anything to Lon, either?" I asked Jess.

"I tried to squeeze him for information, but he wouldn't budge. Boss's orders, he said."

"What does that mean? Do you think that's good or bad?"

"I don't know, honey. Don't worry about it too much, OK?"

"I won't. I'm either writing my own ticket at work – or I'm out of a job. We'll know which one tomorrow."

Jess double-parked in front of my building's entrance.

"That's right, we will. But since you have a difficult night ahead of you, how about reaching into my purse and getting yourself a nice, little muscle relaxant or a sleeping pill?" suggested Ashley.

"I'm fine. Staying awake will be my problem tonight," I said, hoping it'll indeed be the case. We parted with hugs and kisses. Then, standing on the curb, holding the handle of my suitcase, I took a moment to soak up the bustle of my magnificent city. I loved traveling, but nothing felt quite as right as coming back home.

Despite its smallness, I always treasured being back in my apartment, with my things, my art, my view. This time was no exception, apart from the fact that the quiet I usually valued above all else was now a painful reminder that I was alone, a continent away from a man I loved. I collapsed on my bed and cried. Yes, I admitted to myself for the first time, I loved him. Maybe he wasn't the man of my dreams, but I loved him still.

As I cried, I started drifting away, but then I caught myself. It was still too early to go to sleep, and it was best to stay up a little longer to make sure I wouldn't be wide awake in the middle of the night. So I dragged myself to the bathroom and took a long, hot, blissful shower.

I debated whether to make the effort to go downstairs to buy a pint of crème caramel ice cream. Laziness, and the sure knowledge that if I'd buy a pint in this mood, I'd finish it, won, and I stayed in my apartment. I did, however, finish all the chocolates Isabel gave me. As I unpacked, I listened to Otavio's love song over and over again, trying to memorize the lyrics, combating the occasional tears. I felt an overwhelming urge to call him on Skype, to hear his voice again, to see his face – but I didn't. I had to survive this evening alone. Then I could survive all the nights after that.

My new colorful clothes made me happy, but unpacking my lingerie was bittersweet. I was happy to have such sexy undergarments, but I didn't think I could ever use them again with anyone else. They were steeped with memories of Otavio, of my first strip at the bachelorette party, and of me stripping for him at my hotel, with lingerie I had just gotten at Isabel's mom's store. That night, I had modeled him my new bathing suit, matching wrap and bag, and bejeweled flip-flops. My new, revealing bikini made him very happy. Then I put on the new, black, lace bra and panties, garter-belt and stockings.

"Dance for me," he said, sitting up in bed, his laziness gone.

He played a song on his cell. I put on my heels, and started dancing, stopping in front of the full-length mirrors in my hotel room to dance in front of myself, which Otavio enjoyed greatly. I gyrated my butt at him, looking back over my shoulder, then I turned to face him, striking different sexy poses.

I was jolted out of my reverie as a sudden realization dawned on me. I had danced in front of those mirrors with not one ounce of the self-criticism that used to be second nature to me. Nor had I been self-critical toward myself in days, as had been my custom my entire life.

And then I started to laugh; laugh at the bullies, at the mean idiots and poor fools who perpetuated this distorted myth of the 'perfect' body. Because that's all it was. This huge thing that made so many of us miserable, which made it impossible for us to enjoy a morsel of food or the sight of our bodies in the mirror without self-reproach, was nothing but an overblown, out-ofproportion deception. Forget the bet! Forget the scoop! *This* was the greatest secret I had unraveled on my trip!

Glowing inside, I realized it was just the kind of the thing I wanted to write about in my new women's magazine.

I took out my beloved, old journal. Frayed from years of use, it was the book I wrote in when I had new, important ideas or thoughts. My hand lovingly caressed the yellow and magenta patterns on the cover. I opened the book, titling a new page *New Magazine Ideas: How travel has enriched my perspective on life*. I added a sub-header that just came to me: *Travel I.Q.* I smiled to myself, pleased at this possible magazine name.

I wrote *Butt-Attitude*. Then I changed it to *Buttitude* with a grin. I added some bullet points:

- "Be courageous – Maristela."
- "Judge a person within his context – Otavio."
- "Look underneath the beauty – Rio. Chantal."
- "Spread benevolence – Isabel."
- "Seize the Day – like Brazilians during carnival."

The latter was something I've personally endorsed prior to the trip, but not all the way. I'd let my self-reproach get in the way of my happiness. I looked at myself in the mirror and smiled. Now I was free to love myself, not just soul, but body, too. Of all my trip souvenirs, this one was the most precious, and the one no one could take away from me - unless I let them.

CHAPTER 24

Over breakfast, I used the PA to text Ryan, Lon, and Christine, requesting to officially change my name with the company to Raquel Moore. Then I made a note to myself to figure out how to do that on my driver's license and other important documents, too.

Since the weather was still cold, I wore my good, black dress suit. But instead of my old habit of wearing a white, brown, or maroon shirt with that, I wore a violet, satin shirt with a wide, black belt around my waist. The color made my green eyes and dirty-brown hair pop. Why did I ever think that these feminine touches could stand in the way of my success? With some light makeup, the amethyst earrings I had purchased in Brazil, and two-inch heels, I was pleased with the way I looked. To properly deserve a name like Raquel, I felt like I needed to honor my newfound Brazilian sparkle. I wanted to make a statement. And if the looks I got on my way to work were any indication, I had succeeded. I savored those looks as I sashayed into the skyscraper that hosted *Travel Secrets* magazine. Remember those looks and stay brave! I told myself as the elevator doors opened to my floor.

"My, my, my; what have we here?" Chad the sleaze hissed as he caught sight of me. I noticed his blond dreadlocks were tied back for a change, but his brown eyes looked stoned, as usual. I continued to walk tall toward my table, Chad followed me, along with an entourage he picked along the way. I arrived at my desk and set down my briefcase tote, which contained my PA. I fervently hoped I did not have to return it today. Jess and Ashley approached me with coffees in their hands, looking wary.

"Well, well, well; could it be our little Rachel?" jeered Kourtney.

"Apparently, it's national fashion day and we weren't informed," sneered Deidre in her British accent. They all laughed.

I breathed in and replied, "apparently, today is be an *asshole* to your coworker day. No, wait! That's every day for you!" I stood in front of The Trio, keeping my back taut, my expression sealed, and my fingers curled into fists. Good thing they couldn't hear the swift beating of my heart or sense my trepidation. Fear be damned! I told myself. I had to stand up to them once and for all. What was the worst that could happen?

"Cute. Keep up the jokes, Rachel, and, who knows? - We may even let you into our little club," said Kourtney.

"I don't want to be a part of your little clique. And it's Raquel now."

"What's Raquel now?" she asked.

"My new name. Now go on, bring it. I'm sure you have a lot to say about that." Better get it all out now, instead of little by little.

"Ha! *You*, a Raquel?!" heckled Chad. "You wish! As if a Raquel would ever be a plus-size."

"I am *not* a plus-size, and it wouldn't have mattered if I were, *Chadwick*."

"Hey! Who are you calling Chadwick?!" he towered over me. My heart nearly jumped out of my chest, but I stood my ground.

"Meh, forget her. Let's grab a coffee before Brooks arrives," said Kourtney.

Chad bent over and made a crazy face very close to my serious face, trying to make me flinch. I didn't. "Feh," he growled, gesturing dismissively. They all turned and left.

"Oh my God!" Said Ashley.

"Are you OK?" asked Jess worriedly.

"I don't know. I think I'm in shock."

"I *cannot* believe you just did that!"

"Me neither," said Ashley.

"Neither can I!" I said.

"I can't believe you called him by the name he hates most!"

"Chadwick. It's such a funny name. We should use it more often," I smiled.

Jess mimicked a British accent, "the name's Chadwick, and I'm a prick, because I've got a stick up my..." We laughed. "I'm out of rhymes." She handed me a cup of coffee. "You look fabulous, by the way. Those assholes are just jealous."

I smiled at Jess. "You know, not one Brazilian person disparaged me. I wonder why these guys feel compelled to do it."

"Those jerks' motivation isn't important," said Ashley in her lecturing tone. "What's important is that New York is one of the enlightened states with an Anti-Bullying Healthy-Workplace Bill in place. I say, sue Ryan for letting this happen on his watch and you can make a small fortune. Let *him* pay for all your misery!"

"How can I do that when I haven't even told him about the bullying yet. I haven't filed a complaint, or anything."

"Then what are you waiting for?"

I sipped the hot beverage pensively, arranging my thoughts. "In case you've forgotten, I tried that with Todd already and nothing happened." I held up my arm to silence her reply and continued. "I will let Ryan know what's going on, but not quite yet. I want him to regard me as a serious writer first. Then I'll tell him about these pesky fools."

"Meanwhile, you handled yourself just fine with no lawsuit," Jess pointed out.

"She did, but the whole point is, she doesn't have to. Why should she be subjected to such abuse on a daily basis? It's so... last century," insisted Ashley.

"Ashley, give me time. If I can't handle this myself, or if things get worse, I'll involve the boss. And if he doesn't help me, then I'll sue. Or probably just quit."

"You shouldn't even mention quitting. They should be the ones who are out of a job, not you!"

"Okay, okay; calm down," said Jess, rubbing Ashley's shoulders, while shaking her head to me behind her back. Neither Jess nor I were big fans of litigation, as Ashley clearly was.

I sipped on my coffee, realizing that, at least to myself, I had to admit there was another reason why I didn't want Ryan Brooks involved in this. I didn't want him to look at me like my bullies did, or to even suspect some of their wicked thoughts crossed his mind, too. He simply couldn't think of me as a helpless, overweight girl, who needed help defending herself against her coworkers. Nor could I, not anymore that is.

"Rocky," said Jess. I smiled at her first correct use of my new nickname. "Have you already picked a location for when you win the bet?" I smiled widely, and she smiled back. Jess always knew what to say to make me feel better.

"Well, France was already on my radar," I said, seeing Ashley's excitement building up, "so if Ryan approves it, I'll take the chateau tour Ashley talked about. But only if I get a couple of days in Paris, too."

Ashley pulled me into an enthusiastic hug. I hugged her back, handing my nearly empty coffee mug to Jess who was rolling her eyes and shrugging at Ashley's sentimentality. When Ashley pulled back, I could see she was on the verge of tears. "Oh Rachel; thank you, thank you, thank you. I mean Raquel. And yes, you do get a couple of days in Paris before the tour and a couple more after." She was obviously all chocked up and about to cry. She sat down and started fanning herself vigorously with a pamphlet she found on the desk, attempting to stop the tears.

"Oh honey. Just let out. You're among friends here."

"The most wonderful friends," she said, her hand on mine. "But no need," she breathed in deeply, "I'm fine now. I just can't believe you'd do this to save my column."

"Well, I do want to help you, and I do care to learn more about the challenges of women traveling alone. This trip sounds amazing, and with Ryan paying for it, I can finally see the City of Lights *and* France's wine country."

"That does sound perfect."

"What does?" asked a baritone voice behind me. The three of us jumped to our feet. "I apologize," said Ryan, exuding charm as he bowed slightly in front of me. "I didn't mean to take you by surprise. Well, perhaps I did, just a bit," he winked. We smiled widely at one another. His good mood was evident. Does that mean good news for me? I allowed myself a glimmer of hope. "Ready for a little office announcement?"

"Depends what kind," I retorted with sass. Jess and Ashley looked at me furtively, Ashley alarmed at my nerve, Jess in appreciation of it. I allowed a small smile to break out for Jess's sake. Yes, my friend, the silent mouse you knew is no longer.

Ryan grinned widely at me and guided me toward a central table between the cubicles, his hand at my elbow, Jess and Ashley following us. "I bet it was hard waiting to hear back from me," he goaded.

"It was *so* hard that making light of it tempts me to use my kickboxing moves on you," I said, my finger raised in warning. I'd never spoken to any boss like this, nor, in fact, to any man. Jess and Ashley looked shocked.

Ryan roared with laughter. "I like your balls, Rachel. Oh, excuse me; Raquel. That new name looks good on you."

I nodded gratefully and waited. Lon and Christine gathered the rest of the writers around us. "Quick announcement," Ryan said matter-of-factly. "As some of you might know, I and your coworker, Raquel Moore here, had a bet." He sneaked a furtive look at me. *He's supporting me in front of the hyenas,* I thought happily. "We bet she would either find a new scoop about Rio de Janeiro or lose her job. And then she sent me this," Lon handed him a PA, on which was the honeymoon spread of rose petals and candles, which Ryan showed everyone. "This was a few days ago, and I find myself needing to apologize to her now, for keeping her waiting so long to find out if that scoop was usable or not. You see, I *was* blown away by the discovery of the nature of Brazilian motels, but I wasn't sure I wanted to take Travel Secrets in the by-the-hour motels direction, as wonderful and as affordable as some of them may be. I consulted Lon, who confirmed above and beyond that this was indeed a secret unknown to the industry. He and Chris both agreed we could market it respectably, and, to prove it, we secretly polled some of our subscribers. They all said they'd love to visit these motels. In short, my dear Miss Moore," he gestured aside, to where someone had pushed in a cart with chilled Champagne and glasses on top, "I am delighted to tell you you've won the bet!" Jess, Ashley, and some of the others whooped and clapped for me. Over the noise, Ryan added, "let me tell you, this is one bet I don't mind losing at all. I was quite impressed with you."

I grinned as Ryan handed me a cold Champagne flute. "Thanks," was all I could say, feeling choked with pride and happiness.

"Congratulations," he said and clinked his glass with mine. "Have you chosen your next location?"

"I have. I've always dreamed of seeing Paris." Ryan nodded with a smile. "And someone just told me about an amazing Chateau tours that begins there and ends in Bordeaux. What's it called, Ashley?"

"Chateau Diderot women-only tours," Ashley proclaimed excitedly.

"Yes. That tour sounds heavenly to me," I said.

"Hmm, a lavish women-only tour, ha? I bet it's very expensive."

"Most likely. The reason France is so expensive is what kept me from visiting it before. I bet it keeps a lot of people away," I added thoughtfully.

"I bet it does."

"Hmm. I wonder if I can dig up a more affordable way to travel there."

"You do that, and you can choose your next *ten* destinations!"

I stood erect in front of Ryan, ripples of excitement charging through me. "I have a better idea. If I succeed, you let *me* choose my prize." I stretched my hand forward to shake his.

"Only a madman would take a blind bet," said Christine, her eyes narrowing on Ryan, a faint smile of amusement on her lips.

"Which you know very well that I am," he grinned widely at her. "Besides, these bets add excitement to life. Raquel, you've got yourself a deal." We sealed the deal with a firm handshake.

"Oh, girl, don't you ever learn?" Jess whispered in my ear with a grin. I wasn't ready to tell her that what I wanted was to pitch Ryan my new magazine idea. It was too soon to talk about it. First, I needed to get a better idea of what I wanted my magazine to be like.

"Let Chris know as soon as you put together your travel plans. And I expect to see your motels series on my desk A.S.A.P. By the way, good move leaving Chantal and Kevin back in Rio for more pictures, although, God knows, we have enough." I tried to read his expression, wondering if he suspected anything was going on between his girlfriend and her photographer, but I couldn't tell. I wanted to tell him my suspicions, but he was my boss, and it wasn't my place. "Enjoy your victory, Raquel," he winked at me and turned to leave.

"Thank you, sir."

As soon as Ryan, Lon, and Chris left, Jess and Ashley flocked to me. "Oh, my God! I'm so jealous!" declared Ashley, a wide grin on her face.

"*You're* jealous?" said Jess, a warning in her tone. "Check them out."

The Trio looked particularly angry. Our former boss, Todd, sat quietly near them, refilling his Champagne flute, despite the early-morning hour. "First, she steals my spot," complained Kourtney, "then she gets to choose one of the most expensive trips known to man. It's just not fair," she whined.

"Don't worry, darling. You'll get a good destination soon," Deidre assured her, her black eyes looking at me scathingly from behind her glasses.

"Did you ever wonder how we've never found out about this awesome motel scoop, but the moment she got there, she learned all about it?" intimated Chad.

"Yea," Kourtney perked up. "You're right. How *did* our little Rachel find out about these sordid motels?"

"She had a local hottie take her there!"

"Fancy a little romp, Rachel?" said Deidre, making the others laugh.

"Don't mind if I do," Chad said in as high a feminine voice as he could muster. They kept on laughing. Suddenly, Ryan came back.

"What's going on here?" he asked, assessing the situation. "Raquel, do we have a problem here?"

I loved, loved, loved that he said *we*, but I couldn't tell on the others, not without severe repercussions. "No; no problem."

"Fine. I had an idea, which is why I'm back. I've decided to go with you!"

"What?!"

"Yes! You see, part of the reason I didn't like the women-only travel column is that this is not a women's magazine, and I was bothered it had no appeal to men. I've finally found a solution: I'm going to pit Ashley's column against a men-only travel column!"

"What?!" Ashley looked stricken, her face whitening.

"Don't worry; it's going to be fun! I'm going to assemble some of my male friends and, while Raquel is exploring women-only tours, we'll explore the men-only tours in France. And, if we find none, we're going to create some – there, and all over the world! I am *certain* there's a market here!"

"That sounds marvelous, sir!" I said.

"Please, call me Ryan."

"Ryan." I said, smiling widely at him.

Things were about to get a lot more interesting.

THE END

A NOTE TO THE READER

Thank you for allowing this intimate communication between us. As you have gleaned, book one of the *Travel Secrets* trilogy is all about Rachel's journey into womanhood. I hope you will join her in book two where her resolve will be tested in French wine-country among aristocratic vintners and global elites.

EXERCISE YOUR POWER: SHOW SOME MODERN-DAY AUTHOR LOVE

In a market overflowing with writers, a new author like me could really use *your* help!

Little matters more to new authors than reviews. Please leave a review of the book on Amazon and/or GoodReads. Please remember that *Travel Secrets* is a trilogy with one unifying theme, the details of which will only become clear in books two and three.

Please "like" my Facebook page and press "see first" to actually see my posts in your news feed (or turn on notifications). There you will also find a *Travel Secrets* book group you can join. The link is:

http://www.facebook.com/AuthorSharLemond/

You can also follow my blog www.sharlemond.com to get exclusives regarding book two. Sign up for my newsletter and receive chapter one of *Travel Secrets: Book Two – Paris and Bordeaux* as a thank you.

Twitter: https://twitter.com/SharLemond

Instagram: https://www.instagram.com/sharlemond/

Pinterest: https://www.pinterest.com/sharlemond/

A WORD ABOUT LIBRARIES

To most of us, libraries are just there. We take them for granted, use them (or not), and don't really give them a second thought. Until we suddenly find ourselves without them, and then we miss them terribly. That's what happened to me while I lived in the big metropolis of Rio de Janeiro. Other than in his Montessori Kindergarten, my then three-year-old could only access books in stores, where they cost an average of 3-4 times as much as they do in the U.S. And books in English for kids and adults were very hard to find (which is why I consider Kindle a life-saver!)

If my book attracts enough attention and makes enough money, I plan to spearhead a read-in library in Rio's shantytowns (favelas). Something magical happens when we read, and I would like those kids to be touched by this magic, too. In Emily Dickinson's immortal words:

<u>There is no Frigate like a Book</u>

There is no Frigate like a Book
To take us Lands away
Nor any Coursers like a Page
Of prancing Poetry –
This Traverse may the poorest take
Without oppress of Toll –
How frugal is the Chariot
That bears the Human soul

A special thank you to my local libraries, Clear Lake County Freeman Branch, Houston, Texas, and Helen Hall Library for their wonderful staff, private work rooms, fantastic selection of books and movies, and variety of free activities for children. After coming back from Brazil, I never took you for granted!

MY DREAM

Other than writing, my dream is to make the *Travel Secrets trilogy* into a movie series starting someone like Emilia Clarke (see the rest of my dream cast in my Pinterest page https://www.pinterest.com/sharlemond/) and even into an opera series! If you can help by putting me in touch with any actors, opera singers, etc., I'd love to hear from you (especially if you know anyone connected to the Neubauer Family Foundation). My goal is to make opera accessible to today's youth, by which I hope to help keep opera, one of the highest forms of art, alive. Contact me at https://sharlemond.com/contact/

DISCLAIMER

This is a work of fiction. Names, characters, places, and incidents are either the products of the author's imagination or are used fictitiously. Any resemblance to actual persons, living or dead, businesses, companies, events, or locales is entirely coincidental.

You may notice I've acknowledged some ladies below who happen to have the exact name of some of the characters in the book. Let me clarify that the characters in my novel are a product of my imagination and if I've used a couple of acquaintances' names, it's because I like those names.

Permission was obtained from *VaiVai* Samba school to describe their 2012 parade in my novel.

ACKNOWLEDGMENTS

Some acknowledgments will only be given at the final installment of Travel Secrets trilogy.

A big thank you to my aunt, plastic surgeon Dr. Renata, who is the only Brazilian person who ever disclosed the nature of their motels to me. She was also the first person who ever told me big butts are popular in Brazil and that there's nothing wrong with them. And to prove it, she refused to do Liposuction on mine, so she must have really meant it!

Thank you to the inventors of the Internet and Kindle for shattering any barriers to in-depth research, for allowing me to self-publish, and for giving me access to books in English abroad, which was a life-saver while living in a foreign country.

A special thank you to my good friend, Rachel, who never tires of correcting my mistakes and who is a parallelism specialist.

Thank you to my wonderful editor T. Greenwood who took the mess that was the first and second drafts and helped me carve a better story.

Thank you to fantastic editor Sione Aeschliman whose insightful comments helped inspire a third editing session, which was essential in highlighting the theme and character of my book.

Thank you to Dawn Grimes from DW Creations LLC for the wonderful cover, her infinite patience, and her unbeatable price.

Thank you to my mom, Rina, for helping me with Portuguese and by reading and commenting on the book, and for her boundless love and support.

Thank you to my cousin and BFF Ronit who helped me with technical stuff, with Portuguese, and with encouragement and support whenever I needed it.

Thank you to my friend and fellow author Sylvia Sarno for your help and advice.

Thank you to Eliseo for your amazing Zumba classes and for inspiring the character of Andreas. Stick around, because he'll have a bigger role in book three.

Thank you, Ana Carolina, for allowing me to use your amazing photo of Rio.

Thank you to Samba school *Vai-Vai* of Sao Paulo for allowing me to use their brilliant parade in my book. Thank you to my cousin, Gisele, who helped me translate the letter to *Vai-Vai* and to my friend, Maristela, who facilitated this.

Thanks again to my friend the lawyer, Maristela, and to favela advocate Theresa, and to my cousin, public defender Miriam for helping me learn more about Brazilian society, customs, and the language. My brave public defender, Maristela, has been inspired by the three of you.

Thank you to my son's sweet Montessori teachers, Carol and Lianna, who never tired of teaching me Portuguese whenever we met.

Thanks to my sweet cleaning lady, Barbara, for tolerating my fractured Portuguese when others didn't.

Thank you to Steve for volunteering to be the registrar for my husband's history business, which freed more of my time to write.

Thank you to my friend, Adam, for helping with technical matters.

Thank you to my Facebook friends' continuing affection and support and to all my friends in general, including my loyal farmers' market customers. And a big thank you to my wonderful launch team members.

A wholehearted thank you to my dad, Henrique, for inspiring me with his integrity and for acting as my moral compass when I was growing up.

A heartfelt thank you to my friend, Rob, for all he's done for me and Scott and for his unswerving confidence in the both of us.

And lastly, I dedicate this book to my husband, Scott, for his steadfast support of me in all aspects of life, and especially in my struggle to get this far as a novelist. I wouldn't be here if it weren't for him.